"[A] ...TING TECHNO-THRILLER . . .

A highly sophisticated cat-and-mouse game that weaves in glimpses of what the entertainment world could be like in the near future."

—*Arizona Daily Star*

"Startlingly inventive . . . [A] high-tech joyride . . . Child's characters are so interesting . . . [*Utopia*] will take its place beside two Michael Crichton classics, *Westworld* and *Jurassic Park*."

—*People* (Page-turner of the Week)

"[Child's] characters are first-rate, as is his writing. The real icing on the cake is Utopia itself, ingeniously conceived and lovingly described."

—*The Washington Post Book World*

"A roller-coaster adventure . . . It's a fast read and a great place to visit. And Disney parks will never look the same again."

—*Charleston Post & Courier*

Please turn the page for more reviews. . . .

"WHAT A GREAT PLOT!"

"Takes readers on an up-and-down ride every bit as thrilling as one of the roller coasters that populate the fictional thrill park . . . Child also draws wonderful characters and seamlessly blends the thrilling setting of the park with the intrigue of the hunt for Doe."

"Just the ticket for some entertaining thrills . . . Child delivers fast-paced thrills, and you don't have to worry about long lines, whining children, or a $75 admission fee."

"The blend of technological jargon and suspense results in a real thrill-a-minute read."

UTOPIA

LINCOLN CHILD

BALLANTINE BOOKS • NEW YORK

Utopia is a work of fiction. Names, places, and incidents either are a product of the author's imagination or are used fictitiously.

A Fawcett Book
Published by The Random House Publishing Group

Copyright © 2002 by Lincoln Child
Excerpt from *Death Match* copyright © 2004 by Lincoln Child

Published in the United States by Fawcett Books, an imprint of The Random House Publishing Group, a division of Random House, Inc., New York, and simultaneously in Canada by Random House of Canada Limited, Toronto.

FAWCETT is a registered trademark and the Fawcett colophon is a trademark of Random House, Inc.

This edition published by arrangement with Doubleday, a division of Random House, Inc.

www.ballantinebooks.com

ISBN 0-345-45520-7

Printed in the United States of America

First Ballantine Mass Market Edition: December 2003

OPM   9   8   7   6   5

To my daughter, Veronica

ACKNOWLEDGMENTS

MANY PEOPLE HELPED make this book a reality. My cousin, Greg Tear, was involved almost from the beginning, and proved himself both a fount of ideas and a tireless sounding board. Eric Simonoff, my agent at Janklow & Nesbit, did a heroic job of reading (and, bless him, rereading) the manuscript and offering vital criticism. Betsy Mitchell was as always a supportive and shrewd reader, and the novel is much the better for her input and that of her associates. And Matthew Snyder of Creative Artists Agency proved himself once again to be the best gunslinger on the West Coast.

I'd like to thank my editor at Doubleday, Jason Kaufman, for his enthusiasm and his invaluable assistance with the manuscript. To Special Agent Douglas Margini, for his advice on weapons and law enforcement procedures—and for the "ridealong"—my thanks. To my lifelong friend, Mark Mendel, many thanks for the systems background. And I'd like to give special thanks to my co-conspirator and writing partner, Douglas Preston, for his extensive input and for encouraging me to write this book in the first place. Throughout seven joint novels he has proven himself to be both a loyal partner and a close friend, and I look forward to our next seven collaborations. Doug, take a bow.

There are others whose contributions, large and small, must be acknowledged: Bob Wincott, Lee Suckno, Pat Allocco, Tony Trischka, Stan Wood, Bob Przybylski. No doubt there are others I've neglected to name, and to you I offer my cringing apologies in advance.

I want to thank the many members of the Preston-Child online bulletin board; your enthusiasm and dedication won't be forgotten.

* * *

And last, but far from least, I want to thank the three women in my life—my mother, Nancy; my wife, Luchie; and my daughter, Veronica—for making this book possible.

It goes without saying that Utopia—and its cast, crew, and guests—are entirely imaginary. References to persons, places, and things outside the Park are either fictitious or used fictitiously.

u•to•pi•a (yoo•tō'pē•ah)   *n.* **1.** A state or situation of perfection. **2.** An ideal place or location, frequently imaginary.

UTOPIA

PROLOGUE

IT WAS THE ultimate coup, and Corey knew it. Not only had he scored a Jack the Ripper T-shirt—the exact thing his mother had sworn for three months that she would never, *ever* buy him—but now the whole family was about to ride Notting Hill Chase. Everyone knew it was the most amazing ride, not just in Gaslight but in the entire Park. Two of his school buddies had been here on vacation last month, and neither one had been allowed on it. But Corey was determined. He'd noticed his parents were having a blast, despite themselves. Just as he'd known they would: after all, this was only the newest, best amusement park in the whole world. One by one, the little family rules had fallen away, until at last he'd tried for the Big Kahuna. An intensive half hour of whining wore them down. And now, as the line ahead grew shorter and shorter, Corey knew he was home free.

He could see the ride was really fancy, even for here. They were in some kind of winding alley with old houses on either side. There was a faint chilly breeze, with a musty smell to it. *Wonder how they faked that.* Little flames burned atop iron lamplights. It was foggy, of course, like the rest of Gaslight. Now he could see the loading platform ahead. Two women clad in funny-looking hats and long dark dresses were helping a group of people into a low, topless carriage with big wooden wheels. The women closed the carriage and stepped back. It jolted forward, wheels turning in rhythm, and disappeared beneath a dark overhang as another empty carriage came up to take its place. Another group boarded, rolled forward out of sight; yet another empty carriage slid into position. Now it was his turn.

There was a scary moment when he thought he might be too short for the ride, but by drawing himself up with a herculean effort Corey raised the top of his head above the minimums bar. He quivered with excitement as one of the ladies ushered them up into the carriage. Immediately, he darted like a ferret for the forward seat, planting himself firmly upon it.

His father frowned. "Sure you want to sit there, skipper?"

Corey nodded vigorously. After all, this was what made the ride so scary. The carriage's seats faced each other. That meant the two who sat in the front would ride *backward*.

"I don't like this," his sister whined, taking a seat beside him.

He gave her a brutal, silencing jab. Why couldn't he have had a cool big brother, like Roger Prescott had? Instead, he was stuck with a wimpy sister who read horse books and thought video games were gross.

"Keep your arms and legs inside the barouche at all times, please," the lady said in that weird accent Corey supposed was English. He didn't know what a *broosh* was, but it didn't matter. He was riding Notting Hill, and nobody could stop him now.

The lady closed the door, and the lap bar came automatically into position across Corey's chest. The carriage jerked, and his sister gave a small squeak of fear. Corey snorted.

As they began to move forward, he craned his neck over the side, looking first up, then down. His mother quickly reined him back, but not before he'd noticed that the carriage was on some sort of belt, cleverly concealed and almost invisible in the dimness, and that the wheels were just turning for show. It didn't matter. The carriage trundled ahead into darkness and the sudden amplified clatter of horse's hooves. Corey caught his breath, unable to suppress a grin of excitement as he felt the carriage begin to rise steeply. Now, out of the darkness, he could see the vague shape of a city spreading out around him: a thousand peaked roofs, winking and smoking in the night air; and, farther away, a cool-looking tower. He did not notice the tiny infrared camera concealed inside its uppermost window.

FORTY FEET BELOW, Allan Presley watched the monitor disinterestedly, as the kid in the Jack the Ripper T-shirt rose up Alpha lift. That shirt had been the most popular seller in Gaslight the last four months running, even at twenty-nine bucks a pop. It was amazing the way wallets flew open when people came here. Speaking of flying open, the kid's jaw was dropping almost like a caricature: his head swiveling this way and that, leaving faint greenish heat trails in the infrared monitor as his car rose up above the sprawling rooflines of Victorian London. Of course, the kid had no idea he was ascending through a cylindrical screen, displaying a digital image beamed from two dozen projectors onto the fiber-optic lights of the cityscape. It was an illusion, of course. At Utopia, illusion was everything.

Presley's eyes flitted briefly toward the girl sitting next to the kid. Too young to be of interest. Besides, the parents were with them. He sighed.

At most of the first-line thrill rides in the park, cameras were strategically positioned at the final hair-raising descents, capturing the looks on the riders' faces. By paying five dollars at the exit, you could buy an image of yourself, usually grinning maniacally or frozen in fear. But it had become an underground tradition among the more daring young women to bare their breasts to the camera. Of course, the resulting pictures never reached public view. But male members of the backstage crew were greatly entertained. They'd even come up with a term for the practice: meloning. Presley shook his head. The crew at the water flume in Boardwalk got a good twelve, fifteen eyefuls a day. Here in Gaslight, it was much less common, especially this early.

With another sigh, he put aside his copy of Virgil's *Georgics* and quickly scanned the rest of the three dozen monitors arrayed along the control room wall. All quiet, as usual. By Utopia standards the Chase was a relatively low-tech coaster, but it still more or less ran itself. The most excitement Presley usually got was when some fool tried to clamber out of a car midride. Even that had its established routine: the intrusion mats along the ridepath would activate; he'd alert the tower operator to stop the ride; then he'd send Dispatch to escort the guest away.

Presley's eye wandered back to camera 4. The kid was at the top of the ratchet hill now. In a second, what little light there was would go out, the car would head into the first drop, and the real fun would begin. He found himself watching the excitement painted on that little face—clear even through the ghostly infrared—and trying to remember the first time he'd ridden Notting Hill himself. Despite the countless thousands of rides he'd worked as foreman, there was still only one word to describe it: magic.

The console speaker crackled. "Hey, Elvis."

He didn't answer. In America, being a white male with the last name of Presley carried unavoidable baggage. It was like having the last name of Hitler. Or Christ, maybe, assuming anybody had the balls to . . .

"Elvis, copy?"

He recognized the nasal voice of Cale, over on the Steeplechase attraction. "Yeah, yeah," Presley said into his mike.

"Any action over there?"

"Nope. Dead."

"Same here. Well, almost. Had five pukers this morning, boom, one after the other. You should have seen it: unloading looked like a war zone. They had to close down for ten minutes to let Sanitation clean up."

"Fascinating." There was a deep, visceral shudder in the control room as one of the carriages hurtled down the final vertical drop that ended the ride. Automatically, Presley glanced up at the bank of cameras as the carriage moved toward the unloading area. Dazed, happy faces.

"Let me know if you get anything good," Cale continued. "One of the commissary chefs told me they expect a bunch of sororities to come through tonight. Maybe I'll stop by after shift."

A warning light glowed red on the circuit panel before him. "Gotta go," Presley said. He snapped a button to speak with the tower operator. "I'm showing a safety dog failure at Turn Omega."

"Yeah, I see it," came the response. "Where the bots at?"

"Lubrication at the Ghost Pond."

"Okay. I'll call Shop."

"Copy." Presley sat back and scanned the monitors again. Warning lights were always going off. The rides were so over-engineered with redundant safeties there was never cause for concern. Most were false alarms, anyway. The biggest danger was to the mechanics, who had to keep their fool heads and fingers out of the way of the cars when the rides were live.

COREY WAS CLINGING desperately to the lap bar, shrieking at the top of his lungs. He could feel gravity pressing against his chest, tugging irresistibly at his armpits, trying to lift him bodily from the car. At the top of the lift—so the storyboard went—their imaginary horses had been spooked by some ghostly apparition, and now the carriage was a runaway. He was surrounded by a pandemonium of noise: the clatter of the runaway carriage, the shrill neighing of panicked horses. And, above it all, the piercing, constant, gratifying shriek of his sister. He was having the time of his life.

Now they were racing through a series of amazingly realistic set pieces as they sped down the cobbled hill: a deserted, spectral lake; a maze of dark narrow alleys; a dockscape of rotting piers and shade-haunted clipper ships. The carriage jerked upward once, then twice, with gut-wrenching force. Corey clung tighter, for rumors of what awaited at the end of the ride had reached his ears: the carriage would ultimately careen over the side of the hill and hurtle straight down through black space.

"I'M AT DOG 91. Checks out fine. Hey, Dave, do you know why, during a physical, the doc tells you to turn your head when he's checking your johnson?"

"Nope."

Presley listened automatically to the mechanics' chatter over the radio, barely paying attention. He swept the monitors, then dropped his gaze once again to *Georgics*. He'd been a classics major at UCB, always meant to go on to graduate school, but now just couldn't summon the energy to leave Utopia and go back to school. As it was, he was probably the only person in the entire state of Nevada who spoke Latin. Once he'd tried to use this as a pickup line. It hadn't worked.

"Well, somebody explained it to me. The doctors don't want saliva spewed in their face when you cough."

"No shit. That's it? And here I always thought there was some anatomical reason, because . . . hey, Christ, dog 94 is burned out."

Presley sat up, listening intently now.

"What do you mean, burned *out*? It's not a damn lightbulb."

"Just what I said. It's smoking, stinks like hell. Must have overloaded. Never seen anything like it, even in the simulator. Looks like dog 95's the same way . . ."

Presley leaped to his feet, chair spinning and rattling away behind him. He glanced toward the ride's breakout diagram. Safety dogs 94 and 95 controlled the final vertical descent from Turn Omega.

This wasn't good. Sure, the safeties would stop any traffic coming up. But he'd never heard of the dogs failing before, especially two in series, and he didn't like it. He grabbed for the radio and the tower operator. "Frank, drop the plates. Shut it down."

"Already on it. But oh, my God, a car's just passing now . . ."

Presley's trained eyes darted to the bank of monitors. What he saw turned the blood in his veins to ice.

A carriage was hurtling down the final descent of Notting Hill. But it was not the even, controlled descent he had witnessed so many times. The carriage was canted away from the vertical track, its detached undercarriage swinging horribly. The occupants were pressed against the lap bars, clutching at each other, the whites of their eyes and the pinks of their tongues pale green in the monitor wash. There was no audio feed but Presley could see they were screaming.

The carriage canted still farther as it picked up speed. Then there was a jarring wrench and one of the occupants tumbled forward. His small hands scrabbled frantically, but the G-forces were too strong; the hand slipped past the safety bar, past the adult hands that reached desperately for it, and as the rider cartwheeled toward the camera, hurtling down with appalling speed, Presley had just enough time to make out the Jack the Ripper stitching before the impact killed the visual feed.

TWO WEEKS LATER

7:30 A.M.

FROM ITS JUMPING-OFF place at Charleston Boulevard, above the Las Vegas Strip, Rancho Drive makes a casual bend to the left and heads straight for Reno. It arrows northwest with absolute precision, ignoring all natural or artificial temptations to curve, as if in a hurry to leave neon and green felt far behind. Country clubs, shopping centers, and finally even the sad-looking ersatz adobe suburbs fall away. The Mojave Desert, tucked beneath the asphalt and concrete sprawl, reasserts itself. Spidery tendrils of sand trace their way across what the signs start calling Route 95. Joshua trees, hirsute and sprawling, dot the greasewood desert. Cacti stand like standard-bearers to the emptiness. After the frantic, crowded glitter, the gradual transition to vast empty spaces seems otherworldly. Except for the highway, the hand of man appears not to have touched this place.

Andrew Warne tilted his rearview mirror sharply upward and to the right, sighing with relief as the dazzling brightness receded. "How could I possibly have come to Vegas without bringing dark glasses?" he said. "The sun shines 366 days a year in this place."

The girl in the seat beside him smirked, adjusted her headphones. "That's my dad. The absent-minded professor."

"Ex-professor, you mean."

The road ahead was a burning line of white. The surrounding desert seemed bleached by the glare, yucca and creosote bush reduced to pale specters. Idly, Warne laid the palm of his hand against the window, then snatched it away. Seven-thirty A.M., and already it had to be a hundred degrees outside. Even the rental car seemed to have adapted to the desert conditions: its climate control was stuck on the maximum AC setting.

As they approached Indian Springs, a low plateau rose to the east: Nellis Air Force Base. Gas stations began to appear every few miles, out of place in the empty void, sparkling clean, so new they looked to Warne as if they'd just been unwrapped. He glanced at a printed sheet that lay clipped to a folder between their seats. *Not far now.* And there it was: a freeway exit sign, bright green, newly minted. *Utopia. One mile.*

The girl also noticed the sign. "Are we there yet?" she asked.

"Very funny, princess."

"You know I hate it when you call me princess. I'm fourteen. That's a name for a little kid."

"You act like a little kid sometimes."

The girl frowned at this, turned up the volume on her music player. The resultant thumping was clear even over the air conditioner.

"Careful, Georgia, you'll give yourself tinnitus. What's that you're listening to, anyway?"

"Swing."

"Well, that's an improvement, at least. Last month it was gothic rock. The month before, it was—what was it?"

"Euro-house."

"Euro-house. Can't you settle on a style you like?"

Georgia shrugged. "I'm too intelligent for that."

The difference was evident the moment they reached the bottom of the exit ramp. The road surface changed: instead of the cracked gray concrete of U.S. Highway 95, lined like a reptile's skin by countless repairs, it became a pale, smooth red, with more lanes than the freeway they'd just left. Sculpted lights sloped gracefully over the macadam. For the first time in twenty miles, Warne could see cars on the road ahead. He followed them as the highway began a smooth, even climb from the alkali flats. The signs here were white, with blue letters, and they all said the same thing: *Guest Parking Ahead.*

The parking lot, almost empty at this early hour, was mind-numbingly large. Following the arrows, Warne drove past a cluster of oversize recreational vehicles, dwarfed like insects by the expanse of blacktop. He'd snorted in disbelief when someone told him seventy thousand people visited the park each day; now, he was inclined to believe it. In the seat beside him, Georgia was looking around. Despite the practiced air of teenage ennui, she could not completely conceal her eagerness.

Another mile and a half brought them to the front of the lot and a long, low structure with the word *Embarkation* displayed along its roof in Art Deco letters. There were more cars here, people in shorts and sandals milling about. As he eased up to a tollgate, a parking attendant approached, indicating Warne to lower his window. The man wore a white polo shirt, the stylized logo of a small bird sewn on the left breast.

Warne reached into the folder, pulled out a laminated card. The attendant studied it, then plucked a digital stylus from his belt and examined its screen. After a moment, he handed the passcard back to Warne, motioning him through.

He parked beside a line of yellow trams, then dropped the passcard into his shirt pocket. "Here we are," he said. And then, looking out at the Embarkation Building, he paused momentarily, thinking.

"You're not going to try to get back together with Sarah again, are you?"

Startled by the question, Warne looked over. Georgia returned his gaze.

It was remarkable, really, the way she could read his mind sometimes. Maybe it was the amount of time they spent together, the degree they had come to rely on each other in recent years. Whatever the case, it could be very annoying. Especially when she chose only to speculate on his more sensitive thoughts.

The girl lowered her headphones. "Dad, don't do it. She's a real ball-buster."

"Watch your mouth, Georgia." He pulled a small white envelope from the folder. "You know, I don't think there's a woman on earth that would pass muster with you. You want me to stay a widower the rest of my life?"

He said this with a little more force than he'd intended. Georgia's only response was to roll her eyes and replace the headphones on her head.

Andrew Warne loved Georgia intensely, almost painfully. Yet he'd never anticipated how difficult it would be to navigate the world, to raise a daughter, all by himself. Sometimes he wondered if he was making a royal mess of the job. It was at times like this that he missed his wife, Charlotte, most acutely.

He looked at Georgia another moment. Then he sighed, took hold of the door again, and yanked it open.

Instantly, furnacelike air boiled in. Warne slammed the door, waited for Georgia to hoist her backpack onto her shoulders and follow, then hopped over the shimmering tarmac to the Transportation Center.

Inside, it was pleasantly chilly. The Center was spotless and functional, framed in blond wood and brushed metal. Glass-fronted ticket windows stretched in an endless line to the left and right, deserted save for one directly ahead. Another display of the laminated card and they were past and headed down a brightly lit corridor. In an hour or so, he knew, this space would be jammed with harried parents, squirming kids, chattering tour guides. Now, there was nothing but rows of metal crowd rails and the click of his heels on the pristine floor.

A monorail was already waiting at the loading zone, low-slung and silver, its doors open. Oversize windows curved up both sides, meeting at the transport mechanism that clung to the overhead rail. Warne had never ridden on a suspended monorail before, and he did not relish the prospect. He could see a scattering of riders inside, mostly men and women in business suits. An operator directed them to the frontmost car. It was, as usual, spotless, its sole occupants a heavyset man in the front and a short, bespectacled man in the rear. Though the monorail had not yet left the Center, the heavyset man was looking around busily, his pasty, heavy-browed face a mask of excitement and anticipation.

Warne let Georgia take the window seat, then slid in beside her. Almost before they were seated, a low chime sounded and the doors came noiselessly together. There was a brief lurch, followed by silky acceleration. *Welcome to the Utopia monorail,* a female voice said from everywhere and nowhere. It was not the usual voice Warne had heard on public address systems: instead, it was rich, sophisticated, with a trace of a British accent. *Travel time to the Nexus will be approximately eight minutes and thirty seconds. For your safety and comfort, we ask that you remain in your seats for the duration of the ride.*

Suddenly, brilliant light bathed the compartment as the Center fell away behind them. Ahead and above, dual monorail tracks curved gently through a narrow sandstone canyon. Warne glanced down quickly, then almost snatched his feet away in surprise. What he had supposed to be a solid floor was actually a series of glass panels. Below him was now an unobstructed drop of perhaps a hundred feet to the rocky canyon floor. He took a deep breath and looked away.

"Cool," Georgia said.

The canyon we are traveling through is geologically very old, the voice went smoothly on. *Along its rim, you can see the juniper, sagebrush, and scrub piñon characteristic of the high desert...*

"Can you believe this?" said a voice in his ear. Turning, Warne saw that—in flagrant defiance of the "remain seated" edict—the heavyset man had walked back through the car to take a seat across from them. He wore a painfully orange floral shirt, had bright black eyes, and a smile that seemed too big for his face. Like Warne, he had a small envelope in his hand. "Pepper, Norman Pepper. My *God,* what a view. And in the first car, too. We'll have a great view of the Nexus. Never been here before, but I've heard it's outstanding. Out*standing.* Imagine, buying a whole mountain, or mesa, or whatever you call it, for a theme park! Is this your daughter? Pretty girl you've got there."

"Say thank you, Georgia," Warne said.

"Thank you, Georgia," came a most unconvincing reply.

... On the canyon wall to the right of the train, you can see a series of pictographs. These red-and-white anthropomorphs are the work of the prehistoric inhabitants of this region, the period now known as Basket Maker II, which flourished almost three thousand years ago...

"So what's your specialty?" Pepper asked.

"I'm sorry?"

The man shrugged his squat shoulders. "Well, you obviously don't work at the Park, 'cause y'all are riding the monorail in. And the Park hasn't opened yet, so you're not a visitor. That means you've got to be a consultant or a specialist. Right? So is everybody on the train, I'll bet."

"I'm an—I'm in robotics," Warne replied.

"Robotics?"

"Artificial intelligence."

"Artificial intelligence," came the echo. "Uh-huh." Pepper took a breath, opened his mouth for another question.

"What about you?" Warne interjected quickly.

At this the man smiled even more broadly. He put his finger to one side of his nose and winked conspiratorially. *"Dendrobium giganteum."*

Warne looked at him blankly.

"Cattleya dowiana. You know." The man seemed shocked.

Warne spread his hands. "Sorry."

"Orchids." The man sniffed. "Thought you might have guessed when you heard my name. I'm the exotic botanist who did all the work at the New York Exposition last year—maybe you read about it? Anyway, they want some special hybrids for the athenaeum they're building in Atlantis. And they're having some problems with the night-bloomers in Gaslight. Don't like the humidity or something." He spread his hands expansively, knocking both his and Warne's envelopes to the ground. "All expenses paid, first-class ticket, nice fat consultancy fee—and it'll look great on my résumé, too."

Warne nodded as the man retrieved the fallen envelopes, passed his back. That he could believe. Utopia was supposedly so fanatical about the accuracy of its themed Worlds that scholars were occasionally seen wandering around, slack-jawed, taking notes. Georgia was gazing around at the canyon, paying no attention to Pepper.

. . . The twenty square miles owned here by Utopia is rich in natural resources and beauty, including two springs and a catchment basin . . .

Pepper glanced over his shoulder. "How about you?"

Warne had almost forgotten the slightly built man with glasses sitting behind them. The man blinked back, as if considering the question. "Smythe," he said in an accent that sounded faintly Australian. "Pyro."

"Pyrotechnics? You mean, like fireworks?"

The man smoothed his fingers over the tiny toothbrush mustache that grew in the shadow of his nose. "I design the special shows, like the recent six-month celebration. Troubleshooting, too. Some of the late-show indoor chrysanthemums are launching too high, breaking panes of glass in the dome."

"Can't have that," Pepper said.

"And in the Griffin Tower show, guests are complaining the maroons at the end are too loud." The man fell silent abruptly, shrugged, turned his head to look out the window.

Warne shifted his own gaze to the passing russet-colored cliffs, then back to the interior of the monorail. Something had been bothering him, and he suddenly realized what it was. He turned to Pepper. "Where are all the characters, the action figures, Oberon, Morpheus, Pendragon? I haven't seen so much as a decal."

"Oh, they're around, all right—in the shops and some of the kiddie attractions. But you won't see any guys in rodent suits walking around. Nightingale was very particular about that, they say. Very concerned about the purity of the experience. That's why all this—" he waved a pudgy hand—"the Transportation Center, the monorail, even the Nexus—is so understated. No commercialization. Makes the actual Worlds that much more real. Or so I've heard." He turned to the quiet man behind them. "Right?"

Smythe nodded.

Pepper leaned a bit closer to Warne. "Never thought too much of Nightingale's stuff myself. Those *Feverstone Chronicles* animated movies, based on his old magic act? Too dark. But my kids are crazy for it. And they watch his cartoons every week, like clockwork. They almost killed me when they heard I was coming here and they couldn't tag along." Pepper chuckled, rubbing his hands together. Warne had read books where people rubbed their hands in anticipation, but he wasn't sure he'd ever actually seen anybody do it.

"My daughter *would* have killed me if I didn't bring her," he replied. "Ouch!" he yelped as Georgia kicked him beneath the seat.

There was a brief silence. Warne rubbed his calf.

"So, you think it's true they've got a nuclear reactor buried underneath the Park?" Pepper asked.

"Huh?"

"That's the rumor. I mean, just imagine the electrical overhead. The place is its own municipality, for heaven's sake. Think of the juice it must take to keep the whole place going, air-conditioning, rides, computers. I asked one of the hosts back in the Center, and she said they used hydroelectric power. Hydroelectric! In the middle of the desert! I . . . hey, look—there it is!"

Warne glanced forward, then froze despite himself. He heard Georgia draw in a quick breath.

The monorail had just banked around a particularly steep bend, and ahead, the canyon widened dramatically. Stretching from wall to wall, from the top of the canyon to its base, was a vast copper-colored facade, glimmering brilliantly in the morning sun. It was as if the canyon suddenly ended in this massive wall of burnished metal. The cul-de-sac was an illusion, of course—a large, circular rock valley beyond enclosed the Park itself—but it was spectacular, breathtaking, beautiful in its own spartan way. The only break in the facade was two tiny squares dead center, near the top, where the monorail tracks entered. Along the upper edge was the single, huge word, *Utopia,* in letters of some micalike substance that winked and glittered, appearing and disappearing with the angle of the sun. Atop and beyond, a huge geodesic dome arched over everything, a complex lattice of crystal polygons and metal webbing. At its apex, a flag rippled: the stylized logo of a violet bird on a field of white.

"Wow," Georgia said under her breath.

. . . *We hope you enjoy your visit. And remember, if you have any questions or concerns, we invite you to visit one of our Guest Services lounges within the Nexus or the Worlds themselves. Please remain seated until the monorail comes to a complete stop.*

The car fell silent as they glided forward into shadow.

8:10 A.M.

THE NEXUS WAS a broad, gracious space, framed in the same brushed metal and wood of the Transportation Center. Restaurants, shops, souvenir boutiques, and Guest Services lounges lined the walls to the left and right, stretching ahead for what seemed a limitless distance. Warne followed the others down the monorail off-loading ramp, Georgia in tow, gazing about curiously. The ceiling was open to the glass dome far above, framing a huge cloudless sky that arced over the Nexus in a brilliant azure band. Before him, information kiosks and low, graceful fountains gleamed in the slanted bars of sunlight. Signs, large but discreet, directed visitors toward the Park's four Worlds: Camelot, Gaslight, Boardwalk, Callisto. The air was cool, a little moist, and full of muted sound—voices, the patter of water, some softer noise he couldn't identify.

A group of youngish men and women were waiting at the base of the ramp. They wore identical white blazers and carried identical folders. They looked, in fact, as if they could have all been related. Warne wondered, only half in jest, if there were height, weight, and age restrictions for Utopia employees. He dismissed the thought as he saw one of the women walking briskly toward him.

"Dr. Warne? I'm Amanda Freeman," the woman said, shaking his hand.

"So I see," Warne replied, nodding toward the nameplate affixed to her blazer lapel. He wondered how she had recognized him.

"I'll be processing you into Utopia, giving you a brief orientation." Her voice was pleasant, but almost as brisk as her walk. She nodded toward the small envelope he was carrying. A miniature bar code had been impact-printed along one edge. "May I have that?"

He handed it to her, and she tore it open, upending it into her palm. Out tumbled another stylized bird, this one in green. She affixed it to his jacket. "Please wear this pin while you're with us."

"Why?"

"It identifies you as an external specialist. You have your passcard? Good. That and the pin will give you the backstage access you'll need."

"Beats paying admission."

"Keep the passcard handy. You may be asked to show it from time to time. In fact, most crew working the Underground keep them clipped to their pockets. Is this your daughter?"

"Georgia, yes."

"I didn't realize she was coming along. We'll have to get her a pin, as well."

"Thank you."

"No problem. She can wait in Child-Care Services while you're processed. You can pick her up afterwards."

"*Child*-Care Services?" Georgia asked, her voice steely with indignation.

Freeman smiled briefly again. "Actually, it's the young adult division of Child-Care Services. I think you'll be pleasantly surprised."

Georgia flashed Warne a dark look. "Dad, this better be good," she muttered. "I *don't do Legos.*"

Warne looked past her, toward the off-loading ramp. The pyrotechnics specialist, Smythe, was walking purposefully down into the Nexus. Norman Pepper was talking animatedly with one of the white-blazered men. The two began moving away, Pepper rubbing his hands and smiling widely.

They dropped Georgia at the nearby services desk, then proceeded down the central corridor of the Nexus.

"You've got a beautiful daughter," Freeman said as they walked.

"Thanks. But please don't tell her that. She's got a chip on her shoulder as it is."

"How was the monorail?"

"High."

"We like to bring visiting specialists in on the monorail their first day here. Gives them a better feel for what it is that paying guests experience. You'll be given directions to employee parking as part of today's orientation package. Much less scenic, naturally, but it shaves off fifteen minutes or so of travel time. Unless you're staying on-site?"

"No, we're staying at the Luxor." Unlike most theme parks, Utopia was geared toward a full-immersion, single-day experience: there were no overnight accommodations for tourists. Warne had been told, however, that a small behind-the-scenes hotel existed: a first-class resort for celebrities, star performers, and other VIPs, with more spartan quarters for visiting consultants, bands, and overnight staff.

"What's with the clocks?" Warne asked as he struggled to keep up. He'd noticed that, although it was now quarter past eight, the digital clocks set into the towering walls of the Nexus read 0:45.

"Forty-five minutes to Zero Hour."

"Huh?"

"Utopia is open 365 days a year, 9:00 A.M. to 9:00 P.M. At closing, the clocks start a twelve-hour countdown. Lets the cast and crew know how much time they have left until opening. Of course, there are no clocks in the Worlds themselves, but—"

"You mean it takes twelve *hours* to get the Park ready again?" Warne asked in disbelief.

"Lots to do," Freeman said with another small smile. "Come on, we'll take a shortcut through Camelot."

She steered him toward a massive portal in the nearer wall. Above it, the word *Camelot* shone in Old English black letter. This typeface was, so far, the only deviation Warne had seen from the rigidly enforced design of the Nexus: even the doors to the bathrooms and the emergency exit signs were in the same reserved Art Deco type.

Three white-jacketed attendants, standing outside the Camelot portal, smiled and nodded at Freeman. She steered Warne past them, through a forest of crowd rails and into a wide, empty queuing chamber. In the far wall stood half a dozen sets of metal doors. On cue, one of the doors slid back and Freeman led the way into a cavernous, darkly appointed elevator.

The doors closed again and that same silky female voice said, *You are now entering Camelot. Enjoy your visit.* There was a muffled metallic thud and the elevator came to life. Except, Warne noticed, it was neither ascending nor descending: it was moving forward horizontally.

"Is it a long way to the Park itself?" he asked.

"Actually, we're not really moving," Freeman replied. "The car just gives the illusion of movement. Studies showed that guests find the Worlds easier to adjust to if they believe it takes a journey—however short—to reach them."

Then the doors on the far side slid open. For the second time in the last half hour, Warne felt himself stop in surprise.

Ahead lay a wide pavement of dark cobblestones. Quaint buildings—some with thatched roofs, others with peaked gambrels—lined both sides, stretching ahead to what looked from a distance like a large village square. Beyond the square, the cobbled road divided around the bailey of a castle, sand-colored and monolithic. Above its high crenellations flew a hundred multicolored banners. In the distance, he could see more towers and the notched, cruel-looking face of a mountain rising above a grassy hill, snow swirling around its summit. Far overhead, the soaring curve of the dome gave an illusion of endless space. The air smelled of earth, and fresh-cropped grass, and summer.

Warne walked slowly forward, feeling a little like Dorothy, stepping out of her drab monochromatic farmhouse into Oz. *Wait until Georgia sees this,* he thought. Brilliant sunshine blanketed the entire scene, giving it a clean, lustrous edge. Park employees hurried quickly here and there over the cobbles, but not in the jacketed uniform he had seen elsewhere: here were men in particolor tights; women in flowing robes and wimples; a knight in armor. Only a small knot of white-blazered supervisors, with palmtop computers and two-way radios, and a crew member from Maintenance, hosing down the cobbles, broke the illusion.

"What do you think?" Freeman asked.

"It's amazing," Warne replied honestly.

"Yes, it is." He turned and saw her smiling. "I love to watch people entering a World for the first time. Since I can't go back and do it again myself, watching somebody else is the next best thing."

They made their way down the broad thoroughfare, Freeman pointing out attractions as they went. As they passed a bakery, a mortared window opened, releasing an irresistible aroma. Somewhere, a bard was tuning his lute, singing an ancient lay.

"The design philosophy of all four Worlds is the same," Freeman said. "Visitors first pass through a set piece—in Camelot's case, this village we're in—that helps orient, set the mood. Decompression, we call it. There are restaurants, shops, and concessions, of course, but mostly it's a spot for the guests to just observe, get acclimated. Then, as you move deeper into the World, we start integrating the attractions—rides, live shows, holographic events, you name it—into the environment. It's all seamless."

"I'll say." Warne noticed that, except for the signboards of the shops and eateries, there was no modern signage anywhere: rest rooms and the cleverly integrated information kiosks were indicated only by what appeared to be highly realistic holographic symbols.

"Scholars come here because this lane we're passing through is a superbly detailed reconstruction of Newbold Saucy, an English village depopulated in the fourteenth century," Freeman said. "Guests come because Dragonspire is probably the second most thrilling roller coaster in the Park, after Scream Machine over in Boardwalk."

The castle loomed ahead of them as they approached the square. "An exact re-creation of Caernarvon, in Wales," Freeman said. "With selective compression and forced perspective, of course."

"Forced perspective?"

"The upper stories aren't full-size, they're smaller. They give an illusion of correct proportion, but are warmer, less intimidating. We use the technique throughout Utopia, on a variety of levels. For example, that mountain, there, is reduced in size to give the illusion of distance." She nodded through the open portcullis. "Anyway, inside this castle is where *The Enchanted Prince* is shown."

The troubadour's song had long fallen behind them, but other noises came to Warne's ears: birdsong, the patter of fountains, and the same softer noise he had heard in the Nexus. "What's that sound I keep hearing?" he asked.

Freeman glanced at him. "You're very observant. Our research specialists have done pioneering work in womb-feedback research. Once guests fill Camelot, the sound won't be audible. But it will still be there."

Warne threw her a puzzled look.

"It's the science of reproducing certain womblike effects—temperatures, ambient sounds—to foster a subliminal sense of tranquility. We have five patents pending on it. The Utopia

Holding Company has over three hundred patents, you know. We license some to the chemical, medical, and electronics industries. Others remain proprietary."

Three of which were developed by me, Warne thought silently, allowing himself a little twinge of pride. He wondered if the woman knew the contribution he'd made to the day-to-day operation of Utopia: his meta-network, which coordinated the activities and intelligence of the Park's robots. Probably not, considering the way she was showing him around, talking to him like he was some assistant programmer. Once again, he found himself wondering why Sarah Boatwright had summoned him here so abruptly.

"This way," Freeman said, turning down a side alley.

A man in a violet cape and dark knee breeches passed them, practicing his Middle English. Ahead, two burly maintenance specialists walked by, carrying a large metal cage between them. Inside sat a small dragon, tail twitching, crimson scales shimmering in the sun. Warne stared. The damp nostrils flared as air passed through them. He could swear the thing's yellow eyes gleamed as they fastened upon him.

"A mandrake, on its way for installation in Griffin Tower," Freeman said. "The Park's still closed. That's why they're not traveling below. What is it, Dr. Warne?"

Warne was still staring after the dragon. "I'm just not used to seeing skin on them, that's all," he muttered.

"Excuse me? Oh yes: that's your field, isn't it?"

Warne licked his lips. The costumes, the dialect, the fanatical realism of the surroundings . . . He shook his head slowly.

"Can be a bit much when no guests are around to break the illusion, right?" Freeman's voice was quieter, less brisk. "Let me guess. When you arrived, you thought the Nexus was spartan-looking, kind of drab."

Warne nodded.

"People often feel that way when they first enter Utopia. A guest once told me it reminded her of a billion-dollar airport terminal. Well, it was designed that way, and this is the reason." She waved her hand at the scene around them. "Sometimes the realism can get disorienting to guests. So the Nexus provides a neutral setting, a buffer zone, a transition between the Worlds."

She turned toward a two-story half-timbered residence, lifting the iron latch of the front door. Warne followed her inside. To his surprise, the building was merely a shell, open to its roof. A plain gray door was set into the back wall, a finger-geometry scanner and a card reader beside it. Freeman stepped up to the scanner, placed her thumb in the mold. There was a snap, and the door sprang open. Beyond, Warne could see the cool green glow of fluorescent light.

"Back to the real world," Freeman said. "Or as close as we get to it around here."

And she motioned him through the doorway.

8:50 A.M.

SARAH BOATWRIGHT, HEAD of Park Operations, sat at the crowded conference table in her office, thirty feet below the Nexus. The office was frigid—the primary air-conditioning ducts ran behind the rear wall—and she cradled her hands around a large cup of tea. Sarah Boatwright was fanatical about tea. Once an hour, like clockwork, the best restaurant in Gaslight sent down a cup of the day's house selection. Today it was jasmine, first-grade. She watched the small, ball-shaped young flowers uncurl in the hot liquid, and leaned forward briefly to inhale their fragrance. It was exquisite, exotic, alluring.

It was 0:10, Utopia time, and the various park chiefs had gathered in her office for the daily "Pre-Game Show." She took a sip, feeling the warmth slowly spread through her limbs. *This* was the real start of her day: not the alarm clock, not the shower, not the first cup of the morning. It all started now, when she gave the day's marching orders to her captains and lieutenants; when she took the helm of the greatest theme park ever built. It was her job to make sure that, although behind the scenes almost anything might be happening on a given day—two thousand riotous Boy Scouts, irregularities in the electrical grid, a visiting prime minister and his retinue—to the guests, every day had to seem precisely the same. Perfect. She could imagine no job more challenging, or more rewarding.

And yet today, mingling with the usual sense of anticipation, was something else. It wasn't apprehension—Sarah Boatwright had never had much use for fear of any kind—so much as a kind of wariness. *Andrew is here,* she thought. *He's here, and he can't possibly know the real reason.* It was the forced duplicity that made her wary: she felt it quite distinctly as she glanced around, mentally checking off faces. Research, Infrastructure, Gaming, Food Services, Medical, Guest Relations, check, check, and check. Bob Allocco, head of Security, sat at the far end of the table, solid as a bulldog and almost as short, his sunburned face impassive. They all looked back at her, alert, serious, attuned to her mood. She preferred things that way: businesslike, brisk. Few jokes were exchanged unless Sarah made the first overture. Fred Barksdale was the allowed exception, of course: his allusions to Shakespeare and wry English humor had the table helpless with laughter on several occasions. And here he came, café au lait balanced precariously atop a sheaf of computer printouts. Freddy Barksdale, head of Systems, with that oversize mop of blond hair and the cute worry lines scribbled across his forehead. Just the sight of him sent a stab of affection through her that drove away thoughts of Andrew Warne, threatened to upset her brisk professionalism. She gave a brief, managerial clearing of the throat, took another sip of tea, and turned to the group.

"Right. Let's get it done." She glanced down at a sheet of paper on the desk before her. "Estimated attendance today: 66,000. The system is running 98 percent operational. Any word on when Station Omega will be back on-line?"

Tom Rose, Infrastructure chief, shook his head. "The ride seems to check out fine, green board all the way. But the diagnostics keep giving us an error code, so the governors refuse to supply any juice from the grid."

"Can you override the governors?"

Rose shrugged. "Sure, we could. And have an army of safety officials climbing all over us."

"Dumb question. Sorry." Sarah heaved a sigh. "I want you to keep on it, Tom. Keep on it *hard*. That attraction is one of Callisto's biggest draws. We can't afford to give it a vacation. Fred will lend you a troubleshooting team if you want."

"Of course," Barksdale said, smoothing down the front of his tie as he spoke. It was a beautiful tie, knotted with the same extraordinary attention to detail with which Barksdale invested all his actions. Although he was not in the habit of expressing personal emotions in a public meeting like this, Sarah had noticed that this tie-smoothing habit seemed to surface when he had something on his mind.

Her eyes swept the table. "Any other news I don't want to hear?"

The head of Entertainment spoke up. "I just learned the band that was supposed to play the Umbilicus Lounge today won't be making it. Drug arrest at LAX or something."

"That's dandy, just dandy. We'll have to get one of the house bands to cover."

"Firmware could do it, but they're booked to play Poor Richard's."

Sarah shook her head. "Umbilicus pulls in three times the crowd. Get that band down to Costuming as soon as they get in—if they haven't played in space suits before, they'll need to get used to them." She looked around the table. "Anything else?"

"They nabbed a third-time offender in the Gaslight casino," the head of Casino Operations said. "Seventy-five years old, if you can believe it. Eye in the Sky got him on tape, stringing a slot machine."

"Too bad for him. Circulate his picture to Surveillance and Casino Security, get his name on the Guest Services blacklist." Sarah glanced back down at her sheet. "Any progress report on Atlantis?"

"Fabrication's on track," somebody spoke up. "Looks like we'll make the deadline."

"Thank God for that." Atlantis was the new—and quite controversial—World, set for opening late in the year. "Dr. Finch, got the vitals for last week?"

The sallow-faced head of Medical picked up a chart. "Five births, all without complication. Two deaths: one heart attack, one aneurysm. Twenty-nine injuries, broken wrist the worst." He put the chart down again. "Quiet week."

Sarah Boatwright glanced at the head of Human Resources. "Amy, any news on that possible wildcat job action by the sanitation specialists?"

"Nothing. And I don't know whether that's good or bad."

"Keep an ear to the ground. Let me know the minute you hear anything." She looked back at her list. "Let's see. Attendance is down in Camelot, running about 15 percent below the other Worlds. The head office has asked us to put an exploratory committee together, find out what the problem is." She paused. "Let's deal with that when I get back from San Francisco, shall we?"

She scanned the rest of the sheet, put it aside, picked up another. "Okay, drumroll please. The Tony Trischka Band will be performing on the Boardwalk, make sure they get comped for all meals and lodging. Celebrity guests today include Senator Chase from Connecticut and his family, the CEO of Gene-Dyne . . . and the Earl of Wyndmoor."

At this last name, another groan went up.

"Is Lady Wyndmoor going to insist on that castle thing again?" someone asked.

"Probably." Sarah put the second sheet away. "The Nevada Gaming Control Board people will be out here a week from Wednesday—everybody start practicing your best smiles. And just one other thing. The external specialist, Andrew Warne, is arriving today." Noticing some blank looks, she went on. "He's the robotics specialist who created the Metanet. Please give him any assistance he may need."

When this announcement was greeted with silence, Boatwright stood up. "Very well. We're at two minutes and counting. Let's saddle up."

She turned to her desk as the group began to shuffle out of the office. When she turned back, only Fred Barksdale remained. As she'd known he would.

"Why is Warne coming today?" he asked, elegant Home Counties accent sounding ever so slightly aggrieved. "He wasn't due for another week."

So that's it, she thought. "I moved up his visit."

"Couldn't you have informed me, Sarah? I'll have to get workloads reassigned, he'll need the resources of—"

Boatwright put a finger to her lips. "It was Emory's idea; it just came together on Thursday. With the accident at Notting Hill Chase the week before last, OSHA about to get involved, the home office wants us seen as fast on the case. But listen." She drew closer to Barksdale, lowering her voice. "I'm leaving for that entertainment convention in Frisco tomorrow. Remember?"

"How could I forget?" And then a light suddenly dawned behind Barksdale's eyes. A smile returned to his lips, faint but noticeable. "And the convention keeps you far from the irritant—who might, after all, still be suffering the, ah, 'pangs of dispriz'd love'?"

"That wasn't my first thought. I was going to ask if you feel we can trust Teresa Bonifacio to buy in on this, in my absence. To work with Andrew, get this done. He's the only one who can do it, but he can't do it alone. It's not going to be easy on either of them. After all, this is Andrew's life work we're about to compromise. And you know how Teresa feels about the whole thing."

Barksdale nodded slowly. "Terri and I have had our differences of opinion. But they've never been about the quality of her work. She may not like what has to be done, but I think we can count on her to do it."

"And you'll keep close watch on their progress, in my absence?"

Barksdale nodded again.

"Thanks, Freddy." She glanced toward the open door of her office, making sure the corridor was empty. Then she reached for his lapels, pulled him to her, kissed him gently. "I'll make it up to you when I get back," she murmured.

Then she stepped back and reached for her cup. "Now, come on. We've got a Park to open."

9:00 A.M.

MOMENTS LATER, TEN thousand clocks within Utopia shifted in unison. The final seconds were counted down; the clockfaces went blank; then *9:00* was displayed and normal time resumed. Zero Hour had arrived.

The Transportation Center had become a place of controlled pandemonium. Attendants with coned flashlights fanned out through the parking lots and onto the approach roads, directing the heavy flow of traffic in a carefully choreographed ballet. Blue-and-white trams, long and snakelike, wound their sinuous ways between loading points and the Center. Guides in the front cars of the trams, wearing jaunty white berets blazoned with the nightingale logo, spoke into microphones in a dozen languages, laying down the ground rules of the Park between jokes and bits of Utopia trivia.

Within the Center, every ticket window was now in operation, taking credit cards and—for seventy-five dollars a head, all ages, no discounts—distributing personalized nightingale-shaped pins that, when displayed on a shirt or lapel, granted one day's access to the magical lands beyond. Monorails glided beneath the twin metal tracks that curved down the middle of the entrance canyon, running 35 percent faster now in "peak mode," shuttling a thousand people to and from the Nexus every ten minutes.

The Nexus itself, which had been cloaked in a watchful, preternatural silence, now echoed with the sound of countless voices. First-timers stood in the shadow of palm fronds and fountains, scratching their heads, consulting maps and guidebooks. Veteran visitors—"Utopians" who formed clubs and Internet sites to share their passion—strode confidently, neophytes in tow, toward their favorite Worlds.

Inside Gaslight, a fish and chips seller ran past the entrance to

Notting Hill Chase—closed for renovations—and headed for her stand. In Boardwalk, the spotters on the Scream Machine finished their walk-by, typed their authorization codes into the control room console, and authorized the operator to initialize the roller coaster. Deep within Caernarvon castle, an imaging specialist did a final run-through of the computer array that controlled the holographic sequences for *The Enchanted Prince*.

The ninety-minute periods directly after opening and before closing—when the maximum volume of guests entered and exited the Park—were the most anxious for Utopia management. Operations specialists were on full alert, ready to deal instantly with any traffic flow irregularities that might create bottlenecks at the Transportation Center, the Nexus, or within the Worlds themselves. Thousands of cameras—discreetly placed behind one-way glass, within false walls and beams, behind facades—scanned the Park, ensuring that the Worlds filled without hitches or snags. Security specialists, some dressed in black blazers, others in plain clothes, mingled with the crowds, on the lookout for lost children and pickpockets. But none of this was visible to the average guest, who roamed the grounds and midways, smiling and unaware.

One place the guests did not roam—were, in fact, never permitted to enter—was the "Underground," the subterranean levels beneath the Park. Most guests did not even know the Underground existed: they assumed they were standing on ground level, rather than four stories above the canyon floor. Although the Underground sported no lifelike holograms or laser shows, no foamed-concrete fairy-tale confections, this was where the real magic of Utopia occurred. Park employees scurried about, some wearing the costumes of the "cast" who worked among the attractions and tourists above; other "crew," whom guests never saw, wearing an assortment of coveralls, jeans, and suits. Cutaway diagrams on the bare concrete walls showed the layout of staff cafeterias, wardrobe, barbershops, break rooms, storage, computer centers, research labs, and the rest of the thriving secret city below the park. Tour guides and Guest Services specialists used the tunnels as shortcuts between the different Worlds. Technicians, artists, and bureaucrats huddled in a dozen conference rooms and labs, dreaming up new attractions or fretting about market penetration. Electric carts purred their way through the labyrinths, whisking a celebrity performer or a much-needed replacement part from one section of Utopia to another.

Tom Tibbald made his way through the corridors of C Level, humming tunelessly. He was in his early thirties, had a thick head of tightly coiled brown hair, and was beginning to sag a bit around the middle. His white blazer sported the gold logo of an electronics specialist. Despite the humming, he felt uncomfortably self-conscious: of the fellow crew who passed quickly by without remark; of the surveillance cameras mounted in the arched ceiling of the tunnel; and especially of the hard little pieces of plastic and copper in his blazer pocket. He walked past Central Makeup and Machine Shop 3. The humming stopped as he approached the security checkpoint at the staff entrance.

The security specialist in the booth glanced at his identification, nodded, and turned to a keyboard to make an entry. Humming again, Tibbald proceeded through the automatic doors and out into the staff parking lot.

After the cool air and muted light of the tunnels, the heat and brilliant Nevada sunlight struck him a double blow. Tibbald grimaced, turning away for a moment, letting his eyes adjust. Then he sniffed and moved forward, more slowly now, glancing carefully around the staff lot. Looking for the van.

The backside of Utopia had none of the dramatic beauty of its front door. The canyon walls fell sharply away on both sides, running down into the endless brown of the desert floor below. Behind him rose the massive rear wall of the Park, concrete and cinder block, infrequent windows like tiny pockmarks in its bulk. At either side, near the top, were huge green doors, opening onto ramps that sloped gently down in long, curved planes: guest emergency exits, never used except in drills. Between them, at ground level, was a thicket of loading docks, staff entrances, equipment shops, and vehicle sheds.

There it was: a brown, long-wheelbase van, parked to one side away from other vehicles, *Exotic Bird Trainers of Las Vegas* stenciled on its windowless sides. Tibbald made for it, hoping to hell the thing was air-conditioned. Windows were rolled shut: a good sign. But when he reached it and opened the passenger door, there was no welcoming gush of chill air. He sighed regretfully, tugged at his collar, and climbed in.

The stench of guano was almost palpable, and the front seat of the van was covered in olive-colored oilskin. *Not surprising,*

Tibbald thought, *with all the bird shit in this junker*. In the back, he could see a tall white-barred cage containing half a dozen Moluccan cockatoos, huge and pale pink. They regarded him silently, salmon-colored crests flared. Then Tibbald glanced over at the driver and blinked in surprise.

"What happened to the other guy?" he asked with a sniff. "The one I met the first time, I mean."

The man behind the wheel returned the glance. He had almond eyes and wide, sharp cheekbones that gave his face a strange heart-shaped symmetry. "Other engagements," he replied after a moment.

Tibbald thought a moment, decided this was supposed to be a joke, and made the appropriate laugh.

"You've got them?" the man asked. He spoke carefully, with the faintest trace of an accent. Tibbald tried to place it. He had friends in Guest Services who talked to foreigners every day, could name any accent there was with just one word. But Tibbald never dealt with guests, and after a moment gave up.

"Right here." He reached into his blazer pocket, fished out the plastic cards, and held them up, fanning them like a hand of playing cards. "All your favorite flavors: lemon-lime, grape, root beer, and new wild cherry."

The man frowned and made a quick suppressing gesture with his hand. Tibbald dropped the passcards below the level of the window. "You know, for a little bit more money, I could have gotten you the specs for that audio-morphing technology you want. Would have saved you a lot of bother, snagging it yourself like this. What park did you say you work for? Paradise Island? FantasyWorld?"

"I didn't say," the man replied. He pointed to the passcards. "Tested?"

Tibbald nodded proudly. "Reprogrammed every one myself." He began ticking them off with his fingers. "This one gives access to all guest areas, this one to Maintenance, this one to the Hub." His finger lighted on the last passcard, colored a pale red. "And this right here is the real bad boy. All secure sites up to level 3." He withdrew the finger, a nervous look coming over his face. "Look, if they catch you, don't use my name. I know nothing about it. Right?"

The man nodded.

Tibbald smiled, then reached into his pocket and pulled out a handful of nightingale-shaped pins. "Right. And here's the image-tags you asked for. They're generic, can't be traced. Just pin one to your jacket and you're good to go."

"Everything else is set?"

"Today's downlink already took place. Couldn't change things now to save my life." Tibbald licked his lips. "Could I have the money now?" Though this was said casually, it was followed by another sniff: the dry sniff of a habitual cocaine user.

"Sure thing." The man reached into his coat pocket—Tibbald noticed idly the coat was leather, despite the heat—and pulled out a thick envelope of bills. He handed it over to Tibbald. "You've done well," he said.

As Tibbald began to count the bills, the man threw an appreciative arm over his shoulder. The man's other hand went back into the leather jacket, coming out this time with a small automatic pistol.

Tibbald's eyes were on the money, and it wasn't until the man placed the gun between his ribs and pulled him in close that he realized what was happening. His eyes widened, his lips worked to form a protest, but surprise dulled his speed.

Although the bullets were hollow-point, designed to explode inside meat rather than pass through it, the leather-jacketed man angled the barrel carefully downward, toward the struggling Tibbald's spine, to avoid the possibility of hitting his own encircling elbow.

There was a muffled *thunk,* then another. The parrots screamed their approval. Tibbald jerked, sagged. He made a thin reedy sound like air escaping from a bellows. The man released his hold, letting Tibbald flop back, plucking the envelope of money away from the flood of red. Pulling the tarp down over the body, he wrapped it carefully, then rolled it over the seat into the rear of the van. He glanced through the windows quickly, then grunted, satisfied everything had gone unnoticed.

He began to snug the gun back into his coat, then stopped. He'd moved quickly, but not quickly enough: a thin crimson jet traced a damp line up the front of his shirt.

With a curse, he slid the gun home, grabbed the zipper of his coat, and snugged it up tight. Two minutes in a men's room would set things right.

Besides, once inside a costume, it would make no difference.

9:10 A.M.

ANDREW WARNE SAT in a plush chair in a large office on A Level. Amanda Freeman was at a computer terminal, typing. Over the last fifteen minutes, she had asked a remarkable number of questions. Once, years before, Warne had done some consulting work for the CIA. The case officer who'd done the background check for Langley had been far less inquisitive.

Amanda finished typing, then looked over at him. "I knew you were in robotics, but I had no idea you were the brain behind the Metanet. I understand it controls all the robots in the Park?"

Warne nodded. "Except for the few that are totally autonomous."

"Very impressive." Freeman consulted her screen again, then scribbled something on a piece of paper and handed it to him. "I believe we're through here. Your meeting's scheduled for eleven. Here's the office number. Just ask anybody in Guest Services for directions. You might want to use the time to look around."

"Sure thing. Maybe I'll take in the nuclear reactor."

Freeman's eyes darted to his face, her faint ironic smile returning. "So you've heard that one, too. I'm trained to respond that we utilize hydroelectric power." She stood up. "This just leaves the orientation—standard for all external specialists."

"What, like a *training* film? I was hoping to see a bit of the Park with my daughter."

"It takes just five minutes. Follow me, please."

She led the way out of the office and down the corridor. Warne followed, feeling a growing annoyance. He'd already sat through more red tape than he should have. And now, orientation? As if he were just another specialist brought in to do some window dressing. Had Sarah set this up for his personal mortification? But Warne quickly dismissed this. Sarah Boatwright may have been many things, but she'd never been petty.

He hugged himself as he walked, rubbing his arms. "I thought my old computer lab was chilly. But it's cold enough to hang meat in here."

"It's a by-product of the purification process. There's two million square feet of floor space beneath the Park, but the air purity here approaches that of a chip fabrication plant." She gestured down the corridor. "No smoking, of course. And all the scooters and carts are electric. The only nonelectric vehicle allowed is the armored car that makes a weekly pickup."

They were walking past a gallery of offices identical to the one they just left. Warne glanced through their windows, still hugging himself. In one office, he saw Norman Pepper, his friend from the monorail, hands moving animatedly through the air. "Did you know," the eager voice filtered through the open doorway, "that orchids are the sex maniacs of the floral world? Instead of fertilizing themselves like other plants, they go to incredible lengths to have sex with other orchids. Why, the flower of the *Paphiopedilum venustum* has even evolved, right down to the veins, to look exactly like a . . ."

"It's in here," Freeman said, opening an unmarked door and ushering Warne into a small room. Walls, floor, and ceiling were all lined in the same dark material, and there were only two identical chairs, across from each other. He glanced around curiously. This was not the projection room he'd expected. It looked more like the office of a psychiatrist with an underdeveloped sense of interior design.

Freeman directed him to the nearest chair. "You can let yourself out afterwards. You've got my card, feel free to page me at any time. First visits can get a little overwhelming."

She left the room, closed the door behind her.

A moment later, Eric Nightingale was sitting in the opposite chair.

Warne almost leaped to his feet in surprise. He stared in amazement.

The holograph was incredible in its detail. Warne knew, of course, that holographic technology was a specialty of the Park, but he had no idea they'd made such advances. The image in the chair could have been Nightingale himself. There he sat—consummate magician, the visionary behind Utopia—in his trademark top hat, white tie, and tails, the same thin intelligent face and bright black eyes, small goatee on his youthful chin detailed down to the individual whiskers. The fabulously successful, legendarily eccentric performer, notorious for his theatrical extravaganzas, his perfectionism, his penchant for blurring the line between reality and illusion. By combining traditional stage performances with technology and dark role-playing, he had leveraged the art of magic into a vast entertainment engine. Nightingale's two cartoon series, based on characters developed in his act, had become the biggest prime-time shows ever for the five-to-fifteen-year-old set. It was his star power that had brought together the conglomeration of corporations and venture capitalists forming the original Utopia Holding Company. And he had been the singular visionary behind Utopia's development—up until his death in a plane crash, six months before the Park was to open its doors.

And here he sat, a highly processed confection of diffracted light, gazing directly at Warne.

The image spoke. "Thank you for coming to Utopia," it said. "We appreciate the expertise you bring to the System, and we hope your stay here will be a pleasant one."

Warne half listened, still a little numb with surprise. *This* was the man who had sat in his own Carnegie-Mellon lab two and a half years earlier, outlining his dream for Utopia, asking for Warne's help. *This* was the man who had so affected Warne's life: first for the better, then—unintentionally—for the worse.

Nightingale had been dead for more than a year. And yet here he was. Staring at the image, Warne felt the affection he'd had for the man—nurtured over so many cups of coffee, so many brainstorming sessions—return abruptly, almost painfully. He hadn't realized how much he missed the intellectual vigor of their friendship, the unspoken mutual respect. Nightingale had been entranced by Warne's theories of robotics and machine intelligence. The very fact they were so controversial had energized him, and he'd become Warne's most powerful advocate: precisely the kind of advocate he could use, right about now. Warne felt both sad and slightly uncomfortable, as if he were in the presence of a ghost.

He knew a little about holography. 3-D video systems producing images only a meter in size took outrageous amounts of computing horsepower. And yet the figure before him was full-size, full-color, devoid of processing artifacts or tricks like emulsion swelling. And it had none of the ghostly, indistinct quality of first-generation holograms. Warne glanced around the dark walls, looking unsuccessfully for the display system. Then he turned back to the holovideo in the chair opposite him and tried to concentrate on what he—what *it*—was saying.

"Close to 500 million people will visit an amusement park this year," the Nightingale-image was saying. "But I'll let you in on a secret. I have something better than amusement parks in mind for them. You see, I want them all *to come to Utopia instead*. If we can provide a fully immersive experience—that utopian experience which educates while it delights—we can achieve our goal. And we can achieve it without gimmicky rides or cheap amusement park thrills. That's where *you* come in." Nightingale smiled—the broad, excited, almost conspiratorial grin that Warne remembered so well. "You have come here because of your own special skill. And that skill, whatever it may be, will help make Utopia a more realistic place. Or a place that runs even more smoothly. Or a place that pushes even harder at the boundaries of the imagination. Because Utopia is all about challenges. If we don't challenge ourselves, we won't evolve."

The Nightingale-image stood up. Warne noticed that, somehow, the hologram had the same kind of physical energy— abrupt, lithe, electric—that the living magician had always displayed.

"When I first described my concept of Utopia, the pundits told me I was crazy. Nobody would drive miles into the desert to visit a theme park. Las Vegas was a terrible location, they said. It was an adult playground, not family-oriented. People didn't want themed environments that would challenge their imaginations. They just wanted roller coasters. But I know Utopia will live up to its name. It will become the most successful theme destination in the world. And with the skills of such off-site experts as yourself, we will continue to grow."

Nightingale removed his top hat, turned it upside down. "You will find that Utopia is all about illusion. We don't shy away from artifice here. Instead, we strive to immerse guests in illusion. *Drown* them in it." He dipped his hand into the hat. When the hand came back into view, a white dove was perched on the index finger, head cocked, beady eyes staring. "And if they leave with some of the best, most vivid memories of their lives, aren't those memories just as real as any others? And *that* is precisely how we create reality out of illusion." With a flourish, he lofted the dove into the air. The bird raised its glossy head, stretched its wings wide. As Warne watched, the white feathers began to glow with an almost metallic shine. Then, abruptly, it morphed into a small dragon. A jet of fire shot from between parted jaws, and Warne ducked instinctively. The dragon whirled above Nightingale's head, then vanished in a puff of blue smoke.

The Nightingale-image was looking directly at Warne, still grinning broadly, as if enjoying the effect he was having on the listener. No doubt he had carefully crafted this as a performance, not knowing it would become a self-administered eulogy.

The image's black eyes glittered beneath notched brows. "Since the Utopia project first broke ground, we've already made many of the most important innovations in themed entertainment. Highly realistic, *consistent* environments. Subliminal mood stimulus. Breakthrough technologies for holography and other video systems. Intelligent, autonomous robotic agents."

"Thank you," Warne murmured to the image.

"It is with your help that we will continue such innovation. And Utopia will continue to build on what it already is today: the vanguard of a new era in family entertainment. And a crucible for new technology. Enjoy your time with us."

As he spoke, Nightingale had been holding the top hat between his hands. Now he spread his hands apart, and the image began to waver slightly. The outline shimmered gold and silver, glittering strangely in the muted light of the room. The shimmering spread quickly inward, until what had been Nightingale now appeared as a hollow, human-shaped coruscation of magical dust. The glimmering cloud seemed to bow slightly. "Until we meet again," Nightingale said, but already the voice was growing as thin and insubstantial as the image itself. The glittering outline brightened suddenly, firing into countless pinpoints of light, and then with the faintest sweep of strings it was gone.

Warne stood staring, immobile, at the place where Nightingale had stood, torn uncomfortably between present and past. He blinked away the sting that had come to his eyes.

"Good-bye, Eric," he said quietly.

9:45 A.M.

ANDREW WARNE WALKED alongside a white picket fence, blinking in the bright sunlight as crowds streamed past him. The sidewalk was a broad expanse of wooden ties, worn and bleached as if from years of salt and sun. Nearby, a hurdy-gurdy man cranked his music box, tame monkey squatting on one shoulder. On the far side of the thoroughfare was a small jewel of a city park, full of landscaped walks and wooden benches. At its center stood a gazebo, where a ragtime band in straw boaters and red-and-white-striped jackets belted out an irresistibly cheery version of "Royal Garden Blues." And over everything loomed the huge roller coaster named the Brighton Beach Express, its intricate spiderweb of wooden supports and vast ski jump of a first drop like an old postcard brought magically to life.

This was Utopia's Boardwalk, a painstaking re-creation of a turn-of-the-century seaside amusement park, authentic down to the cast-iron streetlights and even—Warne realized with some surprise—the faintest touch of horse manure in the air, oddly pleasant in this context. And yet it was not authentic, of course, because no real boardwalk of 1910 had been this perfect. It was like a fondly remembered nostalgic confection, a past sanitized of its imperfections, buttressed by an arsenal of hidden technology. Warne worked his way through the crowd to the border of the little park, pulled a guidemap from his pocket and consulted it, then started down the nearest pathway.

Ahead now he could see the blue oval of the pond. The smooth bright curve of the glass dome far overhead lent a sense of unreality to what was an already exotic setting. Children and adults knelt along the pond's marble lip, trailing hands in the water, gazing out at the small sailboats that leaned and fluttered their way across the placid surface.

Warne winced inwardly. It had seemed like an obvious spot to meet: centrally located, probably not too crowded. It hadn't even occurred to him there would be sailboats. He wondered how Georgia would react.

And then he tried to dismiss the thought. It was instinctive, automatic, this desire to shelter her. Though nearly three years had passed since Charlotte's death, it never seemed to go away. And the more he allowed it to show, the more Georgia seemed to resent it. *I'm a big girl now,* her look would always tell him. *I can handle myself.* She never said it aloud—just as she never spoke much about her mother—but he knew it, anyway, with a kind of paternal sixth sense. Funny: despite how much closer they'd grown in the last three years, there was still this pocket of terra incognita into which he was not allowed to venture.

And then he saw her, standing between two knots of Asian tourists at the far end of the pond, gazing out over the water.

For a moment, he just stared, love and pride mingling within him. Most fourteen-year-olds were a little awkward, gangly, dangling precariously between the child and the adult. Georgia was different. She stood slender and tall, poised unconsciously, like a thoroughbred. There was so much of her mother in her every movement: in the way she drew the chestnut hair away from her face with a finger, the way her dark eyebrows knitted together as they stared out into the pond. And yet she was beautiful in a way Charlotte had never been. Warne often wondered where Georgia got her looks. Not from *him,* certainly. He looked down into the water at his feet: a thin, tall man with a dark complexion and a lantern jaw stared back up at him. When he went places with Georgia, Warne usually felt both gratified and a little alarmed. The girl turned heads.

He came up to her and she caught sight of him, rolling her eyes in mock exasperation. "It's about time," she said, tugging the headphones out of her ears. "Come on, let's get going."

"Going where?" Warne asked, falling into step behind her as she led the way back out to the boulevard. He was surprised that, with such an abundance of choices around them, Georgia could be so single-minded. But she was striding forward, snaking her way through the crowds, a girl on a mission.

"To *that,* of course," she said without looking around, poking a finger into the sky.

Warne looked up. "That?" he asked. Then he understood: the vast wooden ramparts of Brighton Beach Express towered over them, the sinuous lines of the track bed rising and falling like a massive ribbon.

"Oh, that," he said. "You . . . you sure you want to go on that?"

Georgia didn't bother to answer. "I've got it all mapped out," she said. "I visited a ton of websites, got all the attractions rated, best to worst, for each of the Worlds. So we're going on that first, then the Scream Machine, and then—"

"Hey, slow down!" This was not how Warne had envisioned his first visit to Utopia: dashing madly through the crowds, so busy concentrating on where he was putting his feet that he barely had time to take in the surroundings. "What's the hurry?"

"Well, you haven't told me how long you're going to be tied up. There's a lot to see, and I don't want to miss anything. Jennifer from my homeroom class was out here in February, and they liked it so much they stayed on an extra day, just so they wouldn't miss anything. Cost them five hundred bucks to change their tickets, she said."

"I don't know how long I'm going to be tied up, princess, but it couldn't be for too long." They were passing the Enchanted Carousel—famous, Warne had read, for sporting the most wooden horses of any single carousel—and the languid waltz strains floated toward them over the cool, perfumed air. "The meeting with Sarah's at eleven. I'll know more then."

"What's the big secret, anyway? Why couldn't she tell you what it's about?"

"There's no big secret. I think it has to do with expanding the role of the Metanet." Actually, Warne hadn't spoken directly with Sarah Boatwright; the eleven o'clock meeting had been arranged through her administrative assistant. Although he didn't say it, Georgia's questions were once again echoing his own. He changed the subject. "Hey, guess who I just had a talk with? Eric Nightingale."

At this, Georgia slowed a little. She looked at him, as if trying to fathom the joke. "Come on, Dad. That's bullshit."

"Watch the mouth. Actually, Nightingale did all the talking. It was a hologram, life-size, amazingly real. It was geared to all the visiting specialists. Kind of a pep talk."

"Like you need one! You gave him half the ideas for this place."

Warne laughed at this exaggeration. "Just some of the early AI stuff, the robotics."

"Hey, where are all the robots, anyway?" Georgia looked around as she walked. "Haven't seen one yet."

"They wouldn't really be in character here. Wait until we get to Callisto."

The entrance to Brighton Beach Express was a large brick building, decorated as a nineteenth-century amusement hall, just beyond the Aquarama. Flags hung like bunting from its upper stories; handbills and ancient-looking broadsides were plastered to the facade, peddling everything from dance-hall revues to patent medicines in heavy-bottomed script. Three vaulted archways led into the ride, each bearing a different signboard: *Panopticon, The Burning Ruins, Metamorphoses.* Lines of visitors snaked away from each archway.

"We just studied metamorphosis in biology," Georgia said. "It was boring."

"Maybe, but the line is shortest." Warne eyed his watch. "Let's go."

The line moved quickly—Warne had read about the Park's ability to keep guests entertained, even when queued—and within a few minutes they were in the shadow of the building. Beyond the archway, the hall was dark. The line split in two, and a woman in a severely tailored gown directed Georgia to the right. Warne followed, letting his eyes adjust to the dim light. The air seemed chillier in here, more humid. Up ahead he could hear laughter, subdued *ooohs*. He could make out people lining up single file, staring at what appeared to be tall panes of glass set into the wall of the corridor.

Within moments, Warne and Georgia took their places in front of the first two panes of glass. Warne looked at the pane facing him, saw himself staring back. *So it's a mirror,* he thought. *Big deal.*

Suddenly, Georgia dissolved into laughter beside him. "Oh, my God!" she squealed, staring at her own pane. "Gross!"

Then Warne's mirror abruptly went blank. *What the hell? That's no mirror.* A moment later, his reflection reappeared. But something seemed wrong; the image was off somehow, unsettlingly so. But he couldn't put his finger on it and, with a shrug, moved on to the next pane, which Georgia had just vacated.

Again, he saw a mirror image of himself. Again, it vanished. And again, it reappeared. Only this time it was obvious what was wrong. He had abruptly grown fat.

The Andrew Warne that stared back at him appeared to have put on an instant two hundred pounds. His belly protruded alarmingly, his prominent Adam's apple was obscured by a double chin. It was a surprising, shocking image. And yet it was unmistakably him: or rather, him *as he might have been*. At the next pane, Georgia was pointing and snickering at herself.

Metamorphoses, indeed, he thought. *How the hell do they do it?*

He moved on to the next pane. Now he went from being fat to alarmingly thin. The eyes, sunken within a fleshy face in the prior frame, stared out at him from gaunt hollows. His jaw, large to begin with, now seemed far too big for the chicken-bone neck.

Abruptly, he realized how it was done. It was holographic technology, like the image of Nightingale he'd seen before. There must be an imaging camera behind the glass. It scanned in his image, then used morphing software to change that image—make it fatter, skinnier, whatever—and reproject it. Like the wavy mirrors in a fun house, only light-years more advanced . . .

He realized that Georgia had been standing at the adjoining pane longer than usual. He glanced over, saw her looking intently at the image. Curious, he leaned over. What he saw made him catch his breath.

It was an image of Georgia, computer-aged by about twenty years. The same chestnut hair, thoughtful eyes, rosebud mouth, striking features. But there was somebody else in that face, too: the image of his dead wife, Charlotte, faint but unmistakable. It was like a specter, looking out at him through his daughter's eyes.

They stood silently for a moment, staring. Then Warne licked his lips, placed one hand on Georgia's shoulders. "Come on," he said. "We're holding up the line."

Beyond the gallery, the queue snaked toward the boarding area for the coaster. The space around them was built to resemble a turn-of-the-century subway station. *Brighton Beach Express* was set into the tiled walls in squares of black. *Boarding straight ahead*. Mingling with the queued guests were men and women in period dress, laughing and chattering. A peanut vendor stood against one wall, hawking his wares in a loud voice. Nearby were concession stands, vaudeville acts. Warne shook his head. The illusion was remarkable. If it wasn't for the other guests around him, he'd have sworn they'd traveled back in time, to the Coney Island of a hundred years before.

Beside him, Georgia was uncharacteristically silent. He thought back to the mirror image he'd just seen. "Your mom and I took you to an old-fashioned park like this. When you were seven, maybe eight. Kennywood. Remember?"

"No. Hey, why do we have to wait with all these people, anyway? Can't you get us to the head of the line? You're a big important person here."

"Sweetie, that was a long time ago. By the way," he said with a teasing smile. "I meant to ask. How was *Child*-Care Services?"

Georgia wrinkled her nose at the emphasis. "Actually, pretty cool. You could watch any old *Atmosfear* rerun you wanted, and they had tons of computers and games. But I really didn't spend much time on that stuff. I was busy doing *this*." And she dug into a pocket of her jeans, pulled out a folded sheet of paper.

"What's that?" Warne reached for it automatically.

Georgia held it away from his grasp. "It's a list. Of qualifications."

Warne waited.

Georgia shrugged. "You asked what kind of girlfriend I'd approve of. So I wrote it all down." She looked at him. "You want to hear it or not?"

He returned her gaze curiously. "Yes, I do."

The line moved forward, and Georgia followed it. She unfolded the list, began to read. "Number one: does not wear high heels. Number two: not a vegetarian. Three: plays hearts, chess, and backgammon, but not too well."

At this, Warne chuckled to himself. He was an ace at backgammon, but sometimes forgot to let Georgia win the occasional game.

"Brings presents on every visit. Eats chocolate cake."

Warne loved chocolate cake. He felt touched: Georgia really had him in mind when she made this list, as well as herself.

"Believes in large allowances. Must not have red hair." She smiled slightly as she said this. Sarah Boatwright's hair was a remarkable, intense copper.

"Plays on-line RPGs. Must not be on a diet."

Warne began to notice an uncomfortable pattern: Sarah, though trim all her life, seemed to be constantly on a diet.

"Goes to McDonald's at least once a week. But likes root beer floats more than shakes. Likes the Three Stooges more than the Marx Brothers. Can't be mean to my dad, like Sarah was."

"She wasn't mean," Warne said automatically.

"Wears blue jeans a lot. Must hate anchovies, sardines, and all other kinds of fish."

Warne sighed inwardly. It was growing clear that no woman could ever live up to all these demands.

"Must think that—"

"How long is this list, anyway?" Warne said, snatching it adroitly out of her hands. He smiled at the handwriting: for all her pretensions to maturity, Georgia still dotted her i's with little hollow circles. The smile went away as he scanned the list. "Good Lord. Thirty-seven items."

Georgia nodded proudly. "Took me almost the whole time I was waiting for you. Just one thing got left off, because it was so *utterly* obvious."

"What's that?"

"She has to like Fats Waller. But then, who doesn't?"

You, probably, in another month or so, Warne thought.

They were near the head of the line now. Ahead, Warne could see a man in a conductor's uniform ushering a dozen people into what looked like an open-air elevated train. He swallowed painfully.

"What time is it?" Georgia asked.

"Five minutes to ten."

"Good. That gives us plenty of time to ride the Scream Machine before your meeting. Maybe the Flume, too."

Warne felt his lips tighten. It was going to be a long sixty minutes.

9:55 A.M.

THE MAN CALLING himself Mr. Doe stood on a walkway over-looking the Hospitality Center, leaning against a guardrail. He enjoyed the casual way his linen jacket draped over the freshly painted rail. He gazed down at the Nexus below, its broad avenue sweeping up toward the monorail station. Though it was almost ten, thick knots of people were still streaming down the off-loading ramps. A veritable river of humanity, he thought: it brought the Book of Joel to mind. He quoted aloud: "Multitudes, multitudes in the valley of decision." But no: if he were honest with himself, the scene had a bleaker, postmodernist cast more appropriate to T. S. Eliot than the Bible. He liked the sound of his voice, and he spoke again, a little more loudly now:

> *A crowd flowed over London Bridge, so many,*
> *I had not thought death had undone so many.*

He glanced down again at the Center, but the employees be-hind the crescent-shaped desk were far too busy to have heard. In fact, the only person who seemed to have noticed was a man in a corduroy jacket, stepping out of a nearby men's room. Their eyes met; the man tipped his tweed cap, turned, and went on his way.

John Doe's gaze swept back out over the Nexus. He decided he disapproved of the design scheme: the chrome and wood con-struction seemed like some monstrous synthesis of Walter Gropius and Piranesi.

The security system, however, was another matter. He was impressed by both its extent and its restraint. The passive-motion cameras in the Transportation Center and the mono-rails were all fifth-generation, marvels of miniaturization. He glanced toward the wall nearest the Hospitality Center. Take, for example, that proximity sensor concealed behind the *Cast Only* sign. A normal visitor to the park couldn't find it if he was looking for it. And, even if he did find it, he wouldn't know what it was. But Mr. Doe's practiced eye identified a DeMinima Sensalert—latest release, very expensive, hard to acquire unless one was a major world power. Which, in a sense, Utopia was.

But a system was only as good as its human minders. After all, the fortifications of Troy didn't fall, exactly: it was the fools inside that let the Trojan Horse in of their own free will. And the security grunts at Utopia didn't seem nearly as impressive as the toys they'd been given to play with. Walking around so purposefully, black blazers instead of the usual white, radio cords fitted snugly into their ears . . . they stuck out like sore thumbs, might as well have been toting Uzis and wearing flak jackets. Even the plainclothes operatives were easy to spot. Oh, he'd seen a wide variety of disguises: a fat tourist in a Hawaiian shirt, a tall, thin man laden down with cameras, a supposedly pregnant woman. But they all wore the same thick-soled, standard-issue black shoes as the regular security staff.

Mr. Doe shook his head. It could not have been better if he'd arranged it for himself. Which, in a way, he had.

He waited another moment, enjoying the feel of the warm sun on his shoulders. Then he picked up his leather satchel and made his way down to ground level, heading for the portal into Gaslight.

INSIDE, AWAY FROM the crowds once again, Mr. Doe strolled down the cobbled streets, hands in his pockets, whistling a complicated figure from Bach's Chromatic Fantasy. His eyes remained constantly on the move. But unlike other guests, he was not taking in the spectacles, attractions, costumed cast members. Instead, he was examining what was supposed to remain hidden: security outposts, exits and entrances for Utopia employees, infrared cameras. His mood, already good, improved. The tempo of the whistling accelerated.

Although Mr. Doe had never been inside Utopia before, he commanded an intimate knowledge of the Park's layout. Without effort, he traced the shortest route to Gaslight's casino, a painstaking reproduction of the conservatory in London's Royal Horticultural Gardens. He stopped before its southern portal, gazing in frank admiration at the glittering facade of glass and steel, the graceful outlines. Now, *this* was more like it. He stepped inside.

Within, the atmosphere was quieter, more stately. There was none of the bustle found among the thrill rides and eateries outside. Potted palms and Victorian banners lined the walls. Cocktail waitresses in bombazine and taffeta rustled by, carrying gratis orders of pink gin and brandy-and-soda. Croupiers and dealers, dressed in Edwardian frock coats, held sway over countless tables. Beneath the central transept lay two massive rings of slot machines, each a huge contraption of brass and tin, with mechanical disks and hand-painted cherries. Mr. Doe strolled by, marveling at the way Utopia had deconstructed all the elements of gambling to keep the casino in period with the rest of Gaslight.

There was, in fact, only one element here that was distinctly, intentionally un-Victorian: the Eyes in the Sky, countless bubbles of smoked glass dotting the paneled ceiling. Unlike elsewhere in the Park, security in the casinos was meant to be seen.

Mr. Doe gazed around, smiling broadly, as he watched the hundreds of patrons: bending over the craps tables, placing their chips before the roulette wheels, yanking slot machine handles like automatons. So many people, so busily employed at losing money.

As a student of human folly, he was hugely amused by the great irony the conservatory presented. Now here was a miracle of rare device: a theme park that at its core was built, not around a brand of beer or a cartoon character, but around casinos. It was a wonderful perversion of Eric Nightingale's original vision. The revised, corporate, post-Nightingale scenario seemed perfectly clear to Mr. Doe: people would come, fall under the carefully orchestrated spell, lose their inhibitions, then their money.

It was remarkable, really: Utopia had been open six months already, and there had been relatively little outcry over this dirty little secret. Perhaps it was because Utopia did it so well.

Mr. Doe gave the conservatory a final, careful look. So ironic—and yet, so very necessary.

He made his way back into the fog-heavy streets of Gaslight. Outside a small shop whose sign read *Blackpool Tobacconist and Cigar Emporium,* he stopped. Nearly hidden in shadow was a small, unlabeled door. He glanced casually back over his shoulder. Then he placed his hand on the knob and turned.

Beyond the door, a long corridor of gray concrete curved away in both directions. A patch of the far wall was painted in ersatz wood grain—just enough to fool any passing guest into thinking the open door was part of the attraction. Mr. Doe closed the door carefully behind him, oriented himself to a mental map, then started down the corridor. Reaching a wide metal staircase, he descended to A Level.

At the first intersection, he stopped. A uniformed officer was approaching from a corridor labeled *Central Processing*. Mr. Doe turned toward him, putting a slightly lost look on his face.

The security officer caught sight of him and stopped abruptly. "Can I help you, sir?" he said guardedly.

"Why, yes, you can. I'm looking for Animal Handling. I'm supposed to meet my colleague there."

"You're an external specialist? Where's your pin?"

"Pin? Oh, of course, my pin!" Mr. Doe stammered. He reached into the pocket of his jacket and pulled out the small green nightingale. "I forgot, I was supposed to wear this. Sorry." He fixed it to his lapel.

"May I see your passcard, please?" the guard asked.

"Got it right here." He fumbled in another pocket, pulled out the laminated card.

The officer examined it, then handed it back. "Thank you. Head down this corridor, make your third right, second door on the left."

"Appreciate it." Mr. Doe smiled and nodded, watching the security officer continue on his way. The guard had acted precisely as the training manual specified he should. Clearly, it was as he'd been assured: he could rely on the lower echelons of Security to react reflexively, to follow the book. This was very good indeed.

ANIMAL HANDLING WAS a jungle of cries, hoots, and unpleasantly exotic scents. Wrinkling his nose, Mr. Doe made his way past a small band of quarreling chimpanzees, locating the door marked *External Prep 3*. Inside, the almond-eyed man in the leather jacket stood beside the enormous parrot cage.

"Any problems?" Mr. Doe said, closing the door behind him.

The man shook his head. "They weren't too eager to take a closer look," he said, jerking his finger toward the heavily smeared newspaper lining the cage bottom.

"Of course, they weren't. The rest of the team?"

"Everything's on schedule."

"And our little computer whiz?"

"He's resting comfortably."

"I'm glad to hear it."

Mr. Doe nodded toward the cage, and the man slid open a drawer concealed in its bottom. Mr. Doe drew closer, reached inside, and pulled out a radio transmitter, thin and black, with a stubby antenna protruding from its top. He snapped it on, punched in a code, lifted it to his lips.

"Water Buffalo, this is Prime Factor. Give me a sit-rep, please."

There was a pause. Then the radio crackled into life. "In position," came the voice.

"Ten-four. I'll check back with you at 1300." Mr. Doe changed frequencies, lifted the radio again. "Cracker Jack, come in. Cracker Jack, do you read?"

This pause was much longer. Then the radio squawked, much more noisily this time. "Affirmative."

"We're moving. Are you ready with the smoke and mirrors?"

"Affirmative," the second voice repeated.

"Roger, out." Mr. Doe slipped the radio into a pocket, then turned back to the drawer beneath the cage, examining its contents with a critical eye.

"Now for the weapon du jour." Mr. Doe considered a Ruger, then rejected it on purely aesthetic grounds. His gaze lingered on the nice brushed-metal Colt, but decided he wasn't in the mood for a gun with such a hefty kick. He'd settle for the Glock-9: light, efficient, dependable in case things got out of hand.

He tossed the gun from hand to hand, then snugged it into a vertical-carry holster beneath his jacket. Kneeling beside the almond-eyed man, he opened his satchel, then began placing items from the drawer carefully inside it. He worked quickly, with practiced movements, and the satchel was filled in thirty seconds. He zipped it closed and stood up, passing it to the other, who slung it over his shoulder and turned toward the door. Hand on the knob, the man looked back at Mr. Doe, nodding.

"You know something?" Mr. Doe said, returning the nod. "You look just like Johnny Appleseed." And he smiled.

11:00 A.M.

THE APPLIED RESEARCH Center on B Level looked just like his old lab suite at Carnegie-Mellon, Warne thought to himself—or would have, if he'd had twenty times the endowment. The rooms were spacious, gleaming, brilliantly lit. They passed a data center full of terminals and rack-optimized servers; a lab in which white-coated technicians hovered over the subassembly of what looked like a holographic transmission system.

Georgia walked beside him, guidemap in one hand. "Do you have to meet with Sarah Boatwright *now*?" she asked. "I mean, we've only gotten to two rides."

Thank God, Warne said to himself. Brighton Beach Express had been bad enough, but the second coaster—Scream Machine—had been much worse. His stomach remained somewhere in the vicinity of his gullet, and if he closed his eyes, he could still see the wooden supports, whizzing past scant inches from his face. "It shouldn't be long. We'll be back out again before you know it. Besides," he ventured, "aren't you curious to see her after all this time? It'll be a surprise—I didn't tell her you were coming along."

Georgia's only response was a noncommittal sniff.

Warne glanced at the numbers on the passing doors, then down at the directions Amanda Freeman had given him. Conference room B-23. *Why a conference room?* he asked himself. Odd place for an informal meeting with Sarah. Her administrative assistant had told him the meeting would concern future development of the Metanet, the computer infrastructure he'd designed to run the Park's robots. And he could certainly use an assignment like expanding its functionality. But at first, he hadn't allowed himself to get too excited. After all, his break with Utopia's home office hadn't been exactly amicable. Then, just last Thursday, the assistant had called to move up the meeting by a week. That meant eagerness on their part: after all, the Atlantis rollout wasn't far off. The Metanet would have to be expanded to accommodate the robots in this new World. That must be it. No doubt this initial meeting would be a brief, fence-mending visit, in which the project would be laid out. Then, after touring the Park with Georgia, he'd go home, put together a proposal. And then more, longer meetings would follow. That's the way Utopia worked.

To his right, he noticed a set of double doors. "Here we are," he said, grasping the nearest handle and turning it. His palm was slippery on the polished metal. The thought of seeing Sarah again filled him with a strange mixture of anticipation and dread. He let Georgia in, followed her through the door, and then stopped in surprise.

The conference room was much bigger than he'd anticipated. He closed the door and walked forward slowly, looking around. There was a large table in the center, surrounded by perhaps a dozen chairs. An electronic whiteboard, covered with scribbled logic diagrams, stood at one end. An LCD projector sat at the other. Several computer terminals on wheeled metal racks were crowded together along one wall. Georgia glanced around for a moment, then walked curiously toward the whiteboard. Warne watched her absently.

And then the door opened again and Sarah Boatwright stepped into the room.

He'd wondered what it would feel like to see her again. He had imagined awkwardness, a little reproach, maybe even anger. But the one thing he had never imagined was mere desire. And yet the longing that rose inside him as he caught sight of her was unmistakable.

It had been twelve months since she'd accepted the job as head of Operations, left Carnegie-Mellon, and effectively ended her relationship with Warne. And yet she looked younger somehow, as if the chill air of Utopia had regenerative properties. Under the artificial daylight of the Utopia Underground, her coppery hair looked almost cinnamon, her green eyes flecked with gold. As always, she stood very erect, chin held high. She had always been self-possessed, self-assured, without doubt the strongest woman he'd known. But there was a new bearing about her, a way she carried her statuesque limbs, that he was instantly aware of: an air of command. The omnipresent teacup hovered in one hand, and a small sheaf of papers was balanced under the opposite elbow.

"Andrew," she said, nodding. "Thank you for coming." She placed the teacup on the desk, extended her hand.

Warne shook the proffered hand. Sarah's touch was brief, professional, without trace of lingering affection.

And then she caught sight of Georgia, who was watching them silently from the far side of the whiteboard. Sarah let her hand fall to her side. For a very brief moment, her face registered surprise: a blank, expressionless look that Warne had seen only rarely. Then, as quickly as it had come, it vanished.

"Hi, Georgia," she said, smiling. "I didn't know you were coming. This is a surprise. A nice surprise."

"Hi," was Georgia's reply.

There was an awkward silence of perhaps five seconds.

"You look like you've grown at least five inches since I last saw you. Even more pretty, too."

In response, Georgia walked away from the whiteboard to stand beside her father.

"How's school going? I remember you were having a little trouble with French."

"It's fine, I guess."

"That's good." A beat. "Have you been in the Park yet? Visited any of the attractions?"

Georgia nodded. Her eyes remained low.

Sarah's own eyes moved toward Warne's. *Drew, what's she doing here?* her expression read.

At that moment, two more people appeared in the doorway: a tall, slender man around forty, and a young Asian woman in a white lab coat.

Sarah glanced at them. "Come in, please," she said crisply. "I'd like you to meet Dr. Warne. Andrew, this is Fred Barksdale, CTO and head of Systems."

The man smiled, revealing a set of white, perfect teeth. "A pleasure," he said, striding forward to shake Warne's hand. "Welcome to Utopia. At long last, I might add."

"And this is Teresa Bonifacio, who works with Fred in Robotics."

Hearing this, Warne looked at the Asian woman with fresh curiosity. He'd spoken with her dozens of times over the phone—enough to have become good friends *à la distance*—but had never seen her in person. Teresa was around five foot four, with dark eyes and bobbed, jet-black hair. She returned his gaze, looking at him intently. For a moment, he found himself almost shocked by how attractive she was. Over all their many conversations, he'd never thought to attach a face to the deep, laconic voice in the telephone.

"Teresa," he said. "We finally meet."

The woman responded with a smile and a birdlike duck of the head. "I can't believe it. I feel like I've known you for years." Her smile was warm, but a little impish; it crinkled her nose and the corners of her eyes.

"And this is Georgia," Sarah went on. "Andrew's daughter."

Both Barksdale and Teresa Bonifacio turned curiously toward the girl. Watching them, Warne felt sudden misgiving. Clearly, this wasn't the informal chat, the nostalgic tête-à-tête with Sarah, that he'd been expecting. He'd made a significant miscalculation.

There was another moment of silence. Warne felt Georgia edge a little closer to him.

"Well, we'd better get started." Sarah squared her papers on the desk. "Georgia, listen. We need to speak to your dad for a few minutes. Would you mind waiting outside?"

Georgia did not reply; she did not need to. The knitting of her eyebrows, and the sudden, stubborn jut of her lower lip, were response enough.

"Here," Barksdale spoke into the silence. "I've got an idea. What if Terri takes her to the nearest cast lounge? We've got every flavor of soda imaginable, and they're all free."

Now it was Teresa's turn to look aggrieved, but Warne flashed Barksdale a grateful glance. The man had clearly sensed the awkwardness of the situation and hit upon a tactful solution.

Warne looked back at Georgia. "How does that sound, sweetheart?" he asked. He watched the wheels go around in her head. She knew that she could not easily refuse such a polite gesture from an adult. And—he hoped—she didn't want to embarrass her dad.

The firm line of her lower lip softened. "Cherry Coke?"

"Oceans of it," Barksdale said, smiling.

"Okay."

Teresa Bonifacio looked first at Barksdale, then at Georgia, and then at Warne. "Nice to meet you at last, *Dr.* Warne," she said in a joking contralto. "Come on, kiddo." And then, ushering Georgia before her, she walked out into the corridor and closed the door behind her.

11:15 A.M.

"ANOTHER CHERRY COKE?" Teresa Bonifacio asked as she tried to find a comfortable position in the red plastic chair.

Across the table, Georgia shook her head. "No," she said. And then she added, "Thanks."

Teresa smiled, then glanced privately at her watch. The meeting would take half an hour, maybe forty minutes. But only ten minutes had gone by, and already she could think of nothing else to say to the girl before her. She heaved an ill-suppressed sigh. *I can't believe I turned down a $120,000 research job at the Rand Institute to baby-sit a bratty kid.*

She stirred again in her chair. As annoying as it was to be playing baby-sitter, she was almost glad she didn't have to be in that conference room, see Andrew's face when he heard the news. Over the course of the last year, she'd developed an affection for the man that went beyond intellectual admiration. A robotics lab could be a lonely place. After all, the things didn't usually talk back to you; and when they did, what they had to say was rarely interesting. She'd found herself looking forward to the telephone chats with Warne. It was nice to talk with somebody who understood, who enjoyed, hearing about the little victories, the offbeat theory. He even seemed to appreciate her quirky sense of humor—and that was saying something. Andrew Warne was a great guy; this was a rotten development. And not just for him.

Teresa watched as Georgia pulled a media player out of her pocket, put the headphones over her ears, and then—as if realizing this was rude—took them off again. She wondered why Warne had brought the girl along. But as quickly as she thought this, she realized the answer. *He couldn't have known why he was really asked here. They've been so secretive about it all. He must have thought it would make a good vacation.*

She decided to try a different tack. "What's that you're listening to?" she asked, nodding toward the player.

"Benny Goodman. At Carnegie Hall."

"Not bad. Although old Benny is a little bit too white-bread for me, if you know what I mean. You like Duke Ellington?"

Georgia shook her head. "I don't know."

"Don't *know*? The guy's only the foundation of all modern music. I don't just mean jazz, either. That guy could *swing*. His concert at Newport, in 1956? Check out 'Diminuendo and Crescendo in Blue.' The sax player, Paul Gonsalves, takes a solo for twenty-seven choruses. *Twenty-seven freakin' choruses.* Unbelievable."

This was greeted by silence. Teresa sighed again. She realized she was talking to Georgia like she was an adult. But she had no idea how to talk to a kid. Even as a kid, she hadn't known how to talk to other kids. Hell, she barely felt comfortable talking to other *adults* sometimes. One thing she knew, though: if she had to sit here for another half hour, she'd go stir-crazy.

Abruptly, she stood up. "Let's take a walk."

Georgia glanced at her in mute inquiry.

"Well, you look about as bored as I feel. Come on, there's something I want to show you."

With Georgia in tow, Teresa threaded her way through the complex passageways of B Level, arriving at last at a small, unmarked door. She opened it, revealing a narrow metal staircase. She ushered Georgia ahead of her, and they began to climb.

The stairs seemed to ascend forever. At last, they reached a small landing of corrugated metal, ringed by waist-high retaining bars. On the far side, a narrower staircase rose again, disappearing into an enclosed passage. With unspoken mutual consent, they stopped on the landing for a breather.

"Isn't there an elevator?" Georgia panted.

"Yup. But I hate elevators."

"Why?"

"Claustrophobic."

Silence descended as they caught their breath. Then Teresa turned to Georgia. "So, what's it like to have such a brilliant dad?"

Georgia looked over in surprise, as if she'd never considered the question. "It's okay, I guess."

"Okay? I'd have killed to have a dad like yours. My father's idea of advanced math was counting the beads on his rosary."

Georgia seemed to think a moment. "He's just like any other dad. We have fun."

"You interested in robotics?"

Georgia nodded. "Sure. I was, anyway."

Teresa considered this. It was still hard to believe that she was standing here, talking with the daughter of Andrew Warne: father of the Metanet, controversial pioneer in robotics and machine intelligence, lately departed from Carnegie-Mellon. In the course of managing the Metanet, she'd had so many one-on-one phone conversations with him that it was somehow hard to imagine him with a family. But of course, she knew the history: how his wife, a naval architect, had drowned four years before while testing out a new sailboat design in Chesapeake Bay. How he'd been closely involved with Eric Nightingale in the Park's early vision, but after Nightingale's death had been alienated by the corporate types who'd moved in to finish Utopia. She even knew the gossip: How he and Sarah Boatwright had been seeing each other back at Carnegie-Mellon. How his controversial theories on machine learning weren't bearing their promised fruit. How the start-up company he'd founded after leaving Carnegie-Mellon had recently gone belly-up, victim of the dot-com implosion. Not all Utopia rumors were accurate, of course. But if that last one was, she felt doubly bad for him today.

She pushed herself away from the bars. "Come on," she said. "Only seventy-one more steps. I counted them once."

The staircase beyond led steeply upward, through an enclosure formed by two long, slender beams that arched away overhead, out of sight. There were no windows, and the tubelike passage was lit by long fluorescent lights set into the walls.

"We're almost there now," Teresa panted as she pulled herself up with the handrail.

Gradually, the angle of the staircase lessened. Teresa led the way around a sharp curve, then stepped onto another metal platform and stood aside, gesturing for Georgia to come and stand beside her. She watched the girl step forward, then stop suddenly in astonishment.

"Take a good grip on that handrail, there," Teresa said, grinning at the slack-jawed expression. "It can take a minute to adjust. Close your eyes for a moment, if that helps."

They were standing on an observation platform, tucked high up under the domed glass roof of Utopia. Below them, beyond a panel of one-way glass, stretched the entire Park. The cool ribbon of the Nexus could be seen arrowing down its center. Spreading out from it, like the sections of a halved grapefruit, were the Worlds themselves: each a riot of color and shape, each utterly different from the others. Callisto, the futuristic space-port, had from this height the kind of dark, burnished sheen of a black-light photograph; Gaslight lay enshrouded in veils of fog; Boardwalk was all brilliant light and bright pastel shades. People were everywhere: walking along the boulevards and sidewalks, waiting in lines, snapping photographs, studying maps, talking with cast members, eating, drinking, laughing, shouting. It was like viewing a map of the Park, brought magically to life. And yet it was much more than that; because from this height, all the complex secret machinery that no tourist ever saw was laid bare: the hidden entrances and exits, the false backs of the buildings, the electric carts and props and equipment and access corridors that filled the spaces between the walls and behind the facades.

Teresa pointed to a workman who was trotting, radio in hand, along a narrow corridor almost directly beneath their feet. "Pay no attention to the man behind the curtain," she said with a laugh. "So, what do you think?"

"It's *awesome*," Georgia said, eyes shining as she stared out at the spectacle that lay spread out beneath them. Suddenly, she pointed. "Look! There's Brighton Beach Express. We were on that this morning. And there's the Scream Machine. I didn't know they were that close together."

"That's part of park design," Teresa replied. "You put the exit of one attraction near the entrance of another."

She stood back, still smiling, watching Georgia look around in fascination. Unlike most competing parks, Utopia did not allow backstage tours. No guest except for VIPs ever got to see the Underground. And sure as hell no guest ever got to see *this*. It was too bad, in a way, because it was one sight guaranteed to amaze anybody—even precocious fourteen-year-olds who think they've seen everything.

"Take a look at this," Teresa said. And she pointed to a small placard set into the railing before them: *Eric Nightingale, 1956–2002*. "We call this Nightingale's Nest. It's dedicated to his vision for Utopia." She glanced again at Georgia. "You ever meet him?"

"He used to come over to our house, talk with my dad, about robotics, I think. He played backgammon with me a couple of times. He let me win more than Dad does."

Teresa shook her head, privately amused at the image of the great Eric Nightingale playing backgammon with a kid in junior high. Then she, too, turned her gaze out over the Park. "Everybody who works at Utopia comes here once," she said. "Usually on their first day. It's kind of an initiation. Other than that, though, it's pretty quiet. All those stairs, you know. But I like coming here. God knows I can use the exercise. It's peaceful. And if I'm feeling down—you know, about my job or something—I know that coming up here will remind me of what I'm working for. That makes it kind of appropriate today."

She shut up abruptly, aware that she'd said more than she planned. She looked over to see Georgia regarding her with a strange, intent look. *She's thinking something about me,* Teresa thought. *I wonder what it is. Then again, maybe I don't want to know.*

"What?" she said aloud.

Georgia looked away for a moment. Then she looked back. "I was just wondering. You like Fats Waller?"

"Like? What's not to like? I think I wore out my copy of 'Handful of Keys.' And piano playing just doesn't get any better than 'Carolina Shout.' " Now it was her turn to stare quizzically at Georgia. "Why?"

Georgia's eyes held hers briefly, and then the girl looked quickly away. "Oh, nothing," she said. It was as if she had suddenly grown shy.

Teresa glanced at her watch. "Well, we've managed to kill half an hour. Let's get you back to your dad." And she led the way down the staircase.

11:15 A.M.

ANDREW WARNE LOOKED from Sarah to Fred Barksdale, then back again.

Sarah motioned toward the table. "Andrew, please," she said. "Take a seat." She placed her cup and saucer directly across from him, then sat down herself. Reaching for the sheaf of papers, she squared them once again on the table, then passed them to Warne. "Sign these before we continue."

Warne took the papers, scanned them quickly. He looked up. "This is a nondisclosure agreement."

Sarah nodded.

"I don't understand. I already signed one of these, during development phase."

"It's Chuck Emory and the home office. They want to make sure a tight lid is kept on what we discuss here today."

Sarah offered nothing more, merely returning his gaze. After a moment, Warne sighed, lowered his eyes, and scribbled his name on the signature line. *Bullshit red tape,* he thought to himself. *The bean counters in New York get worse by the year.* And yet it made sense. Expanding the Metanet would require access to new and sensitive Utopia technology.

Sarah took back the papers. "Thank you." She placed them neatly beside the teacup. "I'm sorry we couldn't give you details any earlier, but we just noticed the problems recently and we've been trying to determine a pattern."

Warne glanced at her. "Problems?"

Sarah turned toward Barksdale. "Fred, would you provide background?"

"Right," Barksdale said. He placed his elbows on the arms of his chair and tented his fingers, staring at Warne from beneath a well-combed mop of blond hair. "Over the last two weeks, we've noticed odd things going on with some of the tech at Utopia.

Glitches in the universal translation system in Guest Services, for example. The AI that controls diagnostics for Station Omega—the free-fall ride in Callisto—kept reporting failures, wouldn't let the ride start up. But most of the problems have been with the robotics." He began ticking off points on well-manicured fingernails. "A janitorial bot on C Level tried to mop an electrical panel; it was deactivated just in time. A mail-delivery bot began dropping mail in trash cans instead of in-boxes. Some of the fire-breathers in Dragonspire forgot their timing and misfired. Almost singed a Japanese tour group."

"These problems," Warne replied. "Are they ongoing?"

"That's the most frustrating part. Except for Station Omega, they've been intermittent. And even that problem went away just an hour ago, gave the ride engineers a green light. Nobody knows why. We've run fault-tolerance tests, engineering evaluations, even gone low-tech with oscilloscopes and trace pens. There's nothing wrong."

"Phantom abnormalities," Sarah said. "They're fine one minute, have a psychotic break the next. Then they're fine again."

Warne turned from Barksdale back to Sarah Boatwright. A chill was beginning to form in the pit of his stomach.

"Voltage irregularities?" he asked.

Barksdale shook his head. "Every line in Utopia is perfectly clean. The power grid never fluctuates."

Warne nodded. "That's right, I forgot. The nuclear reactor." When nobody laughed, he asked another question. "Beta-testing artifacts?"

"No," Barksdale said. "Everything's running in production."

"Bugs?"

"After so many processing cycles? And in so many places? And then to have them vanish?"

"Have you set up a clean room, tried to isolate an event?"

"With the number of autonomous bots out there, the truth is, we wouldn't know where to begin."

The room fell silent. The chill was spreading quickly. "Intermittent problems like these often mean external intrusion," he said, choosing his words carefully.

Barksdale shook his head again. "Absolutely not. There's a moat around all the production servers. No external connections. The only portal to the outside is the guest information web, and that's located off-site, firewalled to the hilt."

Sarah Boatwright sipped her tea. "Just to be sure, Fred had the white-hats at KIS work it over last month. They said it was the most secure system they'd ever seen."

Warne nodded absently. He'd worked with Keyhole Intrusion Systems the year before, when the robotics web server at Carnegie-Mellon had been hit with a denial-of-service attack. "White-hats" were licensed hackers, hired by corporations to break into their computer systems and pinpoint weaknesses. The cowboys over at KIS were the best in the business.

Warne licked his lips. He had to ask the question. "Okay, so there's trouble in paradise. I'm sorry to hear about it. But how exactly does this relate to the—what did your assistant call it over the phone—the future development of the Metanet?"

Barksdale and Sarah Boatwright exchanged glances. "Dr. Warne, I don't know exactly how to say this," Barksdale replied. "I was hoping you'd come to the same conclusion we have. The problem seems to lie *with* the Metanet."

Even though he'd already begun to fear just such a reply, Warne was stunned. He felt his mouth go dry. "Don't you think that's jumping to conclusions?"

"It's the only thing all the failures have in common. We've eliminated everything else. There's no other answer."

"No other *answer*?" Warne heard his own voice, faster and louder than he'd meant it to be.

Barksdale nodded. "The Metanet is supposed to be self-learning. Perhaps, over time, it has modified its own rule-set for the worse. You know: 'Striving to better, oft we mar what's well.' "

"No, I *don't* know. The system gets a nervous tic, and you blame the head."

"It's rather more than a nervous tic," Barksdale said. He had a strange look on his finely featured face, like a doctor breaking bad news to a patient. "There's something else. What happened on the Notting Hill ride the Friday before last."

Warne had seen a short blurb about this in the paper. "That was a mechanical failure. Shoddy workmanship or something."

"All of our high-G rides are built by the Swiss firm, Taittinger & Rochefort. The Rolls-Royce of the roller-coaster world."

"Whatever. It was an accident. What's the relevance?"

"Two bots are assigned to that attraction. During the day,

while the ride is operational, they work lubrication. After the Park closes, they do a safety inspection of the entire track. They're programmed to look for metal fatigue, stress points, to make sure the electronic safety dogs that control the movement of the cars on the ratchet hills and descents are secure. For some reason we don't know, seven nights ago they *loosened* a dozen of the dogs instead of tightening them, reversing polarity. During operation the next day, five of the dogs shorted out, two at a critical point. Without the dogs to keep it on the track, a car derailed on the final descent. Backup safety plates in the undercarriage kept the car from leaving the track completely, but it whipsawed severely throughout the entire seventy-foot drop."

"I reviewed video logs of the incident," Sarah said. "It was like watching a dog shaking a rat. A boy in the front seat lost his grip and fell out. He survived, by a miracle. But both legs were shattered, several ribs crushed. He'll be in a wheelchair for months. The other occupants of the car were badly bruised. The father suffered a broken collarbone. Needless to say, lawyers have been circling ever since."

Warne realized he was holding his breath. He exhaled slowly. "You're sure about this?"

Both Sarah and Barksdale nodded.

"That doesn't make any sense. Did you examine the bots' programming?"

"It was the first thing we did after closing the ride. We had a code-review team, led by Terri Bonifacio, check every line from the command stack to the mapping routines. The Metanet had reprogrammed the bots to loosen the safety dogs."

"Both bots?"

"Each loosened precisely six safety dogs."

Warne felt something ridiculously like panic threaten to seize his limbs. He fought it back. "Wait a minute. Let's back up here, think about the Metanet's job. It's a neural network that examines the operating code of the Park's robots, and optimizes that code. That's *all* it does. It's a passive-learning system. It wouldn't just . . ." Warne stopped. "You've considered the possibility of internal tampering?"

Barksdale nodded, smoothing down his tie. "All of our IT staff goes through rigorous psychological testing and background checks. Our compensation and benefits packages are the best in the industry, we have an employee satisfaction rate of 99 percent—"

"Wait, wait," Warne interrupted. "That's all well and good. But this has got 'inside job' written all over it. I mean, what other explanation is there?"

Warne watched as Sarah and Barksdale exchanged glances. He could guess what they were thinking: *He's defensive, lashing out, trying to lay blame anywhere but his own creation.*

Barksdale cleared his throat. "We have a stringent code-promotion process, nothing gets updated without passing up the managerial chain and past me. But, Dr. Warne, the bottom line is, this simply isn't the work of a corporate spy or a disgruntled employee. Diagnostic failures on mail-delivery robots? The hand-writing is all wrong. Besides, it's too broad-scale. Even so, we've begun interviews and log checking, just to be sure."

Sarah took a sip of her tea, replaced the cup in the saucer. "Meanwhile, Andrew, we want to detask the Metanet."

For a moment, Warne was too stunned to respond. *Detask the Metanet. Jesus.* He thought about the bots on Notting Hill Chase, the loosened safety dogs. Was it really possible that he was indirectly responsible for such a terrible . . .

Then he shook his head. It *wasn't* possible, it couldn't be.

He looked once again at Sarah and Barksdale. He could see in their eyes that this conversation was merely for the sake of form. A decision had already been made.

"Sarah," he said in his best abject tone. "I know you must be under a lot of pressure over this. But I think it's a rash decision. Look, we can take a few days to examine the problem. You can show me the specifics. I'm sure something will come to light."

"Actually, Andrew, I'm leaving for San Francisco tomorrow morning," she replied. "Fred will give you whatever you need."

Warne watched the two share another private look. Then he realized: Sarah and Barksdale were an item.

Abruptly, jealous anger mingled with the shock, dismay, and mortification that already filled him. Not that he could blame Sarah, of course; going for someone like Barksdale was almost a given. The guy was charming in that Brit way that had always seemed a little superficial to Warne; good-looking, gallant, re-portedly a brilliant CTO to boot. It was almost too much. Warne felt like a Volvo, traded in for a twelve-cylinder Jag.

He shook his head at the bitter irony. All this time, he'd been worried about seeing Sarah again—how she'd act, how he'd feel, what Georgia might or might not say. He hadn't been thinking much about the meeting itself at all, save how it might jumpstart his stalled career . . . He sat back in his chair, feeling a lot older than when he'd first walked into the room. "You bought the technology," he said, the anger hardening his voice. "It's yours to use as you see fit. Why did you bring me all the way out here to tell me the bad news?"

"We want you to head up the disassembly," Barksdale said.

"Don't you think that's a little cold? Not only are you giving my creation a lobotomy, you want me to wield the scalpel?"

Barksdale seemed to consider this. "It's a nontrivial operation."

"Surely you have enough programming drones on hand to do your plumbing for you. You don't need my help—"

"Dr. Warne, do you think it was *my* idea?" Barksdale was smiling, but the rich English vowels carried the faintest undercurrent of irritation.

"Or maybe what you're really looking for is a scapegoat."

Barksdale shot him a look of surprise, and Sarah rose to her feet.

"I think you've heard all you need," she said briskly. "Let's wrap it up. Fred, I'll see you at the State of the Park meeting. Andrew, why don't you stay behind?"

"Right." Barksdale smiled briefly at Sarah, nodded a little warily to Warne, then left.

Sarah watched him go, then turned to Warne. "Well, I'm glad to see you haven't lost your ability to alienate an audience."

"How'd you expect me to react, after hearing my biggest success is about to be trashed? Pleased?"

"You shouldn't look at it like that. This Metanet exit is temporary, exploratory."

"Come on. I *dealt* with those home office guys after Nightingale's death, remember? You saw the result. Once you take the Metanet off-line, it's not going to go back on."

Sarah reached for her teacup. "I understand how you feel, Andrew, but—"

"And that's another thing. What's with this *An*drew?"

"I think it's better." She withdrew her hand, looked him in the eye. "Don't you?"

Nobody won a staring match with Sarah. Abruptly, the anger drained out of Warne, leaving him feeling defeated. He leaned against the table and crossed his arms.

Then he looked at Sarah. "It just occurred to me. Tomorrow is June twenty-first."

"And?"

"The first anniversary of the day you walked out."

"I did not walk out, Drew. I accepted the job at Utopia."

"Would it have killed you to stay a little longer? Try to work things out? I mean, I know we were both busy, we didn't have as much time as we should for each other. And I know Georgia didn't make it easy for you. But you didn't give her enough of a chance. You didn't give *us* enough of a chance."

"I gave as much as I could. Did you expect me to give up my job?"

"I didn't expect you to pack up and move to Nevada."

"It was the chance of a *lifetime*! Would you rather I'd stayed behind, resented you for holding me back?"

Sarah had stepped toward him with these words. Now she paused. Then, with deliberate movements, she took a step back, reached for her teacup, took a sip.

"Let's not play archaeology," she began again in a quieter tone. "It's pointless, it won't get us anywhere." She replaced the cup with a steady hand. "Bringing you into this was a difficult decision for me. But there was no other choice. Nobody else understands the topology of the Metanet like you. You designed it, after all. And . . . we just don't want any more problems."

Warne didn't answer. There seemed like nothing else to say.

"I shouldn't have to remind you of the original terms of the agreement. Can't you view this as an opportunity? The thing's had six full months to mature, operating in a production environment you couldn't begin to duplicate in your lab."

I'm without a lab at the moment. But Warne simply shrugged. "Sure. It'll make for a nice postmortem."

Sarah looked at him as the silence lengthened. Then she turned back to the table, collected her papers, picked up her teacup.

"Teresa should be back any minute," she said. "I suggest the two of you not waste any time. Mr. Barksdale's expecting an action plan by the end of the day."

She walked out of the conference room, leaving the door open behind her.

11:45 A.M.

CALLISTO WAS UTOPIA'S future world, a bustling spaceport in geosynchronous orbit—visitors were asked to believe—sixty miles above Jupiter's sixth moon. Andrew Warne found it hard not to believe. After a brief, pitch-black shuttle ride, he had walked through the docking area, Georgia at his side, then stepped out into the bustling main concourse—only to stop again and stare around in surprise. Spread before them was a thriving hub of entertainment and commerce that looked as if it had been torn whole from the twenty-fourth century. Strange-looking aliens and cast members in futuristic uniforms walked among the camera-clicking tourists. Ruby- and azure-colored lasers lanced and flickered overhead. Incredibly detailed holographic images were everywhere: pointing the way to rides and attractions, hovering like futuristic signboards above the entrance to restaurant and rest room alike.

As elsewhere, the span of the Utopia dome curved far above. But this was not the stripe of brilliant blue sky he'd seen in the Nexus or Boardwalk. Instead, he saw a deep blackness of limitless space, punctuated by countless stars. The richly colored bulk of Jupiter filled more than a quarter of the sky. As Warne stared, he noticed that the clouds on the planet's surface were moving, roiling convulsively in earth-sized tempests.

"Awesome," Georgia said as she looked around. "Just like in the show. But why are we here? We haven't finished Boardwalk yet."

"We'll have plenty of time for that later on," Warne said. "Right now, there's something I want to show you." He glanced at his watch. He'd agreed to meet with Teresa at one o'clock: that gave them a little over an hour. He tried to keep his step light, his tone relaxed: Georgia was too uncannily good at picking up his moods. Thank God, she hadn't asked him anything about the meeting.

He consulted a guidemap briefly, then steered Georgia out into the current of chattering guests. The excitement and energy grew stronger, the chill, sterile-smelling air was filled with an almost palpable sense of glee. Callisto was the only World where characters from Nightingale's wildly popular cartoon show, *Atmosfear,* could be found in costume. It was also the location of two of the Park's most outrageous thrill rides, Event Horizon and Moon Shot. As a result, children were everywhere: running up to full-size holograms of Eric Nightingale and costumed cast members, dragging parents toward favorite attractions, pleading for money to buy action figures.

But the carnival atmosphere and exotic surroundings did little to penetrate Warne's gloom. *Detask the Metanet.* He could still scarcely believe it. To think that just two hours before, he'd been wandering through Boardwalk, like a prize idiot, wondering what exciting new features they wanted him to add to the robotic network. He shook his head bitterly.

"What's up, Dad?" Georgia asked instantly.

"Nothing. This place is just . . . All these rides, all these shops. It's so commercial. Nightingale would turn in his grave."

"Dad, you are so *utterly* out of it. It's awesome. Look at that." She pointed toward one of the quieter rides: a spiderlike array of child-sized rockets, circling on pearlescent metal legs that seemed to fade in and out of sight, making the rockets appear detached, self-guided. "Even the kiddie rides look great."

Warne nodded. But it was a far cry from the vision Nightingale had described, seated at their kitchen table, coffee untouched, on that night they had first met. He remembered how the magician's black eyes had glittered with an almost manic energy; how he had jumped out of his seat to pace, again and again, as he talked; how his hands had never stopped moving as they sketched out his idea for a virtual environment. He'd been traveling the world, visiting theme parks, castles, temples, medieval villages. He wanted to create virtual worlds complete in every detail; past worlds, future worlds, that would instruct visitors as they entertained. Worlds that relied on immersiveness, not rides, to delight guests. A themed *system,* Nightingale had called it, that would use the latest advances in digital media, holograms, robotics, to weave its magic. And he'd wanted Warne to design the robotics substructure.

Even without Nightingale's intensity and charisma, the idea had held great appeal. It meshed perfectly with Warne's own highly controversial theories about artificial intelligence and machine learning. So he'd pitched the idea of a meta-network—metanet, for short—that would link all the Park's robots to a central processor. The processor would study the robots' activity, create improvements, and download the optimized code daily to the bots over the network. It would be the perfect vehicle to demonstrate his theories about machine learning. But it would be just the start of a vast web of robotics and AI that would ultimately encompass the entire operation of the Park.

At least, that had been the plan . . .

"Is Teresa Japanese?" Georgia asked.

Warne pulled himself away from his thoughts, distantly surprised by the question. "I don't know, princess. I don't think so."

"Dad, I *told* you not to call me princess."

They had threaded their way deeper into Callisto now, and the crowds on the concourse were thicker here, jostling and laughing and pointing. To one side, guests were thronging around a tall, gaunt man in twenty-fourth-century armor and a glossy black cape. This was Morpheus, the demonic, magic-wielding ruler of Earth Prime: a creature 50 million television-watching children loved to hate. He was posing for a picture, hand on the shoulder of a young boy, devilish beard parted in a smile. Warne looked toward him, frowning. Now that he thought about it, he hadn't spoken to Teresa in at least three weeks. That in itself was unusual: they'd developed a habit of making contact at least once a week, mixing shop talk with gossip, sharing jokes, catching up.

She was in charge of running the Metanet. The least she could have done was warn him. Why hadn't she? Anger lanced through him as he wondered if she was somehow at fault for all this; if she'd done something, inadvertently or otherwise, to sabotage his creation. And to think his first reaction, upon seeing her in person, had been one of physical attraction . . . He shook his head.

They had agreed to meet in her lab. And that's what he'd do, he decided: he'd meet her. He'd discuss an exit strategy, make sure there were no impediments to a smooth transition. And then he'd do what he had planned all along: enjoy the Park with his daugh-

ter. Teresa and her people could take the Metanet off-line themselves. To hell with his contract. He'd be damned if he'd be the
one to pull the plug on his own biggest accomplishment.

Up ahead now, he could see a hologram of a skeletal constel-
lation, revolving above the entrance to a brightly lit restaurant:
the Big Dipper. A crowd of people were lined up outside, murmuring and pointing. In spite of everything, Warne felt himself
smiling. He could guess what they were pointing at.

Beside the restaurant entrance was a large take-out window,
framed in chrome and open to the concourse. At its base, a series
of round seats set atop low posts were arrayed along a counter of
some shiny transparent material. Behind the counter, a futuristic
ice cream shop sat bathed in ghostly shades of black light. Tending the shop was a large mobile robot. The mobot was a hilarious,
ungainly-looking thing, a child's unsteady construction of metal
blocks. Its base was a dollylike platform of six synchronously
driven wheels. Atop the drive mechanism was a large cube that
housed the onboard computing. Planted on that was a tall cylinder which supported two arrays of ultrasonic transducers.

Warne reached for Georgia's arm, pointed. She glanced over,
then stopped abruptly. A grin slowly broke across her face.
"Oh, man," she said at last. "It's kind of weird to see him here—
you know?"

It was making a milk shake. Warne watched as the mobot industriously scooped ice cream into a metal mixer, the powerful
pincers moving in short, controlled jerks. That had been the
hardest part: the sonar geometry. Because he knew the robot
would be working in a fixed environment, everything else—the
wheel encoders for the dead-reckoning system, the topological
map—had been relatively easy. But the stereo vision necessary
to carve perfect scoops out of an unpredictably shaped tin of ice
cream had kept him up more nights than he cared to remember.
And it had given birth to the mobot's name: Hard Place. No
doubt its sibling, Rock, was somewhere inside the restaurant.
Warne had designed Rock to tend bar: a far easier job, pouring
premeasured drinks, requiring less of the fine motor control
sported by Hard Place's arm servos.

"Come on," Warne said, throwing his arm over Georgia's
shoulders. "Let's get some ice cream."

As they approached, Hard Place finished the shake and delivered it to a teenage girl at the counter. "Here you are," it said,

pan-tilt camera nodding down toward the girl. "Your passcard, please." Warne watched as Hard Place scanned the card with its sonar cluster, handed it back, then used its pincers to set the shake gently down on the counter. Georgia was right: he, too, had grown so used to seeing the mobot in the cramped confines of his Carnegie-Mellon lab that it was strange to see it here, in this surreal environment, serving up real ice cream to real people.

The mobot swiveled away, trundling down the counter toward the next customer. Warne led Georgia through the knot of on-lookers and found two seats at the far end of the counter. It had been Georgia who'd convinced him to plant a panning ultrasonic sensor atop the robot's central array, and direct it to swivel toward the closest human voice. He could still remember showing it to her for the first time, the way her young face had screwed up in disapproval. "It's got to have a head, Daddy," she'd said.

He had built these two robots as mere eye candy for Nightingale, platforms to demonstrate how voice recognition and image processing could be put to commercial use. But Nightingale was a man who loved details just as much as an overarching vision, and he'd been as delighted with Rock and Hard Place as he had with Warne's prizewinning thesis on hierarchical neural nets, or his scheme for a self-learning meta-network. He'd insisted they find a home within Utopia.

Hard Place was approaching them now. "Good afternoon," it rasped. "How can I help you?"

"A root beer float, please." Warne hadn't even needed to ask: Georgia could subsist on root beer floats alone. It had been the first thing he taught the robot to make.

"One root beer float," Hard Place echoed back. Warne had almost forgotten that artificial voice: digitized samples of his own. And he'd certainly forgotten just how big the robot was, almost eight feet to the top of its sensor array. "Would you like anything else?"

"Yes. A double pistachio chocolate sundae with whipped cream, please."

At this, Hard Place paused. "Dr. Warne?" it asked after a moment.

"Yes, Hard Place."

The robot paused again, slightly longer this time. "A double pistachio chocolate sundae with whipped cream, coming right up. Kemo Sabe."

Warne watched the robot as it pivoted and moved away. That joking nod to *The Lone Ranger* had been his own private embellishment; his signature at the bottom of the painting. He'd decided to add the routine on that day eighteen months before, when Rock and Hard Place were being crated up for delivery to Nevada. Eighteen months, but the difference was like night and day. Then, he and Sarah had just begun seeing each other; she was an amazingly confident woman, an intellectual equal, a potential second mother for Georgia. He'd begun pioneering work for Eric Nightingale, with the promise of much more to come. The future looked bright with promise.

How quickly things had changed. Georgia hadn't warmed to Sarah in the way he'd hoped; in fact, she seemed to resent her, became jealously possessive of her dad. His own work was coming under increasing fire at Carnegie-Mellon, seen as controversial, unproved. And then Nightingale had died. And Warne's relationship with the corporate suits and bean counters who'd rushed in to fill the gap soured, then broke apart completely, leaving his contractual obligation to the Metanet as the lone connection to Utopia. Sarah had moved out, taken the job as Park chief. How ironic that she'd first met Nightingale through Warne himself. With the Metanet money, Warne had left Carnegie-Mellon to start a research company to help prove his theories on machine learning—only to see it lose its financial backers when the dot-com bubble burst. But through it all, he still had the Metanet—or so he'd believed until this morning.

Now Hard Place was gliding back with the root beer float. "Here you are," it said, placing the root beer float on the counter in front of him and turning back to the row of ice cream tins, its AI routines already working toward the goal state of a double pistachio chocolate sundae with whipped cream. The robot's movements seemed a little more erratic, a little more hesitating, than he remembered. Almost as if its pathfinding routines had been deoptimized. Could this be a result of the daily uplink? Was it possible, really possible, that the Metanet had . . . But Warne refused to follow this line of thought. He'd had more than his share of bad news for one day.

"Can I borrow the guidemap?" Georgia asked.

"Sure."

"And forty bucks?"

"Sure, just . . . Wait—forty bucks? Why?"

"I want to get one of those *Atmosfear* T-shirts. The weird shimmery ones. Haven't you seen them?"

Warne had seen them, dozens of them, adorning the torsos of teenagers wandering the concourse. With a sigh, he opened his wallet and passed over the money, watching as she slipped the headphones over her ears and took a sip of root beer.

If he was honest with himself, he'd admit this particular stop was as much for him as it was for her. He needed to see this affirmation of his work, this reminder of better times. Until just today—when he learned it was to be deactivated—he hadn't realized just how important the Metanet was to him. And now, despite the defiant posing, he felt a wave of despair wash over him. What was he going to do now? He'd left Carnegie-Mellon, burned his bridges. He glanced covertly at Georgia again. How was he ever going to explain it to her?

There was a nearby whirring, and Hard Place returned. "Here you are, Kemo Sabe," it said as it set the sundae down before Warne. He waited. Next, the robot would ask for his passcard, charge the ice cream order to his Utopia account.

But Hard Place did no such thing. Instead, it swiveled its sensor array first left, then right. With a low whirring sound, the robot began rocking backward and forward. The movements seemed strangely hesitant, uncertain.

Georgia looked over from her root beer, plucked the headphones away from one ear. "Dad?" she asked inquiringly.

With a sudden, sharp grinding, Hard Place charged toward Warne. Its boxlike central housing collided with the counter, knocking over glasses and straw dispensers. Murmurs of surprise rose from the patrons. Abruptly, Hard Place rolled backward, banging roughly against the backbar, then shot forward again at high speed, servos twisting, sensor arrays spinning.

"Georgia!" Warne cried. "Get out of the way!"

The robot smashed again into the front counter. There were sharp gasps, a scream, as the patrons fell from their chairs, scrambling to get away from the counter. But Hard Place had shot backward once more, colliding heavily with the rear counter. A dozen bottles of colored syrup fell to the ground, shivering into pieces. With a squeal of motors, the robot came forward again.

Warne leaped from his seat, staring at Hard Place in shock and surprise. He'd never seen the robot act like this before. In fact, it *couldn't* act like this; he'd programmed it himself. *What the hell is going on?* It was as if the robot was trying to break free of its enclosure, force its way out into the concourse. But its pathfinding routines were primitive; if that happened, with its speed and size, it would trample anything in its way.

The robot collided with the counter in a shattering crash. The long, transparent countertop shivered, deformed, spilling its remaining contents in a staccato chorus. Hard Place reared backward, then came forward yet again, like a caged and angry bull.

There were shouts of warning from behind Warne, cries of alarm. He looked to his right: Georgia was standing some distance away, staring, eyes wide. He thought quickly. There was only one thing to do: try to reach the manual kill switch in the rear of the central housing and deactivate the robot.

Gingerly, he approached. "Hard Place," he said in a loud, clear tone, hoping to get its attention, interrupt whatever bizarre behavioral loop it had fallen into. As he spoke, he put his left hand up, fingers spread, in a placating gesture; he kept his right hand low, angling it slowly around toward the robot's housing.

At the sound of his voice, Hard Place swiveled its sensor arrays toward him. "Kemo Sabe," it rasped.

And then one set of pincers shot out, catching his right wrist in an iron grip.

Warne cried out with pain as Hard Place clamped down with crushing strength. The robot yanked him forward and Warne threw himself across the counter and against the bins of ice cream, turning desperately with the robot to keep his wrist from breaking.

"Dad!" Georgia ran forward, reaching out to pull him away from Hard Place.

"Georgia, *no!*" Warne gasped, fighting to reach his left hand around the central housing, fingernails scrabbling on the smooth metal. Hard Place slid backward, dragging Warne with him, servos howling under the strain. The robot's second set of pincers shot forward, arrowing toward Warne's neck, just as his searching fingers found the small nub of the kill switch.

Abruptly, Hard Place stopped. Sparks flew from its drivetrain. Its sensor array sagged. The whine of motors spun down. The pincers sprung wide, releasing their hold on Warne's wrist. He fell heavily to the floor, then rose slowly from among the bins of ice cream, rubbing his aching wrist. Georgia ran toward him again and together they moved away from the smoking, darkened robot.

A crowd had gathered around, watching the unfolding events from a respectful distance. Warne swept them with his gaze, breathing hard, dripping chocolate and vanilla, still massaging his wrist. Georgia stood beside him, shocked into silence.

For a moment, no one said anything. Then there was a low, appreciative whistle.

"Great act, man!" somebody said. "For a moment there, you had me convinced it was the real thing."

"Too much!" called another.

And then the clapping started: first one pair of hands, and then another and another, until the air was filled with the sound of cheers.

12:45 P.M.

AS THE SUN climbed its way up the Nevada sky, all color bled out of the landscape below. The reds, yellows, browns, and purples of the sandstone canyons faded, then turned white. The high desert vegetation stood suspended as the shadows ran away to nothing.

Atop the rocky, bowl-like escarpment that surrounded Utopia, the sun illuminated a vast moonscape of hollows and ridges. The mesa top was a crazy quilt of gullies, silent and deserted, punctuated by infrequent junipers and bristlecone pines. The sky itself was a dome of pale blue, empty save for a lone airplane, drawing a white line thirty thousand feet overhead.

In a narrow gully near the far edge of the escarpment, something stirred. The man who had moved little since before dawn now stretched his legs and glanced at his watch. Despite the brutal heat, he had been dozing. It was training, more than anything else, that made this possible. Much of the man's professional life had been spent waiting. For hours, sometimes days, he had waited: in the jungle canopies of Mozambique; in foul Cambodian swamps, surrounded by leeches and malarial mosquitos. The desert heat of Nevada seemed a vacation by comparison.

He yawned leisurely, cracking his knuckles, then rolled his head around, working a kink out of his thickly muscled neck. Behind him, the geodesic dome covering Utopia rose up out of the canyon like the top of some giant's globe. Its ribs of steel and panels of glass, row after countless row, winked and shimmered in the noonday sun. It was encircled by several bands of narrow catwalks, one above the other, separated by perhaps fifty vertical feet. The catwalks were connected by a series of access ladders. Along one edge of the dome, a vast crescent-shaped wedge was dark: the roof that hung over Callisto. Close-up, from this high vantage no tourist would ever enjoy, the dome was almost other-worldly in its massive beauty.

But the man atop the mesa was no tourist. And he had not come for the view.

He turned toward a long, low canvas duffel that lay in the gully beside him. Drawing back its zipper, he reached inside, found his canteen, and took a long, thirsty pull. Although there were no guards or security cameras up on this deserted cliff top, the man's movements remained habitually brief and direct.

He put the canteen to one side, wiping his mouth with the back of a hand. A large pair of binoculars hung around his neck, and now he raised them to his eyes. The laser range-finding system made the binoculars heavy, and he used both hands to steady them as he made a slow scan.

From his place of concealment, he commanded an excellent view of the rear approach to Utopia. Far below, he could clearly make out the heavy-duty access road that snaked its way up from the desert. A large refrigerated truck was making the climb now; he watched the driver silently working his way through the gears. It was a good recon post: any fleeing vehicles or approaching cavalry would be spotted immediately. He raised the binoculars further, and the red numerals of the distance readout quickly rose as he panned over the more distant backdrop.

To build their Park, the Utopia Holding Company had purchased a tract of land bordered by U.S. 95 on the south and Nellis Air Force Base on the north. Deep inside Nellis, at a site called Groom Lake, was an installation once known on government maps as Area 51. It was patrolled by personnel authorized to use deadly force against trespassers. To the east and west, Utopia was surrounded by Bureau of Land Management wilderness. The Park did not need the huge berms and perimeter fences employed by other theme parks: it let nature, and the government, do the job for it.

Perhaps Utopia and its predecessors were lulled by the same unthinking sense of security and well-being they worked so hard to impart to their visitors. When they thought of their perimeters at all, most parks were primarily concerned with keeping non-paying guests from sneaking in. Security measures did not take into account someone whose skills at evasion and penetration had been honed in half a dozen hostile environments.

The man took another pull at the canteen. Then he replaced it in the duffel and pulled out an M24 Sniper Weapon System rifle. Whistling tunelessly, he gave it a quick, automatic inspection. The SWS was based on a Remington Model 700 receiver: there were newer rifles, but none more accurate. At ten pounds it was relatively light for a sniper's tool. The flash hider and lens hood ensured it would not visually betray its presence when used.

Cradling the rifle on his knees, the man fished in the bag and brought out four 308 Winchester cartridges, loaded with 168-grain boat-tails: the most accurate .30-caliber bullet-cartridge combination available. He filled the magazine, ran the bolt to load the first cartridge, then laid the rifle carefully back inside the duffel. He was not concerned about the sun warping the Kevlar-graphite stock, but he did not want the heavy target barrel growing too hot to touch.

The second rifle he pulled from the duffel was a Barret M-82 "Light 50." It was considerably meaner-looking than the M24, and less accurate; but with .50-caliber machine-gun cartridges for ammunition, it would drop anything it hit even a thousand yards out.

With the rifles and other materials in the duffel, the man had lugged more than eighty pounds of gear on the sheer climb up onto the escarpment the night before. But weapons redundancy was a discipline that had been drummed into him since his boot days at Parris Island.

His radio gave a muffled *chirrup,* and he plucked it from his belt, quickly tapping in the scrambler's decryption code.

"Water Buffalo, Water Buffalo," came the voice. "This is Prime Factor. How's your read?"

The man lifted the radio to his lips. "Still five by five."

"Status?"

"Ready to party."

"Very good. Monitor this frequency, we'll update you within the hour. Prime Factor out."

The radio went silent and the man returned it to his belt. He glanced again at his watch: one o'clock precisely. Then he turned back to the M-82, giving it the same check he'd given the first rifle. Satisfied, he ran his hand along the tactical telescopic sight. It was permanently fixed, of course—removable sights couldn't be relied on to hold zero—and the weapon had already been sighted in. He glanced toward the vast dome that rose behind and above him, his eye falling on a small speck of black that was crawling across it. He snugged the beavertail stock against his cheek and fitted his eye to the scope. Now the black speck was a man in a white maintenance uniform, moving slowly across the network of metal ribbing, checking for broken panes. He occupied two grids in the scope's range-finding system: approximately three hundred yards away.

The man's finger snaked inside the guard, caressing the trigger. "Be real careful, now," he whispered. "Wouldn't want you to fall."

Then—carefully, lovingly—he slid the rifle back into the duffel.

1:05 P.M.

HIS SUIT HAD been cleaned and pressed at Valet Services, an incident report logged with Security. And now Andrew Warne found himself pausing in the corridors of B Level, rubbing his chin perplexedly. As a child, he often had one recurring dream following particularly traumatic days: he'd be walking down a school corridor on his way to the principal's office, passing classroom after classroom after classroom, but never getting any closer to the intimidating door at the end of the corridor. He felt as if he were living that dream right now.

Beside him, Georgia stirred restlessly. "Are you lost?"

"No."

"I think you are."

"What's this *you* business? I put you in charge of following the cutaway diagrams, remember?"

They stepped to one side to let an electric cart purr past. Warne glanced again up and down the intersection. Hadn't they been here before? The layout looked familiar. But with the constantly changing streams of cast and crew passing by, it was difficult to orient himself.

Besides, he was preoccupied. His wrist still throbbed where Hard Place had gripped it. He found he had been rubbing it unconsciously.

Georgia looked at him. "You okay, Dad?"

"Just a little banged up. I'm sorry, that must have been pretty frightening."

Georgia shook her head. "I wasn't frightened."

This surprised Warne. "No? *I* was."

"Get real." She looked at him, as if disbelieving such profound ignorance. "You built him, remember? He couldn't do anything bad. He wouldn't let himself."

Warne shook his head. Georgia hadn't been at the meeting,

hadn't heard what he'd heard. If she wasn't asking questions, so much the better. But he sure as hell had some questions to put to Teresa Bonifacio—if they ever found her office, that was.

His eye caught a sign he hadn't remembered seeing before. *New Technology*. Now, that was more like it. He glanced over his shoulder again to make sure they weren't about to be run down by another maintenance cart, then led Georgia in the direction of the sign.

Another minute and, maddeningly, he had managed to get them lost again. This new section of B Level they'd stumbled into seemed reserved for management: there was thick carpeting underfoot, and subdued wallpaper covered the concrete walls. Just as he was about to give up and turn back, he saw a familiar figure ahead. He stopped abruptly.

Sarah Boatwright was standing in the doorway of an office, her back to them, speaking briskly to two men in dark suits. They were listening intently, nodding. Her straight coppery hair shook slightly as she motioned with her arms.

Seeing her like that, facing away from him, brought back a sudden memory: the first morning they'd risen together from the same bed. Before leaving for work, the last thing Sarah had done was stand before a mirror for several minutes, turning, observing all angles of her person. At first, Warne thought this to be mere vanity. But he'd later realized that she was simply scrutinizing herself for anything out of place, any imperfect crease. Sarah liked order in all things. But once she got to work, she would grow so completely absorbed she tended to forget such details as appearance. And so she made this conscious, prearranged effort. Warne had been inclined to laugh—until he realized how, from Sarah's point of view, it was clearly the most logical solution.

Sarah turned and caught sight of them. She smiled briefly and waved them forward, then turned back and said some final words to the waiting men. They nodded again and walked away.

"Didn't mean to interrupt," Warne said as they approached.

"You're not. Those are just the VPs of Transportation and Concepts. Half a dozen new snags on the Atlantis fabrication. Business as usual." Sarah's green eyes went from Warne to Georgia and back again. "You're late for your meeting with Terri. Are you lost?"

"Yes," Warne said.

"No," said Georgia simultaneously.

"Actually, you're not that far afield. Terri's lab is just around the corner." Sarah looked at Georgia again, hesitated. "Why don't you come in for a moment?" she said.

The office was large, well appointed, and unusually chilly, even for the Utopia Underground. After the brightly lit corridors, it seemed subdued, almost dark. Sarah's desk was bare save for a few folders, a computer terminal, and an oversize teacup. As usual, nothing was out of place. Even the pictures on the walls—a photograph of Eric Nightingale with his arm around Sarah; a picture of the *Swope,* the sixty-foot boat she'd helped crew in a Newport–Bermuda race—were carefully aligned.

"Very nice," Warne said, nodding. "You've done well for yourself. I just may have to borrow the key to the executive washroom."

"Utopia's been good to me."

"So I see."

There was an awkward silence, a sense of unfinished business lying between them. Warne wondered, a little absently, if he should apologize for his outburst after the morning meeting. As quickly as the thought came, he realized that, right or wrong, the last thing he felt like doing was apologizing.

"I heard about Hard Place," Sarah said. "I'm glad you weren't injured."

"If you can call it that," Warne said, rubbing his wrist.

"I'll have the logical unit sent over to Terri's lab for analysis." She didn't say it—she didn't need to—but the implication hung in the air.

Warne glanced over at Georgia. She had taken a seat at Sarah's conference table and was leafing through a coffee-table book titled *Utopia Portraits.*

"Sarah," he said, lowering his voice and moving a little closer. "The Metanet isn't responsible for this. It *can't* be. You were at Carnegie-Mellon during the development, you know what it's capable of. Reprogramming bots just isn't part of its behavior pattern."

"How can you say precisely *what* it's capable of? It's a learning-capable expert system. You designed it to improve *itself* as well as the bots; to adapt to change."

"But you're acting like it's some piece of rogue software. The Holding Company wouldn't have authorized its installation if it hadn't proved itself in beta. It ran pre-production for six months without glitches. Right?"

"And now it's run another six months in an environment of constant change. Perhaps it's done self-modification in ways we're not prepared to monitor. That's Fred Barksdale's theory, anyway. And he's in a position to know."

"But—" Warne stopped himself with an effort. There was no point in arguing; he'd save that particular discussion for Teresa Bonifacio. He sighed, shook his head. "Fred Barksdale," he repeated. "So are you two serious, or is it just sort of a spring thing?"

Sarah looked at him sharply. But Warne was careful to smile.

"Is it that obvious?" she said after a moment.

"Stands out like a neon sign."

She smiled wryly. "Fred's a nice guy."

"Wouldn't have taken him for your type. An upper-crust Brit, I mean. He seems so . . . I don't know. Hunt club, pink gins, ironed copies of the *Times,* that sort of thing."

"He's the most sophisticated man I've ever met. I think I've been dating scientists for too many years. No offense meant."

"None taken." But Warne felt the smile on his face freeze just a little.

He could see Sarah looking past him, and he glanced over his shoulder. Georgia had lowered the book and was watching their tête-à-tête with an expression of disapproval.

Sarah took a casual step back. "Georgia, I've got something for you." She walked behind her immaculate desk, knelt down. There was the audible rasp of a key being turned, a low whine of fans coming up to speed. Then she stepped away.

"Come on out," she said in a coaxing tone.

For a moment, it seemed to Warne as if the desk itself suddenly moved. Then something emerged from behind it: a portly, ungainly-looking thing like a beer keg laid on end, mounted on large knobby tires. It stopped, head assembly atop the metal cabinet swiveling. It seemed to catch sight of them, emitted a strange low noise somewhere between a bark and a belch, and came abruptly forward.

Immediately, Georgia scrambled out of the chair and held open her arms. "Wingnut!" she said. "Come here, boy."

Warne watched the large thing roll eagerly across the floor

toward Georgia. It didn't manage to stop quite in time, and Georgia was sent sprawling.

He had forgotten just how much the stereo cameras on the head assembly resembled eyes; how well the yaw-rate gyro he'd installed in the robot base imitated the jerky, impatient motions of an oversize puppy. Even the thing's clumsiness was in character. He'd originally built Wingnut as a demonstration tool, a simple vehicle for explaining robotic concepts like path planning and collision avoidance. Warne was a strong proponent of ethology—using animal behaviors as models for robust AI architectures—and Wingnut had served as the perfect paradigm. It was one of the earliest examples he'd built to implement his theories on machine learning. And it had seemed an ideal pet for Georgia, who was allergic to dogs. But when her interest waned, Wingnut had taken up residence at the institute, where he quickly became something of a curiosity piece. The robot sported dual processors, an extravagant amount of memory, and some expensive—if aging—hardware. By the time Warne was done tinkering, its fifty thousand lines of scheme code included low-level behaviors for fetching, begging, intruder detection, and a score of other doggy tasks. And yet, either Wingnut had been given one software patch too many or one of Warne's graduate students had played a practical joke, because the robot behaved unpredictably, in a way Warne's other creations never did. That is, until this morning.

Now Wingnut had acquired Warne with its sensor array and rushed toward him, butting its head assembly none too gently against his hip, as if asking for a treat. "Hi, there," Warne said. He was fond of the creature and even now felt an irrational impulse to give a gentle box to its nonexistent ears. As he bent closer, however, he was surprised to see that a layer of dust had settled around the microphone input, servos, and actuators. It was almost as if the thing had just been dragged out of a closet—not at all in keeping with the rest of Sarah's office.

He blew carefully at a few areas, then rose to his feet. "Go play with Georgia," he said.

During his brainstorming meetings with Nightingale, the magician had been entranced with the robot. Ultimately, Warne had given it to him as an early promise of more technological goodies to come. He'd always assumed the Park designers would fit

Wingnut into some kind of attraction, most likely in Callisto somewhere.

"How come you're not using him in the Park?" he asked.

"We'd always planned to. But we've been evolving more toward sensory environments—holograms, laser displays, computer-controlled rides. Guest surveys, all that."

"Guest surveys. Chuck Emory and his bean counters."

"There was also a feeling that he might be a little, ah, intimidating for the guests."

"Intimidating? Little old Wingnut?"

"He's not that little."

A man appeared in Sarah's doorway, a sheaf of blueprints and mechanical drawings beneath one arm. "Excuse me," Sarah said, walking over to speak to the new arrival.

Warne watched her for a moment. Then he glanced toward his daughter, who was on her knees murmuring to the robot. He looked around the office once again, his eye coming to rest on the photograph of the *Swope*. At the time, it had seemed a good omen. Charlotte Warne had built sailboats; Sarah had raced them. He hadn't realized this synchronicity would get the opposite reaction from Georgia than he'd expected. And there was something else. His wife had loved boats with a pure and simple passion. As he grew to know Sarah better, he realized her interest in sailing had been primarily the interest of overcoming a challenge.

He glanced back at his daughter. Georgia had been the one challenge Sarah was unable to surmount. He thought back on the awkward interplay in the conference room, when Sarah first saw Georgia. There was no spontaneous hug; just obvious affection, rather awkwardly, formally presented. It was almost as if Sarah just didn't "get" children. She'd tried—in a way she was still trying even now, with Wingnut. But Warne knew it would never succeed. Sarah was a supremely logical person. But relentless application of logic never worked with a child; they would always confound your plans, do the opposite of what you expected.

Abruptly, the phone on Sarah's desk began to ring. Warne glanced toward it, then at his watch. "We'd better be going," he said. "I'm sorry, Teresa's lab is . . . ?"

"Take your second right, third door on the left." Sarah dismissed the man in the doorway, stepped toward her desk. "Andrew, one word about Teresa. She's not a typical Park employee."

"How so?"

"She's brilliant, of course—you can't touch her skill at robotics programming—but she's unconventional. We've had some difficulty getting her into the Utopia spirit."

"You mean, moody? Rebellious?"

"Let's say she swims against the current. For example, a few months ago she programmed a mail-server bot to pinch the rear ends of a dataset of cute mail room guys."

She'd been speaking in a low voice, but from across the room Georgia snorted with laughter.

"You don't say," Warne replied.

"And she's suspected of posting a nude photo of Margaret Thatcher, with Fred Barksdale's head superimposed on the shoulders, in the Systems ladies' room. She's received three disciplinary notices since the Park opened." The line of Sarah's mouth tightened disapprovingly.

"Won't be brainwashed into the feel-good ethic, eh? Sounds like a troublemaker to me."

Sarah opened her mouth to answer, but paused when a white-blazered woman leaned her head into the office.

"Grand Central around here today," Warne murmured.

"Every day." Sarah turned toward the woman. "Yes, Grace?"

"I'm sorry to interrupt, Ms. Boatwright, but you weren't picking up. There's a gentleman here to see you . . ."

"A gentleman?"

"An external specialist. Says you had asked to speak with him."

"I don't remember any appointment." Sarah walked back to her desk, tapped at her keyboard, glanced at the monitor. "Very well. Ask him to wait just a moment."

She took something out of a drawer, came around the desk, and handed it to Warne. "Here's Wingnut's echolocator. I'd better see what this specialist wants."

"Thanks," Warne replied, fastening the locator around his wrist.

"I'm leaving first thing tomorrow morning. If I don't see you again this afternoon, good luck. I hope it all works out."

Warne gave a wintry smile.

"Fred will do all he can to help. Remember, nothing's permanent. With any luck, you'll correct what's wrong, and we can submit a restart request to New York." She turned. "Good-bye, Georgia. Good to see you again. Have a nice visit."

"Thanks," Georgia said, rising from her knees.

Warne nodded to Sarah, then ushered Georgia out the door. In the corridor beyond, the white-blazered woman waited, along with a tall, slender man with a closely trimmed beard. His gaze met Warne's at a distance, and he smiled.

There was a frantic, klaxonlike yipping from behind, and Warne turned to see Wingnut, moving alternately forward and backward across the carpet in jerky motions, his sensors panning wildly.

"Well, what are you waiting for?" Warne asked. "Let's go." And as they made their way down the corridor, passersby gave the threesome—a man, a girl, and a hulking robot that weaved erratically behind them—a wide berth.

1:09 P.M.

ALTHOUGH WARNE HAD disappeared from view around the corner, Sarah paused a moment, staring at the spot where he had stood. The sense of wariness she'd felt during the Pre-Game Show had not dissipated. Yet it wasn't wariness, really, so much as a consciousness of something unresolved within her. She'd never been one for lengthy self-analysis, preferring action over introspection. Nevertheless, she knew it had something to do with the timing of Andrew Warne's visit. It had been Chuck Emory's idea, of course. "Move it up, get him here now," the CEO had told her from New York. "I want the Metanet off-line before anything worse goes wrong. But not a word about why he's coming until he's on-site. We can't afford to let this leak. Say what you need to get him there, but *get* him there." She had disliked the deception, of course. But there was something more: she'd felt relieved, knowing this meant she'd be away in San Francisco through most of Warne's visit. And that was a sign of weakness—something she detested. What was she worried about? She had never feared anyone's disapproval, including Warne's. Perhaps it was sympathy she felt; the days to come would be unpleasant ones for him. They would be difficult to watch, much less participate in.

All these thoughts flashed through her mind in a second. Then she turned to the man waiting outside. "I'm sorry. Won't you come in?"

The man stepped into the office, smiling broadly.

"I don't remember asking to speak with you, sir," Sarah said, taking a seat behind her desk.

The man nodded, folding his arms gracefully in front of him. She noticed, almost unconsciously, that the linen suit he wore was impeccably tailored, clearly expensive. There was something unusual about him, but she was not quite able to put a finger on it.

"There's nothing wrong with your memory, Ms. Boatwright," he said. "You didn't ask to see me. A small deception on my part, I'm afraid."

He came forward, and now Sarah realized what it was. The man's eyes were different colors. The left was hazel; the right, an intense blue.

She felt no alarm. It was a common occurrence. Some of the Utopia groupies were a little too zealous. They were the ones who visited the Park dozens of times; who dressed in the formal garb of Eric Nightingale; who constantly applied for jobs, even menial tasks like "honeycart" driver, in order to get backstage. Occasionally, they found their way behind the scenes and had to be escorted out, graciously but firmly. True, none of them had ever sought her out by name before. But despite the unusual eyes, this man looked neither crazy nor dangerous. His face was handsome and dignified, the smile frank and straightforward. He seemed to radiate a kind of calm composure. For a moment, Sarah was reminded of Fred Barksdale.

"May I ask your name?"

"Of course you may, Sarah—is it all right if I call you Sarah?" The voice was low and melodious, with a faint accent that might have been Australian. "First names are so useful in establishing trust. My name is Mr. Doe, Sarah. But you can call me John."

There was a brief silence.

"I see." Sarah turned to her computer, tapped some keys. "There's no record of any external specialist named . . . ah . . . John Doe scheduled at Utopia today."

"Right again. Another small deception. It *is* awkward, I'm sorry. Say, is that jasmine tea you're drinking? It smells marvelous."

Mr. Doe was still smiling easily at her. Then he did a very strange thing. He came forward, perched on the edge of her desk, picked up the cup and saucer, and took a sip. Then he closed his eyes appreciatively.

"Ah. Very excellent." He took another sip. "But it tastes like a spring harvest—first flush, you know. For this time of the day, a second flush would have been the more appropriate choice."

Sarah let her right hand drift casually back toward her keyboard. A short sequence, typed onto the numeric keypad, would bring Security to the office within ninety seconds. But then the man's jacket fell open as he bent forward to replace the teacup. Inside, the butt of a handgun gleamed from a Mylar holster. Her hand dropped from the keyboard.

"What is it you want?" she asked.

The man looked hurt. "Why the rush, Sarah? Things are going to start happening very quickly, very soon. So let's take a moment to get to know each other first. Like civilized people."

She pushed her chair back a little, watching him carefully. "Okay. Who are you?"

Mr. Doe seemed to consider this, as if he had never heard the question before. "You mean, what do I *do*?" He paused. "I guess you could call me an expediter. I dislike the word— it has such a faddish, ephemeral sound—but I don't know exactly how else to describe what it is I do. I get things that other people want. But 'middleman' sounds much too down-market. Perhaps it would be easiest for you to think of me simply as a man with a gift."

He slid a hand into a pocket of his jacket, and Sarah gathered herself to move quickly, if necessary. The man shook his head reprovingly, as if dismayed by her mistrust. Then he laid a small two-way radio on her desk with slender, elegant fingers. He leaned across the desk, as if to impart a secret.

"Sarah, I have good news for you," he said. "You have it in your power to make sure nobody in your Park dies this afternoon."

Sarah looked at the man, saying nothing.

"I know how much this Park means to you." As the man spoke, he held her eyes at all times. There was a look of empathy, of profound understanding, on his face. "I know you place the very highest value on its smooth operation, on the safety of your guests. Nothing need happen to compromise that; nothing at all. As long as you follow a few simple ground rules." The sympathetic, understanding gaze continued to hold her. "You are not to alert local or federal law enforcement. And you are *not* to try to evacuate the Park. Business will go on as usual. Guests will come and go, just like they do every day of the year. Everybody has fun, nobody gets hurt. And when you come right down to it, isn't that your job, anyway? Please don't break the ground rules, Sarah."

"What is it you want?" she asked again.

Mr. Doe leaned away. "I will be requiring several things of you. It is very important that you follow my instructions completely and precisely. We'll keep in communication by means of this." He pressed a button on the radio, and it made a quiet buzz. "But I wanted us to have this little chat first, in person. You know: to break the ice, put a human face on things, all that."

He adjusted his jacket. "You'll forgive me, I hope, but now I've come to the unpleasant part of the conversation."

Sarah felt her jaw harden. "I don't respond well to threats," she said stonily.

"Oh, it won't take long. And these are such *good* threats, Sarah. Do exactly as I say, when I say it. Don't try to stop me, or hamper me, or deceive me in any way. *Or else.* You'll find I know more about you and your Park than you realize. There are others with me, all of them far more intimidating than myself. We've had lots of time to prepare. We're watching both your entrances and your exits. If you cooperate, we'll be gone before you know it. And you can get on with the job of pleasing the guests."

He slid off the desk. "There. That wasn't so bad, was it? I always think threatening someone should be like administering an injection. Do it quickly, and it won't hurt as much." He reached forward, and Sarah tensed again. But the man merely smiled, brushing his knuckles caressingly across her cheek. "I'll be in touch shortly. Enjoy your tea, Sarah—it's quite exquisite. But remember what I said about the second flush."

As he turned and walked away, Sarah's hand moved once again toward the keyboard. But she thought about the gun, and the preternatural calm behind John Doe's eyes, and she waited.

Near the doorway, the man turned back. "One other thing. You may be inclined to doubt what I've told you. And you're clearly a woman who doesn't scare easily. You may, for example, be tempted to close down the Park to new arrivals. Or not comply with my requests. Either of which would be met by immediate reprisal. So in an effort to avoid any complications, I've arranged for a little show. I mean, you put on so many, shouldn't you get to see one yourself once in a while? It should remove any lingering doubts from your mind."

He glanced at his watch. "It starts at 1:30 precisely. Enjoy."

And then, without another word, he was gone.

1:15 P.M.

"DO YOU THINK perhaps he was daft?" Fred Barksdale asked. "Like that fellow last week, thought he was Abraham and Utopia was Sodom?" He swerved the wheel of the electric cart to avoid a pedestrian. At ten miles per hour, their cart was moving at twice the speed allowed in the corridors of the Underground.

Sarah shook her head. "He didn't sound like the usual bomb crank or telephone jockey. He was too polite. Too solicitous, somehow . . ." She shook her head roughly, as if to clear it. "Remember he sought me out. He knew exactly what he wanted. And then there's *this*." She patted the pocket of her jacket.

They rounded a corner, the rubber wheels of the cart squealing on the bare concrete. Sarah glanced over at Barksdale. The fine features of his face looked set, blond eyebrows furrowed in concentration.

Barksdale glanced over, met her gaze. "You all right, luv?"

Sarah nodded. "I'm fine."

They came to an abrupt stop outside a set of unmarked double doors. Leaving the cart parked diagonally across half the corridor, Barksdale trotted up to the doors, swiping a passcard through the scanner. When the lock clicked open, he pushed the doors inward, then stepped back to allow Sarah in ahead of him.

The Center for Monitoring Operations, known to all Utopia cast and crew as the Hive, was a large circular space filled floor-to-ceiling with rack-mounted monitors. Here, the feeds for the Park's mainline security cameras were channeled into a single command station. Not all video links in Utopia were viewable here: the infrared cameras inside the rides and attractions were closed systems, and the Eyes in the Sky at Utopia's four casinos were controlled from separate locations. But views of more than six thousand locations throughout the Park—from restaurants to queuing stations to maintenance bays to monorail cars—could be independently controlled from within the Hive.

As Sarah walked in, she thought—as on all her infrequent visits—just how appropriate the nickname was. The hundreds of monitors that surrounded her on all sides, glass faces slanting downward at achingly regular angles, were irresistibly reminiscent of the interior of some vast honeycomb.

She was not concerned; at least, not overly so. There had been too many false alarms over the months, too many threatening phone calls and e-mails that never followed through. But none of the cranks or practical jokers had ever introduced themselves by name. None of them had given her a two-way radio. Most especially, none of them had carried a concealed weapon. And so she'd called Bob Allocco, head of Security, and ordered an interdiction. Just to be sure.

Inside the Hive, the air was cold and dry, with the faint, almost sweetish smell of high purification. A dozen security specialists sat at the monitoring stations circling the room, panning across screens or speaking into headsets. Bob Allocco was standing beside the nearest specialist, his impatient fingers drumming on the black composite of the table. He swiveled at their approach, then frowned, motioning them to follow.

In the far wall, a door of smoked privacy glass had been set between two tiers of monitors. Allocco unlocked the door with his passcard and led the way in, closing the door behind them.

The room beyond was small and dark. It contained several large monitors, three phones, a computer workstation, a couple of chairs, and little else. As the door lock engaged, a fan came on, providing a low, scratchy background hum: pink noise, ensuring they could not be overheard in the Center beyond.

Allocco turned toward them. "How serious do you think this is?" he asked.

"I'm afraid we shall have to treat it as serious, whether it is or not," Barksdale replied.

"We'll know at 1:30," Sarah said quietly.

Allocco's eyes darted toward her. "How's that?"

"He said he'd give us a demonstration. To show he meant business, prove it wasn't a bluff."

"And he didn't give you any idea of what he wants?"

Sarah pulled the radio out of her pocket. "He said he'd contact us with this."

Allocco took it from her, turned it over in his hands. "Well, whatever else the guy may be, he isn't hard up for money. Look at this: a military-grade scrambler. With a signal diffuser, I'll bet. No way to get a lock on his position."

He handed it back. "Did he threaten you?"

"He implied that if we didn't do exactly what he wanted, people would die."

"Sounds bloody well like a threat to me," Barksdale said.

"He also told me not to contact law enforcement, not to evacuate the park. Keep things strictly business as usual. Or else."

There was a brief silence as this was digested.

"And then he said something else. That there were several of them. And that they'd had plenty of time to prepare."

She turned, caught Barksdale's eye. Even in the dim light, his face seemed to have gone a little gray.

"What's going on?" he asked. "Terrorists? Zealots? Some lunatic fringe group?"

"No time for speculating," Allocco replied. "We have the gadgets. Let's find this guy." He picked up a telephone beside the workstation, dialed a number. "Ralph? Bob Allocco. I'm in the Hive. Can you join me, please?"

He replaced the phone. "Ralph Peccam, my top video tech," he explained. "Worked in Systems before, knows the whole infrastructure like the back of his hand."

"Discreet?" Sarah asked.

Allocco nodded. "What time did this John Doe leave your office?"

Sarah thought a moment. "About ten minutes after one."

"Okay." Allocco turned to the workstation, moused through a series of menus. "Let's pick up his scent."

There was a quiet rap on the door, and Sarah moved to open it. Standing outside, in the ethereal glow of the Hive's countless monitors, was a short, skinny youth. He had a rooster's crest of red hair, and freckles were splashed across his nose and cheekbones. He could not have been more than twenty. The gold pin on his retro-looking sports jacket identified him as an electronics specialist.

"Ralph," Allocco said. "Take a seat."

The youth glanced at Sarah, then sat down in front of the workstation, sniffing loudly.

"We've got a little project for you. Something that stays inside this room, okay?"

Peccam nodded silently, large eyes flickering once again toward Sarah. He was clearly unused to being in such close proximity to the Park chief.

"Remember the interdiction drills we've run? Well, this isn't a drill. A man left Ms. Boatwright's office around eight minutes ago. Let's follow his trail." Allocco pointed at something on the screen. "I've brought up a list of the cameras in that corridor. Start with B-2023."

Peccam turned to the workstation and typed a series of commands. An image appeared on one of the monitors: the entrance to Sarah's office, taken from a ceiling-mounted camera across the corridor. Displayed along the bottom of the screen was the time the film was taken. As the film ran in reverse, the hundredths of a second flew past, almost unreadable. Beside them was a long series of numbers.

"It's black-and-white?" Sarah asked in surprise.

"All cameras in the staff areas are black-and-white. Only the public areas have color. We went over all this in one of the Pre-Game Shows last month, when the new system was fully installed. Weren't you listening?"

"Not closely enough, it seems. Get me up to speed."

Allocco waved his hand at the monitor. "The video is now entirely in the digital domain. No analog whatsoever. That means no signal degradation, infinite storage possibilities, theoretically infinite resolution. Everything's striped to a uniform SMPTE time code running at—what is it, Ralph?"

"Thirty drop," Peccam said in a hoarse voice.

"Thirty drop frames per second. We can synchronize precisely any two, three, whatever, feeds in the Park. And we can maintain a history indefinitely."

Sarah nodded. "So you journal everything?"

"Up to a point, because the size of—Ralph, what's the architecture again?"

"Each monitor is linked to a fiber-channel RAID array, currently scalable to four terabytes." Peccam sneezed explosively.

"Sounds like you've got a lulu," Allocco said.

"I went down to Medical for some antihistamine two hours ago," Peccam replied. "All it did was make me sleepy."

"Well, we need you awake right now." Sarah turned back to

Allocco. "If I'm understanding this, we can comb through old output, yes? See if John Doe made prior visits? Maybe see exactly what it was that he did?"

Allocco scratched his chin. "Theoretically. But as I was about to say, real-time streaming video takes up bandwidth. A *lot* of bandwidth. You wouldn't believe how fast those four terabytes fill up. That's why we kept the Underground cameras black-and-white. Every night, video storage is handed off to the IT servers." He nodded toward Barksdale. "And that, Buck Rogers, is where your guys come in."

Sarah looked over. "Fred?"

Barksdale, who had been listening silently, cleared his throat. "We store the video feeds on our WAN for two weeks. Then they're mothballed off-site."

"How fast can we get them back?"

"Overnight."

"That's not fast enough."

"We're getting ahead of ourselves here. We haven't even located the guy yet." Allocco stepped up behind Peccam, glanced at the image on the central monitor. "Good. Ten minutes after one. Now go forward, two hundred frames a second."

On the central monitor, figures passed by Sarah's office in blurs of gray. Then a shadow darted through her door.

"Stop," said Allocco. "Back one hundred frames."

Frozen on-screen was Fred Barksdale, stepping into Sarah's office.

"That's too late," Sarah said. "Fred came in maybe two minutes after John Doe left."

"Back at fifty," Allocco said.

Another blur of figures, slower this time, moving backward in silent pantomime. Then one of the figures slid into her office door in reverse; turned; disappeared within.

"Stop," Allocco repeated. "Forward, ten frames a second."

On the monitor, in slow motion, John Doe walked back into view. He glanced up and down the corridor, smoothed one hand across the front of his suit, then walked out of the doorway and disappeared out of camera view.

"That's the sonofabitch?" Allocco asked.

Sarah nodded. Seeing him again—the small beard, the easy, narrow smile—sent a thrust of anger through her, mixed with some other emotion she couldn't identify. Her cheek burned where his knuckles had brushed against it.

"Back one hundred and freeze."

John Doe stood, motionless, in the doorway.

"Bring up the face. Ten x."

The face now filled the screen, striped in the shadow of an overhead light. Sarah saw that the left eye was a darker shade of gray than the right.

"Can you clean that up?" Barksdale asked. "Sharpen it?"

"Yes," said Peccam. "It'll take a little time."

"Then it can wait. Let's find out where he went." Allocco peered at a listing that ran down the edge of the command screen. "Bring up B-2027. Sync the time."

The central monitor went black for a moment. Then another view of the corridor, two doors down from Sarah's office.

"Forward, thirty," murmured Allocco.

For a second, the corridor was empty. Then a woman wearing a Victorian-era crinoline walked by. A moment later, she was followed by John Doe. He strode confidently, even casually, from the top of the screen to the bottom.

"B-2051," said Allocco. "Same sync."

Now the view was of two intersecting corridors. The woman in the crinoline appeared, turned left, and entered a stairwell. A maintenance cart passed laterally across the screen. Then John Doe emerged at the top. Stopping only to look for opposing traffic, he went left, following the direction the woman had taken.

"He's heading for A Level, maybe Gaslight," said Allocco, glancing back at the screen listing. "Bring up A-1904."

"Remember," Sarah said, "I don't want a full-scale interdiction. Not yet. Let's see where he's going, if he's really got something planned for 1:30. Get a security net around him, just in case he's on the level. But don't move in until I give the word."

The A Level corridor now displayed on the monitor was wider, more brightly lit. It was also busier. Knots of Utopia employees passed beneath the camera, talking together, heading to and from lunch at the A Café, the nearby employee cafeteria. The woman in the crinoline went by. She had apparently spotted her boyfriend, and the two of them were now walking arm in arm, at a much slower pace.

"Tsk, tsk," said Allocco. "PDA. Better write them up." Public displays of affection between cast or crew members, while not exactly forbidden, were discouraged.

Now John Doe came into the monitor's range. He strolled forward, then stopped in the middle of traffic. People threaded their way past, ignoring him.

"Now what the hell's he doing?" Allocco asked.

Suddenly, John Doe glanced up, directly at the lens. He smiled and raised his hands to his tie, as if to fix the knot.

"Cheeky," Barksdale muttered. *"Villain, villain, smiling, damnèd villain."*

Unexpectedly, the picture sheered away violently, and the monitor filled with static.

"What's this *shit*?" Allocco shouted.

Peccam's hands darted over the keyboard. "Don't know. Time code's still running. Must be a software glitch."

Within a few seconds, the picture shivered back into place. The throngs of people continued to pass beneath the camera, oblivious. But John Doe was gone.

"Bring up A-1905," said Allocco, glancing at the listing. "Same sync."

There was the same storm of gray static that had appeared on the previous feed. After a moment, it, too, cleared.

"A-1906. Come on, hurry it up."

Once again, no picture.

"Christ," Allocco grumbled.

He moved toward the door, opened it. "Listen up," he addressed the Hive in general. "Was there a problem with the digital feed five, ten minutes back?"

The security specialists turned to look at him. One of them nodded. "Yeah, we lost signal for about ten seconds."

"*What?* System-wide?"

"No, sir. A portion of A Level and Soho Square in Gaslight."

Allocco shut the door and turned back to Peccam. "Let's follow the obvious routes he might have taken. Bring up A-1940. Sync it ahead ten seconds."

They ran through various camera feeds, fruitlessly, for a few minutes. At last, Allocco sighed and spread his hands.

"What do you make of that?" he said.

"Couldn't be the tech," said Barksdale. "It wouldn't fail like that, not with the redundant clustering." He glanced at Sarah. "Another glitch."

"I don't think so," she said. "The timing's too convenient." A new—and disturbing—thought had entered her mind.

"Can we track his tag?" she asked.

"We already tried," Allocco replied. "He must be using a generic. Ralph, keep scanning. Let me know if you stumble across him."

Allocco turned away from the monitor. "What now?"

"We wait," said Barksdale.

Sarah glanced at her watch. It was twenty-five minutes after one.

1:15 P.M.

TERESA BONIFACIO'S APPLIED robotics lab was perhaps the messiest private space Warne had seen since his MIT dormitory days. In an environment like Utopia that thrived on order and precision, it seemed almost belligerent somehow: a statement of independence. Thick technical manuals lay facedown, pages bent, spines broken. A skeletal-looking robot stood in one corner, arm raised in imitation of the Statue of Liberty, gowned in green-and-white-striped computer printouts. "Paradise City" was playing somewhere in the background. Unlike the rest of the Utopia Underground—which had been relatively scentless—there was a faint odor in the air: odd, rather fishy. Warne's nose crinkled involuntarily as he looked around. Teresa's office did not sport the usual shiny murals of key Utopia attractions or framed motivational phrases. Instead, garish posters of Guns N' Roses were tacked to the walls. One was autographed "Peace, Love, Slash" with a large red marker. A postcard labeled *Borokay Beach, Philippines* was affixed to the inside of the lab door. Nearby, someone had taped a handwritten excerpt:

> When a task cannot be partitioned because of sequential constraints, the application of more effort has no effect on the schedule. The bearing of a child takes nine months, no matter how many women are assigned.
>
> —Frederick P. Brooks, Jr.,
> *The Mythical Man-Month*

Teresa was sitting in a far corner, almost invisible behind stacks of trade journals and back issues of *Amusement Industry Digest*. She was soldering something, a thin curl of smoke rising between her hands. When she caught sight of Warne, she put the soldering gun to one side, pushed the eye goggles onto her forehead, and came around the stacks.

"Andrew, it's so great to have you here," she said in her deep, uninflected voice, smiling widely. "I can't believe it, after all this time, you're—oh, Lord."

Warne followed her glance. Georgia had just walked into the lab, Wingnut at her heels. Immediately, the robot stopped, its sensor arrays scanning the landscape again and again, as if unable to process all the surrounding obstacles.

"Don't worry," Georgia said. "It's just Wingnut."

"Sure." Teresa stared at the oversize robot for a moment. Then she looked back at Warne and laughed: the rich, ironic contralto he'd heard so often, long-distance. "You know, you're something of a legend in IT. Nobody's ever seen you. The only people who talked to you over the phone were Barksdale and me. There was a joke going around that you didn't really exist, that you were just some invention of Nightingale's. When word got around you were coming this morning, two people came by to ask me if it was true."

"You don't say." Warne glanced at Georgia, who was now standing next to him, looking curiously at the surrounding mess. With her nearby, he couldn't tell Teresa what he thought of all this. Not yet. Even so, he'd be damned if he was going to buy into this flattery.

The smell was stronger here, and Georgia wrinkled her nose.

"It's *bagoong*," Teresa said, turning to Georgia and laughing again.

"Baga what?"

"Shrimp paste. What you smell. Fantastic on green mangoes. Nobody around here can stand it, though, except me." The impish smile widened. "That's why I usually eat lunch here, instead of the café."

Warne thought of the postcard of the beach. Then he reached far down into his memory. "Smells *mabaho*," he said. "Right? Tastes *masarap*."

Teresa looked back at him. "You speak Tagalog?"

"Maybe five words. I had a Filipino lab assistant once."

"Yeah. We're infesting the halls of science these days." Then she turned once again to Georgia, who was restless, clearly eager to get back to the Park. "I've got something you might enjoy. It's the new Game Boy, 'Archaeopteryx: Perfect Edition.' "

"I've played it," Georgia said.

"Not this one, you haven't." Teresa turned away, opened a drawer, rummaged for a moment. When she turned back, she was holding a pocket video game. But it was unlike any Warne had ever seen: its plastic cover had been removed, and half a dozen alligator clips were affixed to its electronic innards, multi-colored wires trailing away like tails.

"Some of these games have remarkable AI," she said. "I sometimes trace through their instruction sets in my downtime, looking for routines we could cannibalize. Working with this one, I stumbled upon a dozen secret levels the developers never made public."

"The master levels?" Georgia said, eyes widening. "I read about those on the Web. I thought it was just bullshit."

"Georgia!" Warne said in exasperation.

"Well, it *isn't* bullshit." Teresa handed her the game. "Here, knock yourself out. Just don't detach any of the clips, or I'll have to rewire the whole thing. You can have a seat at that far table, there. Just push the stuff onto the floor."

Warne watched Georgia move away, hunched over the game, already absorbed. So Teresa spent her downtime cracking Game Boys. Perhaps if she'd paid more attention to the Metanet instead, he wouldn't be here right now.

He turned back to see the woman regarding him. "So," she said after a moment. "How do you want to start this?" She smiled again. When Warne didn't return the smile, uncertainty began to creep into her expression.

"You tell *me*," he said. "It's your little party."

Teresa's smile faded. "Look, Andrew," she said in a lower voice. "I know how you must feel. And I'm really sorry about—"

"I'm sure you are," Warne interrupted in a rough undertone. "But save it for your report. Bring in your team, I'll get you started. But then we're leaving. You can clean up your own mess."

This hung in the air for a long, uncomfortable moment. Then Teresa turned away. "I'll get the incident reports," she said over her shoulder. She walked to the door of the lab, opened it, and stepped out, not bothering to close the door behind her.

Warne closed his eyes, expelled a long, slow breath. For a moment, the lab was silent save for the beepings of the Game Boy.

"Dad?" Georgia said.

Warne looked over. She was bent over the game, not bothering to look up. "Yes?"

"Why were you mean to her just now?"

"Mean?" Warne repeated, surprised. He'd had no idea Georgia overheard anything. Normally, she paid little attention to his work conversations. Then he remembered her asking if Teresa was Japanese. *Georgia likes her,* he realized with surprise.

Teresa appeared in the doorway again, a sheaf of papers in her hand. She closed the door and walked quickly toward him, head low between her shoulders, mouth set in a straight line. She looked pissed.

"The Metanet control terminal is over here," she said without looking at him. She walked toward a desk in the far corner of the room, Warne following. Two wooden stools, one piled high with printouts, were set before a large computer monitor. Teresa grabbed the chair and shook it with a sharp, angry gesture, knocking the papers to the floor. She took a seat, pulled it close to the terminal. Warne sat on the opposite chair. Teresa leaned her head in close to the terminal, black eyes glittering, and with a crook of a finger motioned Warne to do the same.

"All right, Dr. Warne," she said in a low voice. "It's obvious that you've got—how can I put this scientifically?—a major bug up your ass. And I know what species it is."

"Then describe it to me," Warne replied, keeping his voice equally low.

"You think I'm to blame for this somehow."

"Well, aren't you? You, or somebody on your team?"

"My *team!*" Teresa said in a voice of mock surprise.

"We've been working together, you and I, for almost a year. Sure, it's been by phone, but I thought we'd developed a good relationship. A *friendship.* You know the Metanet isn't capable of this kind of misbehavior. I'll bet you didn't even put up a fight for it. Hell, you didn't even *warn* me about this. You let me walk in like an idiot, with my pants down around my ankles."

"My *team!*" Teresa repeated, as if still unable to believe what she had heard. She sat back. "Oh, my God. You're a smart guy, I thought you'd have figured it out by now."

"Figured what out?"

"Who have you ever spoken to about the Metanet besides me?"

Warne thought a moment. "There was that lab assistant, Clay—"

"Barnett? Clay's been working in Imaging Technology for the last five months." She leaned closer again. "I *have* no fucking team, Andrew. There's only me."

"What?" Warne said in disbelief. "You're the only person assigned to the robots?"

"There's a maintenance staff that does the blue-collar work: servo replacement, diagnostics. But I'm the only tech."

There was a brief silence. Warne struggled with this fresh surprise.

"As for warning you, I was forbidden to say a word of this to anybody, I mean anybody, *especially* you."

"Dad?" came Georgia's voice from across the lab. "What are you talking about? Why are you whispering?"

"Nothing, sweetie," Warne said, straightening up. "We're just—working on a little problem here, that's all."

Then he leaned back toward Teresa.

"You think I didn't fight for the Metanet?" she whispered fiercely. "I *did,* tooth and nail. It's my bread and butter. Especially now."

Warne looked at her closely. "All right. Tell me about it."

She pulled the goggles from her head, ran her fingers through her hair. "It started shortly after the park opened. At first, I was told we were temporarily in maintenance mode. That we'd be expanding the robotics staff as soon as the Future Attractions Committee issued a report. Well, the report came out, but I never saw it. The new hires budgeted for robotics were funneled elsewhere: imaging, acoustics. And then, a couple of months ago, they started scaling back."

"Scaling *back*?"

"Taking nonessential bots off-line. Replacing them with humans, or simply detasking altogether. In fact, the only bots we've added aren't real, autonomous bots at all. They're just animated machines, like the dragons and mandrakes in Camelot. And the World line managers, not me, take care of those."

Warne passed the back of his hand over his forehead. "But why?"

"Can't you *see* why? It's the bean counters in the head office. Robots aren't sexy enough. Too academic, too high-concept. Sure, it's nice to keep a few around for eye candy: wow the tourists in Callisto, give the PR types something to write about. But they don't sell tickets. The home office thinks robots are passé. Barksdale told me himself. They had a lot of promise, just like AI did, but it's not panning out. Every kid has a robot toy these days, little brain-dead things that give the genuine article a bad name. Nobody cares whether it's bots or mouth-breathers that clean the floors on C Level."

"Eric Nightingale cared. He told me so himself."

Abruptly, Teresa sank back. "Nightingale was a visionary. He saw Utopia as something more than just a New Age theme park with fancy gadgets. He meant it as a crucible for new technology."

"A crucible for new technology. I heard him give that speech just this morning."

"And I *believed* in it!" she countered defiantly. "I still do. That's the reason I signed on here. But Nightingale's dead now. And the Park doesn't run on his vision any longer. It's run on exit polls and demographics. All the attention's on the superficial. Bring in art history scholars, make it look more real. Add bigger and better holograms. Speed up the rides." She lowered her voice again. "And nobody was prepared for just how much those casinos would bring in. The whole attitude of the place has changed."

Warne watched as she lapsed into silence. She had a most un-Utopian candor. Here he'd burst in, full of righteous indignation, chip firmly on shoulder, only to release Teresa's own pent-up frustration.

"Dad?" Georgia called again. "You ready? Let's get back to the Park."

"Hold on a sec," Teresa called over. "We've almost got it worked out."

There was a brief moment in which the two exchanged glances.

"Sorry, Teresa," Warne said. "I guess I jumped to the wrong conclusion."

"It's okay. Like I said, I know how you must feel. I feel the same way. And call me Terri, please. I hate 'Teresa.' "

"Named for the saint, I suppose?"

"Of course. I must be the only non-Catholic Filipina on earth. Haven't been to mass in ten years. My parents would roll over in their graves."

There was another brief silence. Warne felt confused, uncertain of what to say or do next.

"Well, Nightingale would be pleased by the holograms, at least," he said at last. "They're truly amazing."

"You're right." Her expression seemed to change. "You'd better take me with a grain of salt, Dr. Warne. Some of it's just jealousy talking. There's plenty of new technology here. It's just that, after their big discoveries, the hologram staff got all the goodies. And the budget to match. Originally, Imaging Technology was assigned eight people. Now they've got forty."

"What big discoveries, exactly?"

"Figuring out how to make holographic images life-size, instead of the size of a cigarette pack. That was first. But the biggest breakthrough came after Nightingale's death. The Crucible."

Warne looked at her quickly.

"Ironic, isn't it? I suppose they named it after his famous little speech. I don't know the technical details—they're still keeping it under pretty tight wraps. But it's a system for creating fantastically complex holograms using computers. Of course, it takes massively parallel CPU power to work. But there's no more need for lasers, photopolymers, anything. It's almost like the 3-D modeling programs used for computer-animated movies. Except instead of creating two-dimensional figures, the Crucible can create full-motion holographic projections."

"Jesus." Warne fell silent a moment. "Imagine the potential."

"You're telling me. But those particular patents aren't being licensed. They're keeping the magic to themselves, making it Utopia's signature. It's been building ever since the Park opened. The first holographically enhanced attraction was Ripper, over in Gaslight."

"Don't know anything about it."

"At first it was more like a trial balloon than anything. See, the audience is in this theater, supposedly to watch some Victorian revue. Then somebody yells that the bobbies are chasing Jack the Ripper, they've cornered him outside. Then somebody else yells that the Ripper's run *into* the theater. And then the lights go out."

"Sounds effective."

"Try sphincter-slackening. Incredibly realistic holograms of the Ripper, running through the theater, popping up behind your seat, bloody knife raised. People screaming." She shrugged. "It developed an immediate buzz. The powers-that-be pricked up their ears, saw the potential. So next, they decided to add holograms to Event Horizon, which was still being developed."

"That's the roller coaster in Callisto, right? I saw it on the guidemap."

"Try next generation *after* coasters. Completely dark. A bank of seats bolted to a platform, synced by computer to lurch up, down, side to side, in time to images hurtling by you. Except here it's not just a flat screen you're staring at—it's three-dimensional comets and meteors, hurtling right by your face. No need for trick glasses. You're basically *inside* a hologram."

Warne shook his head wonderingly.

"Then somebody got the bright idea of leveraging the technology. You see the Mind's Eye galleries in Callisto and the Nexus?"

"Nope."

"They're studios where you can get a holographic portrait of yourself—alone, with one of the characters, even with Nightingale himself. And you know what? They can't churn 'em out fast enough. So you're a Utopia accountant, watching the money pour into the casinos, seeing dads fighting each other for the privilege of slapping down a hundred bucks for a holographic portrait of their kid. Then you look at Terri Bonifacio and her robotics program. Who do you think's coming up short when they prepare the next quarter's budget?"

The question hung in the air, unanswered.

"But that's just the beginning." She turned around, stood up. "Hey, Georgia, you want to come over here a minute? I want to show you something." Terri waited for Georgia to walk over, Game Boy in hand. Then she turned toward a small object Warne had assumed to be a robot: a black cylinder on wheels, no more than forty inches tall. "They're also working on this." She bent over it, pushed a few buttons. There was a brief flickering in the nearby air, and then, suddenly, a baby elephant was standing shoulder-to-shoulder with Warne.

Warne shrank back instinctively, almost tripping over Georgia in surprise. The elephant was perfect in every detail. The small black eye, buried within intricate folds of gray, glistened as it regarded him intently. The fine hairs on the upper lip shone. It was a hologram, but far more realistic than even the image of Nightingale he'd seen that morning.

"Good Lord!" Warne said.

"Awesome!" Georgia breathed.

The elephant vanished as Terri pressed another button on the cylinder. "It's a portable holographic projector," she said. "Still under development. I've only got this old prototype because they're thinking of incorporating some memory chips from my deactivated bots. They plan to use these in the Nightingale magic shows opening in all of the Worlds next year." She jerked a thumb at the black casing. "That elephant was the last thing in its image buffer. It's easy to use. Here, watch."

She adjusted a small lens on the housing, pressed a button marked *sample.* Then she stepped back a few feet, positioning herself in front of the lens, pressing her hands against her head in a Stooge-like imitation. There was a series of warning beeps, then a short whirring noise. Stepping forward again, Terri pressed another button marked *display*. Instantly, a second Terri Bonifacio was standing next to her, incredibly lifelike: Terri, as her image had been captured by the machine just seconds before.

"It can only render stills," Terri said. "But the detail surpasses anything else around." She looked at the frozen image. "Hey, Moe!" she said in a squeaky imitation of Curly.

"Can you make one of me?" Georgia asked.

"Sure thing." Terri ushered them over, showed Warne how to work the device. Within moments, two Georgias were standing side by side.

"Does my face really look that fat?" Georgia asked, scrutinizing the hologram.

Despite himself, Warne shook his head in mute admiration. Terri switched off the device, and the image disappeared.

"But what are they using all this technology *for*?" Terri asked suddenly. "Entertainment. To project a monster into your car on the dark rides, give the kiddies an extra scare. Do you really think Nightingale would approve of *that*? I think he'd call it shortsighted, and—"

There was a sudden roar directly overhead: a massive, bone-jarring sound, like ten volcanoes erupting at once. Georgia shrieked, clasped herself instinctively against her father. Warne cringed, throwing his arms over her head. The stool behind him went clattering to the floor. Wingnut made a frightened-sounding *chirrup* and moved quickly into the nearest dark corner.

The aggrieved look on Terri's face dissolved into a grin as Warne slowly lowered his arms.

"What the *hell* . . . ?" he began.

"Sorry, should have warned you two about that. We're right below Griffin Tower, in Camelot. The 1:20 show's going on."

Warne righted the stool, glanced up at the ceiling. "How many shows are there a day?"

"One in the morning, two in the afternoon, one in the evening."

"You have to deal with that four times a day?"

Terri's grin widened a little. "It's better since they moved me to the smaller lab. Before, they had me underneath Thames Tempest, in Gaslight. The river used to leak."

Warne waited a moment, letting the ringing in his ears ease.

Georgia glanced from one to the other impatiently. "So are you guys done? I mean, how long does it take to unhook the Metanet, or whatever you have to do?"

Warne turned to her in surprise. "You knew?" He turned to Terri. "Did you say something to her?"

"Come on, Dad. It's been written all over your face ever since that meeting."

Warne shook his head, scratched the back of his neck ruefully. There was another, softer explosion overhead. He thought he could hear the screams and cries of an excited audience.

"This whole thing is pretty stupid, if you ask me," Georgia added.

"What is?"

"Taking it off-line. I mean, there's no bug, or glitch, or anything like that in it, whatever *Sarah* says."

Terri's eyes twinkled mischievously. "How would you know?"

Georgia sat up straight, looked at her squarely. "Because my father made it."

Warne glanced away, blinked his eyes. For a moment, he was afraid to speak. The lab fell into a brief silence.

"Sarah told me they want an action plan by the end of the day," Warne said at last.

"Yup. Emory's bean counters in New York have given us a week to detask the Metanet. Basically, that means removing a hundred-odd robots from its control. Fred needs to know the safest, fastest way to do that."

Warne settled back on his stool. He took a deep breath. "First, you'd need to take the uplink capability off-line." He thought for

a moment. "The way it works now, each night the Metanet ana-
lyzes the data streams it gets from the individual bots, looking
for ways to improve efficiency. If it finds any, it transmits new
code to the bots during the next morning's downlink. Right?"

"Right."

"So first, you disable the machine learning subsystem. Once
that's done, you simply turn off the uplink. That way, you can
still send new instructions and firmware patches to the bots remotely. But the Metanet won't make any modifications of its
own."

Terri nodded. "Makes sense."

"Disabling the intelligence will be the complicated part.
You'll have to model the process in a test environment first, of
course. But once that's done, the rest is easy. Compile a list of
bots and their processes. You make recommendations as to es-
sential or nonessential tasks."

"You, you," said Terri. "What's all this *you* business?"

Warne stared at her. He'd been planning on spending just a
few minutes here: assess the situation, give brief instructions,
then leave Terri to do the lobotomy herself. But now a new
thought came into his mind.

He glanced quickly at Georgia, who was fiddling with the
holographic projector. *There's no bug, or glitch*, she'd said. *My
father made it.*

"Terri, I have to ask," he said, turning. "There's nothing
you've done to the Metanet, as administrator, that could possibly
account for this?"

Her brown eyes widened, flaring with sudden indignation.
"Nada. It's autonomous. I've simply logged its updates."

"So you've been monitoring the changes the Metanet made to
bot activities?"

"Most were pretty minor. Streamlining behaviors, updating
rule systems, that kind of thing. It pretty much ran itself."

Warne stood, thinking, rubbing his bruised wrist, still aching
from when Hard Place had gripped it.

"What's going through your mind?" Terri asked, frowning.

Because my father made it.

Besides Georgia, the Metanet was all he had left. It was the
credibility he needed if he was ever going to secure another academic or research post. Hell if he'd give up on it without a fight.

Warne looked back at Terri. If he understood things right,

with the robotics work being scaled back, the Metanet would mean almost as much to her as it did to him.

He reached out suddenly, put his hand on her arm. "Correct me if I'm wrong, but haven't we just developed our action plan?"

She nodded cautiously.

"Well, that gives us some free time. What do you say if, instead of taking it to the scrapyard, we open the hood and try to fix the damn thing?"

Terri looked at him for a moment. Then, slowly, the frown faded from the exotic face and her impish smile returned.

"I think I'm beginning to like the way you think. Sailor"—and at this she leered at him and lapsed into pidgin English—"you just bought youself a girl."

1:17 P.M.

"LISTEN UP," THE voice crackled across the backstage sound system. "House opens in three minutes."

Jogging toward Wardrobe, Roger Hagen checked the clock. Prompt to the second, as always. Sometimes the punctuality was almost depressing.

All around, the usual last-minute preparations for the Griffin Tower show were being made. The front-of-house engineer was in his booth, prepping the control board. The stage manager was going down the event checklist with her assistant. Maintenance workers were milling about, checking gas and fog effects, firing up the colored smoke generators. Grips, gaffers, electricians, set decorators, and makeup artists trotted back and forth. A close-proximity shooter was busy setting up squib connections to a bank of theatrical flash pots. A few cast members already in costume worked on their fencing moves. Others sat huddled in corners, practicing Middle English with diction coaches.

Performers "behind the show" at other parks were known to act as if they were attending frat parties. At Utopia, however, they sometimes seemed more reminiscent of law students prepping for their bar exams. Hagen ducked across the wings—careful not to trip on the rivers of coax and light-pipe cabling that ran across the floor—then headed down a small series of steps.

Wardrobe for the Griffin Tower show was packed: wizards, wimpled maidens, and knight-errants stood around in various stages of undress. There was a frantic whirring of sewing machines, assistants rolling racks of antique clothing back and forth. Harvey Schwartz, portly wardrobe master for the show, caught sight of Hagen and broke into a grin. "Hey, look, everybody!" he cried, stepping out from the bank of commercial washers and pointing in Hagen's direction. "It's the lame duck!"

"Yeah, yeah," Hagen muttered, pulling off his shirt, opening his locker, and shrugging into the fire-retardant Nomex jerkin that hung inside. He glanced around a little uneasily. Despite the occasionally studious atmosphere, Utopia backstage had its traditions, like every other park. And one of those traditions was to play a nasty practical joke on somebody's last day at work.

One of the costume assistants came over to help him into his own armor. Hagen inspected every piece—mail shirt, leggings, boots—searching suspiciously for unwelcome presents. Last month, they'd stuck a dog turd in the helmet of some guy on his last day in the show. The poor slob hadn't discovered it until it was too late, and he'd had to go through the whole performance with the thing rolling around inside his armor.

Everything checked out, though, and Hagen gave the dresser the okay to lower the helmet over his head. Immediately, Hagen's world contracted to the small rectangle of light allowed by the forward visor. It wasn't the armor he minded so much—after all, the aluminum was light and relatively flexible—it was the loss of vision. That, and the smell: by the end of a performance, the suit of armor usually smelled like a ripe locker room.

He could hear the fanfare, the rising cheer of the audience, as the curtain went up and the show began. The dresser fastened the final snap, switched on the small IR transmitter attached to his helmet, handed him his shield and sword, and gave him a go-ahead rap. With a nod in the direction of Harvey Schwartz, Hagen made his way up the stairs to the backstage area. It was much harder, walking in the armor. He had to be careful where he stepped: if he tripped and fell, he would not be able to get up without assistance.

He approached the wings, peering out behind one of the blackout curtains. It was a good crowd: the three-thousand-seat theater was packed. The Battle of Griffin Tower had been introduced about four months before and had quickly become one of Utopia's hottest live-action shows. Little kids especially were eager to see, firsthand, the characters from *The Feverstone Chronicles*, Nightingale's animated movies about a mythical, magical Camelot. Watching the smiles of the children, illuminated by 25,000-watt strobes and flickering lasers, Hagen felt a little nagging tug of self-doubt.

Utopia had been a good place to work. Years before, during college, he'd worked as a Disney riverboat captain, spieling for guests. Utopia was very different. True, the insistence on realism, the background classes, grew old pretty fast. At every show, there were always one or two "nannies" on hand, checking for historical accuracy, awarding points to the best performers. But the pay scale was the best in the industry. Each week, everyone got two hundred bucks' worth of free tokens for the casinos. And hard work was rewarded: you did well, you got your pick of show times, an accelerated promotion path to lead, or even foreman.

The truth was, Hagen just didn't like the desert. Many cast members—the ones who didn't relish the daily thirty-mile commute from the northern suburbs of Vegas—had made their homes in the town of Creosote, a few miles north of the Park on U.S. 95. Over the past year, what had once been little more than a desert truck stop had transformed into a bustling agglomeration of trailer parks and bungalows, with a boisterous nightlife and the air of a college campus. But for Hagen, living the life of a thirty-year-old student just wasn't much fun anymore.

Onstage, Mymanteus the Archmage was now weaving his evil spell, bent on bringing the griffins of Griffin Tower to life. Somebody knocked on his armor, and Hagen backed away from the curtain, swiveling to get a glimpse of Olmstead, the guy who would be playing his shield bearer . . . or *écuyer*, as the nannies kept insisting they say.

"Hey, hey," Olmstead said, his narrow grinning head sticking out of a chain-mail hauberk liberally smeared with fire gel. "How's it hanging?"

"Pretty damn high, in this rig."

Olmstead's grin widened. "Come on. Enjoy. It's your last day, remember? Me, I've got another eight performances before the weekend."

Dramatic music swelled, pounding from batteries of speakers hidden behind false walls. The archmage's spell was almost complete, and backstage the tension had grown almost palpable. This was when the real fun started. Hagen glanced over at the stage manager, standing in the wings below a bank of monitors, her finger poised above the effects enable button on the forward console. Nearby, the theatrical tech stood by the pyromusical firing panel, monitoring the computer-choreographed firestorm that was about to launch. Behind them was a short, spectacled, scholarly-looking little fellow Hagen didn't recognize, a decibel meter in one hand. *Probably that fireworks specialist they were talking about bringing in,* he thought. The maroons—the low-level indoor salutes used in the finale—were spectacular. But they were loud as hell. Guests were always complaining, and two of the crew had developed tinnitus. Hagen stole another glance at the bald guy brought in to fix things. *Quiet fireworks,* he thought. *Jesus, what a concept.*

They wouldn't be quiet today. In seconds, all hell would break loose. The griffins would wake, surrounding Queen Kalina and the prince regent. The evil archmage Mymanteus would set upon them with ice bolts and magic missiles. All the children in the crowd would start to scream. And then Hagen himself would wade into the thick of things. Race onstage, fight heroically, die two minutes later. Three times daily. Except at the end of *this* day, he'd die for the last time. Then hang up his shield, turn in his sword. And hope to get back to Creosote without getting fire-hosed or otherwise abused by his fellow cast members.

The crews were really sweating now: the fog machines were working overtime, pouring rivers of gray mist out into the theater. The stage manager had armed the electronic pyrotechnic system, and now she punched the enabling button, nodding to the control booth.

There was a tremendous, floor-shaking crash, accompanied by yells and shrieks from the audience. The griffins were on the move. *Thirty seconds.* Low flickers of orange and red shone through the gauzy drapes and fire curtains. Now and then, a brighter flash cut through the murk: the laser effects of the archmage's spells. Olmstead grinned again, nodded. Stage adrenaline began to course through Hagen's veins. A tech climbed a catwalk at the far right wing, ensuring the small laser-firing robot was on track and ready to go. The floor rumbled again as the subwoofer array beneath the stage cut in. Hagen glanced up at a clock: 1:28. More flashes, then a cackle of evil laughter: his cue.

The stage manager gave him the high sign. "Hagen! Go!"

With a deep breath, Hagen took a tight grip on his sword, raised the shield across his breastplate, and began lumbering forward. The assistant manager gave him a thumbs-up. A stagehand parted the blackout curtain, veils of smoke and cordite-heavy fumes wafting between the folds. And then he was onstage.

He'd done the show maybe three hundred times before. But on this, his last day, he tried to look at it again with fresh eyes: to implant the memory of what it looked like, smelled like, *felt* like, to be onstage at Griffin Tower.

Most obvious was the noise. The screaming of the audience, the roar of the enraged griffins prowling the stage, the sharp crackle of the archmage's magical bolts, provided a suffocating, surrounding presence. As he stepped into the light, and the streams of mist and fog fell away, there was a fresh cheer from the audience.

Griffin Tower was a remarkable space: a vast, rectangular bailey that rose eight stories, open all the way to its distant ceiling. It smelled of mold and damp stone. Light flickered from flaming torches and braziers set high into the walls. The air was alive with blasts of searing color. Overhead, the archmage cackled once again as—with the help of the effects crew backstage—he hurled fireballs down upon the terrified queen and prince regent. One of the fireballs hit the far wall of the tower: with a roar, a massive piece of masonry cracked, split, then hurtled down toward the audience on invisible truss rods, sheering to one side at the last minute. There were shrieks of delight.

Downstage, poor Olmstead was getting mauled by an enraged griffin, right on schedule. Swinging Perilous above his head, Hagen raced forward to attack. One of the griffins turned toward him, its mechanical eyes glowing bright red. Careful to keep the creature between him and the audience, Hagen gave a mighty thrust with Perilous, missing the griffin by a good six inches. Offstage, the handler worked his remote control, and the mechanical beast jerked and fell over, writhing on the ground, smoke darting from its mouth. It was a very realistic effect, and the crowd cheered wildly.

Now, Hagen leaped over the body of his fallen shield bearer and raced toward the queen, dispatching a second griffin in the process. Already it was getting hot inside the armor. Sweat was beading on his forehead. There was a bank of small monitors, concealed behind the footlights at the front of the stage, providing the actors with views from the audience perspective. Hagen had learned to keep a careful eye on them. Even though his part lasted only two minutes, it was easy to get disoriented amid the smoke and laser light.

He came forward, placing himself before the queen and raising his shield toward the archmage.

"Varlet!" he cried. *"By Goddes herte, cease thy alchemy!"*

The wizard gave another menacing laugh, gathered himself for another spell. The lights flickered, and the stage trembled as the subwoofers cut in again. Hagen glanced down through his visor toward the monitors, checking his placement, making sure he was half-turned toward the audience. When Mymanteus launched his spell, a laser would bounce off Hagen's helmet, then carom wildly around the set, synced to more explosions. He'd fall, arms outstretched, victim of the evil archmage's mind-blast. It was a great effect, a real crowd pleaser. Hagen wanted to get it right his last day on the job.

There was an unearthly shrieking noise; the wizard lifted his arms; a bluish beam shot from his outstretched fingers. Hagen kept his eyes on the monitor. He never tired of seeing this.

Only this time, it looked different. The wizard's beam did not reflect off his helmet, shimmering and coruscating into the smoke and haze. Instead, the laser pierced the helmet and lanced straight through Hagen's head, emerging out the other side and heading stage left in an unwavering line. In the monitor, it looked as if a glowing knitting needle had been thrust through his jaws. The crowd roared its approval.

But Hagen did not hear them. There was no pain, really: just a steady heat that refused to go away, and a pressure inside his skull that grew, and still grew, until one by one the rest of his senses dropped away and he crumpled to the stage.

MOMENTS LATER, THE curtain rang down to a thunderous cannonade of fireworks that burst below the tower rooflines and threw delicate traceries of color down toward the audience. The violent echoes quickly gave way to clapping and wild cheering as the crowd, with one mind, rose to its feet.

The other side of the curtain was a scene of frenetic activity. Actors trotted toward dressing rooms, high-fiving each other; wardrobe assistants feverishly checked costumes for wear and tear; engineers began resetting props for the next performance. All ignored the booming wall of noise from beyond the curtain. The fireworks specialist examined his decibel meter, jotted some notes. In a distant corner, one of the nannies was scolding the sennet-player—a waif no older than ten—for holding his trumpet improperly. Only Roger Hagen remained motionless, sprawled facedown across the boards of the stage.

Now Olmstead, his shield bearer, ambled up. "Hey, no laying down on the job," he grinned, nudging Hagen with a booted foot.

When Hagen remained still, Olmstead's crooked grin widened. "What is this, Method acting?" he said. "I'm fresh out of Oscars, pal."

Still no response, and now the grin began to fade. "Hey, Roger, what's the gag?" Olmstead asked, kneeling beside the motionless knight and shaking him gently.

As he shook Hagen a second time, Olmstead noticed something. His gaze shifted to Hagen's helmet. He bent closer, sniffing, detecting an odor of cooked meat.

And then he leaped to his feet, his frantic shouts barely audible over the unceasing roar of the crowd.

1:34 P.M.

BOB ALLOCCO, HEAD of Park Security, had seen or heard just about everything in the six months since Utopia had opened. But he'd never seen anything like this.

He stood in the monitoring station at the exit to Griffin Tower, watching through privacy glass as the audience streamed out of the theater. There was laughter, whistling, a little horseplay: the usual antics of a crowd keyed to fever pitch by the excitement of a show. If anything, they seemed more enthusiastic than usual. He snapped the mike channel open to listen to the exit chatter.

"Awesome!" one kid was saying to another. "You check out those cool-looking dragons?"

"They weren't dragons, lamer," said the other. "They were griffins. Don't you know *anything*?"

An old lady passed by the hidden doorway, fanning herself with a guidemap. "Merciful heavens," she said to an even older woman at her side. "Those fireworks, practically in my face . . . you know, I thought I'd have to leave, with my heart and all."

"See how that knight died?" a man pushing a baby stroller said to his wife. "Zap, right through the head. Wonder how they managed that?"

"That wasn't so great," the woman replied. "They can do anything with special effects these days. But that big old chunk of tower practically falling on top of us—now, *that* was something else."

Allocco waited, silently running a balm stick over his lips, as the last of the crowd filed out. Then he opened the door, nodded to the costumed hosts and hostesses, and stepped into the theater. The fallen tower section was being lifted back into position with a whine of hydraulics. Huge air scrubbers were venting the pall of smoke and gunpowder out through overhead ducts.

He stood between the rows, glancing up at the high walls of

artificial stonework. He had a bad feeling, of course: but then, he always seemed to have a bad feeling whenever the Park was open. Allocco liked Utopia best at 6:00 A.M.—the way it was meant to be seen, when staff was at a minimum and no guests were around to sully the illusion. Then he could walk through the cobbled streets of Gaslight or the skyways of Callisto without worrying about lost children, or poor health risks, or lawsuit seekers. Or drunken frat boys.

Just last week, three motorcycle thugs had decided to go skinny-dipping in the Boardwalk boat pond. It had taken eight security officers to convince them to put on their clothes and leave. The week before, a Portuguese tourist objected to the two-hour wait to get into Event Horizon and pulled a knife on the cast member working the queuing line. Allocco shook his head. Security specialists were forbidden to carry weapons, even in self-defense. No Mace, no billy clubs—and sure as hell no firearms. They had to rely on their smiles, their powers of persuasion. Not exactly a match for a nine-millimeter. A Portuguese-speaking security officer had managed to talk the guy down—but it had been touch and go for a couple of minutes.

Allocco walked down the carpeted aisle to the front of the house, then climbed onto the stage and ducked behind the curtain. Cast members were standing around in small groups, still in costume, speaking in low tones. Allocco shooed them away. Then he walked toward a white-clad figure kneeling over the man in armor, lying motionless on the boards.

The knight's helmet had been placed to one side. Allocco picked it up, turning it over in his hands. Puncture holes, small and very precise, had been drilled through each cheekplate. Allocco hefted the helmet, sighting through the holes. There was remarkably little blood. The helmet smelled of scorched metal and overdone hamburger. He put it aside and turned toward the kneeling doctor.

"How is he?" he asked.

"The laser cut clean through both cheeks," the doctor replied. "Skin abrasions, tissue damage, muscle trauma. What you'd expect. The tongue is scorched, and he'll probably lose two, maybe three teeth. And he'll have one hell of a headache when he wakes up. But he's lucky to be alive." He glanced up. "If that beam had been a couple of inches higher, we'd need a body bag instead of a stretcher."

Allocco grunted.

"We can suture him up in Central Medical, but he'll probably need some cosmetic surgery down the road. Shall I call Lake Mead, get an ambulance up here?"

Allocco thought about John Doe. "No. Not yet. Just stabilize him downstairs. Let me know if his condition changes."

The doctor signaled to an orderly hovering nearby, and Allocco turned away. Downstage, near the wings, the stage manager was watching a couple of techs bring something down on a ladder. As Allocco drew closer, he could see it was a robot. It looked like a cart on wheels, topped by a long white tube—a laser head—with a lens at one end and a bundle of control wires snaking out from the other. The lens was shattered and hanging loose in its coupling. The top of the laser head had been peeled back like a zipper, jagged ends of bare metal charred and smoking.

The techs placed the robot gingerly on the ground.

"Which one of you is the laser safety officer?" Allocco asked.

The taller of the two turned toward him. "I'm the LSO for Camelot, sir."

"Want to tell me what happened?"

"I don't know, sir." The LSO swallowed painfully. He looked very frightened. "It's only a thirty-watt head, I can't understand, it doesn't make sense . . ."

"Slow down, son." Allocco pointed at the robot. "Just tell me what went wrong."

"It's an argon laser with a multiline air-cooled head. We needed argon because the beam had to match the blue color of the archmage's blasts."

"Go on." If he let the guy blab long enough, he might say something important.

"And we couldn't use a standard light-show controller because there's no script to follow. You know?"

Allocco nodded sympathetically. He knew the procedure. "It had to hit the knight, every time. But you couldn't know precisely where the knight would be standing when the effect went off."

The man nodded. "There was an extra bot hanging around. They used to use it for some maintenance duty and didn't want it anymore. Somebody got a bright idea."

The man's look of fear grew even more pronounced. *I can*

guess who that someone was, Allocco thought. He remained silent.

"Anyway, so they mounted an argon head on it, fixed the bot to that overhead track, stage right." He pointed. "That woman in Robotics—Teresa? She modified it to track an infrared beam on the knight's helmet. At the trigger event, it fired the laser right down the IR signal."

"And how long has this been in operation?"

"Since a couple weeks after the show opened. Almost three months now, four times a day. No problems."

"No problems." Allocco pointed at the ruined housing. "What could make it overload like that?"

"Never seen anything like it, sir. It must have exceeded its normal output by a factor of one hundred."

Allocco gave the man a sidelong glance. "You know, OSHA's going to want to evaluate this incident."

The laser safety officer paled. For a moment, Allocco wondered if he might faint.

"Your compliance chart is up to date?" Allocco asked in a more soothing tone.

The man nodded again. "We follow Z-136 like a book." ANSI Z-136 was the set of laser safety standards set by industry, research, and government. "Weekly evaluations, as specified. Hazard zone re-evaluation, maintenance, interlocks—"

"Good boy. Now, I want you to take this thing downstairs, do a postmortem. Let me know what you find."

He glanced toward the stage manager, who had been listening in silence to this exchange. "No more lasers for the archmage, at least for the foreseeable future," he said. "Can you cobble something together for the 4:20?"

"I'll have to, won't I?" The stage manager turned and followed the techs backstage, disappearing into the dim tunnel that led toward the dressing rooms.

Allocco watched her leave. Then he plucked his radio from his pocket and spoke into it. "Command Nine Seven, this is Thirty-three."

"Yes, sir."

"Pull up the Griffin Tower history. Any intrusion alerts over the last twenty-four hours?"

"Just a moment." Allocco waited through the faint whisper of static. "No, sir. One beam is open, otherwise it's clean."

"One beam's open? Where's the interrupt?"

There was a tapping of keys. "Griffin Tower 206. West aspect, catwalk 4."

"And what time did the beam transmit an open signal?"

"About five minutes ago, sir. You want me to send someone up to clear it?"

"No, thanks. I'll check it myself. Ignore any more tower alerts until I radio back."

Allocco returned the radio to his pocket and walked farther backstage, looking thoughtfully up at the webbing of spars and metal beams that formed the skeleton of Griffin Tower.

The public areas of Utopia were surrounded by networks of intrusion mats and more modern infrared beams. They ensured that guests stayed safely inside their cars during rides; that they didn't wander, intentionally or otherwise, into potentially dangerous backstage areas. Somebody passing by and interrupting an infrared beam would cause only a temporary break. When a beam stayed open, it almost always meant hardware failure.

Besides, what guest would climb up into those metal rafters—avoiding all other intrusion sensors—and then sit, motionless, in the path of one?

Allocco looked up at the metal track the laser-wielding robot had run along. Then he glanced back at the spot on the stage where the wounded knight had lain a moment before.

It was crazy. Yet Allocco knew he had to check it out nevertheless.

The gray-painted rungs of the metal ladder were cool to the touch. He pulled himself up carefully, hand over hand. It had been a long time since he'd climbed a backstage ladder—or jogged, or swum, or done much physical activity other than walk—and in less than a minute he began to puff. He rose past various strata of backstage gear: guy wires, curtain pulleys, black conduits of communications and power lines.

It grew darker. The sounds of life from below—the murmur of voices, the brief tinkle of a troubadour's song—grew very faint. Overhead now, he could make out a catwalk, the number 2 stenciled on its underside in white paint. He pulled himself up onto it, puffing more heavily. To one side was a spotter's station, equipped with binoculars and a telephone. During performances, this span would be alive with activity. Now, it was deserted. A narrow band of fluorescent lights was set into the wall above the catwalk, ensuring that the stagehands would not run into each other as they scurried to and fro.

Allocco walked twenty feet along the catwalk to the next ladder. With a sigh, he grasped the rungs and began to ascend once again.

It was a longer climb to catwalk 3. When he reached it, Allocco swung himself up, took a seat on the hard grillwork, and rested his back against the walkway railings. He could feel the sweat on his back, damp where his shirt touched the metal railing. This was crazy. He should have let them send up a standard security team. Or, better still, just have Maintenance look into it. But he'd come this far, might as well follow through. God knew he needed the exercise.

He looked around, breathing heavily. He was now at the level of the backstage ceiling. The light was fainter here, but at the far end of the catwalk he could make out a large bulkhead: housing for the hydraulics that dropped the breakaway section of masonry toward the audience at the climax of the show. Above his head, the interior and exterior walls came together: a narrow vertical channel forming the facade of Griffin Tower. Down catwalk 3 he could see the base of another ladder, rising into darkness overhead. He waited a minute, then another, catching his breath. And then he pulled himself to his feet. Too much to do to sit around here all day.

Climbing up inside the skin of the tower proved much more difficult. If he leaned out too far from the ladder, his back would brush against the surface of the inner wall, the fake stonework coarse and nubbly. He was forced to stay close to the rungs, using his arms to pull himself up. By the time the shadowy outlines of catwalk 4 came into view overhead, the muscles of his arms were shaking. Gasping for breath, he heaved himself upward.

This catwalk was only used for maintenance and infrequent safety checks, and it was very dark. Hard to believe that just on the other side of the outer wall were bright sunlight, strolling minstrels, the laughter of tourists. Allocco leaned against the ladder, feeling the hammering cadence of his heart. Great: he'd have a heart attack up here, and nobody would find him for at least a week.

After a minute, as his breathing slowed, he reached into his shirt pocket and drew out a penlight. It threw a puny, threadlike beam onto the catwalk overhead. Why hadn't he thought to bring a real flashlight?

He climbed the final rungs, stepping onto catwalk 4. It was narrow, with a high railing. Even though he could see only darkness under his feet, Allocco was all too aware of the great drop to the stage below. He felt unpleasantly like a small insect, crawling along the inside rim of a Mason jar.

The catwalk ran in both directions, vanishing into blackness. *West aspect, they'd said.* Allocco took a moment to orient himself, then moved forward cautiously, penlight sweeping a path ahead of him.

After a moment, his light picked up the telltale housing of an IR sensor, fixed to the railing about a foot above the ground. Artfully concealed, but still easy to find if you knew what to look for. Allocco knelt beside it, directing his light over the faceplate. GT-205. That meant the defective intrusion sensor must be the next one down the line. *Thank God.* He rose to his feet and began to move forward again.

Suddenly, he stopped, limbs tense, listening. He opened his mouth to call out a challenge, but some sixth sense told him to stay quiet.

Then something strange happened: his right hand dropped toward his belt. Only to clutch empty air.

Allocco looked down at his hand with a numb kind of disbelief.

Years before—in another life—he had been a member of the Boston police force. He had not pulled a gun in the line of duty in a dozen years: what kind of atavistic impulse would prompt him to reach for one now?

He looked back down the catwalk, shining the penlight into the darkness, searching for a flicker of movement, a glint of metal—anything that might represent a threat. His heart was racing, his instincts still going off three-alarm. But there was no sound, no hint of motion, and after several minutes he forced himself to relax. With a sigh, he straightened up, reaching for his radio, bringing it to his lips. Then he dropped it back into his pocket. He was already at the sensor. What good would it do to call in a backup team now?

He shook his head at his own foolishness. He'd allowed John Doe to spook him. Thank God Sarah Boatwright couldn't see him now. She hated weakness of any kind. And here he was: sweating, panting, heart pounding in his chest like some rookie cop on his first taste of action. It was embarrassing, unprofessional. For all he knew, the guy was just a bullshit artist. It was a game, like the phony bomb threats they got so routinely. What kind of terrorists, or thugs, or professional mercenaries, or whatever, would assault a *theme* park? Utopia had nothing they wanted.

Laughing quietly to himself, Allocco eased forward once again, penlight sweeping the catwalk in search of the defective sensor. There it was: near the ground, in the same position as the last, maybe twenty feet ahead.

Instantly, he could see the sensor was not defective. There was something there—something in the path of the beam.

Allocco crept forward, more slowly now. Then he drew in his breath with a sharp rasp.

"Jesus Christ," he whispered. He sank to his knees, eyes riveted to the floor ahead of him.

Now he knew—beyond any trace of doubt—that, whatever else was going on here, it was most definitely not a game.

1:42 P.M.

SARAH BOATWRIGHT WATCHED as Allocco carefully shut and locked the door to her office. He jerked the blind cord, shutting out the view of the corridor beyond. Then he came forward, placing a metal case on the conference table. Fred Barksdale, who had been standing on the far side of the room, stepped up. He was frowning, the aristocratic curve of his lips compressed into a hard line.

Sarah leaned forward in her chair. "Okay, Bob. Let's hear it."

Allocco's face was red, and beneath the suit jacket his shirt was damp with perspiration. "I've got the laser safety officer examining the unit. He thinks it overcharged. Fired at over three hundred watts instead of the rated thirty. Ripped the hell out of it, the head's totally destroyed."

"That's not possible. The Park only uses Class 2 lasers, and they're not—" Sarah stopped. "Was the laser robot-controlled?"

"Yup. Ran along a suspended line, tracking a signal on the poor jerk's helmet."

There was a brief silence.

"The Metanet again," Barksdale said in a low tone.

"I'm just getting started," Allocco went on. "There were reports of something tripping an intrusion sensor in Griffin Tower. I checked it out. And found this."

He snapped the locks on the case, swung it open, and hefted something out by the edges. To Sarah, it looked like a plank of gray plasticine, wrapped in a clear membrane that was stamped with a series of numbers.

Allocco placed the plank very carefully on the surface of the table. "C-4," he said.

"C-4?" Sarah echoed, standing up to take a closer look.

"High explosive. Military grade. Five-pound package."

Sarah froze midstep. Then—slowly—she sat back down behind her desk, eyes on the gray brick.

"I found it on a catwalk in the tower. It had been deliberately placed against the intrusion sensor."

"My God," Barksdale said. "They planned to blow up the tower."

Allocco shook his head. "I don't think so."

"And why the bloody hell not?"

A strange little smile came across Allocco's face. "Because look what I found stuck in it for a detonator."

He dipped his hand into the breast pocket of his jacket and pulled something out: a Tootsie Pop, wrapped in purple paper.

Nobody spoke. Sarah stared at the round little lollipop, balanced on the end of its white stick.

"Grape," she murmured.

"I talked to the stagehands, the catwalk jockeys. Nobody saw anything. But somehow, somebody managed to elude all the sensors, place the explosive, and get away."

"I'm afraid I don't understand," Barksdale said.

"I think I do." Allocco laid the lollipop beside the case. "He's simply telling us he can hurt people. Destroy rides with impunity. In fact, now that I think about it, all these glitches we've been noticing may not have been glitches at all. We got our show: and I think our friend John Doe's sending us a double message. That he controls both the vertical *and* the horizontal."

Barksdale looked from Allocco to Sarah, then back again.

"What Bob's saying is they've got us both ways." Sarah spoke slowly, carefully. She was aware of several feelings—surprise, concern, anger—and she did not want any of them to cloud the decisions she had to make now. "They've reprogrammed some of the robots to wreak havoc around the Park—loosen the brakes on roller coasters, overload lasers. But they've also got the means to blow us to hell and gone."

"What was it John Doe told you he wanted to do?" Allocco said. "Dispel any lingering doubts? Well, I'm a believer." He walked toward the desk, picked up Sarah's phone.

"What are you doing?" she asked.

"Ordering a level 1 phased evacuation of the Park," he said, dialing. "Then I'm going to contact the state police. My pals in Troop E will be very interested to hear about this. We'll need two, maybe three SORT teams, as well as plainclothes federal agents trained in crowd dispersal within a fire zone—"

Barksdale stepped forward and abruptly placed his hand over the phone's switch hook. It was such an uncharacteristic gesture for the CTO, so full of unseemly haste, that Sarah stared at him in surprise.

"What the hell are you doing?" Allocco roared.

"I might ask you the same question. Don't you recall why they *gave* us this demonstration? To warn us against making rash moves."

Allocco glared. Without a word, he raised the handset again.

"Put down that phone," Sarah said instantly.

Allocco froze, looking at her, conflict clear on his face. But Sarah's tone of cold command could not be resisted. The security director released his grip, letting the handset drop into its cradle.

"Before we do precisely what we were warned *not* to, we need to learn more about what we're dealing with," she said, softening her voice slightly.

Allocco was still looking at her. "What we're dealing with? Let me tell you what we're dealing with. I watched the guests leaving Griffin Tower after the show. Guess what? They all had a great time. Nobody knew—nobody had the faintest *inkling*—that somebody got hurt." He waved his hand at the explosive. "If that semtex had detonated, it would have blown away the inside wall of the tower. Sent it crashing down into an audience of three thousand people. It would have brought the house down—literally. And do you know what would happen? They'd be loving it—right up to the moment it crushed the life out of them. Because they'd just seen another tower come crashing down on the other side of the theater. A crash that was *part of the show*."

He walked slowly around the table, then approached Sarah's desk again. "We have, what, 66,000-odd guests here today? And not one of them retains even an infant's sense of self-preservation. They checked their fight-or-flight instincts at the door. That's what they're paying for. They see a fire, hear an explosion, feel their roller coaster begin to shear off its track—what are they gonna do? Laugh all the harder. Because they think it's *part of the act*. That makes every last one of them a sitting duck."

He turned to Barksdale. "How many robots do we have operating in the Park?"

Barksdale thought a moment. "Connected to the Metanet, you mean? After last month's cutback, eighty, plus or minus five."

"Eighty, any one of them a potential time bomb. Even if we could take them all off-line without creating major problems, there's no time to get to every one of them. But it's not just the bots. We've given this John Doe the perfect playing field." He leaned across the desk. "He planted explosives in the walls of Griffin Tower. But he could just as well have sabotaged the gas lines for the flame effects. Or—"

"And that's precisely the point!" said Barksdale. "You said it yourself. We can't check everything. These beggars hold all the cards. We've got our guests' lives to consider. Right now, evacuation, calling in the police, is *not* an option."

"Excuse me, but that's the *only* option. We're not equipped to defend ourselves against this kind of threat." Allocco gestured at the plastic explosive. "As for our guests, do you think the people who planted this give a shit whether a bunch of tourists live or die?"

"Probably not," Barksdale replied. "That's precisely why we can't incite them."

The two men turned toward Sarah, as if appealing for a ruling. She returned their gazes: Allocco, stone-faced and resolute; Barksdale, distress evident on his patrician features.

"We're not calling in the police," she said.

Relief broke like a wave across Barksdale's face, while Allocco flushed deeply. "What?" he said. "Are you simply going to lie down for this bastard?"

"No," Sarah said. "I'm not going to lie down for him." As she spoke, she felt her jaw harden as cold anger displaced other emotions. The arrogance with which John Doe had sauntered into her office, drunk her tea, made his demands. Caressed her face. The way he was deliberately, almost casually, violating her Park, hurting her people . . . He had assumed she would simply roll over before his threats. He had assumed wrong.

"John Doe told me he's watching the entrances and exits," she said. "He implied guests will be killed *if* we evacuate. I have no reason to think he's lying. And flooding Utopia with cops isn't the answer. We'll deal with John Doe. But on *our* terms, and with *our* people." She turned toward Barksdale. "Fred, you said they hold all the cards. I don't think so. This is our Park. And that gives us a home court advantage."

Barksdale raised his hand to protest. Then he dropped it again, drew back.

"But first things first. They implied they were watching the monorail, so we can't do a general evac—not yet, anyway. So we'll start with limited bomb threat procedures. Bob, put the security leads on alert. But no details. Round up the VIPs, get them into the hospitality suite. Tell them the president's coming, tell them *anything,* but get them there. Meanwhile, I'll put in a call to Vegas, cancel the milk run. Fred, you'll alert your financial processing staff?"

Barksdale nodded. Although most financial transactions in the park went through the credit lines on the guests' passcards, cash was still used in many places, particularly at the casinos. The "milk run" was Utopia-speak for the weekly armored car run from Las Vegas.

Sarah looked back at Allocco. "We can't close down the entrances. But let's start taking the ticket booths out of service a little early: say, four every half hour. We can move up the monorail schedule by a couple of hours, increase outflow."

"We can take one or two A-list attractions off-line," Allocco said. "If people think they've seen everything, or if the lines start getting too long, they might decide to leave early."

"Very well, but keep it low-profile. And let's get that robot assembly from Griffin Tower down to Terri Bonifacio's office. Dr. Warne should take a look at it. Maybe there's some commonality we can use to find which other bots have been tampered with."

"I can do that right now." Allocco reached once again for the phone.

Barksdale watched him, frowning. Then he turned to Sarah. "But if you want to keep things quiet—"

"We won't tell Andrew any more than we have to. But right now, we need his kind of help. Especially since . . ." She paused. "Especially since it looks like the Metanet may not be to blame, after all."

Barksdale stood beside her, smoothing his tie with an absent hand, a troubled look on his face. Sarah felt a sudden, unexpected throb of affection. Then, quite consciously, she put it away. There would be time, later.

"What's on your mind, Fred?" she asked.

"I'm just having difficulty understanding this. If the Metanet isn't dodgy, then what could be happening? How could these chaps be downloading instructions to the bots? Our site's totally secure. There's no way anybody on the outside could . . ."

Barksdale fell silent. The only sound in the office was Allocco hanging up the phone.

Sarah watched Barksdale's face intently. Freddy Barksdale was the most polished and charming man she had ever met. But he was also a strange hybrid: a youth of privilege spent in English public schools, a career spent in the upper echelons of Information Services. If there was a problem, he turned, by instinct, toward machine failure. It would not occur to him to consider the possibility of *human* failure or betrayal. That was not cricket, not sporting. Simply not the way it was done. But now, as she watched, Sarah could see something dawning in his eyes—the glimmerings of something she already knew must be the truth.

"Freddy," she said, lowering her voice, "I want you to get me a list of everybody on your IT staff with the access and the skills to pull off this kind of thing. And which of them are on-site today."

Barksdale stood still for a moment, as if the mere thought had frozen him to stone. Then he nodded slowly.

"And I think you should do it now."

Barksdale turned to leave.

"And Fred? Keep quiet. Keep as quiet as the grave."

Sarah watched the door close behind Barksdale. Then she pulled her eyes away and turned toward Allocco.

"I want you to do the same," she said. "Get me a short-list of security personnel with either the means or the motivation. Anyone with a beef about their job, a grudge against their boss. Anyone with a drug problem, a money problem."

As Sarah said these last words, a far more significant look passed briefly between them. Then Allocco nodded.

"This tech of yours, Ralph Peccam. Has he found anything?"

"He's still checking the video logs."

Sarah paused, thinking. "He couldn't have staged that glitch in the Hive himself, could he? When we lost the video tail on John Doe?"

"No. At least, not without adequate preparation."

"You said he used to work in Systems. You have complete confidence in him?"

"I'll vouch for him personally. He wouldn't be involved in this kind of thing. I know him too well for that."

Sarah nodded. "Very well. Keep him on the logs, then." She walked away from the table, toward a cutaway diagram of the Park. "You've got my ear, Bob. If you can come up with a plan to end this preemptively, without undue risk to our Park or our guests, I want to hear about it."

She was interrupted by a low buzzing noise.

For a moment, Sarah didn't recognize the sound. And then, with an electric current of recognition, she wondered how she could have forgotten it, even for a moment.

She reached into her pocket and pulled out the small radio.

"Ms. Boatwright?" came the pleasant, mildly accented voice of John Doe. "Sarah?"

Sarah glanced at Allocco. The security director dug into a pocket, pulled out a microcassette recorder, and tossed it to her.

"Sarah? Are you there?"

"I'm here," she replied, snapping on the recorder and holding it close to the radio.

"Did you see our 1:30 show?"

"Not personally. I heard the reviews."

"So we can get down to business without any further unpleasantness?"

"Get on with it."

"As you wish. I've got a little story to tell you. Please listen very carefully. It isn't long, and I think you'll find it very interesting."

1:45 P.M.

"CAN I USE one of these terminals to access the Net?" Georgia had beaten the last Game Boy level and was now sitting disconsolately on the floor, cross-legged, throwing a wadded paper ball out for Wingnut to fetch. "I'd like to, maybe, download some Duke Ellington stuff."

Across the lab, Terri Bonifacio was industriously spreading brown shrimp paste over a slice of green mango. "No can do, kiddo."

Georgia looked around at the dozen vacant computer terminals with a look that clearly said, *What, you can't spare even one of these?*

Terri caught the look and grinned. "It's a sealed system, no portals to the outside. Too big a security risk. I've got a bunch of bootlegged Guns N' Roses concerts, though, if you're interested."

"No, thanks."

Warne had been staring at the Metanet terminal. Now, he pushed himself away and glanced blearily over. "She went through her California postpunk hard-rock phase last December." His eye fell on the mango. "I'm sorry, but that looks really disgusting."

"You got off lucky. Some days, I bring *dinuguan* for lunch."

"I'm afraid to ask what that is."

"Pig's head, heart, and liver, in a sauce of pig's blood. And then there's *balun-balunan*, which—"

"Okay, okay."

From her position on the floor, Georgia made an elaborate pantomime of sticking a finger down her throat. Terri's grin widened.

Georgia tossed the wad of paper toward a far corner of the lab. Immediately, the robot shot after it, sensor swiveling away. Reaching the paper, Wingnut's pan-tilt head assembly bent forward, large, mouthlike pincers opening. It grasped the ball between the pincers and rolled back toward Georgia at an alarming speed—still managing, however, to drop the paper into her outstretched hand with surprising gentleness.

"Good boy, Wingnut!" Georgia cooed. The robot yipped excitedly, spun in an awkward circle.

"Look, he's chasing his tail," Terri said. "Just like a real dog."

Georgia let the paper fall to the ground, turned toward Warne. "Dad, aren't you done *yet*? We've been here an hour, at least."

"Half an hour, princess."

"Don't call me princess." She glanced at her watch. "It's almost two o'clock."

"Just a little longer." He glanced at Terri, then gestured toward the terminal. "There's nothing wrong with the Metanet. I've tried to break it every way I can think of. Multi-threaded downlinks, missing arguments, everything. It always crashes gracefully."

Terri finished the mango, shrugging as if to say, *I told you so*.

"It's like you said. All the Metanet changes have been benign." Warne turned back to the terminal and began mousing his way down the screen. "What really gets me are the incident reports. I've checked almost all of these robot glitches. You know what? According to the Metanet logs, none of those bots were ever even *touched*. The Metanet made no modifications to their code. And that doesn't make sense."

He stared at the terminal. He could see his own face—pale, a little drawn—staring back at him from the reflecting glass. Just sitting at this terminal brought back potent, bittersweet memories. The last time he'd sat before it, in his lab at Carnegie-Mellon, he'd felt an almost paternal pride for the creation that was about to be shipped off to Nevada. The Metanet was to be the first in a series of revolutionary developments that would no doubt be emerging from his lab. His theories about machine learning were the buzz of the robotics community. And he'd found a powerful champion in Eric Nightingale . . .

How different things were for the face that stared back at him now. He closed his eyes, bowed his head. *What's happened?* he asked himself. *How could everything go so wrong, so quickly? It's like I just can't catch a break.*

There was a whir of stepper motors, a loud, metallic, clangorous yipping. Wingnut rolled back and forth across the center of the lab, as if searching for something. Then he came to a stop below a bank of fluorescent lights.

"What's he doing?" Terri asked.

"Recharging his solar cells. Since his avatar—most recently, that was Georgia—isn't moving, he's in a wait state, doing background tasks. Like locating the brightest light source and moving toward it. Remember your graduate school cybernetics? Grey Walter's tortoise, its primitive light-seeking, light-avoidance behaviors? Same idea."

Terri watched the robot, motionless beneath the light. "He's completely autonomous. Right? If he'd been plugged into the Metanet, I'd have known about it."

"Yup."

"I assume he's using the A-star algorithm for pathfinding? How did you avoid the usual zigzags?"

"By adding some postprocessing tweaks."

"And his architecture—totally reactive? Must be, given all the random processing the poor thing has to do."

"Right. But there's a hierarchical core to give him some personality traits, make him seem more real. Not that they all work the way they're supposed to, though. He can be an unreliable little spud when he feels like it."

He stole a glance at the woman. Clearly, she knew her stuff.

The robotics community was split into two camps. The older camp believed in creating robots with "deliberative" AI: highly structured, hierarchical systems with fixed internal world models and hardwired assumptions about that world. The newer camp—of which Warne himself was a controversial leader—believed that "behavior-based" robotics was the way of the future: reactive systems that based their actions on what their sensors told them, rather than relying on pre-coded instructions.

"There's something a bit unsettling about him," Terri said. "As if you never knew what he was going to do next. And why's he so damn big?"

"When I first built him, components weren't as miniaturized as they are now. Over the years I swapped out his innards for smaller, more powerful replacements. That cut his weight in half, freed up space for bigger motors and servos. That's why he's such a speedy brute, too." Warne looked at her. "You sound as if you'd never seen him before."

"Only from a distance. It was sitting in a corner of Sarah Boatwright's office. Or maybe Barksdale's, I can't remember."

Warne sighed. Somehow, he wasn't surprised.

"Tell me about Fred Barksdale," he said. "What's he like?"

"Let's see. He's charming, suave, cultured, debonair . . . if you like that sort of thing in a man, of course. Can quote Shakespeare for hours on end. All the women in Systems are madly in love with him. Which is precisely why I'm not."

Warne chuckled.

"According to the grapevine, he and Sarah Boatwright are quite the thing."

Warne's laugh died in his throat. He looked over at Terri. He could have sworn there was the slightest, teasing edge to her tone.

"Don't worry, Dr. Warne," she said. "I know all about it. *And* you. Utopia's even more fond of gossip than Peyton Place."

He sighed, looked away. "That's ancient history."

"Not ancient enough," Georgia muttered.

Terri let out a whoop of laughter. "You know, I like this daughter of yours."

Georgia grinned, blushed.

Warne looked back at the screen, moving the mouse from one code window to another. Once again, a mix of feelings washed over him: part fear, part desperation. He was losing the Metanet; it was happening right before his eyes. And yet *there was nothing wrong with it*—he'd just run every test he could imagine. But clearly, something *had to be* wrong. The accident on Notting Hill Chase. And just this morning, his own construct, Hard Place . . . It made no sense. He lifted his hand from the mouse, rubbed his bruised wrist absently.

There was a sudden commotion nearby as Wingnut—batteries now fully recharged—darted in, grabbed the mouse, then rushed away. There was a loud bang. Warne looked over at the hulking robot, who was staring back at him, mouse between his metal jaws, severed cord hanging down like a flaccid tail, waiting for Warne to give chase.

"Wingnut, *no chase*," he said in a tired voice. He turned toward Terri. "Got another mouse handy, by any chance?"

"Sure. Does he always grab things like that?"

"He developed a fondness for chasing cars, robots, anything with wheels. Don't ask me where it came from. It got so bad I was forced to hard-code a special instruction into him: 'no chase.' And it's still hit-or-miss." *My career in a microcosm,* he thought as he stared ruefully at the robot. No wonder the thing had become a dusty relic.

Terri walked off to fetch a new mouse. Somehow, the natural sway of her body was able to make even a lab coat look alluring. Warne glanced over at Georgia, riffling disconsolately through an industry journal, then back at the screen.

There it was again: the sense that something was wrong.

And then, suddenly, he realized what it was. It was so simple, so obvious, that he'd never made the connection.

"Terri," he said. "If the Metanet modified certain bots for inappropriate actions, why are there no internal modification logs for any of them? I've examined the Metanet's logs. None exist for any of the bots that went haywire."

Terri shook her head. "That couldn't be."

"And there's the *other* thing. In the meeting this morning, Barksdale said the problems were intermittent. The bots would misbehave one day, be fine the next." Warne paused. "If the Metanet instructed those bots to misbehave, *who told them to behave again?*"

Terri looked at him, dark eyes troubled. "Only the Metanet could do that."

"Exactly. But there are no internal logs showing either the introduction or the correction of these glitches." Warne pushed the incident reports aside. "How many cases of inappropriate code have you actually seen with your own eyes?"

"Only one. Notting Hill Chase."

"How did you determine what went wrong?"

"Maintenance walked the ride, found the loosened safety dogs. I found incorrect behavior in the onboard code."

"What kind?"

"The code had been altered to specifically loosen, rather than tighten, the safety dogs."

Warne winced involuntarily. There were only two ways for the bots to receive such specious instructions. Only Terri was authorized access to the Metanet terminal. Either she had deliberately hand-coded the errant bots, or the Metanet had modified their programming. The Metanet had *caused* the accident. He felt the sense of desperation grow stronger.

"Dad," Georgia spoke into the silence. "Come on. *Please.*"

"Georgia!" Warne turned sharply. Then he took a breath,

mastered his annoyance. "Look, I'm sorry, but I have to finish this." He glanced at the screen, considered a moment. Then he turned back to Georgia. "Tell you what. I'll let you take in a few rides on your own. How about that? Give me an hour. No, ninety minutes."

"I don't want to go by myself," Georgia said. "What fun is that?"

"That's the way it has to be, sweetie. I'm sorry. Just ninety minutes. I'll meet you at . . ." He fished in his pocket for a guidemap, unfolded it. "At Guest Services in the Nexus. Quarter after three. We'll finish up Boardwalk together. Okay?"

Georgia chewed her lip a moment. Then she nodded, stood up. "Thanks for the Game Boy," she said to Terri. She tugged her headphones onto her ears, shouldered her backpack, headed for the door.

"Georgia?" Warne asked.

She stopped in the doorway, turned back.

"No big coasters, no tall rides, okay? Save those for me."

She frowned.

"Promise?"

She sighed. "Yeah." Then she slipped around the corner, closing the door behind her.

A brief silence settled over the lab. Warne found himself staring at the door.

"She's a cute kid," Terri said. "As far as kids go." And she smiled roguishly.

Warne turned his gaze to her. "You don't like kids?"

"It isn't that. I guess I just never had much use for them. Especially when I was one myself." Terri shrugged. "Never had a lot of friends my own age. Never had many friends at all, actually. Somehow, I always felt more comfortable around adults."

"Sounds like Georgia. I worry about that sometimes. Since her mother died, it's almost like she's pulled up the drawbridge. I'm the only one she's really close to."

"At least she has a loving father."

"You didn't?"

Terri rolled her eyes. "Don't ask. The Wicked Warlock of the East."

Warne stretched, glanced back at the terminal. "Let's get back to it. There's a mystery here that I don't understand." He waved at the stack of incident reports. "Only the Metanet could have caused these glitches. But why did you actually see the altered code in only one: the Notting Hill ride? What was different about *that* particular glitch?"

Terri looked down. "There was a casualty," she said.

For a moment, Warne lowered his eyes.

"And you shut the ride down," he resumed. "When did you examine the two Notting Hill bots?"

"The following morning."

"Were they connected to the Metanet at that point?"

"Of course not. The whole ride was taken off-line."

"Naturally." Warne picked up the pile of incident reports. "And the problems with all these other bots. When were they checked?"

"Usually, the afternoon following the day the reports were filed."

"Were they ever checked earlier?"

"If it was a high priority, we'd check them first thing."

"Which means?"

"Around 9:30. Right after downlink."

"Right *after* downlink." He glanced at her quickly. "That's it. That's why you only saw the altered code in the Notting Hill ride. Not the others."

"I don't think I understand."

"And I'll bet if we examined the internal routines on Hard Place, we'd see it, too. Jesus, don't you *see*? All the rest must have been—"

At that moment, a rap sounded on the door.

"Come in!" Terri called.

The door opened, and a tall, thin man in a lab coat stepped in, pushing a metal cart before him. Sitting on the cart was a metal box the size of a milk carton, multicolored wires streaming away: the central processing unit from Hard Case. Beside it sat a low-slung robot. Warne recognized the type: a late-model Autonomous Systems controller assembly, frequently used for simple maintenance duties. This one's upper plate looked oddly scorched, though; almost as if somebody had held a blowtorch to it.

Wingnut turned his head array toward the new arrivals. He emitted a low, muttering growl and began rolling toward the cart.

"Wingnut, *no chase*," Warne said in a warning tone, enunciating the command carefully. The creature rolled to a stop.

"What are those doing here?" Terri asked.

"Ms. Boatwright asked me to bring these to a Dr. Warne. Said

I'd find him in your office." The slender man glanced over at Warne. He was pale, and shrank back nervously from Wingnut's attentions. "Would that be you?"

"The big one is Hard Place's brain," Warne said, nodding at the cart. "I told you how he went postal on me today. I had to hit his kill switch manually. I don't recognize the other one."

"It's from the Griffin Tower show," said Terri. She turned back to the technician. "What's it doing here?" she repeated, her low voice a little louder now.

The man licked his lips. "The laser went nuts during the 1:20 show."

"What?"

The man nodded. "Overloaded. Shot right through a guy's face."

Hearing this, Terri seemed to go gray. She moved toward the cart, then stopped, as if unable to bring herself to touch it.

"Oh, my God," she said. "I *programmed* that. *I* did that . . ." She glanced back toward Warne, a look of horror on her face.

But Warne did not notice. His mind was far away.

1:47 P.M.

SARAH BOATWRIGHT WAITED. Over the dedicated landline, there was no sound: no digital artifacts, no whisper of static, nothing.

Then, at last, Chuck Emory's gravelly voice came again. "High explosives."

"That's right, Mr. Emory."

"You're sure about that?"

"There's a brick of it sitting on the table in front of me."

"Excuse *me*?"

"Bob Allocco found it. Without a detonator. Left there to send us a message."

"Some message. And you're sure it's not a hoax?"

"Allocco says it's the real deal this time. And the glitch with the laser-firing robot, the accident on Notting Hill Chase—those certainly weren't hoaxes."

There was another silence. Waiting, Sarah felt ambivalent about bringing Emory into this. But she reminded herself there was no way she could proceed—one way or the other—without talking to Emory first.

If Eric Nightingale had been the creative genius behind Utopia, Charles Emory III was the man who had taken Nightingale's idea and breathed life into it. In the wake of the magician's death, Emory had quickly moved from chief financial officer to CEO of the Utopia Holding Company. He had managed to keep the corporate backers and venture capitalists together through the Park's final design and fabrication. Many people credited Emory with saving the Park, for guiding its development in the face of unexpected tragedy. Others—Utopia purists, or people who, like Andrew Warne, had been drawn in by Nightingale's original vision—felt differently. They believed Emory sold out, took Nightingale's dream and sullied it with commercialism.

Emory had added thrill rides, concession areas, merchandising tie-ins. And, most controversial of all, he had added the casinos. Nightingale had planned to have a single, small emporium in Boardwalk, where guests could play turn-of-the-century games of chance with buffalo-head nickels. Emory had replaced this quaint Emporium of Chance with four full-blown casinos that catered in real money.

Sarah respected Emory's business sense. She knew that the entrance fee covered only half the Park's overhead. The rest came from food, beverages, souvenirs, concessions, and most especially the casinos—a business reality that Nightingale had never been able to accept. To his credit, Emory had spotted new trends—like holographic technology—and been quick to leverage them when there was a profit to be made. He excelled at managing from a distance, letting the Park's creative designers and administrative staff run the day-to-day operations. But he seemed less good at handling crises. There had been only one in recent memory—a salmonella scare in Camelot that had proved to be unfounded—but his indecisiveness, at a time when prompt action had been called for, remained uncomfortably strong in her mind.

There could be no indecisiveness, no hesitancy, here. The longer she thought, the more convinced she became: bold action was required.

"Do you know how many people are involved?" Emory asked.

"No. Judging from appearances, it's a well-planned operation. And they couldn't have done it without help from inside the Park."

"Jesus *Christ*. Do we know who?"

"Not yet. But it's a good bet whoever the insider is works in either Security or Systems."

A pause. "What *are* these people? Fanatics? Some kind of cult?"

"I don't think so. I just got off the radio with their spokesman. He told me what it is they want."

"And that is?"

"The Crucible, Mr. Emory."

Once again, the line faded into silence. Then Sarah heard—or thought she heard—a long, slow release of breath.

"The Crucible," the voice repeated.

"Yes. All the source code, image banks, everything."

More silence.

"We can burn it all to a single, noncopyable DVD," she went on. "But first we'll need three digital keys—yours, mine, and Fred Barksdale's—to decrypt the core routines."

"And have they told you what will happen if we don't comply?"

"He was very explicit about that. He claimed he would take out rides, blow up queuing lines, bomb restaurants. Injure, kill, hundreds of people."

"Can we locate the devices? Take the robots off-line? Evacuate the guests?"

"We've been warned that trying anything like that would bring prompt retaliation. He says the monorails are being watched, and he implied that they have been rigged with explosive charges. Besides, we have to deliver the code to them in half an hour. There's no time to put any kind of large-scale plan together."

"I see. Who in the Park knows about this, besides you?"

"Security heads have been put on general alert. But only Bob Allocco and Fred Barksdale know the whole story."

"Let's keep it that way as long as possible." Sarah heard the creak of a chair. "But, Sarah, I don't get the angle. The Crucible technology is too distinctive. Nobody would dare use it. If we saw holograms like ours popping up in another park, or some Vegas act, we'd know who the culprit was right away."

"Fred Barksdale has a theory about that. He doesn't think these guys are going to use the Crucible for entertainment at all."

"I don't follow."

"According to Fred, the Crucible technology can be altered for other uses. Like reproducing the holograms used for anti-tamper seals on software and DVD movies. But Fred thinks maybe they're after something much bigger than that. Like maybe a new supernote."

"Supernote?"

"That's what they called the phony hundred-dollar bill found in circulation a couple of years back. Remember? It was almost indistinguishable from the real thing. Nobody knew where it came from. But speculation was it was so good that only a medium-size world power, or a terrorist state, could have produced it. It scared the U.S. Treasury so badly they developed the new currency. With, you know, anticounterfeiting safeguards: color-shifting inks, holographic watermarks, security threads. Except . . ." She paused.

"Except that the Crucible could be programmed to re-create it."

"It's a theory. Fred also thought they might want the Crucible for some kind of military use: creating false heat signatures or radar images to confuse smart bombs, that kind of thing. You know how eager the government has been to get their hands on our patents."

"Did Fred tell you how difficult it would be to pull this off?"

"It isn't the coding so much as the processing power. Reproducing small holograms is relatively trivial. But for the kind of stuff Fred's talking about, you'd need access to supercomputers. Lots of them. You'd need the resources of a medium-size power."

"Or a terrorist state."

As Emory fell silent, Sarah could almost hear the man's mind working its way through the options. He was a money guy; he'd be putting it in financial terms. So much for the loss of the technology, so much for the collateral damage the loss might cause, so much for the death of a dozen, two dozen guests. When you thought about it, it really wasn't that complex an equation, at all.

"This contact of theirs," Emory said. "What kind of assurances did he give you if we hand over the source code?"

"No assurances. He just said that, if we did what he asked, nobody would die. They'd leave. The Park would be ours again."

There was a long inhalation of breath, another squeak of the chair. "I'd like your thoughts on this, Sarah. You're on-site, you've talked to their spokesman. Is this on the level?"

So Emory was asking her opinion. Sarah did not know if this was a good sign or a bad one. "He's brazen. He's arrogant. He sat there in my office, grinning like Brer Rabbit." At the memory, she felt hot anger swell once again. "He's well funded: at least, so far as we've seen. And that's just the problem Bob Allocco and I have been discussing."

"Go on."

"Our first reaction was knee-jerk: he's dangerous, give him what he wants. But then we started to think. What *have* we seen? A gun, a stick of explosive, a few radios. Maybe they're real, maybe they're expensive fakes. What we *haven't* seen is the manpower. We know he must have someone on the inside; there's no other way he could have manipulated the bots and the video feed. But that could still just mean a two-person show. For all we know, we've already seen everything he's got. And he's bluffing the rest."

"Or else he's deadly serious."

"Correct. But the Crucible is the crown jewel of this Park. What if it's just two men, with an elaborate scam? We can't just give it away without a fight."

There was a pause. "If there's a fight, guests will be the casualties."

"And that can't be allowed to happen. But even Brer Rabbit eventually met the Tar-Baby. Allocco's developed a plan to intercept John Doe at the drop point."

"That's a very dangerous game, Sarah. If things go wrong—"

"Bob will play it safe. He'll have John Doe tailed, take him down as he leaves the Park. Recover the disc with the Crucible technology. If it turns out John Doe's on the level—there is a team, and they are heavily armed—we back off immediately, notify the police to intercept. But *only* once they're outside, away from the Park."

There was another pause.

"There are only two other options," Sarah spoke into the silence. "Call John Doe's bluff, refuse to give him the disc at all. Or give him the disc and just let him walk away. With our most crucial technology in his pocket."

There was a sigh. "And you can trust Allocco to do this? You get my drift?"

Sarah got his drift. Of all Utopia staff, only she and Emory knew that Bob Allocco had left the Boston police force ten years before because of money troubles, a result of compulsive gambling.

"This operation will be my call, and my responsibility. But, yes, I trust Allocco. What happened, happened a long time ago. Besides, at this point, I think we have no choice."

This time the silence was so long, Sarah wondered if the line had gone dead.

"We've only got twenty-six minutes," she said at last. "I'll need your digital key if we're going to create that disc."

Still nothing.

"Mr. Emory? I need a decision."

Finally, the CEO of Utopia replied. "Give it to them," he said. "But let Allocco place his tar-baby. And, for God's sake, be careful."

1:50 P.M.

AT THE ICE cream counter in the Big Dipper restaurant, a cast member in a copper-colored flight suit was mixing a chocolate banana malt. It was more crowded now, in the early afternoon, and a horde of hungry, disappointed onlookers were standing on the concourse, staring perplexedly at the counter, wondering what could have happened to the robot they had come to see. Overhead, the bulk of Jupiter filled the empty darkness of space, the great red spot coming into view, roiling and turning, bright as an angry boil. Callisto's speaker system, hidden within air ducts and hollow walls, pumped its own blend of low-frequency noise: ambient electronic music, drowned by the chatter of adults and the delighted cries of children.

At a large circular portal a hundred yards down the concourse from the ice cream counter, these cries were particularly strong. This was the entrance—"access port," as the loading crews were reminded to call it—to Galactic Voyage. It was a newer attraction, devised by Utopia's design team after Nightingale's death. Most of Callisto's rides were much too intense for younger children. Galactic Voyage was the result. It was a standard amusement park "dark ride," in which small cars ran along an electrified bus bar past a series of moving images: asteroid belts, horsehead nebulas, supernovas.

Infants loved Galactic Voyage. Anybody older than five, however, found the attraction paralyzingly dull and gave it a wide berth. With young children and numbed parents as its only passengers, Galactic Voyage boasted the lowest rate of security incidents in the entire Park. As a result, there were no lookouts or cameras, no infrared intrusion beams. And since the ride practically ran itself, there was very little for the operators to do. This made Galactic Voyage almost as unpopular with Utopia cast members as it was with adult guests.

Just about the only employees who enjoyed working the ride, in fact, were the romantically inclined. Like all mainline rides, Galactic Voyage had a large, labyrinthine backstage area for service and maintenance. One particularly remote spot was Fabrication, where the dark meshing and black velour that served as backdrops were sized and repaired. Operators had found this an ideal place to bring amorous fellow employees, or impromptu dates plucked from among the visitors. Fabrication became so popular a trysting spot that its large cutting table was dubbed the "groaning board." When management learned of this, strategic shifts in personnel were made. Now, Galactic Voyage workers were mostly women in their fifties and sixties. The ride had the oldest employee demographics in Utopia, and its fabrication area was now used only—and infrequently—for its designed task.

Except that, at present, John Doe sat on the edge of the cutting table. His legs, crossed at the ankles, swung casually above the floor. It was dark, and the whites of his eyes glowed dimly with the subdued phosphorescence of outer space. Like Sarah Boatwright in her office far below, he was speaking into a telephone.

"That's very interesting," he said. "You did the right thing to inform me. I'll be expecting the particulars from you soon." He listened briefly. Something must have struck him as funny, because suddenly he burst into good-humored laughter—although he was polite enough to put a hand over the mouthpiece as he did so. "No," he said as echoes of the laugh died away. "No, no, no. I don't think it's cause for concern, let alone cancellation. My dear fellow, that would be *unthinkable*." A pause. "I'm sorry? Yes, that was unfortunate, I agree. But we're talking lasers and high explosives, not brain surgery, you know. They're a little hard to predict."

He listened again, longer this time. "We've had this conversation before," he said at length. "As recently as last week, I believe." His voice was calm, informal: a man of breeding, speaking to a respected equal. "Let me repeat what I said then. There is nothing to worry about. The time we spent in planning, in removing bugs and ironing out the kinks, was well spent. Every possible outcome has been analyzed, every contingency planned for. You know that as well as I. One must keep up one's nerve. 'Our doubts are traitors, and make us lose the good we oft might win, by fearing to attempt.' "

John Doe repeated the quotation for the listener's benefit. He chuckled. And then the tone of his voice abruptly changed. It grew cold, remote, condescending. "You'll remember what else I said, no doubt. It was unpleasant, and I'd hate to repeat it. We have passed the point of no return. We're committed. There has been too much accomplished *already* for you to waver now. Remember that a word in the right ear would be all it takes to expose you, arrest you, lock you up the rest of your life with inmates in need of—well—diverting companionship. Not that things would ever get so far, of course. My own companions would find much more rapid and permanent ways of expressing their dissatisfaction with you."

As quickly as it had come, the ominous tone disappeared. "But that won't happen, of course. All your hard work is already done. In fact, your assignment now is to *not* do something. Isn't that a delightful irony?"

He switched off the cell phone, let it drop to the table beside him. Then, reaching into a pocket of his suit jacket, he pulled out a radio, punched in a code, selected a frequency. "Hard Case, this is Prime Factor," he said. The cultured accent he had employed for the prior call was now gone. "Message delivered at 1:45. Pickup at 2:15, as scheduled. However, I've just learned of a slight problem. There's a fellow in the Park today, one Andrew Warne. It appears he built the Utopia Metanet, and they've brought him back to fix it. Wasn't scheduled to arrive until next week, but he's here early. No, I don't know why. But we can't have him rooting around, turning over rocks with his snout and uncovering bugs. Snow White is getting me a description and most recent location—I'll pass them on. You do what's necessary to remove the threat. I'll leave the creative details to you. Out."

Mr. Doe lowered the radio, gazing around the secluded room. In the distance, he could hear the faint sounds of childish laughter as a car made its way through the ride. After a moment, he glanced down at the radio, switched frequencies, and raised it to his lips once again.

"Water Buffalo, this is Prime Factor. You copy?"

There was a squawk, a brief crackle of static. "Affirmative."

"How's the weather up there?"

"Sunny. Zero percent chance of precipitation."

"I'm sorry to hear that. Listen, we're in business. You may lay the eggs when ready."

"That's a rog. Water Buffalo, out."

The radio fell silent. Mr. Doe slid it back into the pocket of his linen jacket, then crossed his arms and leaned back upon the groaning board, swinging his legs with a sigh of contentment.

1:52 P.M.

THE MAN ON the escarpment let the radio drop slowly from his ear. This time, instead of returning it to his belt, he placed it inside his duffel, next to a thick, battered paperback. For a moment, he let his eye linger on the book: volume one of Proust's *Remembrance of Things Past*. Then on impulse he picked it up, fanning through the dirty pages to the dog-ear he'd made moments before.

Water Buffalo was not, by nature, a reader. During his youth, there had always been too much trouble that needed getting into, too little time for books. Once, in reform school, a priest had given a sermon. He'd told the boys that books were the doorways to new worlds. Water Buffalo had paid no attention. But later, as a marine scout sniper—waiting endlessly in tiny hidden blinds where there was nothing but time—he'd found himself going back to that sermon, wondering about those worlds.

One thing about civilian work: you could read on the job.

He'd decided that, if he was going to read a book, it had better be a long one. He didn't understand why somebody would go to all the time and effort of reading something, just to have it end after a couple of hundred pages. You'd have to start all over again with another one. There'd be the trouble of learning new names, figuring out a new story. It was highly inefficient. It didn't make sense.

So, after some recon in a Denver bookstore, he'd settled on Proust. At 3,365 pages, *Remembrance of Things Past* was certainly long enough.

The cry of some desert bird roused him, and he returned the book to the duffel, pulling out a Bausch & Lomb spotting scope and the M24 sniper rifle instead. He turned in his shallow gully, swiveling the scope in the direction of the huge dome of Utopia. He ranged across the countless polygons of glass until at last he found the maintenance specialist. The man had recently crossed over into the fat, crescent-shaped wedge of blackness that formed the ceiling over Callisto.

Water Buffalo grunted. That was good. Very good.

He put the spotting scope down and picked up the rifle, screwing the silencer into place, then fitting his eye to the telescopic sight and aiming toward the dome. The scope was a Leupold M3 Ultra, with range-finding reticle and a built-in compensator for bullet drop. He'd been careful to keep the sight against his canteen inside the duffel, and the metal felt cool and familiar against the orbit of his skull.

He scanned the dome slowly. John Doe once told him that, in World War II, Japanese snipers had been known to climb palm trees with steel hooks, tie themselves to the trunks, and stay up there for days at a time, waiting for a target. Water Buffalo could understand that. There was something about scope work that was almost comforting. You couldn't really explain it to anyone who hadn't done some themselves. All of a sudden, the world shrank to just that little circle at the end of a tunnel. If you'd done your setup right, you could forget about everything else. All you had to worry about was that little circle. It simplified things enormously.

He thought back to John Doe, how the man had recruited him in a Bangkok joss house. When it came to team leaders, Water Buffalo was extremely picky. But John Doe's credentials had been impeccable. And his leadership and tactical skills had been proven to Water Buffalo's satisfaction time and again since, over the course of half a dozen successful ops. For a civilian, he had a rare understanding of the kind of anonymity a solo operator like Water Buffalo preferred.

But then, John Doe had not always been a civilian.

He shifted the rifle slightly and the specialist jumped back into view, ten times normal size. He was about a third of the way up the curve of the dome, making his way cautiously along the narrow horizontal catwalk, lifting his rubber-soled feet and placing them down again precisely, like a cat. A palm-sized data entry pad dangled from his belt. Water Buffalo watched as he reached a vertex of windowpanes. Carefully, the man unhooked a tether, clipped it to a rail on the far side of the vertex, and stepped around. He moved forward again, paused, then reached for his data pad and tapped in an entry: perhaps he'd found a cracked pane. Then he moved on. Water Buffalo watched him through the scope.

At the next vertex, a metal ladder intersected the catwalk, running vertically up and down the curved surface of the dome. The man hooked his tether to the ladder and began climbing downward, hand over hand, between the dark panes of glass. There was something about the worker that reminded Water Buffalo of Proust. Maybe it was the white jumpsuit he was wearing. Somewhere in the book's introduction, it had said Proust liked to dress in white.

He'd reached a point in volume one where Proust was describing an elderly aunt. The woman's sphere of life had gradually contracted until she kept herself confined to just two rooms of her apartment. That, too, Water Buffalo could understand. He'd had a grandmother who'd been like that. Of course, her shabby tenement only *had* two rooms. But when she grew older, she'd never left them. It was as if the world beyond her door had been a different universe, something to be feared and avoided. If people wanted to see how she was—to check on her health, give her soup—they had to come to her.

Proust talked of visiting his aunt, making her lime-blossom tea. Water Buffalo had visited his own grandmother, once or twice. Then he'd stopped visiting for good. He wondered what lime-blossom tea tasted like.

When he'd first started reading the book, it hadn't made any sense to him. From what he could make out, it was just some Frenchman blabbing about his childhood. Who gave a shit how long it took the guy to fall asleep? But then Water Buffalo had found himself on an op—a very long and tedious op—near the Mexican border. He'd given the book another chance. Bit by bit, memory by memory, Proust's life began to take on shape and structure. And then he thought he understood. Maybe the priest was right: books really were doorways to other worlds.

The worker had stopped descending the dome and was making his way along another lower horizontal catwalk, only thirty-odd feet now above the surface of the escarpment. Water Buffalo settled himself carefully in the gully, spreading his legs wide, digging his toes into the stony soil. He placed the rifle's bipod against a small ledge of rock at the gully's edge, made sure it was firm. One hand slid forward to grip the rifle's forearm, while the other snicked off the safety and settled around the trigger guard. He took a breath, then another.

The worker unclipped his tether, moved around the metal skin of the vertex to the next window. Water Buffalo timed his shot between heartbeats, pulling the trigger just as the man was reaching forward to reclip the tether to the catwalk.

The man jerked his head upward as if someone had called his name. Through the scope, Water Buffalo watched the red plume blossom against the white cloth. Automatically, he ran the bolt, still sighted in, ready for a second shot. But it was unnecessary: the slug had mushroomed inside the body as intended, taking out most of the vital plumbing. The man was already sliding, head-first, down the dark face of the dome.

Water Buffalo followed him with the scope, watching as the man came to rest in a shallow gully at the dome's base. He was almost invisible there, one hand cradling a rock as if he'd stretched out for a catnap. Water Buffalo watched for a minute, then two. At last, he let the scope fall away from his eye. There had been nothing to see against the dark roof of Callisto, nothing to raise any alarm. It had all gone exactly to plan. And now, he was alone.

He slid the rifle back into the duffel, took a long swig of water from the canteen. Then he pulled out a government-model .45, which went into a shoulder holster. The radio came next, followed by a loaded backpack. Last to emerge were two camouflaged utility belts, their oversize pockets bulging. Crouching in the gully, Water Buffalo snapped these around his waist. Then he turned back to the duffel. He hesitated a moment, hand on the zipper, looking down, a little regretfully, at the paperback.

Then he tugged the zipper closed, rose cautiously from the gully, and began making his way through the rocks toward the dome.

1:55 P.M.

SARAH BOATWRIGHT SAT behind her desk, microcassette recorder cradled in one hand. Fred Barksdale stood close beside her. They were silent, listening to the calm, pleasant voice of John Doe.

"Pay attention now, Sarah," John Doe was saying. "At precisely 2:15, you are to notify Dispatch at the Galactic Voyage attraction to send five empty cars through the ride. You will place the package in the middle car. When the cars reach the Crab Nebula turn, the operator is to stop the ride for ninety seconds. Ninety seconds. Then he can proceed. In every other way, business should continue as usual. Once I've verified the contents of the package, you will hear from me again. If all goes according to plan, that's the last time you and I will speak."

There was a brief silence in which Sarah heard the whispered rattle of the tape.

"Sarah, do you understand everything I've just said? It is very important that you understand everything I've just said."

"I understand."

"Please repeat what I told you."

"At 2:15, send five empty cars through Galactic Voyage. Leave the disc in the middle car. When the cars reach Crab Nebula, halt the ride for ninety seconds."

"Very good. And—Sarah—I don't need to remind you there are to be no tricks. This isn't the time for cleverness. *All* the source code, the latest iteration. And no heroics. Understood?"

"Yes."

"Thank you, Sarah. Now, you might want to get started. You have a busy half hour ahead of you."

Sarah snapped off the recorder and turned to place it beside her teacup. As she did so, the faint scent of Barksdale's cologne reached her nostrils. As always, it reminded her, somehow, of

tweed and hunting horses. She turned toward him. He was staring at the recorder, a strange, faraway expression on his face.

"Are things set on your end?" she asked.

At the sound of her voice, Barksdale recollected himself. He
nodded. "Once all three of our digital keys are entered, the security protocols will be satisfied. We'll be able to download a single decrypted copy of the core routines onto a glass master. Then
I'll transfer over the low-security files. I assume you want the
disc rendered uncopyable?"

"Of course."

"Right, then. Burning the intentional read errors takes a little
time, but still we're talking about ten minutes, I'd say."

"What about the other question?"

"I'm sorry? Oh, yes." His blue eyes grew more troubled.
"Clearly, whoever's behind this has an intimate knowledge of
our systems. And they have the access necessary to move around
at will."

"How many people on your staff are capable of that?"

Barksdale reached into the jacket of his suit and withdrew
a folded piece of paper. As always, his movements had a habitual, graceful economy. "To hack the Metanet, override intrusion alerts, reprogram passcards, access the Crucible's security
protocols—eight people. Nine, including myself. Here's a list."

Sarah glanced quickly over the names. "And how many are in
the Park today?"

"Six. I've located all of them except Tom Tibbald. Nobody's
seen him since this morning."

"Get a copy to Bob Allocco, please. Ask him to put an alert
out on Tibbald, but quietly. And we should check the security
logs. But first, you'd better burn that disc. Emory's standing by in
New York. Call when you're ready for our digital keys."

Barksdale nodded, brushed her cheek with the palm of his
hand. The troubled look had not left his face.

"What is it, Fred?" she asked.

"It's nothing, really." He hesitated. "I was going to ask if you
had the bot from Griffin Tower sent down to Andrew Warne."

"Bob Allocco was going to see to it. Why?"

"It's nothing, really." He stroked an eyebrow. "But putting that
list together made me think. Shouldn't it wait?"

"What?"

"Involving Warne. This doesn't seem at all the time. He has

his own agenda here, and it's not the same as ours. Remember Shakespeare's words: 'love all, trust a few.' Not the other way around."

"You're not suggesting he could somehow be *involved* in this? The Metanet's his baby. You saw his face in this morning's meeting." She looked at him sidelong. Then—despite everything—she broke into a smile. "You know what, Frederic K. Barksdale, Esquire? I think you're just a wee bit jealous. The ex-boyfriend, and all that." She drew closer. "Am I right? *Are* you jealous?"

He returned her gaze. "No. Not yet, anyway."

She took his hand, caressed it. "You've got a funny sense of timing."

Barksdale looked away a moment. "Perhaps I was wondering," he said. "His coming back like this. If I wasn't around—in the picture, I mean—do you think the two of you might—"

Her fingertips froze in mid-caress. "How can you even ask that? I've got you now. I don't want anybody else." She took hold of his other hand, drew him toward her. And still the troubled look did not completely leave his face.

The door to the office opened and Andrew Warne stepped in.

To Sarah he seemed like a specter, summoned abruptly by their conversation. His eyes went from her, to Barksdale, to their joined hands. For a moment, a look of pain lanced across his face. Almost as quickly, it was gone.

"Didn't mean to crash the party," he said from the open doorway.

"No party," Sarah said, casually dropping Barksdale's hands and stepping back. "Fred was just leaving. Fred, I'll see you at the Galactic Voyage pre-show, ten minutes after two. *Precisely* ten minutes after, okay?"

Barksdale nodded again, then moved toward the door. Sarah watched the two men exchange passing glances.

Abruptly, Wingnut rolled into the office behind Warne, forcing Barksdale to half leap, half sprawl into the corridor to get out of its way. Behind the robot came Teresa Bonifacio, short black hair swinging across her face. Normally, that face wore a private little smile, as if contemplating a practical joke. Right now, the smile was absent.

"Sorry about that," Warne said, approaching Sarah. "Interrupting an intimate moment, I mean."

"It wasn't all that intimate," she replied, moving back behind her desk.

"And such a nice man, too," Warne said. "I'm so happy for you both."

Sarah looked at him curiously. There was the same speculative arch to the eyebrows she'd always known. At Carnegie-Mellon, he'd stood out like a wasp among moths: the brilliant bad boy of robotics, with his controversial theories and remarkable creations.

But she had seen a different Warne in the meeting this morning: a man besieged, under fire. And this bleak sarcasm was something newer still.

"I don't have time for this right now, Drew," she said.

Terri looked back and forth between them. "I think I'll go grab a cup of coffee in the staff lounge," she said.

"No. Stay put. You of all people deserve to hear this." Warne pulled up a chair, collapsed into it with a laugh. He glanced back at Sarah. "*You* don't have time for this right now? My God."

The bitter words echoed in the chill air.

"Okay," Sarah said. "Let's hear it."

"You lure me out here with a phony story. Then you sit me down in a conference room, give me a dog and pony show about how the Metanet's misbehaving. You even guilt me about it, make me feel responsible for that boy on Notting Hill Chase. You ask me to pull the plug."

She watched him lean toward the desk.

"All that *shit*. And you didn't even have the decency to tell me what was really going on. Instead of scaling up robotics development, you were cutting it to the bone. Compromising the program, knocking Terri's legs out from under her."

"I didn't tell him to say that," Terri said.

Sarah's eyes rested on her a moment, then returned to Warne.

"I'm not happy with the way you were brought here, Andrew. That was the decision of the home office. As for the robotics, it's a shame, but this is a business, not a think tank. I told you as much right here, when I gave you Wingnut. It's all about demographics." She raised her teacup, glanced at the clock: 1:57.

"Demographics, sure. Nightingale would turn in his grave if he knew how accountants and pollsters were running his Park." Warne laughed again, mirthlessly. "You know, in another context this might almost be funny. Because we've learned there's nothing wrong with the Metanet, after all. It's your goddamn *Park* that's broken."

Sarah lowered the cup. She looked at him more closely. "What do you mean?"

"Oh, Barksdale was partly right. The Metanet has been doing these things, changing robot procedures and the like. But he was also partly wrong. Because the Metanet wasn't transmitting its *own* instructions to the bots. It was transmitting somebody *else's*."

When Sarah was silent, he went on. "Here's the way it must have worked. Somebody on the inside—let's call him Mister X—would write a routine instructing some bot to misbehave. He'd slip it in with the rest of the Metanet's instruction set. The next morning, the Metanet would make its regular downlink to the bots. Except along with the usual program updates and firmware patches, Mister X's program would be sent to a particular bot. And that particular bot would act naughty. An incident report would be duly logged. But Mister X would make sure to slip that bot's *regular* programming back into the *next* morning's downlink. And cover his tracks by instructing the Metanet not to log either change. So when a team got around to inspecting the misbehaving bot, it would appear normal, the victim of some phantom glitch."

He glanced at Terri. "How am I doing?"

She gave him a thumbs-up.

"The only time things didn't happen this way was with the Notting Hill bots. And that's because they were taken off-line after the accident. Cut off from the Metanet. There was no chance for Mister X to restore their normal programming."

He looked at Sarah. "Why don't you look surprised by any of this?"

But Sarah was thinking quickly. "Let's accept your hypothesis for the moment. You know the Metanet better than anybody. Could you search for a hack trail? Find out which robots have been—*are* being—affected?"

Warne didn't look up. "Maybe. It would take some time. One of the things that clued me in was the lack of—" He stopped. Then he glanced up at her. "Wait a minute, I recognize that look. You know something, don't you? You're holding something back."

Sarah glanced down at Barksdale's list of possible moles. Teresa Bonifacio's name was number three.

"Sarah, answer me. What the hell's going on?"

Her mind raced through the possibilities. Warne was in a

unique position to help. Here was somebody who could strike back; who could hit these bastards where they live. Sarah glanced down at the list again. She could order Terri from the room. But Warne would probably tell her regardless. And chances were, he couldn't do this alone; not in time, anyway. He'd need help.

Sarah had always disapproved of Terri's un-Utopian attitude, her rebellious streak, her habit of voicing her opinions whether solicited or not. But in her gut, Sarah didn't think Terri would betray the work she loved. And Sarah always trusted her gut.

"Teresa, close the door," she said quietly.

She waited until Terri returned. "What I am going to tell you must be kept in strictest confidence. *Strictest* confidence. Do you understand?"

She watched the two exchange glances. Then they nodded.

"Utopia's being held hostage."

Warne frowned. *"What?"*

"There's a team of operatives inside the Park. We don't know how many. Remember that man who entered my office just as you were leaving? He calls himself John Doe. He's their leader. They've sabotaged some of the bots, probably in just the way you suggest. They also claim to have placed high explosives throughout the Worlds. Maybe the threat is real, maybe it's not. But we have to assume it is. We have to hand over the source code for the Crucible, our holographic engine, or . . ."

Warne had gone pale. His eyes locked on hers.

"Or what?"

Sarah did not reply.

There was a moment of stasis. Then Warne jumped to his feet. "My God, Sarah. Georgia's in the Park."

"We're making the handoff in fifteen minutes. We've been promised that no harm will come to anybody. Drew, if you can use the Metanet to track down which bots have been affected, maybe we can—"

But Warne wasn't listening. "I've got to find her," he said. *"Drew."*

"How the hell *do I find her*?" he cried, leaning across the desk. "There has to be a way. Help me, Sarah!"

She looked at him a moment. Then she glanced again at the clock. Two o'clock.

"We can trace her tag," Terri said.

Warne turned abruptly. "Trace her tag?"

"Every guest is given an imagetag, a unique multicolor sticker, to wear while they're in the Park. You've got one, too. It's embedded in your pin."

Warne glanced down at the stylized bird on his lapel. Then he wheeled toward Sarah. "Is this true?"

Sarah stared at him. She could feel this opportunity fading, right before her eyes.

She exhaled in disappointment. Then she turned to her computer. She'd have to do this fast.

"There are cameras throughout the Park, taking photographs of guests and Utopia personnel," she said as she began to type. "Each night, after the Park closes, we run pattern-recognition algorithms against the photos, isolating imagetags of the guests. We process them together with the cards people use to buy food, souvenirs. Knowledge-discovery software helps us track attraction flow, purchasing patterns, the like."

As Warne listened, his tense look seemed to ease a little. "Big Brother does data-mining," he said. "But I'm not complaining. Come on, let's find her."

Sarah typed additional commands. "I'm bringing up the tag retrieval application," she said. "I'll enter Georgia's name."

They waited a moment.

"Okay, there's her tag. Now I'll request a chronological breakdown of camera sightings."

There was another wait, longer this time.

"What's taking so long?" Warne asked impatiently.

"I'm requesting a special job. It takes a lot of horsepower. Normally, we only run this in the evening, when the computers aren't busy handling Park operations."

Then her screen cleared and a new window appeared, a short list inside it. "Here it is," Sarah said.

Warne and Terri came up behind her, and together they peered at the screen.

"I don't understand all those abbreviations," Warne said.

"She's in Callisto. Four minutes to two, Rings of Saturn."

She swiveled toward him.

"That was five minutes ago," she said.

Warne looked at her for a moment—an intense, hunted look. Then he turned and raced away.

"Wait!" Terri called after him. "I'm coming with you." And

she, too, disappeared from the office. Wingnut, taken by surprise, wheeled around quickly, then began lurching toward the corridor.

"Wingnut, stay!" Sarah commanded. "Stay with me."

The robot stopped. Then slowly, it backed into the office with a loud bray of frustration.

For a moment, Sarah stared at the open door. Then she squeezed her eyes shut, massaging them with her fingers.

There was a low beep from the computer. She glanced over at the screen.

This was odd. Somebody else was using the tag retrieval program.

She stood up, sweeping John Doe's radio into her pocket. There was no more time; she had to get to the Galactic Voyage ride right away.

But still she lingered a moment, curious.

She glanced back at the screen. Except for emergencies, nobody was authorized to run a tag retrieval while the Park was open.

She lowered herself back into the chair. Placing her hand on the mouse, she navigated through a series of menus, displaying the anonymous request on her own screen. Then she went rigid in surprise.

Whoever it was, they were looking for Andrew Warne.

2:10 P.M.

"THE ONE RIDE in Utopia without security cameras," Bob Allocco said over the babel of voices filling Callisto's main concourse. "Tell me that's a coincidence."

They stood within a rest area of curved Lucite benches and alien-looking potted palms, a small oasis of relative calm not far from the entrance portal to Galactic Voyage.

"Eleven minutes after," Sarah said, glancing at her watch. "Fred should be here by now." On cue she spotted Barksdale, jogging down the concourse, threading his way between strolling knots of visitors.

She motioned to Peggy Salazar, a Callisto line manager who was standing nearby. "Everything's set?" she asked as the woman came over.

Salazar nodded. "I've explained it to the cast member working Load. He's a little surprised." She glanced at Sarah speculatively.

"Just an impromptu drill. The home office wants to keep everybody on their toes. Practice the same emergency procedures each week, and you grow stale."

Salazar nodded slowly, as if digesting this.

Sarah took another quick look around. The knowledge that John Doe was somewhere nearby sharpened her senses, increased her heartbeat. She felt her hands balling into fists.

"Come on," she said to Allocco. "We'd better get inside."

They crossed the concourse, stepped through the Galactic Voyage portal, and entered the pre-show area. Salazar came in behind them, and they took up an inconspicuous position away from the queue line. Sarah watched as the dispatcher at the loading station ushered the next group—a woman and three small children—into a waiting car, then lowered the grab bar over their waists. Although she couldn't see the worker's face through his space helmet, Sarah knew he couldn't be too happy, working under the gaze of his department supervisor and the head of Operations.

As with the other mainline rides, the Galactic Voyage "pre-show" served two purposes: a queuing area for guests waiting to board, and a taste of what they could expect when the ride began. Early on, Utopia designers had learned that it didn't matter how many warning signs were placed around the entrances to intense attractions like Moon Shot and Notting Hill Chase. Parents insisted on taking young children on the rides, anyway—and then complained bitterly afterward about how terrified their toddlers had been.

The answer had been to modify the pre-show areas. Event Horizon, one of the worst offenders, was the first to get the treatment. In keeping with the Callisto theme, its original pre-show area had looked like the loading dock of a warp-capable spaceship. The Utopia designers carefully detuned it, adding subauditory rumbles, sparking electrical lines, and a floor that trembled ominously underfoot. After this change, young children often grew so alarmed on entering that they demanded their parents take them on a different ride. The technique worked so well that the intrusive, un-Utopian warning signs could be done away with entirely.

The Galactic Voyage pre-show could not have been more different from Event Horizon's. It was bright, cheerful, decorated like a kindergarten of the future: the jumping-off point for a child's field trip through the cosmos.

Sarah's gaze lingered on the queue. Some of the youngest children were dozing. Others pranced in place, impatient after the wait yet eager, now that they could see the ride ahead of them. Often, there was only one parent on hand: adults, especially those who'd been through Galactic Voyage before, weren't eager to repeat the bland experience.

In her mind, she could once again see the careful way Allocco had placed that big brick of high explosive on the conference table. Sarah dropped her eyes, forcing the image from her mind.

Barksdale came up beside them. He nodded to Peggy Salazar, then reached inside his jacket and withdrew a slender jewel case. Silently, he handed it to Sarah.

"What's that?" Salazar asked.

"Part of the drill," Sarah replied quickly. "Peggy, would you excuse us for a minute?"

"Of course." Salazar glanced curiously at the three of them, then walked over to the dispatcher.

Sarah glanced at the DVD within the jewel case. It was hard to believe that this slender little circle of aluminum and polycarbonate held the most precious of all Utopia's possessions: the specifications and software that made up the Crucible technology. The disc was branded for internal use only, with the words *Proprietary and Confidential* stamped below the imprint of a nightingale, along with dire warnings in smaller type of what would befall anyone who put the disc to unauthorized use. She handed the case to Allocco.

"Go over it one more time," she said.

Allocco gestured toward the ride entrance. "Like I was saying, this guy's a clever bastard. He picked Galactic Voyage for the drop because it has the least security of any ride in the Park. But what he didn't know was, right beside the Crab Nebula turn—the spot where the cars will stop, where he's making the pickup—there's a blind."

"What's this?" Barksdale asked, surprise writ large on his face. "A blind?"

"A maintenance conduit, big enough to conceal one man. My operative's already in place. He'll see John Doe grab the package. Then he can tail him. Or—if we get really lucky—he can take him down."

Sarah frowned. "We discussed tailing John Doe *out* of the Park before making an apprehension."

"This guy's slippery. Remember what happened back in the Hive? If he seems to be working alone, if we get any signals that this is in fact just a ruse, we should snag him while we can."

Sarah considered this. John Doe's threats could not be treated lightly. He had to be regarded as deadly serious. Her first responsibility was to their guests. And yet the idea of subduing this threat—of neutralizing him now, rather than letting him roam through the Park like a loose cannon—was very attractive. Her sense of anger and outrage ran steadily, like a turbine. Her cheek burned where he had stroked it.

"It's too dangerous." Barksdale spoke with uncharacteristic vehemence.

"My guy's good, an ex-cop like myself. He's taken down hundreds of perps over his career. He'll be under strict orders not to do John Doe unless there's 100 percent certainty of success. I've got another man concealed near the ride exit." Allocco motioned discreetly toward a plainclothes security specialist standing by the loading dock. "And Chris Green, here, will be watching from within the entrance. They're three of my best. Together, they'll set up a three-way tail. Or, if John Doe can be safely contained, they'll neutralize him, escort him to Security."

Allocco nodded at the security specialist named Green. The man nodded back, then slipped through a partially concealed door beside the loading dock. None of the guests in the queuing line so much as glanced in his direction.

"This is irresponsible," Barksdale went on. "We can't take the chance."

Sarah checked her watch again: sixty seconds to make a decision.

"Look," Allocco said. "You've ruled out a police response, so it's up to us to take action, while we still can. Assume for a moment this whole thing *isn't* a ruse. Who knows what else they really have in mind? Who knows what they'll demand next, what hostages they'll take? One thing we do know: John Doe's the ringleader. If we can cut off the head, the body will die. This is the perfect chance to take him without any casualties."

"Do you want the responsibility for what happens if we take him?" Barksdale asked.

"Do you want the responsibility for what happens if we *don't?*"

Sarah looked from one to the other. She hesitated briefly. And then she turned to Allocco.

"Your operative is not to take John Doe unless he's absolutely positive of success. On the first sign of trouble, anything unexpected—*anything*—you call your men off. Even if it's just a tail. Agreed?"

Allocco nodded vigorously. "Agreed."

"Then get started." She turned to Barksdale, who was looking at her with an expression akin to horror. "Fred, come over here a minute. Please."

She led Barksdale a few steps away, toward the wall opposite the queue line.

"Sarah, don't do this," Barksdale said. His intense blue eyes held hers almost pleadingly.

"It's done."

"But you don't know what you're dealing with, what you're up against. Our first responsibility is to the guests. They're paying us not just to entertain them, but to keep them safe."

Hearing Barksdale echo her own thoughts brought an unexpected mix of emotions to Sarah: irritation, impatience, uncertainty. She pushed them away. "Look, Freddy," she said in an undertone. "Do you remember our first dinner together? At Chez André, in Vegas?"

Barksdale's narrow, handsome face grew puzzled. "Of course."

"Do you remember the wine?"

He thought a moment. "Lynch-Bages, '69."

"No, no. The dessert wine."

Barksdale nodded. "Château d'Yquem."

"Right. Remember how I'd never even heard of a dessert wine before? How I thought all sweet wine tasted like Manischewitz?"

Barksdale allowed himself a brief, wintry smile.

"You explained to me about *Botrytis cinerera,* remember?"

Barksdale nodded again.

"Noble rot. It attacks the skin of the grape, enriching the sugars, creating the best sweet wine in the world. I couldn't believe it when you told me—a fungus the growers actually *encouraged.* I made you explain it twice." She leaned closer, fingered his lapel. "Freddy, we have a rot in this Park. Here, today. And there's nothing noble about it. If we don't do something—if we let ourselves look vulnerable, an easy target—who's to say it won't happen again? And again?"

Barksdale looked at her silently, jaw working.

She applied gentle pressure to the immaculate lapel. Then she turned away and walked back toward Peggy Salazar and Allocco. After a few moments, Barksdale followed.

Together, the group approached the loading dock. A Hispanic woman with twins was being shown into a car.

Sarah waited until Dispatch had sent the car on its way. "Send on two empty cars, and cue up a third," she said to the loading attendant. He nodded, middle-aged face oddly magnified by the Plexiglas helmet.

The two cars went bobbing off into the darkness at the end of the ramp, and a third car shot up the bus bar from the unload boosters. Allocco stepped forward, leaned over to note the number of the car, then placed the disc on its floor.

"Send it," Sarah told the attendant, and the car trundled away. She watched until it disappeared from sight around a dark corner, into the ride.

"Now, send on two more empty cars," she said.

Behind her, there was a discontented murmuring from the party waiting to board. Sarah turned, flashed them a smile, then told the load attendant to proceed as usual.

A trip through Galactic Voyage took just over six minutes. The empty cars would reach the Crab Nebula in four.

Sarah stepped back from the dock and looked around the pre-show area. A baby was crying somewhere, its wails cutting sharply through the crowd chatter. A maintenance specialist stepped out of one of the ride's side portals. As always in public areas, he was in costume: only the color of the nightingale pin on his space suit indicated his occupation. Sarah scanned the faces in the line: excited, impatient, bored. The scene looked utterly normal. Everything was business as usual.

Except for the package. And the person waiting for it, deep inside the ride.

"Let's get to the tower," Allocco said.

Still, Sarah waited, scanning the bright space. Then she turned toward him and nodded.

THE CONTROL TOWER for Galactic Voyage was a cramped space even for the operator: with three additional visitors crowding inside, Sarah found it difficult just to draw breath.

"We don't have a whole lot of leeway," Allocco was saying. "The ride's completely computer-controlled. We'll have to cut juice to the bus bar temporarily."

He leaned over the dispatcher. "Keep an eye on the mimic diagram. When car 7470 reaches the Crab Nebula, I want you to shut it down."

The tower operator looked uneasily from Allocco to Sarah and back again. He'd been eating pistachios and reading *Roquefort for Dummies*, and clearly hadn't been expecting managerial company.

"Hit the E-stop?" he asked.

"No, no. Not all the power. Just do a service interrupt. As if there was an exit alert. Ninety seconds, no more, no less. Then put it on-line again." He took the radio from his pocket. "Thirty-three to Forward, you in position? Very well. Do not, I repeat, *do not* apprehend the suspect unless you have 100 percent confidence."

He glanced at Sarah. "I instructed the spotters near the entrance and exit to maintain radio silence."

For a minute, then two, the tower was quiet as everyone watched the white call numbers of the cars make their way along the fluorescent curves of the diagram.

"Ten seconds," said the dispatcher.

Allocco raised his radio again. "Forward, acquisition in ten seconds. Get ready." This time he did not lower the radio.

Sarah watched the digital label numbered 7470 continue its slow progress along the diagram. She realized that, unconsciously, she was holding her breath.

"Springes to catch woodcocks," Barksdale murmured beside her. His voice was tight, strained.

"Now," said the dispatcher, leaning forward with a red scatter of pistachio shells and punching a button on the tower console. An alarm sounded. The cars stopped their progress along the mimic diagram; the call numbers turned red and began to flash.

"Ninety and counting," murmured the tower operator.

Sarah found herself staring at car 7470, now motionless beside a label marked *Crab Neb*. Somewhere beyond the control tower, in the actual world of the ride, men were hiding in the blackness surrounding the empty car. She took a deep breath. One way or another, it would all be over in less than two minutes.

"Forward?" Allocco said into the radio. "Anything?"

"I've got a visual," a voice squawked from the radio. "There's somebody in the car."

"You mean, removing something from the car."

"I repeat, in the car. Sitting *in* the car."

Allocco turned to the dispatcher. "You sure you stopped the right car?"

"Positive." The dispatcher pointed at the mimic diagram as proof. "Fifteen seconds."

"Forward? How many passengers in the car?"

"Looks like one."

"Roger. Come forward and examine. Slow."

Sarah put her hand on Allocco's arm. "No. Maybe it's John Doe."

"And just what the hell would he be doing? Enjoying the ride?"

"Waiting for a trap. To see if we're going to try something."

Allocco looked at her a moment. Then he spoke into the radio again. "Forward? Cancel that. Remain in position."

"Time," the dispatcher said, pushing another button. The car numbers on the mimic diagram stopped blinking, went white, and began to move again.

"What just happened?" Sarah asked.

Allocco glanced up toward the mimic diagram. "I think our boy messed with that board, just like the monitors in the Hive. Made us stop the cars in the wrong position, or something. No doubt the bastard's already nabbed the disc and left." He raised the radio. "Alpha, Omega, this is Thirty-three. Subject may have already acquired the item. Maintain your positions. Report any sightings, but do not apprehend. Repeat, do not apprehend."

"Omega, roger," came a voice.

Allocco let the radio fall to his side. "That disc is long gone," he said, voice suddenly weary.

"Let's check unloading," Sarah replied. "Just to be sure."

BY THE TIME they made their way through the back of the ride to the unloading area, the woman with twins was already being helped out of her car. Sarah could hear the elderly unload attendant apologizing for the delay during the ride.

"Watch yourselves," Allocco said to Sarah and Barksdale. "I don't think John Doe is stupid enough to just come strolling out the ride. But at this point, nothing would surprise me." The first two empty cars came trundling along the bar, and he moved up the unloading ramp toward them.

Sarah motioned to Barksdale, and together they followed Allocco up the ramp. *Sarah, there are to be no tricks. This isn't the time for cleverness.* She became aware of an emotion she had little experience with: uneasiness. She glanced over her shoulder. Except for the woman with twins, the corridor leading back to the concourse was empty.

As she turned back, the third car lurched into position at the unloading dock. A lone man was sitting within it, and for a moment Sarah froze, thinking it was John Doe. But the man was too short, too heavyset. He was slumped forward, as if sleeping.

Suddenly, Allocco was running toward the car. And Sarah recognized the man inside as Chris Green, the security specialist who'd ducked into the front of the ride.

The car eased to a stop. Green sagged forward heavily.

Maneuvering around the unload attendant, Sarah came up beside Allocco. She glanced inside the car, suddenly flooded with a terrible misgiving. Beneath one foot of the security specialist, she could see the jewel case, crushed to pieces. Shards of the disc lay within and around it.

"Chris?" Allocco said, putting his hand on the guard's shoulder. Green remained motionless, slumped forward.

Gently, Allocco pulled the guard up into a sitting position. His head lolled back. Sarah felt herself go cold with horror.

"Oh, good Christ," Allocco groaned.

Chris Green's eyes stared back at them: wide, sightless. Below—where a large shard of the DVD had been thrust deep into his mouth—a single rivulet of blood traced a slow course down the chin, and along the neck, before disappearing out of sight against the dark shirt.

2:22 P.M.

THE BODY OF the security officer had been moved discreetly to Medical and placed under locked quarantine. No one, not even doctors, was allowed to approach it until the police could be summoned.

They had returned to the Hive and were running through the video logs of the few security cameras that monitored Galactic Voyage: trying to make sense of what happened, to piece together what had gone so terribly wrong.

"All right, stop it there," Allocco told his video tech, Ralph Peccam. These were the first words that had been spoken in several minutes. They'd just completed a high-speed review of the camera in the ride's unloading area. Nothing out of place. No sign of John Doe lurking among the parents and children.

"What else we got?" Allocco asked wearily.

Peccam consulted a table. "Just the camera in pre-show," he said, sniffing.

"Very well. Bring it up, same time reference, two hundred frames a second."

Peccam tapped in a few commands, then adjusted a hat switch set into the oversize keyboard. Sarah stared at the screen as the tourists, accelerated into languid rivers, flowed around the barriers and dropped, a few at a time, into the empty cars that shot up to meet them. She knew she should feel something right now: grief, anger, remorse. But all she felt was an overpowering numbness. The image of Chris Green—the staring eyes, the gleam of the jagged shard peeping from parted lips—refused to leave her. She glanced toward Fred Barksdale, the contours of his face spectral in the artificial light of the Hive. He shifted his eyes toward her for a moment, then turned back to the screen. He looked stricken.

"All routine," Allocco muttered bitterly as he, too, stared at the screen. "Another day in paradise."

Sarah was holding a sealed plastic bag, containing the fragments of disc left on the bottom of the car. They were crushed by what must have been a terrible struggle. Without realizing, she had been turning the bag over and over in her hands. She thrust it into the pocket of her jacket.

On the left edge of the screen, there was movement as a handful of figures took up positions beside the loading area.

"Slow to thirty," Allocco said.

Now the figures to the left of the screen resolved themselves: Allocco; the line manager; herself. Sarah forced herself to watch as the scene, not yet half an hour old, replayed itself. Freddy walked into the picture, disc in hand. A little drama unfolded as both he and Allocco pleaded their cases to her. She made her decision; Chris Green, the security officer, vanished through a door into the rear of the ride. Sarah watched herself take Fred Barksdale aside to explain the wisdom of launching a pre-emptive strike against John Doe. To explain why, in effect, she had just condemned a man to death.

On-screen, they placed the disc, sent on the empty cars, then vanished from view, heading for the control tower.

"Cut it," Allocco told Peccam. The monitor went blank. "That's it. We've checked all five cameras. Nothing."

A silence settled over the small, dark room.

At last, Allocco spoke. "Chris Green was a stand-up guy," he said slowly. "The best thing we can do for him right now is try to figure out what the hell happened." He sighed, turned to Peccam. "Ralph, bring up that last camera once again. Cue on the empty cars as they enter the ride."

Peccam restored the view of the pre-show area. Once again, Sarah watched Allocco place the package in the empty car. It trundled forward along the bus bar, then vanished out of sight into the blackness of the first turn.

"It doesn't make sense," Allocco muttered, more to himself than anyone else. "The Crab Nebula is deep inside the ride. That's where John Doe would have to be for the pickup. But Chris Green was stationed at the ride entrance. Why would he encounter John Doe there?"

The question hung in the air, unanswered. All eyes remained on the screen.

"Stop!" Allocco barked suddenly. "Okay. Ahead fifteen." He pointed at the monitor. "Look at that."

Sarah watched as the maintenance specialist she'd noticed in passing stepped out of the side portal and ambled, slow-motion, across the pre-show area. Abruptly, the numbness that had enveloped her like a cloak fell away.

In the bulky helmet and obligatory space suit, there was no way to be sure. And yet Sarah knew—in some instinctive way—that she was watching John Doe.

From the expressions around her, she realized the others had reached the same conclusion.

"Shit," Allocco said. "The whole thing with the ninety-second stop was a phony. John Doe wasn't waiting by the Crab Nebula turn. He was going to pluck the disc from the car as soon as it *entered* the ride, then just walk away before we even stopped the damn thing. But he ran into Chris Green instead."

"You want me to track him?" Peccam asked.

"No. I mean, yes. But on your own time. No doubt he's worked that out, too." Allocco glanced over at Sarah. "I'll get Costuming over there, run an inventory. See if any uniforms are missing."

Sarah nodded. She already knew exactly what they would find.

A low buzzing sounded from the radio in her pocket.

The control room fell silent. All eyes turned to Sarah as she drew out the radio.

She snapped it on, raised it slowly to her lips. "Sarah Boatwright here." They were the first words she had spoken since entering the Hive.

"Sarah."

"Yes."

"Why, Sarah?" It was John Doe's voice, yet it sounded different somehow. The tone of bantering civility was gone. It was chillier now; more businesslike.

"Why what?"

"Why did you set a trap for me?"

Sarah struggled to find words.

"Haven't I always been honest with you, Sarah? Hasn't honesty been the basis of all our dealings?"

"Mr. Doe, I—"

"Didn't I take the time to visit you personally, to make your acquaintance? Didn't I spell out *precisely* what you should and should not do?"

"Yes."

"Didn't I go to the trouble of giving you a demonstration? Didn't I make every possible effort to make sure that, at the end of the day, there would be no deaths to weigh upon your conscience?"

Sarah was silent.

"Oh, dear God," Barksdale murmured. "What have we done?"

"Mr. Doe," Sarah began slowly. "I'll see to it personally that—"

"No," came the voice. "You lost your chance to speak when you betrayed my trust. I'm the teacher now. You're the student. And you will now attend to my lecture. Do you know what the subject is? No, don't speak—I'll tell you myself. It's *panic*."

Sarah listened, radio pressed against her ear.

"Did you know, Sarah, that there's an art to orchestrating panic? It's such a fascinating topic, I've been planning a monograph on it. It would make me famous, the Aristotle of crowd control. What's especially interesting is the opportunity for creativity. There are so many tools at one's disposal, so many ways to proceed, that choosing the most effective becomes a real challenge. Take—oh—fire, for example. Something unique happens to crowd dynamics during a fire, Sarah. I've studied all the greats: the Triangle Shirtwaist fire, the Iroquois Theater, the Cocoanut Grove, the Happyland Social Club. All very different. And yet they all have something in common. Extremely high mortality rates, even without the benefit of artificial accelerants. People bunch together at the exits, you see. The *closed* exits."

"Our exits are open," Sarah murmured.

"Are they? But all this is beside the point, and I'm getting ahead of myself. I have to go. I'll be in touch."

"One person is already dead—"

"One person is not even a statistical blip."

"You'll get your disc—"

"I know I will. But there's something I have to do first. You think your Park is famous now, Sarah? I'm about to *really* put it on the map."

"No! Wait, *wait*—"

But the line had already gone dead.

2:22 P.M.

GEORGIA WARNE LEFT the exit portal for the ride known as Ecliptic and joined the crowds moving along the broad concourse. She had just purchased Callisto's version of cotton candy—an iridescent rainbow of spun sugar, shot through with carbonated crystals that popped noisily on the tongue—and was devouring it with resolute single-mindedness. She did not hear the crackling of the crystals, or the hoots and laughter of the guests passing by her, or the faint background wash of Utopia sonics: she was wearing her headphones, and the surrounding landscape was drenched in the call-and-response of Count Basie's "Jumpin' at the Woodside."

A group of older teenagers, sporting purple hair and wearing Dragonspire T-shirts, were making their raucous erratic way toward her, and Georgia veered to one side to let them pass. She hadn't expected much from Ecliptic—after all, it was a Ferris wheel, get *real*—but it had turned out to be pretty cool. It revolved around a planet with a vertical ring, sort of like Saturn, only set on end. Dark, like most of the rides in Callisto, but with this amazing sense of depth, of being in outer space. And the holographic rings had been so *utterly* real she felt sure she could have touched them if she'd reached her hand out from the car.

But she'd been alone, so they'd stuck her with this squirmy, wriggling girl from a large family, who'd insisted on pointing out everything in sight. She'd been too stupid to just shut up and enjoy the ride. So halfway through, Georgia had put on her headphones and cranked the volume.

She paused, scowling at the memory. Ahead and to the right, she could see a ramp curving away from the central concourse, ending in a people-mover that disappeared into a low tunnel, arched over by bands of neon and flickering lasers. It was the entrance to Dark Side of the Moon, a ride she'd read great things about on the Web. She pulled her homemade itinerary from her pocket. Sure enough: a four-star ride. She angled toward it. Then she stopped. She'd promised her dad no big coasters, no tall rides. Dark Side of the Moon sure fell into that category. So did Ecliptic, probably; but what did Dad expect her to do? She'd tried some of the kiddie rides, like Rings of Saturn, but she felt stupid crowded in among six-year-olds.

She stared at the ride entrance, her scowl deepening. Then she turned away unwillingly and continued down the concourse until she reached a bench. She sat down, fished out her guidemap, glanced over it, put it back in her pocket. Finishing the last bite of the cotton candy, she turned to toss the long white tube into a trash receptacle. Then she paused, looking at the slender cone of paper in her hand.

Earlier, she'd told her dad she had no memory of the trip they'd taken, many years before, to Kennywood Park. But that wasn't quite true. She remembered the way her mother had surprised her there with a tall cloud of cotton candy, balanced precariously on a white stick, just like this one. She remembered how the pink confection had seemed impossibly large to her eight-year-old eyes. She remembered the heat of the sun beating down upon them, the tanned lines of her mother's face, her pale lipstick, the way the edges of her eyes crinkled up when she smiled.

She had other memories of her mother, too: taking one of her boat prototypes out for a test sail; riding ponies in a leafy park; sitting in a window seat, smothered in blankets, reading Kipling's *Just So Stories* together. They were fragmentary memories, pale and faded like old photographs, and she kept them to herself, as if speaking of them—even to her father— would break a magic enchantment, cause them to vanish forever.

She glanced at the paper cone for a moment, turning it around in her hands. Then she dropped it in the trash, stood up, and continued down the concourse.

Ahead, she could see the Mind's Eye gallery. Above it, a life-size hologram of Eric Nightingale hovered, beckoning people inside with a wave of his silk top hat. A small knot of people crowded around, staring at the portraits in the gallery window, pointing at the image of the magician. Georgia slowed, staring curiously. She remembered Nightingale, too. He never seemed to keep still, always moving, always gesturing. She remembered how, even though he wasn't very tall, even for a grown-up, the room had always seemed too small for him. There had been nights he'd visited with her dad, where the men had talked around the kitchen table for hours and hours, it seemed. She remembered the smell of coffee, pipe tobacco. She'd crawled under the table and played there, listening to the voices, knowing that if she didn't call attention to herself she could stay up way, way past her bedtime.

"Jumpin' at the Woodside" ended. There was a brief moment of silence on her digital player, and the sounds of Utopia rushed in: hoots, a babel of voices, a distant echoey loudspeaker, a child's shriek of delight. Then "Swingin' the Blues" started and the sounds were lost once again. Georgia stuck her hands in her pockets and moved on. She remembered how Nightingale had this way of looking at her when she talked, listening, as if what she had to say really mattered. He wasn't dumb, like most adults seemed to be. He didn't say the same dumb things that everybody else did, like how pretty she was, or how much she had grown since he last saw her.

For some reason, Georgia's thoughts turned to Terri Bonifacio. She didn't seem dumb, either. She probably even liked cotton candy. Usually, Georgia had little interest in what adults had to say. But she found herself very curious to hear Terri's opinions on things: what she thought about bluegrass or bop; what books she'd read as a kid; what colors she liked to wear; what her favorite food was. She sure hoped it wasn't that nasty, fishy-smelling stuff. That could be a problem.

By now, she had reached the end of the central concourse, and she stopped, hopping from one foot to the other on the reflective pavers. Ahead, the thoroughfare widened into what looked like a vast, circular terminal. This was the Callisto Skyport, with half a dozen "embarkation zones" leading to some of the World's most popular rides. The space throbbed with chatter. Georgia glanced at her guidemap. Moon Shot, Event Horizon, Afterburn. Every one an awesome ride. And every one exactly the kind Dad didn't want her to go on.

As usual, there were no clocks anywhere. She glanced down at her watch. Forty-five more minutes until she was supposed to meet her dad.

It wasn't fair, it wasn't *fair*. Just a couple good rides that morning. Then, nothing but dumb meetings and hanging around in labs. And it wasn't any fun going on rides alone. Especially when you couldn't even go on any of the *good* rides.

Georgia sighed disconsolately and turned to retrace her steps. As she did so, her eyes landed on an embarkation zone labeled *Escape from Waterdark*.

She stared up at the shimmering holographic letters. She'd read all about this ride on the Web. It was modeled after her favorite scene in *Atmosfear,* in which the young band of heroes escapes Morpheus's prison on the sea planet of Waterdark Four. The ride was new; nobody at her school had been on it. And it was especially cool for two reasons. It took place entirely inside a world of water and rain. And it was supposed to be the first ride anywhere to employ low-gravity technology. And no fakes, either: real, live low-gravity.

Georgia noticed that most of the people were walking toward her, rather than away: they had already been on the Skyport rides and were streaming back into Callisto proper. Although these six rides were some of the most popular anywhere, the lines were shorter than the ones she'd waited on already.

The fanzines published by the Utopia fan clubs contained exhaustive listings of ideal times to visit specific rides: times at which, for no easily explainable reason, lines seemed to be shorter. Georgia didn't care about any of this. She only knew she was sick of kiddie rides, sick of hanging around. And it looked as if she'd be able to get inside Waterdark in under ten minutes. Anyway, it wasn't a coaster—not really. Her dad wouldn't mind; not much, anyway.

She was abruptly jostled to one side. She looked up: two little kids, holding their mother's hands, had passed her on their way to Waterdark. The mother was young, attractive, her tan dark against her red dress.

Georgia pulled the headphones from her ears. Then she jogged forward, and—smirking at the kids from over her shoulder—took her place in the Waterdark line ahead of them.

2:26 P.M.

"STOP SHOVING, DICKBREATH."

"*I'm* not shoving, scrotum-sack. *You're* shoving. Do it again and I'll pound ya."

Angus Poole listened, without interest, to the petty squabbling of his cousin's youngest boys. It had erupted on every single line they'd waited in. At first, Poole had been mildly intrigued by the remarkable arsenal of foul names the two boys had for each other. In line for the Brighton Beach Express, over in the Boardwalk, he'd even started counting. By the time they'd reached the very next ride, Scream Machine, he'd given up at fifty.

Thank God, at least *this* line was short.

Around him, the Skyport was a vast echoing citadel of conversation. From his place in line, Poole glanced around. The designers had done an excellent job of making the place feel like some futuristic transportation terminal, right down to the departures board and the steady drone of the dispatch loudspeaker. Today it held an added benefit: with six rides all boarding from the same convenient place, he could sneak off for a cool one and let his cousin deal with her own family for a while.

As if on cue, Sonya turned toward him. Three cameras slanted across her ample midriff, and atop her head the archmage's cap had gone slightly askew. "What did you say the name of this ride was, Angus?"

"Escape from Waterdark." Never mind that a hologram of the damn name was hovering right above their heads; she had to ask anyway.

"And where do we go next?"

"Well, there are five other great rides you can catch from this spot. See? It's sort of like a huge airport, except each gate leads to a different attraction. You should ride them all." *Please, ride them all.*

"How about you?" Sonya asked.

"After Waterdark, I think I'll go grab a beer at the Sea of Tranquility. It's that bar outside the casino—I pointed it out from the concourse, remember? You can meet up with me there."

At the mention of beer, Sonya's husband, the insurance readjuster, came out of his daze and glanced over at Poole: a brief, hunted look.

Sonya and Martin Klemm of Lardoon, Iowa, and their three charming boys. Until he'd knocked on the door of their motel room this morning, Poole hadn't seen his cousin Sonya in at least a dozen years. But then, it had been the same with his sister, Vicki, and his nephew Paul, or any of the other relatives, near or distant, who'd come out of the woodwork over the last six months. It was as if, in their minds, Utopia had finally given him purpose in life. Strange Uncle Angus, who had moved to Las Vegas after leaving the Corps and never gotten married. Odd cousin Angus—or half-nephew Angus, or quarter-sister Angus, or whatever—who professed to work for a living, but doing what, no one seemed to have asked. And Poole had never offered details.

But now, by some unspoken agreement of the extended family, he had been appointed tour guide to Utopia.

In a way, he didn't mind. It wasn't that he enjoyed the reunions—he could have done without those—but, to his surprise, he became fascinated with the Park. In earlier years and earlier lives, he'd been to Disneyland, Universal Studios, Busch Gardens. By and large, they had left him cold. But Utopia was different somehow. And it wasn't just because it was slicker, and newer, and had cooler toys. It was the immersiveness, he guessed: somehow, you almost found yourself believing you'd been transported back to nineteenth-century London or medieval Camelot. Of course, you knew you were in the middle of the Nevada desert. But they'd done such a great job of integrating the rides and attractions into each separate World that you *enjoyed* taking part in the fantasy. And for someone as unimaginative as himself, that was saying something.

But every fascination has its limits. And, as of 2:26 P.M., Poole had officially achieved Klemm family saturation.

"This low-gravity stuff is a crock." Now it was the oldest Klemm kid talking. "It's a trick. The acceleration due to gravity is 9.8 meters per second per second toward the center of the earth. To create a weightless condition, you'd need to create a force opposite the force exerted by gravity, and . . ."

Poole stared at the kid: buckteeth, gangling, adenoidal. All that was missing was a plastic protector in his shirt pocket. A walking, talking argument for infanticide if there ever was one. Besides, the kid didn't know what the hell he was talking about. He'd shut up once he got inside the air lock.

With a yawn, Poole gazed around the Skyport again. It was crowded, of course, but not nearly as bad as usual. There was the normal sea of happy faces, peppered with an occasional harassed-looking parent or impatient child. Characters in space outfits wandered about, working the queue lines or posing for pictures.

One distant figure stood out to Poole's practiced eye. Unlike everyone else, standing in line or moving deliberately from one destination to another, a lone man was rushing about, helter-skelter. Poole looked on in mild curiosity as the man darted between the throngs on the concourse beyond: now rushing up to a concession stand, now approaching a queuing line, looking here and there, craning his neck around as if searching for something.

The man trotted off again, disappearing into the milling crowds, and Poole turned away. His own line had moved forward steadily and they were almost at the embarkation air lock. Escape from Waterdark was the only reason Poole wasn't already enjoying a beer in the Sea of Tranquility. It was his favorite ride in the Park. If the low-gravity environment was faked, it was done so cleverly that it didn't matter to him.

He wondered, a little idly, what it was he found so appealing about the ride. You couldn't call it a thrill ride, like Moon Shot over there to the left, or Station Omega, at the top of that futuristic-looking escalator. In fact—outside of the first few jolts as the pods "escaped" from Waterdark Prison and made their way up to the orbiting mothership—you couldn't call it thrilling at all. It was the utter realism of the ride, probably, that did it: you really felt you were scrambling up through the rain-drenched sky toward outer space. He'd have to pay closer attention, this time, to exactly what subliminal buttons they were pushing; how they made it seem so realistic. One thing he could remember vividly was the way, as they climbed higher and higher into the atmosphere, the fat drops of rain that poured down around the pod seemed to slow, and then—as gravity's hold grew fainter—

practically stood still outside the capsule, floating and dancing in the darkness of space. He remembered how his gut had pressed against the lap bar as the mothership came into view, how his soft-drink cup had seemed to rise out of its holder. Wait until the Klemm kid got a load of *that*.

Now, this was interesting: the man he'd seen running around the concourse had blundered into the Skyport and was standing dead center, staring around. Beside him was a young Asian woman. They exchanged a few quick words. Then they separated, running in different directions. No doubt about it, they were looking for somebody, and in a big hurry, too. *Good luck finding anyone in this place*, Poole thought to himself. The rides in the Skyport had no pre-show areas. Everybody was made to queue up in the Skyport itself—maybe to enhance the illusion of a bustling transit center—and there had to be at least a thousand people milling around. That didn't seem to deter this guy, though: he broke away from the woman and headed toward Afterburn, trotting along the ride's entrance line, oblivious to the looks he was getting.

Poole looked at the man more carefully, trying to type him. He didn't seem to fit any obvious profiles: dark hair, light complexion, tall, medium build, early forties. No red flags, other than the obvious agitation. Odd, though: this was the second time today he'd gone through this exercise. Dismissing this from his mind, Poole turned his attention back to his own queue.

There were no more than four, maybe five groups waiting ahead of them now, and even his cousin's kids had shut up in anticipation. They'd definitely come at the right time—the lines behind them were at least twice as long as they'd been when he first arrived. If the brats rode all six rides here, he'd have at least two hours of blessed solitude in Sea of Tranquility: just him, Sam Adams, and the crossword of the *Las Vegas Journal-Review*. It would be . . .

His thoughts were interrupted by a series of faint shouts. He glanced back. It was that man again. He was standing at the head of the Afterburn queue, calling out what sounded like a name, looking directly at him. No, Poole realized instantly: not at him, but at somebody at the head of the line. Maybe it was that girl, the pretty one, who was just being shown through the air lock into the ride. Now the man was racing across the Skyport toward them, dodging guests as he approached. Instinctively, Poole let his arms drop loosely to his sides, placed his feet apart. But the man's eyes were fixed on the air lock. He raced up the line, elbowing his way past the guests ahead of Poole. He began speaking to one of the loading attendants, gesturing quickly, pointing toward the air lock. The other attendant, a tall figure in a quicksilver space suit, came over, placing his hand solicitously on the man's arm. The man shook it away.

"What do you suppose he wants?" Sonya asked.

Poole didn't answer. For the briefest of moments, he considered intervention. Then he relaxed. *Hell with it.* This was vacation. The man had paid his seventy-five bucks like everyone else; let him have his little scene.

2:26 P.M.

ANDREW WARNE PAUSED on the reflective pavers of the concourse, breathing hard, looking around. It was a useless effort, trying to find his daughter among the countless guests. The chances of something happening to her were minimal. And yet the thought of spending the time until their planned meeting, waiting, *not knowing,* seemed unthinkable. They had been searching the queues and souvenir emporiums for twenty minutes, hoping to catch a glimpse of Georgia's slim figure and chestnut-colored hair. So far, nothing. And it seemed that the more time that went by without finding her, the more anxious he became.

The look in Georgia's face, just before she had left Terri's lab, was burned into his memory. *I don't want to go by myself,* she'd said. She was all he had left. And he'd sent her out here, into a theme park mined with high explosive. It had been unwitting, it had been well intentioned, but he had done it just the same.

Terri trotted up beside him.

"Anything?" he asked.

She shook her head. "I checked the entrance and exit lines to Ecliptic and Atmosfear," she panted. "No sign of her."

"She could be anywhere."

"I think we've just about *searched* everywhere."

Impatience and frustration filled him. Could she have left Callisto already, gone to one of the other Worlds? They had reached the end of the concourse, and only the Skyport lay ahead.

He glanced at Terri. "Do you think I'm crazy?"

"I don't know. Maybe." She paused. "But if it was my kid, I'd be doing the same thing."

He gestured toward the Skyport. "What's in there?"

"Those are all thrill rides. She promised you she'd stay off those."

"We'd better check them out, anyway. You don't know Georgia."

"Sure thing. I'll take the rides on the far side of the departures board, meet you back here." And she took off.

Warne watched gratefully as she jogged away. Most people would have brushed off his distress, tried to talk him out of searching for Georgia. Not Terri. Perhaps she couldn't identify with a widowed father's concern for his only daughter. But she'd volunteered to help, searched as hard as he had.

Turning, he trotted into the Skyport, glancing over the queue line for Afterburn, the first ride he came to. As expected, nothing but the same curious or amused glances from the tourists he'd seen everywhere else. He turned away. There were two other rides on this side of the departures board. He'd try their lines next. Then he'd meet up with Terri, and . . .

Abruptly, he caught sight of Georgia.

Relief coursed through him. She was at the head of the line for—what was it?—Escape from Waterdark. *Thank God,* he thought as he shouted her name. If he'd looked over a moment later, she'd have already vanished through the embarkation portal . . .

And then, almost before he realized what was happening, one of the loading attendants helped Georgia through. As he watched, the pearlescent hatch slid closed behind her.

Relief fled instantly. Seeing her like this—*knowing* she was about to enter one of the rides—galvanized him.

He broke away from Afterburn and raced across the Skyport, heading directly for the portal. He elbowed his way toward the front of the line. A woman caught her breath in surprise, and he heard a man's voice behind him, calling out, "Hey, buddy, what the hell?"

As he ran up, the loading attendant was ushering a woman in a red dress and two children inside. Warne caught a brief glimpse of what lay beyond—some kind of heavy pressure hatch bearing a sign that read *Warning: Low-Gravity Area*—before the portal closed again.

He wheeled toward the attendant. "Stop it!" he cried.

The woman blinked at him through her helmet. "Excuse me?"

"I said, *stop* it! Stop the ride!"

The other dispatcher came toward them. "I'm sorry, sir," he said, placing a hand on Warne's arm, "everyone here's in a hurry to escape from the prison, and I'm afraid you'll have to wait your turn like—"

Warne yanked his arm away. "My daughter just went in there. I'm getting her out."

The second dispatcher—a tall, thin man—blinked back at him through his helmet. Warne knew he was mentally reviewing his *Guest Relations Handbook,* deciding which strategy to use with this difficult visitor.

"It's impossible for me to stop the attraction, sir," he said in a lower voice, dropping out of character. "I'm sure your daughter is having a wonderful time. Everybody loves Escape from Waterdark. If you'd like to wait for her, the best place is the debarkation area, over there." He pointed a silvery glove. "The attraction lasts only twelve minutes, she'll be out in no time. Now, if you'd kindly step away, we can continue accommodating other guests."

Warne stared at him a moment. *He's right,* he thought. *This isn't rational.*

Mutely, he stepped back.

"Thank you, sir," the attendant said. He turned to the group at the front of the line, ushering them forward: an overweight couple with a single child. The father glared balefully at Warne.

The loading attendant turned to his console, pressed a button. The portal glided open with a hiss of escaping air.

Warne stared at the opening. Then, abruptly, he thrust his way past the attendant and darted through.

Inside, the airlock felt cool and dry. The bluish light was faint. He was surrounded by a low rumbling noise, like the murmur of giant turbines. An empty escape pod was waiting here, low and smoothly contoured, hovering at his feet without any obvious supports. It had windows of clear plastic, but no roof. Beyond it lay the far wall of the airlock. A ponderous circular door had been cut into it, secured by massive metal bolts, a single small window of thick glass in its center. Through the glass, Warne could see the woman with the two children, ascending inside their own pod. They were smiling. Faintly, he could hear a voice crackling over their pod's comm system: *Please remain as still and quiet as possible. The less you move, the less chance there is of alerting the Waterdark guards. Once we've cleared the prison, we'll begin to ascend toward the mothership. As gravity decreases, you'll begin to feel some effects of weightlessness. This is normal. Full gravity will be automatically restored as we dock with the mothership . . .*

With a muttered curse, he realized there was no way he could reach Georgia. Even if he somehow managed to commandeer this waiting pod, it wouldn't do him any good.

He whirled around, exiting the portal as quickly as he had entered it. There was a scattering of excited voices. The male attendant was speaking into a radio: "Tower, this is Load Two. We've got a Five One One, say again, a Five One One at the loading area."

Warne paid no attention. He ducked past them, left the platform, and headed in the direction the attendant had pointed to earlier. He threaded his way through the Skyport's milling crowds, heading for the small hologram that read *Mothership Debarkation, Exit Only*. Terri was nowhere to be seen.

The off-loading ramp was a spare, neutral corridor, carpeted gray-blue on walls, floor, and ceiling. He passed a small group of exiting riders, smiling and chattering, and followed the corridor as it curved gently up to a brushed-metal access port. The port whispered open to allow another group out onto the debarkation ramp, and he ducked inside.

This was the mothership: a large, low-ceilinged control room ablaze with blinking lights. Along the lower half of one wall ran a large, smoked-glass tube. Almost every other vertical space was arrayed with a riotous variety of futuristic-looking electronics.

With a sudden whoosh of air, a pod slid into view within the smoked-glass tube, coming to a stop at a short platform. Water ran down its windows and engine cowling. The lone attendant working unload approached it, lifting the visor of her helmet. "Welcome to the Callistan mothership," she said, unfastening an access panel in the side of the pod and swinging it open. "Congratulations on your escape from Waterdark."

"Cool ride!" said a youth of about twelve, scrambling out of the pod and staring around. His hands and arms were damp, and his eyes were shining. "Can we go again?"

"That low-gravity part was amazing," said the boy's father. "How did you do that?"

"There was nothing to do," the woman said, remaining steadfastly in character. "Weightlessness is part of space travel. But the mothership's docking at the Skyport now, and you'll find it maintains a gravity equal to 100 percent of Earth."

"I heard they licensed the technology from NASA," said the boy.

The unload operator turned to open the access port and usher the family out of the ride. As she did so, she caught sight of Warne.

"You can't enter this way, sir," she said.

"Where's the maintenance access?" he demanded.

The woman's eyes narrowed. "I don't understand," she said. But as she spoke, her eyes made a betraying shift toward the wall beyond Warne's shoulder.

Immediately, he turned, running across the control room in the direction of her glance. The wall was a solid mass of ersatz technology: telemetry machines, environmental controls, cryogenic monitors. He swept his hands over it all in frustration.

The unloader approached him. "Sir, I'm going to have to ask you to leave," she said.

As she spoke, Warne made out a faint rectangular outline among the instrumentation. He placed his hands along its edges and pushed. A door-sized bulkhead swung back, revealing a dark walkway beyond. He ducked inside, closing the door behind him and shutting out the protests of the operator.

Inside the bowels of the ride, it felt utterly different. The air was dense with humidity, and from above came the impatient drumming of rain. There was a catwalk here: the grating dripped water, and its railing was slippery to the touch. Warne glanced around in the darkness, trying to orient himself. As he looked upward, feeling beads of moisture gathering on his face, he could hear a cold little voice in the back of his head. *This isn't normal behavior, pal*, it said. *What exactly can you do, anyway? Why don't you just go wait outside? She'll be out in a couple of minutes.*

But it didn't matter: rational or irrational, he wanted to be with his daughter, *right* now. Just in case. He pushed the voice aside.

He kept to the primary catwalk, which ascended in a broad spiral. To his right, along the inner edge of the spiral, the catwalk hugged an endless wall of black glass. To his left were banks of computers, heavy hydraulics, a complex network of pipes that rose from below and disappeared overhead in the darkness.

He continued to climb, growing more and more confused. Where were the pods? They were supposed to *rise* through space toward the mothership—right? And yet the mothership was at the *bottom:* the ridepath seemed to come in from above. It didn't make any sense, the architecture was all wrong. Was it possible he'd become disoriented and was moving in the wrong direction? Whatever the case, in a few minutes Georgia would be exiting the ride—and he'd still be climbing around futilely in here. The little voice came back again, louder this time. Maybe he should go back out, wait for Georgia to emerge, find Terri, explain his way out of this. He slowed to a walk, then stopped, hands on the slick railing, in an agony of indecision.

Then he noticed, a few steps up the catwalk, what looked like a break in the black wall: a low, narrow archway, etched in the faintest yellow glow. As he stared, he noticed small ribbons of water drizzling in. He approached the open arch, curious, and crouched to peer through.

With a roar and a howl, something dropped out of the darkness to hover six feet in front of him.

Warne fell back onto the catwalk, crying out in surprise. He barely had time to register what it was he was seeing—a pod, full of laughing, smiling faces—before it lurched downward again, out of sight.

He picked himself up off the catwalk and crouched cautiously in the opening. Ahead of him, framed by the surrounding wall of glass, lay a field of stars. On the far side of the archway was a narrow platform, maybe two feet on a side. It was painted black and almost invisible against the swiftly moving starfield. It was surrounded by a railing, also black.

Warne waited a moment. Then, taking a deep breath, he ducked through the opening and stepped out onto the platform.

It was like walking out into the vastness of space. He was surrounded by stars, infinite and infinitely far away, all racing hell-bent for the vortex beneath his feet. For a moment, the illusion was so overpowering that he closed his eyes and swayed slightly, grasping for the railing. Dimly, he was aware that water was soaking through his clothes. He waited, breathing slowly, fighting vertigo, focusing on the reassuring solidity of the railing. He waited another moment, then opened his eyes again, squinting against the rain.

Gradually, he began to understand what he was looking at. He was standing atop a platform on the inside edge of a huge, hollow cylinder. Its curved surface was some sort of one-way mirror, onto which the countless hurtling stars were reflected and re-reflected, giving an alarmingly realistic sense of depth.

There was a rumble above him, which turned quickly into a roar. Glancing upward, he saw another pod descending toward him at a sharp angle, wheeling through the rain. It seemed to be heading straight for him, and he shrank back toward the low archway. But then the pod curved and slowed, stopping beside the platform. The roar subsided to a whine as, against all reason, the direction of the rain seemed to alter subtly. The motion of the stars on the surrounding walls slowly ceased, until they hung motionless in the void. Inside the pod, he could see a family of five, all wearing the same dazed, happy expressions he'd seen in the previous car. They were clutching their lap and shoulder belts as if to keep themselves from floating out of their seats. *Attention, please,* came a voice over the pod's comm unit. *We've been given clearance to approach the mothership. Initiating docking sequence now.*

One of the children, looking around, caught sight of Warne. For a moment, she simply stared, as if disbelieving her eyes. Then she jabbed her mother and pointed toward him.

The woman looked over, not seeing him at first. Then her eyes seemed to focus and her expression changed from wonder to consternation. At that moment, the roar returned and the pod dropped away from the platform, en route to its final destination.

Warne watched it drop out of sight as once again the stars went into motion around him. Like everything else about the ride, the platform had clearly been designed to enhance illusion and disguise reality. No doubt any spotter in position here would be dressed in black, invisible from the perspective of the riders inside their pods.

He was beginning to fully comprehend the clever artifice that lay behind Escape from Waterdark. The ride was built inside this cylinder—cone, actually, wider at the top than at the bottom. Although the pods actually *descended* in a tightening spiral toward the mothership at the base, riders inside the pods would have the sensation of *rising* into space. Even at this extreme moment, he was struck by the almost brazen brilliance of the conception. In the ride, the pods were supposedly flying up from the castle to the orbiting ship. And yet the castle dungeon was the highest physical point of the ride: the mothership was at the bottom of the cone. Everything—the utter darkness of space, the computer-controlled motions of the pod, the wheeling of the stars, the direction of the wind-controlled pulses of rainwater—

was precisely calibrated, synchronized, to allow Utopia's designers to superimpose their own reality over the laws of physics. As
the pods revolved on their hidden spokes, the rate of descent increased, creating a false sense of low gravity. The angle of the
pod was constantly adjusted so the riders remained unaware they
were traveling in descending circles. And he himself was standing on a spotter's platform, used for covert observation of the
passengers, or perhaps in case of . . .

There was a whine overhead, the roar of another escape pod
descending into its holding position. As it came into view,
Warne's train of thought dissolved instantly. Inside sat Georgia,
mouth open, wide delighted eyes reflecting the stars.

Warne did not stop to think. As the pod hovered, he dashed
forward, reaching over the railing and fumbling with the access
handle. Georgia looked over as he climbed over the rail and half
jumped, half fell into the pod.

The look of wonder on her face changed quickly to alarm
and confusion. "Dad? What are you doing here? How did you
get here?"

"It's okay," he said, closing the access door and kneeling on
the floor of the pod, taking her hand. "It's okay."

"Gross," Georgia said. "You're all *wet*."

He sat a moment, embarrassment beginning to mingle with
the overwhelming relief. He felt water rolling off his nose and
ears, dripping onto the molded interior of the pod. Once they
reached the mothership, he'd explain everything. *Well, not quite
everything*, he thought as he waited for the pod to begin its final
descent.

"What's going on, Dad? Why—?"

And then Georgia looked away from him suddenly, her fine
features backlit by the starfield, dark brows knitting together.

Then Warne, too, heard the voices—distant at first, but coming closer.

"There he is. Platform 18."

"Waterdark tower, I need an E-stop. Repeat, emergency stop."

There was a clattering of feet, and then vague forms appeared
on the platform beside him. From inside the pod, it was difficult
to make them out against the illusion of space, but Warne
guessed they were security officers.

"Excuse me, sir," one of the men said, "but you'll need to
come with me."

"No," Warne said. "It's okay. Everything's okay now."

"Sir, please exit the pod and step onto the catwalk," the man said again, his voice a little harder this time.

Warne felt Georgia tighten her grip on his hand.

It was all so ridiculous. He was with Georgia, she was safe now. Everything would be all right if they'd just get the ride under way.

He turned to explain this to the men on the platform, but found he could not hear himself speak. In fact, he could not hear anything, except for a sudden harsh eruption of sound that seemed to come from everywhere.

There was a flicker of light overhead. He looked up just in time to see two huge spurts of orange-colored flame lick down toward him. For a moment, in the blinding illumination, he glimpsed the secret architecture of the ride—the expanding cone of glass, the central hub with its umbrella-like supporting spokes—before the glare, magnified off the infinite mirror, overloaded his vision. He jerked his head away, closing his eyes. There were shouts of alarm and surprise from the platform. The pod gave a sudden lurch to one side. The terrible noise faded, replaced by the crash and shriek of rending metal.

"Daddy!" Georgia cried.

Warne turned toward her.

Then—with a sudden, convulsive instinct—he leaned forward, shielding the girl with his body as the pod gave another sickening wrench and enfolding darkness abruptly claimed them.

2:40 P.M.

UTOPIA'S CENTRAL MEDICAL Facility was located on A Level, directly beneath the Nexus. It had been designed so that, in case of calamity or natural disaster, it could be reached from any area of the Park, public or private, in a minimum amount of time. And it had been diligently stocked with enough emergency equipment to make a world-class trauma center envious: respirators, ventilators, defibrillators, intubators, monitoring systems, crash carts. Most of this high-ticket equipment stood silent and unused within darkened bays and storage areas, lifesaving objets d'art that, in a nonsterile environment, would have been collecting dust. In the hectic seas of Utopia, Medical had always remained an archipelago of calm: soft-voiced nurses tending the occasional scraped knee or sprained ankle, orderlies stocking supplies, technicians running obligatory diagnostics on machines that rarely saw use.

But now, Medical had been transformed into a frantic triage operation. Cries of pain mixed discordantly with calls for plasma. Paramedics darted from room to room. Orderlies who would normally be doing drug inventories were shuttling equipment between operating theaters. Guests clustered in waiting rooms, huddled around sobbing figures or sprawled in chairs, looking vacantly at the ceiling.

Warne pulled the light blue curtains around the recovery bay, shutting out the noise as best he could. His left shoulder throbbed as he dragged the rings along the overhead rail. As he turned back toward the bed, he caught sight of himself in the mirror above the small basin: face drawn, eyes deep-set. A gauze bandage on his temple, dark with drying blood, made him look like a brigand.

Georgia lay in the bed, her breathing slow and regular, eyes motionless beneath parchment lids. Her music player was grasped in one hand. His arm still ached where that hand had held him. She had not released her grip, not ever; not when the rescue team brought them down from the crippled ride on a backboard, not when the electric cart had sped them through the backstage corridors toward Medical.

Now her eyes fluttered open, looked up at him.

"How do you feel?" he asked gently.

"Sleepy."

"That's the Demerol. The shot the doctor gave you. You'll rest for a while now."

"Mmm." The eyes slid shut again. He looked at her, at the ugly bruise coming up on one cheekbone. He reached forward, stroked her hair.

"Thanks for coming to get me. Back there, I mean."

"Sleep well, Georgia," he replied.

She shifted slightly beneath the covers. "You didn't call me princess," she murmured.

"I thought you didn't like being called princess."

"I don't. But say it, anyway. Just this once."

He leaned forward, kissed her bruised cheek. "I love you, princess," he whispered.

But she was already asleep.

He stood for a moment, watching the rise and fall of her chest under the thin hospital blanket. Then he smoothed the corners of the blanket beneath her chin, eased the music player from her hand, plucked her small backpack from a nearby chair, unzipped it. As he stuffed the player inside, something fell to the floor. Placing the backpack on the chair once again, he knelt down, picked the object up. Then he stopped dead as recognition burned its way through him.

It was a bracelet, made of a simple chain of silver. Dangling from its loops were half a dozen sailboats: yawls, ketches, trim sloops. He turned it between his fingers, feeling tears well up in his eyes. His wife had given this charm bracelet to Georgia for her seventh birthday. Whenever she had finished a new boat design, she'd given Georgia a replica to add to the bracelet. He'd forgotten about it, had no idea his daughter had been carrying it around with her all this time.

His fingers found the graceful lines of *Bright Future,* the last boat his wife had designed. The boat she'd drowned in, that day off the Virginia coast.

"Charlotte," he said under his breath.

There was a subdued rustling noise, then a man's face appeared at the edge of the curtain: middle-aged, balding, small mustache over an even smaller mouth. Catching sight of Warne, he stepped into the bay, another man following behind. They did not wear the usual white blazers of Utopia crew: instead, they wore dark, understated suits.

"Dr. Warne?" asked the first man, consulting a metal clipboard.

Warne rose, turning away a moment to wipe his eyes. He nodded at them.

"I'm sorry to disturb you," the man with the mustache said. "My name's Feldman, and this is Whitmore. I wonder if we could ask you a few questions."

"And perhaps answer a few of yours, too," the man named Whitmore said. He was tall, with a high, reedy voice, and his eyes blinked rapidly as he spoke.

Before Warne could answer, the curtain parted again and Sarah Boatwright entered briskly, Wingnut whirring along in her wake.

Sarah's eyes landed first on Warne, then on the men in suits. "Don't bother him," she said.

The two men nodded at Boatwright and quickly left the recovery bay.

"Who were they?" Warne asked without much curiosity.

"Feldman, Legal. Whitmore, Guest Relations."

Warne watched as an invisible hand pulled the curtain shut from outside. "Damage control," he said.

"Keeping the incident contained."

Warne nodded. "How much do they know?"

"They know what they've been told. That it was a minor mechanical glitch." She came closer. "How are you feeling?"

"Like I had a close encounter with a Peterbilt. What happened in there?"

"I was going to ask you the same question."

"I don't know." Warne took a deep breath, remembering. "There was this explosion, a flash of light. The whole ride was bucking and shuddering. I thought it was going to come crashing down on us." He stopped. "I shut my eyes, held Georgia close. That's all I remember until your emergency teams arrived." He looked back at her inquiringly.

"I won't lie to you, Andrew. It was a near thing. Some kind of explosive was attached to the ride's central shaft. That shaft is critical to the structural integrity of the entire ride. If it had snapped, the pods would have all broken free and plummeted to the ground. But they miscalculated when they set the device. A retaining spar held, kept the shaft from collapsing. It allowed us to evacuate the guests."

Miscalculated. For the briefest of moments, Warne felt something almost like relief. Whoever they were, these bad guys weren't invincible, after all. If they screwed up once, they might screw up again.

Sarah nodded toward the bed. "How's Georgia?"

"A little banged up. The doctor says she'll be fine. She's a brave girl."

Sarah stared down at the sleeping form for a moment. Then she stretched out a hand, touched Georgia's forehead.

Warne followed her with his eyes, really looking at Sarah for the first time since she'd entered the bay. There was an expression on the proud face that he didn't remember ever seeing: a look of pain, almost of vulnerability. He thought back to their last conversation, in her office. He realized, quite abruptly, that she had never asked for his help before. *This Park means everything to her,* he thought, watching her. *Just like Georgia means everything to me.*

A spasm of anger cut through him: anger at those who had done this, hurt the people he cared about.

"What can I do?" he asked.

Sarah looked up.

"In your office, you asked for help. I'd like to help you, if I can."

She hesitated, her eyes returning to Georgia. "Are you sure?"

Warne nodded.

After a moment, she let her hand slip from the girl's forehead. "We've been warned not to alert the police. We don't know what's been touched, and what hasn't. We know there's at least one rotten apple inside the Park, but we don't know who. All we know is that the Metanet was used to hack the operating code for some of the bots."

"You can't evacuate?"

"They've rigged the monorail with explosive charges. We've been told they're watching the emergency exits, as well."

"Do you know why they set off that explosive charge in Waterdark?"

The pain grew stronger in Sarah's face. "We—I— underestimated these people. We arranged to give them the Crucible technology. But we were planning to put a tail on John Doe, the leader, when he picked up the disc. He found out." She fished her hand into a pocket, pulled out a plastic bag containing half a dozen silver shards. She put it on the edge of the bed with a bitter smile. "A security guard was killed in the struggle, and that's all that remains of the Crucible disc. Waterdark was our punishment. Now I'm waiting for them to contact me again, arrange the delivery of a second disc."

She met his gaze, held it.

"So what can I do?" Warne said after a moment.

"If you can use the Metanet to narrow down which bots have been affected, and how . . . Anything, any scrap, would be useful. If we know what they've done, maybe we can figure out their next move. Prepare ourselves."

She looked down. "Let's hope to God it doesn't come to that."

There was a brief silence.

"I'll do what I can. As long as—" He gestured toward the bed.

"I'll personally make sure that Georgia's looked after. We've had security teams sweep a few select areas—Medical, the VIP suites—for any signs of tampering. She's safer here than anywhere else in the Park." She lowered her voice. "There's something else you need to know."

"What's that?"

"Teresa Bonifacio is on the short-list of possible suspects."

"Terri?" Warne said incredulously.

"I don't believe it, either. But there are only a handful of people with the skills and the necessary access to pull this off. She's one of them. Keep that in mind. And another thing. You remember how, in my office, we traced Georgia from her imagetag? Well, I noticed somebody was tracing you, too."

"Me?" Warne felt surprise, followed by an uncomfortable trickle of fear. "Why?"

"No idea. But be careful. And maybe you'd better take off your tag. I'll have somebody drop it in a trash can on the far side of the Park."

Warne glanced down at his lapel, found it empty. "Gone. Lost it in the ride, I guess."

"Just as well. If any cast member stops you, show them your passcard, tell them to talk to me."

The curtain parted again, and a man in a white coat came in. "Ah, Sarah," he said. "They told me I'd find you here."

"Dr. Finch." She nodded. "What's our status?"

"A lot better than it could have been, thank heaven. It was a miracle, that retaining spar catching where it did. Kept the entire structure from collapsing. Otherwise, we'd be needing a fleet of coroner's vans. As it is, we've got some two dozen casualties, the worst being the boy with two broken legs."

Sarah's lips set in a tight line. "Keep me posted."

The doctor left, and Sarah turned back to Warne. "You left something in my office," she said. Taking one of his hands, she strapped the echolocator around his wrist. "Remember?"

Warne's skin tingled at the forgotten touch. "Is that why you brought him along?"

"He's *your* dog. Remember?"

Warne looked at the hulking, canine robot, which was looking back at him. His hand dropped unconsciously to the echolocator. The moment—with its shock, grief, anger—had taken on an almost surreal cast.

The curtain drew apart yet again. A short, heavily built man came in, nodding at Sarah. He carried himself with an air of self-assurance; his tanned face made his thin blond hair look almost gray. "Is this him?" he asked Sarah.

"No, this is Andrew Warne," she replied. "I think Poole's in the next bay, with Feldman and Whitmore."

The man scowled. "The guy's a damn hero. You shouldn't let him be pestered by PR flaks."

Warne turned to Sarah with a look of mute inquiry.

"This is our head of Security," Sarah explained. "He's here to thank a guest named Angus Poole. Seems Poole was on the ride a few pods behind Georgia. Risked his life to save the other passengers."

Allocco nodded, grunted, then parted the curtains and disappeared.

"I think I'll go pay my respects, too," Sarah said.

Warne turned back to the sleeping Georgia. As he bent forward to kiss her cheek, he noticed Sarah had left the bag of disc shards on the edge of the bed. He scooped it up with one hand,

and then—with a backward glance at his daughter—turned to follow Sarah and Allocco through the curtain.

A man sat on the bed in the next bay, worrying at a freshly dressed cut on his right wrist. He was clearly a guest: brown tweed cap, corduroy jacket, black turtleneck. Fortyish, muscular but not heavy. His lips seemed to be set in a fixed, distant smile. In fact, his entire face seemed immobile save for the alert, faded-denim eyes, which never fell still, shifting from object to object with implacable curiosity. Feldman and Whitmore were nowhere to be seen.

The blue eyes shifted to Warne, then widened slightly in surprise. "You!" the man said.

Sarah stepped forward. "Mr. Poole, my name is Sarah Boatwright. And this is Bob Allocco, head of Security here at Utopia."

"We wanted to thank you for your bravery, back on the ride," Allocco said with an approving nod. "Helping those people safely escape that broken pod took guts."

"Those people are relatives of mine," the man named Poole said. Though he spoke to Allocco, his eyes were still on Warne.

"We're terribly sorry this happened," Sarah said. "Utopia has the best safety record of any park, but I'm afraid even the most stringent checks can't guarantee against every mechanical—"

The man's alert eyes darted from Warne to her. "You're in charge?" he asked.

"I'm head of Operations, if that's what you mean. And I'd like to do something for you, compensate you in whatever small way I can, for what you did here."

The distant smile deepened slightly. "Actually, I thought I could do something for *you*."

Sarah frowned. "I don't quite understand."

The man looked at her in surprise. "Well, how many of them are there?"

"Them?" Sarah echoed.

"The bad guys. What kind of a force are we talking about? Tactical? Rogue cell?"

Warne watched as Sarah Boatwright and Allocco exchanged glances.

"Sir," Allocco said, "I think maybe you should rejoin your family—"

Sarah motioned him to be silent. "I'm sorry, we're just a little confused."

"By what?"

"By what you're saying. There's just been a serious accident, and—"

The man named Poole laughed: a short bark almost like a cough.

"It's serious, all right," he said. "But it's no accident."

When nobody spoke, he continued. "I can't believe you turned on all those lights," he said, baritone voice almost mournful. "Escape from Waterdark was my favorite ride. But now I know how it's done. You ruined it for me."

Once again, Warne saw Allocco and Sarah exchange glances. But they remained silent.

"I was up at the start of the ride when the thing went off. After I got my relatives out, I spent quite some time up there, waiting. And then, later on, they lowered me past that ruined spar. By then all the lights had come on, and I got a real good look. Quite a blast signature. C-4, right? Three charges, placed laterally. What's known as a club sandwich. Remarkably precise work, really. And cleverly done, considering the working environment."

There was a silence in the recovery bay.

"Keep talking," Allocco said.

"Do I need to? Unless you guys are in the habit of using high explosives for your special effects, I'd say you've got some party-crashers on your hands. Or else one seriously pissed-off guest." Poole waved his hand toward the curtain. "But where's law enforcement? Why isn't the crime scene being stabilized? Instead, there are all these suits rushing around, apologizing for the accident. The *accident*. Smells like a cover-up to me. Someone's scaring you, bad. And I think I know who he is."

"You do," said Sarah.

Poole nodded. "Early this morning, in the Nexus, I saw this fellow talking to himself. That's what caught my attention first: it was like he was reciting poetry or something. He had a South African accent, that was the second thing. And the cut of his suit—no tourist wears a five-thousand-dollar Italian suit to an amusement park. But what really struck me was the way he was looking around. I recognized that look. As if he was casing the joint. Or, actually, as if he *already* owned it. As if there were no surprises left."

Poole shook his head, chuckled. "But it's my day off, so I forgot about it. Until, sitting in that broken pod, I started to put two and two together."

"Are you a cop?" Sarah asked.

The man laughed again. "Not exactly."

"What, exactly?"

"Armed guard. Personal protection services. That sort of thing."

Allocco rolled his eyes. "And here I thought you were Sherlock Holmes." His tone had changed significantly in the last minute or two.

There was another silence, longer this time.

At last, Sarah drew a deep breath. "You said you could do something for us, Mr. Poole. What, exactly, did you have in mind?"

"I don't know. What do you need?"

Allocco broke in abruptly. "That's enough," he said. "Mr. Poole, would you excuse us for a moment, please?"

"Certainly."

Warne followed Sarah and Allocco back into Georgia's bay.

"What the hell are you doing?" Allocco said, rounding on Sarah. "He's just some kind of guard for hire. And we've got work to do."

"That's the problem," Sarah whispered back. "What *kind* of work, exactly? Anything pan out on Barksdale's list of internal suspects yet?"

"Nothing suspicious. The tech named Tibbald logged out at a security checkpoint early this morning and hasn't returned, so we haven't been able to question him. And the video logs have checked out clean so far."

"See what I mean? We don't have anything to do but lick our wounds and wait for the phone to ring."

Allocco jerked a thumb over his shoulder, toward the curtain. "For all we know, he's one of them."

"Come on, Bob. You know that's crazy. His relatives were on that ride; he risked his life to save them."

"So he's a guest. That's even worse. Do you know how this is going to look? What he's going to say?"

"What do you think he's going to say if we tell him to get lost? We need all the help we can get. You send your security specialists crawling over everything, it's going to look suspicious. But this guy—a tourist in khakis and a tweed cap? Probably not. He obviously knows what he's talking about. I'm inclined to bring him on board. And last time I checked, this wasn't a democracy."

Allocco looked at her in disbelief. He opened his mouth to protest. Then he shut it and gave his head a disgusted shake. "You're right, it's not. But I don't want anything to do with him. And keep him the hell away from my people."

"No promises." Sarah motioned them back into Poole's cubicle.

"You've got some relatives here, Mr. Poole?" she asked as they re-entered.

The man nodded. "My cousin's family. Good, solid Iowa stock."

"Are they all right? After the—the accident, I mean?"

"You kidding? The way your PR storm troopers have been passing out meal vouchers and casino chips around here like they were candy? They're already back in the fray."

"And you don't want to join them."

"It's like I told you. My favorite ride's just been ruined for me." Poole shook his head, the perpetual smile drooping a little mournfully. "Couldn't enjoy a Sam Adams now."

This was greeted by another silence.

"You mentioned personal protection. You mean, like a bodyguard?"

"That's not the term we prefer. It's on a case-by-case basis. Business executives, foreign dignitaries, VIPs. That sort of thing."

"Okay." Warne watched Sarah wave in his direction. "Mr. Poole, meet Andrew Warne."

Poole nodded at him. "I saw you in the Skyport. I thought you were just another guest. Getting some jogging in, as I remember." He peered more closely at Warne. "Feeling okay, pal?"

"Well, he's not just another guest. Think of him as your VIP."

The man considered this. Then he nodded.

"And Mr. Poole?" Sarah said.

Poole rolled his faded blue eyes toward her.

"Keep him alive for the rest of the day, and maybe you'll get your lifetime pass."

Poole smiled.

2:40 P.M.

NORMAN PEPPER SAT on a wide leather couch in the External Specialists' Lounge on B Level, sipping a glass of soda and reading the National Edition of the *New York Times*. He'd just spent a delightful half hour with the A section, and he intended to spend an equally delightful half hour finishing up the rest.

The day had gone even better than he'd hoped. The Utopia personnel all seemed intelligent, businesslike, eager to help. His proposal for the orchid beds in the Atlantis athenaeum had been accepted without question. In fact, they'd given him an even bigger budget than he'd requested. And Atlantis itself was remarkable. When it opened, he was sure it would become the biggest draw of all the Worlds. Calling it a water park didn't do it justice. It was almost like an inland sea, or something, with those special boats that propelled you between the individual rides and the half-sunken city. But the best touch was the actual entrance to the World. Even in an unfinished state it was outstanding, out-*standing,* undoubtedly the cleverest portal in Utopia. And he, Norman Pepper, had seen it before anybody. Wait until his kids heard about this—they'd die. He felt a secret smugness, as if he'd been made privy to state secrets. He chuckled softly to himself.

And this lounge was just the icing on the cake. Free food and drink, videos of all the Nightingale shows, showers, pool tables, a small library, private "breakout" rooms with televisions and phones. Best of all, nobody seemed to use it. The place was dead. It was probably the name, Pepper guessed. "External Specialists' Lounge" conjured up bus-station images: plastic chairs, year-old magazines, instant coffee in Styrofoam cups. Nothing could be further from the truth, but what else could explain why it was so deserted? There was only one other person in the lounge, and he'd just come in about five minutes ago. Maybe the other visiting specialists were all out, taking in the Park. But

Pepper didn't want to rush that. He was scheduled to visit Gaslight at six, to check on the problems with the night-bloomers. Tomorrow, more meetings, finalizing the design and installation schedule. And then on Wednesday, he'd do the Park. He'd do it right: nine to nine, soup to nuts, Camelot to Callisto. He sighed with satisfaction and laid the paper aside to fill his glass with the dregs from his Dr Pepper can.

Ever since childhood, Pepper had been teased about his choice of soft drink. He couldn't help it; he just had a weakness for the stuff. No amount of teasing had ever changed his mind. Nowadays, he liked to tell people that the Doctor had been his great-great-grandfather. Just a joke, of course. But, my, the mileage he got out of it. He took a huge swallow and picked up the paper again, keeping the glass in his right hand as he did so. Now, *this* was living.

As he turned over the pages, he got a glimpse of the lounge's other occupant. The guy was dressed in an outlandish getup: Inverness cape, tight wool suit with skinny lapels and lots of buttons. One hand held a tall silk hat, the other the brass head of a long walking stick. The man had been wandering the lounge, peering in here, glancing around there. Now he approached Pepper.

"Very quiet," the man observed.

"Like the grave. You're the only one I've seen come in."

The man nodded at this. "Been here a while, then?"

"Sure have," Pepper said. *And what of it*? he thought to himself. He didn't like the man's tone. After all, he was an external specialist, right? He had every right to be here. Which was more than he could say for this guy. In that getup, obviously a cast member. What was he doing in the lounge? Snagging the free food, probably.

Now the man was scanning the ceiling with his eyes. They were almond eyes, set into a wide, almost heart-shaped face.

With a careful, almost delicate motion, the man placed his hat on a nearby table, then turned deliberately toward Pepper. He was holding the polished wooden stick in his right hand now, tapping its oversize brass head into his palm. Pepper watched the sharp bright ferrule winking in the fluorescent light. He lowered the newspaper.

"You're a difficult man to track down, Mr. Warne," the man said as he walked toward Pepper. Only for some reason he didn't stop in time. He kept right on walking until his shins pressed against Pepper's knees.

Pepper had become so lulled by the tranquil, friendly atmosphere of Utopia that, for a moment, he felt merely curious. Then reality set in, and he shrank back into the leather folds of the couch. His fingers went slack and the glass dropped, ice cubes and soda spreading across the newsprint. What was this about? The man was violating his personal space. More than that: his voice—what was that accent? French? Israeli?—was clearly menacing. Pepper had become so alarmed, so quickly, that it took a moment for the man's last words to sink in.

"Warne?" Pepper babbled. He felt the cold soda crawling in around the seat of his pants, soaking the small of his back. "I'm not Warne. That's not my name."

The man took a step back. He lowered the heavy cane to one side, waiting.

"Oh, no?"

"No. But wait, wait! I remember now. Warne, sure. He was the guy on the monorail with me this morning. I'm not Warne. I'm Pepper. Norman Pepper."

The man's eyes swiveled from Pepper's face to the soda can.

"Of course you are," he said with a smile. Then he came even closer.

2:55 P.M.

FROM HIS UNCOMFORTABLE perch at Terri Bonifacio's console, Warne watched the man named Poole unlock the laboratory door, open it cautiously, peer out into the corridor, then close and lock it again. In his tweed cap, corduroy jacket, and turtleneck, he looked like a tourist playing at secret agent. It was not a reassuring image.

"You know, I get nervous just watching you," Warne said.

Poole glanced over and showed his teeth, startlingly white against the tan. "Good," he replied. "Nervous is good. Keeps your pecker at the ready." He eased away from the door, then began a slow turn around the office, glancing at the walls and ceiling tiles. Circuit complete, he came over to stand behind Warne, arms folded.

Warne shook his head. Having a bodyguard seemed ludicrous. Okay: so perhaps the bad guys, whoever they were, had learned of his presence. But could they really consider him much of a threat? Surely, they'd be more worried about security. And who was this Poole, exactly? His own feeling of unreality seemed to increase. There had just been too many surprises, too many traumas, over the last few hours.

"Shouldn't you be standing over there, between me and the door?" Warne asked. "I mean, so you can take the bullet for me, and everything?"

"I'd just as soon not take a bullet on my day off. Just do whatever it is you have to do."

Warne glanced a moment longer at the impassive face, then sighed heavily. "Do what I have to do," he said, turning to Terri, seated next to him. "Where to begin?"

Terri was silent. She had eventually found him in Medical, as he'd been preparing to leave, Poole in tow. When Warne explained what had happened in Waterdark—as well as what Sarah had told him was going on in the Park—she'd paled visibly. But now, as she returned his gaze, her dark Asian eyes were clear and steady. "If you've told me everything, it sounds like Sarah gave you two jobs," she said after a moment. "Figure out which bots have been affected. Then learn who's responsible."

"Two jobs." Warne rocked back and forth, staring at the terminal screen. "And I think they're connected."

"Yeah? How so?"

"Every thief—hacker, in this case—leaves a trail. If we can learn how the bots were hacked, maybe we can use that to trace our way back to whoever did this."

"Then shouldn't we talk to Barksdale? I mean, it's his department that's being messed with. If anybody has the tools, he would."

"The bad guys know that, too. They would have taken precautions." Warne paused. "The problem is, this is all speculation. We don't have enough information."

"So take the head shot," Poole interjected once again.

Warne looked at him in silent query.

"Take the head shot," Poole repeated, as if it were obvious. "First thing our CO taught us. You're in a combat situation, you've got your choice of targets. Which one do you shoot?"

Nobody answered.

"The one who offers a clean head shot," Poole answered his own question.

"Your CO," Warne echoed. "So you were in the armed forces?"

"Sure, we were armed."

Warne looked back at Terri. "If we strip away the homicidal veneer, I think he's suggesting we do the most obvious thing first."

"Find the affected code."

"Yeah. If we can pinpoint how the Metanet's been altered, maybe we can reverse the procedure, pinpoint the affected bots."

"That means putting on our detective's hats."

Warne nodded, sighed.

"Detective?" Poole echoed.

Warne's left shoulder throbbed, and this time he didn't bother to look back. Now, here was a bodyguard who took an unusual interest in his client's doings.

"We dig through the system," he replied. "Look for crumbs the bad guys left behind."

Terri jerked one thumb toward the metal cart that contained pieces from the misbehaving robots. "We could start with those," she said. "Run a diagnostic, get a dump of their most recent operations."

"We could." Warne shifted in his chair, looked at the jumble of wires and chips that made up the brain of what, until a few hours ago, had been Callisto's premier ice cream vendor. "You know, I've been thinking about Hard Place."

"What about him?"

"It just seems strange. Obviously, he was reprogrammed to go nuts, wreak havoc. But why did he go off *when* he did? It seems premature to me. I mean, this John Doe hadn't yet made his play."

Terri thought a moment. "Did you notice anything unusual right before it happened?"

Warne shook his head. "Hard Place was acting just like he had in all the trials. He made a root beer float for Georgia. Then I gave him a special order that identified me as his creator."

"A special order?"

"Just a back door I built in. No big deal. A double pistachio chocolate sundae with whipped cream. When he hears that, a special process is activated. He calls me Kemo Sabe, makes the special order. But right after giving me the ice cream, he went nuts. Started breaking up the place. I managed to activate the kill switch before he did any real damage or hurt anyone. Except me." He rubbed his wrist ruefully.

"Hmmm. A back door." Terri glanced at him. "You can bet whoever altered his code didn't know about that. Even *I* didn't know. Did you consider that, by activating your back door code, you might also have activated the rogue instruction set? Set him off early, so to speak?"

Warne looked at her in surprise. "No, I didn't. And I'll bet that's what happened. That's brilliant thinking, Terri."

"Shucks. I'll bet you say that to all the girls." But she was unable to conceal the faint flush that rose in her cheeks.

"We can verify it later. But Hard Place and the others are still just individual bots. I think we'd do better to inspect the Metanet itself." Warne placed his hands back on the keyboard. "In the meeting this morning, Barksdale said the Utopia Intranet was a hardened system, entirely isolated from the outside world. Is that right?"

"Yes."

"So whatever tampering was done, was done from the inside. That means we can skip over external hacker steps like footprinting, enumeration. We can assume he's already done a privilege escalation. Right?"

Terri nodded again.

"So we can move right to the final steps any hacker would take. Do you archive directory listings?"

"Every week."

"Could you get me the last six months or so, please?"

"Sure thing." Terri slid off her chair and headed toward a particularly high stack of papers on a nearby table.

Poole had taken several steps closer and was standing beside Warne, looking down at the screen. "What are you doing?" he asked.

"Taking the head shot," Warne replied.

Poole raised his bushy eyebrows.

Warne pointed at the Metanet terminal. "Somebody has compromised this computer. They've used it to send bogus programming to the Park's robots. But Utopia is a highly secure environment: a hacker, even somebody on the inside, couldn't just take a seat and start typing. They'd have to use a Trojan of some kind."

"Wise precaution these days. Ribbed, or regular?"

"Not that kind. I mean a Trojan *horse*. It's software that hides itself within another program, does its dirty work in secret." Warne shrugged. "Of course, that's just one scenario, but it's the most likely one. So we're going to look for any signs of tampering in recent months."

Terri returned, a sheaf of yellowing printouts in one hand. "I thought you'd want hard copy," she said. "Low-tech, but more reliable."

"Agreed." Warne typed a quick series of commands at the terminal, and a window opened, a detail listing scrolling within it. "Let's compare these old printouts to the current state of the Metanet. We'll start with the most recent and work back."

The two fell silent as they bent over the sheets. Poole watched for a moment, then did another circuit of the room. Wingnut, idling beside Warne, observed the man's movements closely, rolling back and forth on his oversize wheels. In the background, the ragged voice of Axl Rose struggled for supremacy over the frantic, soaring guitar lines of Slash.

"I don't suppose I could convince you to turn that off," Warne said, nodding at the CD player.

"Helps me think." Terri turned over a sheet. Then she giggled.

"What?"

"I was just thinking. A double pistachio chocolate sundae with whipped cream. Sounds absolutely hideous."

"That, coming from a woman who spreads brown shrimp paste on unripened fruit." He hesitated, then looked up from the printouts. "It's a funny thing."

"What is?"

"Here we've been talking to each other, every week, for just about a year. And all this time I thought, with a name like Bonifacio, that you were Italian."

"I see. You had fantasies of Sophia Loren, bending over the Metanet terminal in a low-cut blouse. Instead, you've got little old me, the friendly Pacific Islander. Disappointed?"

"No." Warne shook his head. "Not in the least."

Maybe it was something in the heartfelt tone of his voice. But the broad smile this comment elicited had none of the impish irony of Terri's usual grins.

"Sheesh," Poole said. He walked to the door and unlocked it. "I'm going to check the corridor," he said. "Don't let anybody in but me."

Warne watched as the door shut behind him. Terri locked the door, then returned to her chair. Their eyes met again.

"You think he's some kind of plant?" she asked, her smile fading.

"I don't know. Anything's possible. According to Sarah, you're a suspect, too."

"Figures." Terri rolled her eyes.

"But in my gut, I just can't see Poole as one of the bad guys."

"I know what you mean. Besides, what terrorist would dress like that?"

Warne returned to his printout. After a minute he sighed, let it fall to the desk.

"What is it?" Terri asked, putting her hand lightly on his shoulder.

"Have you ever worried about something you knew was

crazy, only to have it come true, after all? Like just now. I knew that searching for Georgia was nuts. The chances of anything happening to her were minuscule. But then *something did*. And now I can't shake this feeling of dread." He stopped. "Does that make sense?"

Terri looked at him, dark eyes holding his. Then she let her hand slip from his shoulder, dropped her gaze to the printouts. For a moment, she stared at them in silence.

"When I was growing up in the Philippines," she began, "my parents put me in a convent school. It was awful, like something out of *Oliver Twist*. I was the youngest, and the smallest, and I got picked on a lot. I don't like being bullied, so I always fought back. But it seemed like I was the one who always got punished. The nuns used paddles. Sometimes I couldn't sit down for hours." She shook her head at the memory. "I could deal with that, though. What I couldn't deal with was confession. I hated it. I hated that little, dark space. I was sure that one day I was going to get locked in, forgotten about. I don't know why it bothered me so much. I just knew if that ever happened, I'd die. It scared me so much that, one day, I refused to go. It was unheard of. As punishment, the mother superior locked me in a broom closet. A tiny room, with no lights."

Although Terri was still staring down at the printout, Warne could see she had gone rigid at the memory. "What happened?" he asked.

"I collapsed. I guess I fainted. I don't remember anything, don't even know how long I was there. I woke up in the convent infirmary." She shuddered. "I was only nine, but I was convinced I had died in that closet. The next day, I ran away. I've been claustrophobic ever since. Can't even go on the Park's dark rides."

At last, she looked up at him. "So I guess what I'm saying is, I *do* know how you feel. Even your craziest fears can come true sometimes."

The silence that followed was broken by Poole's whisper at the door. Terri rose, unlocked it. "Let's get back to it," she said as she returned.

It was a tedious business: pick a file on the screen, note its date and size, then compare the same file to the old hard-copy dumps, looking for any discrepancies, any change in file size or date accessed, that would signal external tampering. Warne finished one listing, then another and another. *It's like looking for a needle in a virtual haystack. I'll* . . .

Suddenly, he stopped. "That's odd," he said, pointing at a printout. "Take a look."

He was indicating a file named */bin/spool/upd_disply.exec.*

"I don't recognize it," Terri said. "What's it do?"

"Hmm. It's a routine to refresh the display before the morning downlink to the bots."

"Sounds pretty benign."

"You aren't thinking like a hacker. Are you going to hide your code in a file named *worm_infect_reformat,* or in something boring and insignificant?" He jabbed at the paper. "The important thing is that this is a maintenance file, part of the core routines. There's no reason for it to be altered. But look at the file size."

Terri looked closer. "Seventy-nine thousand bytes."

"But look at the same file as it exists now on the Metanet." He pointed toward the listing on the computer screen.

Terri whistled. "Two hundred and thirty-one thousand bytes."

But Warne was already flipping through the other printouts. "Look, the file size stays consistent all the way up to . . ." He turned over another page. "Up to a month ago."

They looked at each other.

"What?" Poole asked.

Quickly, Warne took the printout and ran his finger down the listing, comparing the files as they had existed a month before to the way they existed now, on the screen. Except for a smattering of temporary files, nothing else had changed.

"That's it," he murmured.

"Any chance we're wrong?"

"Nope."

"It's a binary file."

"Tell me about it."

Terri rolled her eyes.

"What?" Poole asked again.

Warne dropped the printouts, rubbed his face with his hands. "Somebody's modified one of our core routines. It's three times as big as it should be. It's been turned into a 'rogue executable.' Each time the Metanet runs, this file is doing things we don't know about. And if we're to have any hope of finding out what, we have to reverse-engineer it."

"Reverse what?"

"Disassemble. Take it apart at the machine-instruction level, try to figure out what it does. Not a fun thing to do."

"And it takes time," Terri added.

"But I'll bet *this* is what caused the bots to go native. If we can figure out what it does, maybe we can reverse the tampering it's done." Warne pushed away from the terminal. "Any reason not to proceed?"

"Only the obvious one," Poole said.

They both turned to look at him.

"Go on," Warne said. "Go on, drop the other shoe."

"The perpetrators said no interference, right? Well, this sure sounds like interference to me. They're not going to be too happy."

Warne held the man's placid gaze for a moment. Then he turned to Terri. She was looking back at him: a searching, inquiring look.

"Only if they find out about it," Warne said. "And they won't. Not unless they're even better coders than they are terrorists. Now, let's get to work."

And he turned back to the keyboard.

3:12 P.M.

ALMOST AS QUICKLY as it had filled with clamor, the Central Medical Facility fell silent once again. Except for a few small groups, huddled around curtained recovery bays, most of the guests had departed. While one or two had marched resolutely toward Debarkation, threatening legal action, a remarkable number had seized upon the free meal vouchers and casino chips and headed back into the Park.

Sarah Boatwright watched them leave with mixed feelings. Much as she hated lawsuits—an aversion shared by all Utopia cast and crew—she wished that more had decided to head for the monorail. Watching them all stream back up into the various Worlds was almost like watching wounded soldiers, wandering unwittingly back into battle.

She walked down the brightly lit central corridor of Recovery, nodding at various nurses as she passed. She stopped to confer with a security tech. And then she continued on, slipping at last between the curtains of Georgia Warne's bay. Dr. Finch had said the girl would be fine, but that the sedative would keep her asleep at least another hour.

Sarah settled into a seat by the foot of the bed, fixing her gaze on the still form beneath the covers. Georgia was sleeping naturally, hair spilled across her forehead, lips parted slightly, the ordeal she had gone through on the Waterdark ride consigned temporarily to oblivion.

Sarah sat, listening to the distant murmur of voices at the nurses' station. There were many things she could be doing: updating Chuck Emory in New York; touching base with the line managers, keeping up the pretense of business as usual. And yet, somehow, they seemed pointless. It was up to John Doe now. Everything was up to John Doe. She leaned back in the chair, willing her muscles to relax, feeling little surprise when they refused.

Her eyes turned back to Georgia, to the fresh bruise on her cheek, to the way the slender hands clutched the cotton blanket. Funny, that her own feet should have taken her back to the bedside of the first major failure in her life.

When she'd moved in with Andrew Warne, she had been determined to make Georgia like her, accept her. Sarah knew that any problem could be solved by a sufficient effort of will. And yet it seemed the harder she tried, the more Georgia resisted.

Of course, if she was honest with herself, she knew Georgia wasn't only to blame. It was true Sarah had appeared on the scene when Charlotte Warne's death was still fresh in the girl's mind, and Georgia had been very possessive of her father. But perhaps the girl had also sensed, with some childish instinct, that Sarah could never have been a full-time mother. Sarah herself now understood that such a commitment would have been impossible. Her career was simply too important. After all, hadn't she taken the Utopia job without a moment's hesitation? She could still remember the look on Andrew's face when she'd told him: he was so sure she'd be coming along to Chapel Hill, help him get his new technology venture off the ground. But the chance to run a place like Utopia was the dream of a lifetime. Nothing could have kept her from taking the job.

To run a place like Utopia . . .

She stirred restlessly in her chair. Order was critical to Sarah; she thrived on it. Utopia was the ultimate ordered system; a complex, perfectly knit closed system. And John Doe was the random element that had introduced disorder, even chaos.

She leaned forward, rested her chin on her hands. "What should I do, Georgia?" she asked. "For the first time, it seems I don't know what to do."

Her only reply was a stirring from the bed, a muttered sigh.

Suddenly, Sarah found herself wishing Fred Barksdale were there. Normally, she would have rejected such an emotion as being sentimental or weak. Not now. Freddy would know just the thing to say to help her through this.

When she first arrived at Utopia, romance was the furthest thing from her mind. And the last person she could ever imagine falling for was Fred Barksdale. She had always gone out with men like Warne: charismatic in an astringent sort of way, a little arrogant, unafraid to hang their brilliance out for all to see. Freddy was just the opposite. Oh, there was no denying *his* brilliance—the way he had taken on the incredible IT challenges of a place like Utopia, overseen the construction of its digital infrastructure, was a remarkable achievement. But he was just too perfect: his aristocratic British manners, his movie-star looks, his literary erudition, were almost a cliché of the ideal man.

But then, one evening two months ago, they'd met, accidentally, at a roulette table in the Gaslight casino. That had been shortly before the New York office decided management attendance at Utopia's gambling palaces should be discouraged. Barksdale had just lost a lot more money than he'd intended to, but had nevertheless charmed her with some bons mots from Falstaff on the evils of gambling. They'd ended up having a drink in nearby Moriarty's. The following week, dinner at the best French restaurant in Vegas. And Fred had been a revelation. He'd spent twenty minutes discussing the wine list with the sommelier. But it had not been mere posturing or affectation; he was genuinely interested, and clearly knew a lot more about the *châteaux* of Saint-Emilion than the wine steward did. He'd passed much of the meal answering Sarah's questions about Bordeaux, explaining *grands crus* and *appellations*.

Sarah was all too familiar with men who felt they needed to come on as strong as she was, act macho, posture like boardroom commandos. She hadn't realized how much she simply wanted to be treated like a woman: to be taken to an elegant dinner, told she was pretty, admired for her mind, flirted with, schooled in the good life, maybe put on a pedestal now and then. Was it really only three weeks ago that she had awakened one sunny Saturday morning to realize her feelings for Fred Barksdale were much stronger than she'd ever expected?

She sighed, sat up in the chair. Utopia and Freddy were now the two most important things in her life. The *only* things, in fact. She had to protect them, at all costs.

Sarah stood up, walked to the head of the bed, composing herself. She should leave Medical briefly, show her face in a few choice spots. Then she'd locate Bob Allocco, talk damage control . . .

There was a low rapping on the wall outside the recovery bay. The curtain parted and Fred Barksdale's face appeared. His watery blue eyes traveled along the bed, then met hers.

"Sarah!" he said. Then—darting his eyes toward the sleeping form—he winced slightly and lowered his voice. "Hullo. They told me you might be here."

For a moment, Sarah found speech difficult. The surprise of his presence, after what had just passed through her mind, brought an unexpected swell of emotion. She stepped toward him.

"Fred," she said. "Oh, Freddy. I feel broken up inside."

He took her hands. "Why? What is it?"

"I've made terrible mistakes. I let my anger at John Doe cloud my judgment. Chris Green, what happened at Waterdark—it's my fault."

"How can you say that, Sarah? John Doe's the responsible party here. Blame him, not yourself. Besides, the plan was Allocco's. You just approved it."

"Which makes me responsible." She shook her head, refusing to be consoled. "Remember what you said outside Galactic Voyage? You said our plan was dangerous. Irresponsible. That our first responsibility was to our guests. In my rush to take on John Doe, I forgot that."

Barksdale said nothing.

"I keep thinking about the way he came into my office, talked to me the way he did. I can't explain it. It was as if he *knew* me, somehow; knew what I wanted to hear, knew what was important to me. *Me*, personally. I know it sounds odd, but he talked like all he wanted was the best for me—all the while slipping in the knife. And the oddest thing was, *I wanted to believe him*." She sighed. "Christ, who *is* this guy? And why did he pick us to torment?"

Barksdale did not answer. He looked stricken.

"Freddy?" She was shocked to see how deeply he felt her distress.

His pale eyes returned slowly to hers.

"Doesn't Shakespeare have something appropriate to say, right about now?" she asked, forcing a smile. "Something consoling, uplifting?"

For a moment longer, Barksdale remained silent. Then he roused himself. "Something from, say, *The Two Terrorists of Verona*?" He returned her smile, wanly. "I can't think of anything suitable, actually. Save perhaps a title: *All's Well That Ends Well*."

He seemed to be in the grip of some profound inner turmoil.

"Sarah," he added suddenly. "What if we were to get away from here? Just leave this all behind?"

She looked back at him. "We will. When this is all over, you and I, we'll go away. Someplace where there aren't any telephones, where nobody wears shoes. We'll pick a small spot of beach and claim it for our own. A week, maybe two. Okay?"

"No," he began. "That's not what I meant. I—" Then he stopped. "Do you mean it, Sarah?"

"Of course."

"No matter what happens?"

Seeing his distress somehow restored her own strength. "Nothing's going to happen. We'll make it through this. I promise."

"I bloody hell hope you're right," he said in a voice so low she barely heard.

The moment passed. Her eyes dropped to the bed.

"Warne's daughter, right?" Barksdale said, following her gaze. "How is she?"

"Bruised, but otherwise fine."

He nodded. Now she freed one of her hands, stroked his face, leaned forward to kiss him.

"One way or the other," she said, "this will all be over soon. You'd better get ready."

"Of course," he said. He held her gaze a moment, then turned toward the curtain.

"Remember my promise."

He hesitated. Then he nodded without turning and slipped out of the bay.

She listened as his footsteps faded into the background hum. Then she straightened the covers around Georgia, caressed the girl's forehead, and turned to leave herself. As she did, the curtain parted and a nurse stuck in her head.

"Ms. Boatwright," she said. "Mr. Allocco is on the phone at the admitting desk. He says it's important."

"Very well." But as she began to follow the nurse, the radio in her pocket buzzed softly.

She stopped immediately, still inside the recovery bay. Then she reached for the radio, snapped it on.

"Sarah Boatwright."

"Sarah." John Doe's voice was slow, almost honeyed, affable once again.

"Yes."

"I hope you didn't find the lesson too painful."

"Some would disagree."

"It was actually intended to be much harsher than it was. Consider it a lucky break—in a manner of speaking." A dry laugh. "However, there will be no such luck next time."

Sarah remained silent.

"I don't mean that as a threat. I just want you to be fully aware of the consequences of any more irresponsible actions."

Still Sarah remained quiet, listening.

"You wouldn't care to atone for your betrayal, would you?" John Doe asked mildly.

"What do you mean?"

"To make up for all the trouble your little welcoming committee caused. It would go a long way toward mending fences between us. You wouldn't, say, like to give me Andrew Warne? He's proven very elusive."

Sarah's grip tightened on the radio, but she did not reply.

"I didn't think so. You're a charming woman, Sarah Boatwright, but I weary of this dance. You will be given one more chance to turn over the Crucible."

"Go on."

"The handoff will take place in the Holo Mirrors, at precisely four o'clock."

She looked at her watch: 3:15.

"You will see to it that the place is emptied of all guests, cast, and crew members beginning at ten minutes to four. Are you with me so far?"

"I am."

"And Sarah? I've been thinking. That nasty bit of business in Galactic Voyage was your own idea, wasn't it?"

Sarah did not reply.

"So this time, you'll deliver the disc personally. It seems the most prudent course of action. Given the rapport between us, I mean."

Silence.

"You understand, Sarah?"

"I understand."

"Enter the Hall as a guest normally would. I'll be waiting inside. Just yourself, now. I'm sure I don't need to warn you about any more unwanted visitors."

Sarah waited, the hard unfamiliar line of the radio against her cheek.

"I don't need to warn you, do I?"

"No."

"I knew I wouldn't. But let me leave you with this parting thought. In *The Soul of Man Under Socialism,* Oscar Wilde said any work of art created in hope of profit is unhealthy. In part, I disagree. You see, I've made Utopia my work of art. It is my intention to profit, and profit handsomely. But it *will* be unhealthy for any who stand in my way. Sometimes art can be terrible in its beauty, Sarah. Please remember that."

Sarah forced herself to take a breath.

"I look forward to seeing you again."

3:15 P.M.

AS THE AFTERNOON lengthened, and the unrelieved blue hanging over the Nevada desert began to pale with the promise of approaching evening, the estimated crowd of 66,000 strolling the boulevards of Utopia reached what Park psychologists termed the "mature" stage. The initial peak of excitement had crested. The pace slowed slightly as parents—feet a little sore and limbs a little weary—sought temporary refuge in restaurants, live performances, or shows like *The Enchanted Prince,* where they could relax in comfortable seats. A small percentage of visitors, unwilling to face the parking lot delays at closing, made an early start for the Nexus and the monorail, where they found a few more outgoing trains than usual. The vast majority, however, stayed on, preferring to return yet again to a beloved ride, or perhaps tour a World not yet visited, marking time until 8:30. That was when Utopia's biggest spectacle began: four simultaneous indoor fireworks displays, computer-synchronized and launched from spots within each of the Worlds, bursting with awe-inspiring brilliance beneath the dark canopy of the dome. This was followed by an even more massive outdoor display, rising high above the dome: a farewell gift to the guests as they left the Park and pointed their cars toward Vegas or Reno.

One place where the midafternoon slump was not apparent was in the queues outside Utopia's roller coasters and free-falls. At mainline attractions like the Linear Induction–powered Event Horizon and Dragonspire, thick crowds continued to mill, and the atmosphere of excitement and apprehensive glee was as heavily charged as ever.

This was especially true at the entrance to Boardwalk's most notorious ride, the Scream Machine. The Machine, as it was universally known, was a re-creation of the kind of roller coaster made famous on Coney Island in the 1920s. It looked like the consummate midway relic: a vast, sprawling forest of spars and timbers, carefully distressed by the Park's illusion engineers to a dangerously weathered appearance. Just the sight of its near-vertical drops and cruel corkscrew twists convinced many would-be riders to seek tamer diversions.

The Machine, like all roller coasters, was more about psychology than engineering. It was actually a tubular steel ride, cleverly disguised to look like a traditional wooden coaster. The metal construction allowed for sharper banks, tighter loops, and more "air time"—moments of negative gravity when riders were actually lifted out of their seats. The complex timbered shell, on the other hand, enhanced the "picket fence" effect of a wooden coaster: spars and beams, rushing past only a few feet from riders, made the fifty-mile-per-hour speed seem several times greater. And the ride's designers intentionally heightened the sense of menace by placing some very un-Utopia warnings about the dangerous effects of high-G turns at its entrance, installing a full-time nurse at the unloading ramp. Small wonder that "I Survived the Machine" T-shirts, available only in Boardwalk, were one of the Park's hottest-selling concession items.

Eric Nightingale had mandated that the Scream Machine boast the tallest first drop—290 feet—of any coaster west of the Mississippi. This proved a challenge: at such height, the monumental lift hill would have risen close enough to the dome to destroy the artificial perspective. Engineers solved this problem by constructing the ride so that the bottom of the first drop was below "street level." A portion of A and B Levels underneath Boardwalk was carved out and the double tracks of the Machine fitted into place. After climbing the initial hill, riders on the Scream Machine would plunge down a nearly vertical drop, its bottom section a tunnel of complete darkness. The track would then rise abruptly, bringing the riders—grimacing under a "pull-out" of 3 Gs—back into the light and up over Boardwalk again, never realizing that, for a few seconds, they had actually been traveling beneath the Park.

This solution, however, created a fresh problem. The roar of the cars, passing by at one-minute intervals, was so intense that no Utopia employee working in the Underground wanted to be anywhere near the areas of A and B Levels closest to the tracks.

Once again, engineers found a solution.

During the Park's construction, the underground levels were

awash in a sea of wires: the *Tour Guide's Manual* stated the backstage areas contained more wiring than two Pentagons or the town of Springfield, Illinois. Designers decided to use the no-man's-land around the dip in the tracks as a hub for Utopia's internal wiring. They encased the dip in two layers of sound-proof walls. Between these soundproof walls—in a narrow compartment forty feet high—lay Utopia's central nervous system. Endless rivers of cabling—coax, cat-5, light pipe, digital—climbed the walls, punctuated by fiber-optic couplings and electrical junctions. The entire Hub was autonomous, requiring no maintenance beyond monthly inspections. As a result, it was a "lights out" area, unoccupied save for a lone sanitation bot.

Today, however, the sanitation bot had company.

In one corner of the routing Hub, a man sat on a folding camp chair. He was dressed in the blue jumpsuit of a Utopia electrician, and his back rested against an oversize utility case, strapped to a red handcart. Within the open case sat a powerful minicomputer. Diagnostic lights on its front panel glowed like fiery pinpoints in the dim light of the Hub. A dozen cables of various thicknesses led from the computer to the nearby wall, where they were fixed by alligator clips and digital couplers to trunk lines and data conduits. A keyboard was on the man's lap, and two small flat-panel displays were propped on the floor in front of him. As he typed, his eyes darted from one screen to the other. Beneath the camp chair was a profusion of litter: crumpled napkins, stained with peanut butter and jelly; empty Slim Jim wrappers; a can of Cherry Coke, drained and dented.

Behind the man, the inner wall of the Hub began to vibrate slightly. A second later, a terrific roar came from beyond as the cars of the Scream Machine hurtled down, bottomed out in the lightless cube, then rose again up into the light and air of Boardwalk. The man paid no attention, typing on as the din receded, then vanished. The pair of military grade noise-suppressing headphones he wore canceled out any sound over fifty decibels.

Now the typing slowed, then ceased. The man pushed himself forward, massaged his lower back. Then he stretched out his legs, rubbing first the left, then the right, forcing the circulation to return. He had been sitting here—monitoring Utopia's video feeds, scrambling selected camera views, tapping Intranet bandwidth—since early morning. At last, his work was almost done.

He glanced up, rolling his head from side to side, working the kinks out of his neck. His eyes strayed to the two monitoring cameras, placed high on opposing walls. Even here, in the tenantless Hub, security was ever-present. But the man's glance was indifferent rather than anxious: he himself had put both cameras into looping routines, patched in from week-old video logs. To the surveillance specialists in the Hive, these cameras showed a space that was shadowy, utterly empty.

The man was young, no older than twenty-five. And yet, even in the dim light, the dark nicotine stains on his fingertips were clearly visible. Smoking would have meant instant detection, so the man chewed nicotine-laced gum instead, swapping pieces as a chain-smoker swaps cigarettes. Still massaging his neck, he fished a spent piece of gum from his mouth and stuck it to a nearby cable port. Several dozen wads had already been pressed into place beside it, hardening in the still air of the Hub.

Leaning back against the utility case, he picked up the keyboard and began to type once more, checking the state of the various secret processes he was running within the Utopia network. Then he stopped typing and frowned, staring at one of the screens.

Everything had gone as planned, without a hitch or a hiccup.

Until now.

As a precaution, he had installed keystroke monitors in a few of the most critical Utopia terminals. These monitors hid in the background, secretly collecting everything typed on the keyboard they were watching. Once an hour, each monitor sent its captured keystrokes, encrypted and disguised, over the Utopia Intranet to his terminal in the Hub.

So far, all the good little Utopia employees had been acting just like they were supposed to. With one exception: the computer that controlled the Metanet. That was turning into a different story.

The man scrolled back through the most recent keystroke file pilfered from the Metanet terminal. Someone was using that terminal to go over old logs, examine routines and instruction sets. Clearly, this was not some random search: this was a deliberate analysis, done by somebody who knew what they were doing.

The man glanced over his shoulder, down the corridor of the Hub. It rose up into the darkness overhead, tall and narrow as a giant's chimney, its walls covered in a complex filigree of wires and cable. Slowly, thoughtfully, he raised one hand to his head, pulling the headphones away from his ears. He could hear the distant tick of machinery, the whir of the sanitation bot's propulsion assembly, rumbling in some far quadrant.

Behind him, the soundproofing on the inner wall began to tremble again.

Placing the keyboard to one side, he glanced toward a radio that stood beside the monitors. It had a large amber blinker fitted to its upper edge, alerting him to incoming transmissions if the headphones were on. He picked up the radio, punched in the descrambling code, raised it to his lips.

"Cracker Jack to Prime Factor," he said. "Cracker Jack to Prime Factor, do you copy?"

There was a brief hiss. Then the cultivated voice of John Doe sounded over the speaker, clear despite the digital encryption. "Cracker Jack, your signal is five by five. What's your status?"

"Except for the passives, another ten minutes and everything will be complete."

"Then why the report?"

"I've been going over the keystroke logs of the terminals we're shadowing. All seem normal except for the Metanet's master computer. Somebody has been spending quite a lot of time on it the last hour, digging around."

"With any results?"

"Of course not. But whoever it is seems to know his business."

"Let me guess. B Level, right?"

"Right."

"It would appear we missed our target. Very well, I shall arrange a visit. Out."

The radio fell silent. A moment later, with a fearsome shrieking noise, the cars of the Scream Machine hurtled past the far side of the inner wall. The floor of the Hub shook. Cracker Jack cringed involuntarily. Then he snapped off the radio, placing it where its amber blinker would be clearly visible. As the clatter of the coaster faded and silence once again settled over the Hub, the man replaced the headphones, dragged the keyboard back onto his lap, popped another rectangle of gum into his mouth, and began to type.

3:15 P.M.

"WHAT THE HELL is that thing doing now?"

It took Andrew Warne several seconds to realize the question was directed at him. Unwillingly, he pulled his gaze away from the monitor. Poole—who was sitting on a nearby table, arms propped on two stacks of printouts—stared back with his usual look of mild inquiry.

"Excuse me?"

"I said, what's that thing doing now?" Poole nodded at Wingnut.

The robot was making its way around the room with ungainly, back-and-forth movements. It would approach an object, back away, then approach it again. Now and then it would move its head assembly forward, directing a thin spray of colorless liquid onto a bench or chair leg.

"He's marking his territory," Warne said, turning back to the monitor.

"What?"

Warne sighed. "It's his behavior programming. He's spent enough time in this place to consider it part of his world model. He figures he's likely to be here again, so it's worth the effort to plot out a topological map. Now that he's optimized his routes through the room, he's marking them with ultraviolet ink. Actually, I'm surprised the poor thing has any ink left."

"Well, can you tell him to stop? He's distracting me."

"Distracting you?" Terri asked. "From what?" She was sitting beside Warne, a large printout balanced on her knees.

"From my homework."

"Homework."

"Yup. I'm trying to figure out exactly how many laws these guys have broken already."

Terri turned over a page of the printout.

"So far, I'm up to thirty-nine."

Terri looked up.

Poole began ticking items off on his fingers. "First, there's burglary in the third degree. Knowingly and unlawfully entering a building or premises with intent of committing a crime. Then there's criminal possession of a dangerous weapon in the first degree. That's possession of an explosive substance, with the unlawful intent of using said substance against a person or property. Next comes criminal possession of a weapon in the second degree—"

"I get the picture," Terri said, rolling her eyes. "What kind of homework is this?"

"Written tests for TEA."

"TEA?"

"Treasury enforcement agent."

"Well, it sounds to me like you'd ace it."

Poole shrugged. "Passed every time."

"*Passed?* As in, past tense?"

"Three times. Also the written and oral exams for the Secret Service, the ATF, and the DEA."

"So why aren't you a federal agent by now?"

"Not sure. I think maybe it has something to do with the polygraph tests."

Warne tuned them out. He was staring at the columns of hexadecimal numbers crawling up his screen.

He had accessed Terri's kernel-mode debugger and was attempting to crack the hacker's hidden code. But it was like threading a needle while wearing gloves. All he had to work with was raw assembly language: no symbolic names, no source-code comments. He leaned forward, raising an inquiring hand to the bandage on his temple. He wondered what Georgia was doing right now; whether she was still asleep, what she'd think if she woke up and found he wasn't there. She'd put on a brave front after what happened. Still, he should be with her, not sitting in a lab, messing around with this jigsaw puzzle. The intrusion was far more complex and subtle than he'd ever imagined. He'd been crazy to think he could make a difference. Besides, the crisis might already be over: for all he knew, the mysterious John Doe had gotten what he wanted and was at this very moment riding off into the sunset.

Terri's voice intruded on his thoughts. "Anything?"

He dropped his hand from the bandage. "The bastard optimized his code. It's as if he, or she, is making it as hard as possible."

"A reasonable assumption," she said, impish grin returning.

"I've been able to reconstruct lines here and there, but not enough to have any clear sense of what's going on." He pointed at the screen. "This routine seems to add unauthorized instructions to the daily download." He paused. "But there seems to be something else. Something beyond just the Metanet hack."

"Like what?"

"I don't know exactly. It looks like data's being secretly channeled out into the main Utopia network. I'm trying to get a handle on it now."

He returned to the keyboard, set another breakpoint, then stepped through a few dozen lines of assembly language instructions. The persons responsible for this had done more than infect the Metanet: by causing its malfunction, they had jeopardized his own credibility. *Not unless they're even better coders than they are terrorists* . . . He realized he'd been wrong about this hacker. Whoever had done this was highly skilled.

He glanced at Terri. "It's definitely transmitting something to a port on the Utopia Intranet."

Terri put the printout aside and came up behind him, looked at the screen. "How?"

"They've hidden a piece of hardware somewhere in the system. They're probably using it to sneak information past the Utopia firewall."

"Can you pinpoint it? Find its physical location on the network?"

The subtle scent of her perfume drifted toward him. She was bending close now, a few strands of her jet-colored hair brushing across his cheek. With an effort, he kept his mind on the problem. "I'm trying, but the code is just too well protected. We'll have to try a different tack. Do you have access to a packet sniffer? Or, better yet, a protocol analyzer?"

Terri frowned. "Sure, up in Network Administration. Why?"

"If these guys have attached a router to the network, we should be able to scan for it. I've found enough crumbs here to give us a head start. Maybe we can track down which TCP/IP port it's listening on."

Terri's frown deepened. "No way."

"Each type of router has its own unique handwriting. The one they're using might not match the rest of Utopia's hardware. And even if it did, we could check for packet leakage. Or send out a tracer ping, see which node doesn't send back the right kind of response."

Terri shook her head. "*Inay*. Where'd you learn how to do that?"

"Misspent youth. Hanging around the MIT computer lab when I should have been cruising for babes."

She looked down at him dubiously. "Will it work?"

"Yes or no, we'd know in ten minutes. It beats sitting here, banging our heads against this code."

The phone rang, startlingly loud. Terri reached for it. "Applied Robotics. Yes. Yes, he's here. Okay, sure, I'll tell him."

"It's Sarah Boatwright," she said as she hung up. "She wants to see you in the VIP suite. Right now."

Poole, who had been silent through this exchange, spoke up. "Where?"

"The VIP suite. I'll take you."

Warne stood, wondering what could have drawn Sarah away from Medical.

"Okay," he said. "But first, let's spend a few minutes with that packet sniffer. We'll stop by Network Administration, see if we can track down that unauthorized router. Then we'll head on to the VIP suite."

They left the office, Poole cursing extravagantly as Wingnut, interrupted while marking territory, shot past him in frantic eagerness to catch up to Warne. Terri locked the door behind them and began leading the way down the corridor.

"How far is Network Administration?" Warne asked.

"It's on the way, actually. It's just around the corner, near the—"

Terri's voice was abruptly drowned out by the squealing of tires. Wingnut had caught sight of an electric cart turning into the corridor ahead of them, and had taken off in frantic pursuit.

"What's he doing?" Terri asked.

"It's like I told you. He likes to chase things. Wingnut!" Warne yelled, breaking into a trot. "No chase! *No chase!*" He jogged around a corner and out of sight, Terri and Poole at his heels.

THE SOUND OF Warne's calls quickly fell away. For several minutes, the hallway outside Applied Robotics remained quiet. An occasional Utopia crew member went past, hurrying from one Underground location to another. Then a costumed figure appeared at the end of the hallway. He was clearly Gaslight cast: Inverness cape, wool suit, heavy wooden cane, buttoned black shoes. Almond-shaped eyes moved from door to door, reading the labels as he moved down the corridor.

Outside the door to Terri's office, the man stopped. He looked, quite casually, in both directions. Then, keeping out of view of the door's window, he put his hand to the knob. Turned it slowly and quietly. Found it locked.

He remained—hand on the door—for some time, listening for sounds from within. At last, he let his hand drop away from the knob. Then he walked away, without particular hurry, disappearing in the direction from which he had come.

3:25 P.M.

THE VIP HOSPITALITY center looked more like an Italian palazzo than the concierge suite Warne had been expecting. Intricately carved alabaster columns rose toward a high ceiling, painted a blue and white trompe l'oeil sky. Between the columns, baroque fountains burbled. The walls were decorated with large landscape oils in heavy gold frames. A dignified-looking string quartet played chamber music in a distant corner.

A knot of half a dozen security specialists stood inside the entrance. Warne gave his name to the closest one, who—after an uneasy glance at Wingnut—nodded and motioned for them to follow. Warne made his way down the long, broad space, shoes ringing against the pink Carrara marble, Terri following. Poole came last, head swiveling around curiously above the turtleneck.

The room ended in a wide set of double doors, which led into a narrower, carpeted corridor. The security officer escorted Warne through. Doors, most of them closed, lined both walls. From behind one of the closest, Warne could hear a woman's voice, very British and very stern, raised in indignant protest. "We've been here an hour," the voice was saying. "An *hour,* mind you! We're guests, not prisoners. My husband's a peer. You can't . . ."

The voice faded away behind him. Then the security officer stopped at one of the doors, knocked, waited for it to open. A man's face appeared on the far side and nodded to the security officer, who turned and walked back down the corridor.

"What took you?" the man at the door said. "We were getting worried." Warne recognized the stocky features, deep sunburn, and pale thin hair of Bob Allocco, the security chief.

"We made a detour on the way," Warne said, stepping in behind Allocco. The room was small, but tastefully appointed. As elsewhere in the Utopia Underground, the artificial light was a close approximation of daylight to compensate for the lack of windows. A large-screen TV stood in the near corner, tuned to one of the Park's closed-circuit channels. Warne's gaze traveled around the rest of the room, stopping when it reached Sarah Boatwright. She was kneeling beside a chair, speaking intently to a seated man, his back to the door. Seeing Warne, she stopped talking and stood up, her mouth set in a narrow line. A look he had never seen before was on her face.

"What is it?" he asked, moving toward her quickly. "Where's Georgia?"

"You're safe. Thank God. It's okay, Dr. Finch is watching Georgia personally. He says she'll be asleep another hour, at least." She paused, glanced at Allocco.

"What is it?" Warne asked again.

"Drew. Do you remember meeting a Norman Pepper this morning?"

"Pepper," Warne murmured. The name was familiar. "Pepper . . . Sure. The orchid specialist. I rode in on the monorail with him."

"He's dead."

"Dead?" Warne asked in surprise. "How?" *Heart attack, probably,* he thought. *Fifty pounds overweight, not used to all the excitement. What a tragedy! The guy seemed so happy to be here. And he said he had kids, how awful to . . .*

"He was beaten to death."

"What?" A chill suddenly enveloped him. He looked mutely at Sarah.

"With a heavy, blunt instrument." Allocco's gravelly voice filled the small room. He nodded toward the chair. "This poor guy found him. Went into the External Specialists' Lounge hoping to find a cup of cocoa. Found Pepper instead."

The man in the chair turned around. He was bald, slightly built, with a tiny toothbrush mustache beneath and a thick pair of round spectacles above his nose. He looked even paler than Sarah. Still in shock, it took Warne a minute to recognize the man: Smythe, the external consultant, fireworks or something.

"Jesus," Warne murmured. He could see Pepper in his mind, rhapsodizing about the Park, rubbing his hands together with almost staged eagerness.

"Why?" he asked.

"That's what we wondered," Allocco said. He moved away

from Smythe, and the others followed. "At first. He wasn't robbed, his wallet was still in his jacket pocket. But it was so soaked with blood we had a hard time getting a readable ID. So we took the imagetag from his lapel and scanned it instead."

The room fell silent.

"And?" Warne said.

Allocco's gaze shifted to Sarah. Warne turned toward her with mute inquiry.

"He was wearing your tag," she said.

The chill gave way to a sudden gust of fear. Warne swallowed.

"My tag?" he asked in a dry, stupid voice. "How could that be?" But even as he spoke, he remembered: in the monorail, Pepper had knocked the small white envelopes to the floor, reached for them, handed his back . . .

"Our tags were switched on the way in," he said. "They must have been. That tag I lost in the Waterdark ride—*my* tag—it must have been Pepper's."

Sarah took a step toward him. "I know," she said. "This is a terrible, terrible thing."

A terrible thing . . . In this moment of extremity, Warne could not get the image of Norman Pepper out of his mind. *That could have been me. That* should *have been me* . . .

"What are you going to do about it?" Poole asked.

"The only thing we can do. Leave the body where it is, seal off the suite. Alert the police." Sarah exchanged glances with Allocco. "As soon as we can."

There was a knock on the door. Allocco opened it, and a young woman in a white blazer entered, bearing an oversize cup of tea, which she handed to Sarah. She murmured her thanks, turned and offered it to Smythe, who declined with a quick little shake of his head.

"Of course, you realize you'll need to stay here for the duration," Allocco said, turning toward Warne. "Or in the hospital with your daughter, if you'd rather. We've secured both areas."

Warne, still thinking about Pepper, was slow to absorb this. "I'm sorry?" he asked.

"We already knew they were looking for you. Now we know they want you dead."

The fear made his limbs feel heavy and sluggish. "But why? Why me? It doesn't make sense."

"It makes perfect sense." It was Terri who spoke up, and all eyes turned toward her. She flushed slightly, as if surprised to hear her own voice. Then she took a breath, stuck out her chin. "It proves you're right. About the Metanet, I mean, and that Trojan horse."

"I don't follow," Allocco said.

"Dr. Warne wasn't supposed to arrive until next week. These guys, whoever they are, couldn't have planned for such a contingency. And they wouldn't be trying to kill him now unless they knew he could hurt them."

"Makes sense," Poole said. He had moved to the coffee machine and was pouring himself a cup.

Allocco glared at him, then muttered something under his breath.

"I suppose that's right," Warne said slowly. Then he turned toward Sarah. "I can't stay here. There's something I have to do."

"Like what?" Allocco asked sarcastically. "Enjoy a few rides? Take in a show?"

"I think I've found something. Something important."

Sarah said nothing, waiting, looking at him intently.

Warne went on, trying to ignore the dryness of his mouth. "I think I've located the port these guys are using."

"Port?" Allocco said. "What are you talking about?"

"You know, the port. The physical node where they've tapped into the Utopia system."

"Do you understand this?" Allocco asked Sarah.

"How do you know?" Sarah was still looking at Warne.

"That's why I was late getting here. Sarah, I found a Trojan horse hidden in the Metanet. It's transmitting information from Terri's terminal out into your network. I was able to reconstruct part of an internal address; not much, but enough for a start. Using that, we went to Network Administration, ran a sniffer over the network, looking for anomalous activity—you know, packet leakage, anything that might betray tampering—" He stopped. "Look, I can explain afterward. The point is we found an unauthorized router, listening over a port in the"—he turned to Terri—"what's that place called?"

"The Hub."

"It might be nothing. Chances are, it's just an improperly configured switch. But if the device *was* placed by these people, we ought to examine it, figure out what it's doing."

"Let me get this straight," Allocco said. "We just told you

'these people' are trying to kill you. Somebody has *already* been killed in your place. And you want to go out there and take them on?"

"I'm not taking anybody on. I'm just tracking down a piece of hardware." Warne looked around the small room, at the faces staring back at him. Then he turned back to Sarah. "You asked for my help, remember? Don't get me wrong, I'm scared as hell. Fact is, I'm *too* scared to just sit here on my hands, doing nothing. At least out there I'll be a *moving* target."

"This router, or whatever," Allocco said. "Could it be what's playing havoc with our video surveillance?"

"Very likely."

Allocco glanced at Sarah. "What do you think?"

Sarah's eyes remained on Warne. "Andrew, I want you to listen to me. These people aren't afraid to kill to get their way." Her voice was remarkably steady; Warne wondered how she was managing to keep herself together under such terrible pressure. "John Doe himself told me we'd been lucky on that explosion in the Waterdark ride. They've killed an innocent man thinking it was you. Do you understand what I'm telling you?"

I think you're telling me that Georgia's already lost one parent. You need my help. But you don't want to be the one responsible for sacrificing me. Aloud, he said, "Yes."

"And?"

"And if somebody's going to do this, it might as well be me."

Allocco sighed deeply. "Christ. Well, I'll send a security detachment with you."

Warne shook his head. "No. I'd rather you send them to watch my daughter instead."

"Good," Poole said from the coffee machine. "A security detachment would just attract attention. We need a small team for this job."

"Did I ask your opinion?" Allocco said, his voice tight with irritation.

"These individuals you're dealing with are clearly well prepared," Poole went on, as if he hadn't heard. "We can assume they're well armed, too. They see a phalanx of security drones, in protective formation around a single civilian . . ." He shrugged, took a sip of coffee. "All it would take is one low-pressure grenade. The M433A1 Dual Purpose would be my choice: forty-five grams of composition A5, with a base-detonating fuse. Toss one of those into the group, and *boom*! Their whole day is ruined."

Allocco scowled, not answering.

"This is a recon job. You'll want a small team. Get the right man, have him ride shotgun."

"The right man," Allocco echoed dryly. "Right. Who would that be?"

Poole smiled demurely, tugged on his tweed cap.

Allocco scoffed. "You trust this guy?" he said to Warne.

"At least we know he's not a mole. He's a guest, not a Utopia employee. A random element."

"Random, you say." Allocco drew Sarah and Warne to one side.

"And how do you *know* he's not one of them?" he asked Warne.

"Because if he wanted to kill me, I'd already be dead." Warne hesitated. "Look, I'm no hero. But I'm the best qualified to check this thing out."

Allocco seemed to consider this a moment. Then he let his hands drop to his sides and stepped back.

"I want you to take my man, Ralph Peccam," he said. "He's my top video tech, and he's trustworthy. He's also the only guy in Security who really knows what's going on. If this device is messing with our feeds, I want him to see it."

Warne nodded.

"I'll call Fred Barksdale," Sarah said. "Get a network tech to accompany you, as well."

"Okay," Warne said. "No, wait a minute. That'll take too long. Terri here knows the network inside and out." He turned to her. "You willing to come along?"

She shrugged with attempted nonchalance. "Probably safer than sitting around in my lab."

Warne watched as Sarah looked at each of them in turn. Then she unfastened the turquoise imagetag from her own lapel and fixed it to Warne's jacket.

"This is a management tag," she said. "You shouldn't be stopped or questioned while you wear it."

She turned away from Warne, toward the man in the chair. "Mr. Smythe, why don't you just rest here for the time being. Take it easy, lie down if you'd feel better. All right?"

The man named Smythe nodded silently.

Warne glanced at the robot by his feet. "Wingnut, *stay*," he commanded sternly. The robot swiveled its stereo cameras at him, as if begging for a repeal of the order. When none was forthcoming, he emitted a bray of dissatisfaction and rolled backward slowly, reluctantly, toward a nearby corner.

Sarah turned back to Warne. "I've got to deliver the second disc to John Doe at four o'clock, at the Holo Mirrors. After that, I'll stay with Georgia, supervise things from Medical until you return. Be careful, don't do anything that might provoke retaliation. But let me know what you find, and if there's some way we can—"

"Wait a minute," Warne interrupted. "*You* have to deliver the disc?"

Sarah nodded. "He specifically requested it. To ensure there were no tricks this time."

"Jesus." Warne lapsed briefly into silence. Then, impulsively, he embraced her. "Be careful."

"I could say the same to you," she replied. She kissed his cheek and pulled away. From over her shoulder, Warne saw Terri's dark eyes regarding them intently.

3:30 P.M.

"WHAT IS THIS Hub, exactly?" Warne asked. They were walking along a wide corridor on B Level, past the complex of offices that made up the Casino Operations Division.

"It's Utopia's central routing station," Ralph Peccam answered. "You do robotics at, where, Carnegie-Mellon?"

"I did."

"The network guys have a wiring closet there?"

"Of course."

"Well, think of the Hub as a wiring closet. Only several orders of magnitude larger."

The man sneezed, burying his face in the elbow of his busy-looking sports jacket. "Man" was a bit of exaggeration, Warne thought: with his big shock of red hair and generous scattering of freckles, Peccam looked more like a kid on his way to algebra class than Utopia's top video tech. Just looking at him made Warne feel old.

His thoughts returned to the VIP suite and the expression on Allocco's face as he'd looked at him. It hadn't been that far removed from scorn. *We just told you these people are trying to kill you*, he'd said. *And you want to go out there and take them on?*

Warne knew, from the tightness in his chest and from the quick thud of his heart, that was the last thing he wanted to do. But he also knew he couldn't just sit in the VIP suite, eating coffee cake and watching *Atmosfear* reruns. And he couldn't stay in Medical, pacing, waiting for Georgia to wake up, waiting for the next flood of casualties to pour in. The scene within Waterdark replayed itself again in his head: the sudden, wrenching jolt; the agonized screams tumbling out of the darkness above; and, most of all, the look in Georgia's eyes.

He felt an upwelling of anger at the people who were causing all this suffering. If he could discover anything, learn anything, that might help save Sarah's Park, he'd do it. It wasn't much, but it was all he had.

"What can we expect to find inside?" Poole was asking.

"Network switches," Peccam replied. They had come to an intersection, and he led them around a corner and down a narrower, utilitarian hallway. "T-1 and T-3 connectors. Electrical junctions. Lots and lots and lots of wires. It's basically a big, narrow wrapper around an underground dip in the Scream Machine coaster. A box outside of a box. Nobody ever goes in there except for Maintenance. I even had trouble finding somebody with an access card." He brandished the plastic rectangle that hung from a cord around his neck. "And dark, too, I hear. I hope somebody brought a flashlight."

Poole's eyes darted from Peccam, to Warne, to Terri. "Damn," he muttered. "And what are we looking for, exactly?"

"A router," Terri said. "A gray box, probably about a foot long and four inches tall. Installed there illicitly at some point." She waved a folded set of papers. "I've got the network architecture here, so I know the approximate location. Once we're inside, we can run a trace on it."

"There's probably a hundred routers in the Hub," Peccam said. "What makes you think this particular one is unauthorized?"

"I did an internal sweep across your net," Warne replied. "Its banner didn't match the rest."

Now it was Peccam's turn to look stumped. "How do you mean?"

"Every piece of network hardware has an identification banner it'll announce if you ping it right. I stumbled on one banner that didn't match the standard configurations. According to Terri's schematics, it's a router in the Hub."

"Mmm," said Peccam, his tone laced with professional skepticism.

Warne glanced at him, his tension falling away beneath an upswell of uncertainty. He was probably leading them all on a wild-goose chase. What had seemed such a clever idea in Terri's lab now seemed foolish. They'd probably search for an hour and find some malfunctioning circuit board. They should be back in the lab, working that code, trying to track down and disconnect the errant bots.

The corridor ended in a small door with no sign except a

red label that read *Warning: High Voltage. Unauthorized Entry Forbidden*.

"This is it," Peccam said, lifting the cord over his head and raising the passcard toward the access reader.

Abruptly, Poole grabbed his wrist.

"What are you doing?"

"We haven't set the rules of engagement."

"Rules of engagement?" Peccam sniffed. "It's just a cable room."

"I don't care if it's a charity tea at the Ladies' Luncheon Society. To fail to plan is to plan to fail." Poole waved at the locked door. "Listen to a trained professional here. We have to treat this as an infiltration. Once inside, we'll do a quick recon. If it's safe, you can proceed with locating this . . . this router."

"Damn," Peccam said. "If I knew I'd be playing G.I. Joe, I'd have worn my cammos."

Poole looked him up and down. "It might have helped," he said disdainfully.

Peccam swiped the passcard through the reader.

There was a click and the door sprang ajar. Poole motioned them to wait. He looked over his shoulder once. Then, keeping himself pressed against the door frame, he nudged the door open with a finger. Warne noticed the door was unusually thick, padded on the inside with what appeared to be soundproofing.

With a quick, snakelike movement, Poole twisted his head around the doorway. For a moment, he remained motionless. Then he ducked his head back out, nodding for the rest to follow.

Inside, it was poorly lit. Cables and wires of all thicknesses, colors, and descriptions crawled up the walls on both sides of a narrow corridor. Warne felt like he was within the walls of some monstrous, nightmarish house. He looked up, squinting in the gloom, trying to make out the ceiling. Communities of tiny lights blinked and flickered everywhere. Twenty feet down the cramped passageway, a metal ladder rose to a catwalk running along the outer wall. Circuits and relays rustled and clicked in the darkness like mechanical insects, and underlying everything was a low, trembling sound, almost beneath the threshold of hearing.

Gazing around at the endless electronics, Warne's heart sank. The conviction already growing within him intensified. This was a pointless exercise, they'd never find the router in all this . . .

The low trembling suddenly grew louder, rising in pitch as well as volume until it filled the Hub with a bansheelike keening. The walls seemed to dance around him.

"Sweet sister Sadie!" Poole shouted against the noise. "What's that?"

"The Scream Machine," Peccam called back. He pulled a tissue from his pocket, blew his nose, replaced the tissue. "Its tracks dip beneath the Park, just on the far side of *that*." He jerked his thumb toward the inner wall. "This Hub is like a skinny box wrapped around that dip. Why do you think they put all this wiring in here? No other use you could put this space to."

Warne winced, turning his face away from the noise. Above the din, he thought he could hear shouting, delighted screams.

The group waited, motionless, as the sound eased, then died away completely. In the wake of the terrible roar, the returning quiet seemed all the more pronounced.

Warne glanced back at Terri. Her eyes were wide and pale, her lips compressed. Her white lab coat seemed to gleam in the dim light.

"Didn't you say you were claustrophobic?" he whispered.

She nodded. "Subways. Tunnels. I won't even go on any of the rides."

"So how can you stand it in here?"

"It's dark. Somebody's got to hold your hand."

They made their way down the walkway, single file.

The Hub was laid out in the shape of a square: four long, narrow corridors, each meeting at a ninety-degree angle. At the first bend, Poole stopped. Slowly, he peered around the corner.

In the stillness, Peccam sneezed explosively.

Poole lunged back from the corner, glaring at the technician and putting a reproving finger to his lips.

Warne felt his breathing quicken. He reminded himself the place was empty. At most, they'd find some uninvited metal box full of circuit boards and ribbon cables—and they'd be lucky to find even that. Yet somehow, tension within the group was rising so quickly it was almost palpable. Part of it was Poole's doing: Poole with his habitual caution, his absurd paramilitary posturing. Part of it was the silence, which in this darkness was almost a presence: watchful, hostile. And the sudden roar of the coaster had set his nerves on edge. Whatever the reason, the group that followed Poole around the corner and deeper into the electronic thicket had begun moving as stealthily as possible.

They encountered a sanitation bot, moving slowly along the outer wall. A miniature vacuum brush, mounted beneath a long eyestalk, moved gently over the numberless couplings. Warne slid past, making a mental note to check its programming with Terri later.

Halfway down this second leg of the square, the faraway rumble returned: another coaster was hurtling down toward them from above. This time, Warne didn't wait. He turned away from the inner wall, ducked his right ear toward his shoulder, covered his left with one palm. He watched as Terri did the same. The rumble transformed into a roar; the trembling grew, then eventually receded; and again the group moved forward.

In less than a minute, they reached the next corner. Once again, Poole snuck a look around. *Why bother*, Warne thought to himself: the light was so dim one couldn't see more than twenty feet ahead. He followed Poole around the corner and down the third leg of the square, shivering. Christ, it was cold in here. Just one more corner, one more corridor, and they'd be back where they started. Then maybe this pointless reconnaissance would end and they could get on with the business of finding the router. Assuming, of course, that . . .

Engrossed in his thoughts, Warne walked directly into Poole's back.

The man had stopped dead in his tracks, motionless in the darkness. Slowly, Poole extended his right hand, palm forward. Warne could hear Ralph Peccam's labored breathing behind them. He strained to see through the thick murk.

There seemed to be a form ahead, vague and dreamlike, at the point where vision failed. Warne squinted, leaning forward. Poole's caution was infectious, and he felt his nerves tighten. He was sure of it now: a figure, squatting near the floor, crouched over something.

Poole took a cautious, catlike step forward, arm still raised in warning. Warne followed. The figure became more distinct: a slender man in a blue jumpsuit, seated on a stool, his back against some kind of cart. Headphones covered his ears, and his head was angled away from them. He seemed to be typing, staring at a small screen between his knees.

The low tremor of another approaching coaster began to vibrate through the Hub.

Very slowly now, Poole gestured to Warne, indicating he should fall back. The rumble of the train grew, the shriek of wheels against metal clear through the soundproof walls.

At the end of the corridor, the man looked up.

Immediately, Poole froze. Warne saw the man scan the dim hallway, saw the sheen of his eyes as his gaze locked upon them. As he stared, the man began to type again: slowly at first, then more quickly.

Poole took a step forward.

The man in the jumpsuit continued to stare at them. He typed, hit the return key, typed again. Then, quite casually, he moved one hand toward a nearby utility case, fingering something within. The roar of the passing train filled the chimneylike space with an almost physical presence.

Poole took another step forward.

Instantly—with unexpected, terrifying speed—the man was on his feet, keyboard spinning away behind him. Poole was yelling but Warne couldn't hear him over the clamor. The man looked around for a moment, as if searching for something. Then he dipped his hand into his jumpsuit, withdrew it.

Poole spun around, pushing Warne roughly to the floor. As he fell, Warne saw a sudden flash brighten the vague outlines of the corridor. Immediately, Poole shot down the walkway in a scuttling, crablike motion. The man in the jumpsuit pointed something, and again the flash came. There was a whining sound above Warne's ear, and as the sound of the coaster receded, he heard the echoing crack of gunfire. He shrank back instinctively, shoulders pressing into the sharp edges of circuit boards. He turned toward Terri, pulled her head down protectively.

Poole and the man in the jumpsuit were now locked in a desperate struggle. As Warne looked back, Poole raised a fist, elbow cocked high, and drove it against the man's face, once, twice. The man staggered, shaking his head as if to clear it. Then he lunged forward suddenly, raising his gun hand: Poole chopped at the man's wrist with the edge of one palm and the gun went clattering to the floor. The man reared back into a martial arts stance, then swung around with great rapidity, aiming a roundhouse kick at Poole's stomach. Poole tumbled backward, the man following, aiming vicious kicks at his head. Poole rolled into a crouch and the man broke away, racing around the corner, vanishing abruptly.

"Jesus!" Terri cried.

Warne continued to stare, hugging Terri tightly against his chest, dumbstruck, ears ringing. The fight had been so brief, so unexpected, he wondered if he had really seen it at all. Though it had lasted less than ten seconds, it had been brutal, horrifyingly deliberate. This was a professional confrontation, each man working as fast as he could to incapacitate the other. For all his military airs, Poole had always seemed an unthreatening, even faintly ludicrous, figure to Warne. But in less than a minute, his opinion had changed utterly.

Poole disappeared around the corner, in the direction the man had taken. Now he reappeared, gesturing for them to come forward. Beside him, the stranger's utility case was flickering brightly, as if lit from within. A stream of smoke billowed outward.

Warne slowly relaxed his grip on Terri and stood up, leg muscles quivering. He took her hand and together they moved cautiously down the passage, Peccam following.

Poole had snugged the fallen handgun into his waistband. "Stop there," he said as they approached the corner. Then he motioned Peccam forward.

"Where does that door lead?" he asked, breathing heavily.

Peering around the corner, Warne made out a small doorway on the inner wall of the Hub. The door was open, blocking the view of the corridor beyond. Instead of a card scanner, it had an old-fashioned metal hasp for a lock.

"The tracks of the Scream Machine," Peccam said. "It's what the Hub is built around."

"Any other way out of there?"

"Not unless you walk up the coaster's railbed. But that dip is incredibly steep. Safety inspectors are roped when they walk that track."

Poole hesitated. The acrid smoke from the utility case wafted toward them, stinging Warne's eyes. Then Poole reached over to a nearby rack of equipment and, with a grunt, yanked out a retaining rail.

"I want you to bar that door behind me," he said, handing the piece of metal to Peccam. "Don't open it unless you hear me tell you to. If I'm not out in five minutes, go for help. All of you. Stay together, don't split up." He pulled the pistol from his waistband, racked the slide, then began walking quickly but deliberately down the passage.

Warne began to follow automatically, then stopped as his foot hit something heavy. He looked down. It was a large duffel, almost invisible beneath a low rack. This must have been what the man in the jumpsuit was looking for. From the end of an open zipper gleamed the muzzle of a large weapon.

There was movement beside him, and Warne turned. It was Peccam. He, too, had seen the duffel. For a moment, they stared at the weapon together in silence.

"I'd better take that," Warne said, a little uncertainly.

Peccam looked at him. "No, I think I'd better."

"I saw it first."

"I'm a Utopia employee."

"But I'm the one they're trying to kill—"

"Hey!"

Both men looked over. It was Poole.

"Don't touch *anything*. Just bar the door behind me."

He slid up to the open door, pistol raised. Then he nodded at them, ducked around the door frame, and disappeared within.

3:33 P.M.

POOLE STEPPED FORWARD into the gloom, shrinking from the dim rectangle of light that slanted in the open doorway. Dim as the Hub was, this cube it encircled was blacker still. He slid back against the wall, breathing slowly, waiting. The rectangle of light attenuated, then disappeared as the door shut. Poole heard the rattle of metal as Peccam slid the rail through the hasp.

He crept a few steps along the wall, gun at the ready. He didn't believe the man in the jumpsuit had another weapon, but he wasn't going to take a chance. Years of training, half-forgotten, reasserted themselves. He took a series of long, slow breaths, scanning the indistinct perimeter.

Gradually, his vision adapted. He was inside a vast box, bounded on all sides by the walls of the Hub beyond. Before him stretched a forest of steel pillars, rising from anchors in the concrete floor to a complex architecture of spars and beams. Somewhere far above hovered a narrow circle of light: the thin opening through which the descending coaster shot briefly beneath the Park. As he stood, back to the wall, he thought he could hear song or laughter floating down from Boardwalk. Here in the blackness, it seemed impossibly far away: a dream kingdom imagined, not seen.

He turned his eyes from the faint light. Right now, he needed the darkness.

He began to move stealthily along the wall, muffling each footfall, scanning the monochromatic landscape before him. He wasn't sure why the man in the jumpsuit had run in here. No doubt their arrival had taken him by surprise. Even so, he'd continued to work as he watched them approach. That had taken balls: clearly, this was one hacker that was no slope-shouldered wimp. Poole wondered what could be so important that the guy would delay his own exit just to type something in.

But right now, that didn't matter. The important thing was, this guy wasn't the type who'd panic. He had come here for a reason.

Poole continued edging along the wall. If he heard the squawk of static, or anything that sounded like a radio, he'd have no choice but to take sudden action. Otherwise, the best option was to keep to the shadows and wait until . . .

With brutal suddenness, bedlam descended upon him. The steel beams shivered, and a wave of overpressure tore at his eardrums. He crouched, shielding his face. The roar was like an engine of God. He was abruptly surrounded by a coruscation of sparks; screams and happy shouts peppered the walls as the coaches of the roller coaster bottomed out above his head, then rose again, trailing cries and yells and curses as it shot up the ramp.

Once more, silence settled over the blackness. Poole raised himself, then stood motionless. *Why the sparks? Must be some special effect of the underwheels.* Whatever the case, sixty seconds and another coaster would come through, bringing light as well as noise. He'd have to find a place where he couldn't be so easily spotted.

Easing himself from the wall with his elbows, he crept forward, ducking from pillar to pillar, gun raised. Something crunched beneath his feet and he cursed, ducking back behind a supporting column. Overhead, the giant double tracks of the Scream Machine swooped downward. The rails gleamed dully in the heavy air.

From a vantage point behind the column, Poole looked around, listening in vain. *What the hell was the guy up to?*

He tried to put himself in the man's shoes. The hacker wouldn't have expected them to show up like that. There was no way the hacker could have known they were as surprised as he was to find somebody there. So he'd have to assume they were tracking him deliberately. He couldn't know how many were confronting him, whether or not they were coming from both sides.

That had to be it. The guy thought he'd been surrounded. So he ducked in here.

But this was a dead end. If the guy in the jumpsuit was going to get out, he was going to have to climb . . .

This time, Poole was ready when the trembling came. Shrinking back against the column, he turned his eyes downward, away from the approaching cars. Once again, the shrieking fell upon him like a heavy mantle of sound. Manufactured sparks shot from the wheels, and for a brief instant, Poole saw the floor around him light up. He started in surprise. He was surrounded by a dense litter of objects: earrings, hairpins, caps, glasses, coins. A set of false teeth gleamed within a small pool of lubricating oil. At first, Poole assumed it was all trash. Then he realized: all these things had been jolted from the riders of the passing coaches.

As the coaster mounted the tracks again and the horrible overpowering noise began to recede, he glanced upward. The flicker of sparks died away, and he saw—or thought he saw—a figure close by. Its hands were above its head. As the faint light died away, the figure fell still, hands locked in position.

Poole fell back behind the column. It was the man in the jumpsuit, all right. Hard at work at something.

And whatever he was doing, the man needed light to do it.

Poole waited, counting the seconds until the next train would hurtle down toward them. He allowed himself no movement, not even the merest flicker of an eyelid: here, between trains, the man in the jumpsuit would be watching, too.

There it came again: the tremor that seemed to start in the gut, then spread outward toward fingers and toes. A low rumble grew all around him. And then came the descending roar of the train.

As the noise reached its crescendo, Poole peered around the edge of the steel column. There was the man, illuminated by the passing glare. His hands were once again over his head, and his forearms were rotating, as if he was screwing something into place.

As Poole watched, the man finished, dropping his hands and ducking out of sight.

But Poole had already recognized the movements. Now he knew—all too clearly—how the man planned on getting out.

Without another thought, he tucked the gun into his waistband and sprinted forward, racing toward the spot where the man had been standing. Raising his own arms, he felt his way up the railings, his fingers spreading in a desperate search. There it was: the cool, rubbery texture of plastic explosive. Enclosing it in his hands, Poole gingerly swept his fingers inward, palpating, searching.

There was a sudden, terrible blow to his temple, and he sagged to one side, feet giving way beneath him. The gun came free of his belt and fell to the floor, spinning as it slid away out of sight. The man in the jumpsuit leaped for it, scrabbling in the gloom. Pulling himself up, Poole raised his hands once again, found the C-4, searched as quickly as he dared for the detonator. His fingers closed over it.

There was a pattering behind him.

Slowly, almost lovingly, Poole pulled the tube loose from the charge, catching his breath as the end bobbed free. He turned, tossing the detonator out into the gloom.

The roar of another car; and over the traceries of sparks he caught sight of the man in the jumpsuit, on his hands and knees a few feet away, still searching for the gun. Poole launched himself toward the man, who rolled away. Then they were both on their feet and dashing from beam to beam.

Poole raced after the sound of retreating footsteps, careering first off one steel truss, then another. The faintest glimpse of a form to one side—black against black—and Poole veered toward it, catching the man by the knees, both of them tumbling to the floor in a disorganized heap. The man kicked fiercely but Poole kept to one side, arcing a blow down into the face once, twice, three times. The man moaned, then lay still.

"Tag," Poole gasped, leaning back against a support.

In the distance, there was a sharp crack, then a flash and a puff of smoke as the detonator fired. Poole did not bother to turn. The coaster descended again, filling the space with sound and fury. Poole paid it no heed. He leaned against the column, taking one deep breath after another, until at last blessed silence returned once again.

3:40 P.M.

TO WARNE, THE anteroom of Utopia's Security Complex looked more like an elementary school than a law enforcement station. The molded-plastic chairs in bright primary colors, sparkling tile floor, large analog wall clock behind a wire mesh, all sent a message of cheery institutional solidity. Even the posters on the walls—touting the Park's safety record, or diagramming the nearest fire exits—played their part. Like everything else about Utopia, it was carefully planned. Most of the people who found their way to Security, after all, would be paying guests: victims of pickpocketing, parents looking for missing children, youths picked up for horseplay. It was important that Security present a benign, reassuring appearance. It neither expected nor was built for hard-core criminals.

Warne pulled his gaze from the walls, glancing back at the surrounding chairs. Terri Bonifacio was sitting beside him. To her right, Peccam was gingerly sorting through the heavy duffel they'd brought back from the Hub. Beyond, Allocco was talking to Poole.

Warne put his arm around Terri's shoulder. "You okay?"

"Me? I've been accused, accosted, stalked, shot at. And the day's still young. Why shouldn't I be okay?"

He drew her toward him affectionately. "This is my fault. I'm sorry you had to get involved in this."

"Hey, don't fool yourself. It's more exciting than programming servos and doing code reviews." She smiled, but the usual impish gleam was missing.

Warne turned back toward Allocco. He knew that he should be listening. But it was as Terri just implied: the whole afternoon had taken on such a surreal cast that he seemed set free from any normal script. As in a dream, he felt he could do, or say, anything, no matter how unexpected or outrageous, and the situation around him would adjust itself to . . .

There: it was starting again. He forced himself to listen.

"You're telling me this punk set the thing *himself*?" Allocco was saying.

"Affirmative. There was *already* a hefty shaped charge in place beneath the rails of that big old coaster of yours. One of several, no doubt, they'd previously distributed around the park. With me so far?"

Allocco had turned a little gray, but nodded. "Go on."

"Well, when this guy found himself ambushed, he ran inside, where the track supports were. He'd dropped his weapon, didn't have time to grab another. But he *did* have a detonator. He planned to set the charge, then take cover until it blew. Once the next set of cars came plummeting down the track . . ." Poole shrugged, waved one hand. "Well, he'd escape in the aftermath."

"Jesus, that's cold," Allocco said in a tone of disbelief. "Those Scream Machine trains hold a hundred and twenty people each."

There was a brief silence as the little group digested this.

Allocco glanced at Warne. "Maybe this thing still has me a little loopy. But I thought you said you were searching for a piece of *equipment*. Were you just feeding us bullshit? You knew we wouldn't let you go if you told us the truth?"

Warne shook his head. "No. It was very clever. He'd set up a remote command post, concealing it as a simple hardware router. One of a thousand. Nobody looking for an intruder would have ever found him. If I hadn't picked apart his code, known what to look for . . ." He paused. "Even so, it was mostly luck."

"We'll see how lucky we are when John Doe finds out we've nabbed one of his goons. If he doesn't already know."

Warne shot Allocco a glance. "What do you mean?"

"Because, while you were playing hide-and-seek in the Hub, we lost our video feeds."

"Lost? What do you mean, lost?"

"As in all our surveillance cameras. In the Park itself, the Underground, everywhere. The only places not affected are the casinos, which have their own closed-circuit surveillance, and C Level, below us. We're basically blind."

"Sweet sister Sadie." Poole gave a low whistle.

"I think our touch-typist friend can be thanked for that," Warne said. He thought back to the darkness of the Hub, and how the man had just stared at them, fingers still moving across the keyboard. "He entered something on his keyboard after he spotted us."

"You've got to hand it to him," Poole said. "Quite a cool customer."

"The only thing I'm handing him is a one-way ticket to Nevada Correctional," Allocco said. "So, what scraps did he leave us? Can we appropriate his equipment, reverse the damage, figure out what he was up to?"

Warne shook his head. "He had a state-of-the-art minicomputer concealed in an equipment box. But it was rigged somehow. When he ran away, he set it off. Torched it."

"A thermite charge," Poole added. "Fused everything solid."

"I see. So these boys are still two steps ahead of everything we do." Allocco turned to Peccam. "What have you got, Ralph?"

The youth's hands were deep inside the satchel. "Let's see. There's a spare radio"—he brought it out with a sniff, placing it on a low table—"but with a scrambler, just as useless as the one in the Hub. Various clips and cables and whatnot. And some very high-end networking equipment. About fifty packs of Nicorette gum. Some of these things, I don't know what they are." He held up a small strand of cablelike material.

"Det cord," Allocco and Poole said in unison.

"Det cord. A couple of peanut butter and jelly sandwiches."

Poole reached over and withdrew one, unwrapped the waxed paper, peeled apart the bread. "I'd guess Jif, chunky style. Excellent choice."

"Get on with it," Allocco growled, running a balm stick over his lips.

"Then there's this." Peccam held up a black plastic object with three buttons: two gray, one red. It looked like an oversize television remote.

"What's that?"

"It's an infrared transmitter. Boosted for long-range transmission." Peccam fell silent, an odd expression on his face.

"Go on, go on."

"Well, it doesn't make sense. Boosting infrared for long range, I mean."

Allocco sighed. "Just explain it, please."

"Well, there's basically two kinds of remote controls: infrared and radio frequency. Normally, RF is preferable because of its longer range." He hefted the black cylinder. "But this infrared transmitter has been boosted well beyond any RF range. Half a mile, at least. Very expensive gizmo. But like I said, it doesn't make sense. Because RF can transmit through walls, around corners. But with an infrared like this, you can go much farther, but you need a clear line of sight. So why bother making such an expensive, powerful transmitter when you have to see what it is you're aiming at?"

In the silence that followed, Warne caught Poole's eye. The man looked grave.

"Thanks for the lesson," Allocco said. "Anything else?"

"No. Oh, yes, one other thing." Peccam reached into the bag and gingerly pulled out a weapon: a short, low-slung submachine gun, with a wooden stock and a heavy magazine. Its barrel was obscured within a cone-shaped piece of metal.

"Heckler & Koch MP5SD," Poole said, nodding his approval. "Note the integrated silencer. As long as you use subsonic ammo, it's so silent there's practically no bullet report—all you hear is the click of the bolt. If you hear anything."

For a moment, nobody replied. They sat motionless, staring at the weapon. Finally, Allocco rose from his seat.

"I'd better get back to our friend," he said. "Though I doubt he's said anything since I left. Not exactly a talkative kind of fellow."

"I'd like to come along," Poole said.

Allocco looked back at him. "Why?"

"Why not?"

Allocco made a scoffing noise. Then he turned to the video tech. "Peccam, put that stuff away. And keep an eye on these civilians for me."

Poole watched the security director's retreating back. "Comrade Allocco doesn't seem to like me very much," he said mildly as he stood. "I wonder why."

So do I, Warne thought. He rose automatically to follow. Then he glanced over his shoulder at Terri. She was sitting upright, hands pressed against the white knees of her lab coat.

"You don't mind waiting here?"

"Are you kidding? I hate jail cells even more than I hate locked closets."

"We'll be back soon." He turned away, leaving her with Peccam, who—very carefully—was replacing the submachine gun in the duffel.

UTOPIA HAD ONLY one high-security holding cell, at the end of the lone, utilitarian corridor that led away from the anteroom. Even this was not especially secure: a small room, with a heavy door and a single cot bolted to one of the padded walls. A group of security specialists stood in the open space outside it.

"You searched him again, right?" Allocco asked.

"Yes, sir," one of the guards—a black-haired youth—replied. A small bronze rectangle with *Lindbergh* stamped on it was pinned to his left pocket. "No wallet, no money, no ID, nothing. He's clean."

"Good. Open up, please."

Warne, coming up behind, peered curiously and a little cautiously over Poole's shoulder. The hacker—so he had begun to call him—was lounging on the lone cot. He was still wearing the blue jumpsuit, but the electrician's pin had been removed from the collar. He was wiry and young, with a dark complexion and long black hair gathered into a ponytail. To Warne, he looked South American. His legs were crossed at the ankles, and his nicotine-stained fingers were laced behind his head. Several ugly bruises were coming up on his face, shiny pink just beginning to give way to mottled yellow and blue. He gazed up at the group without interest.

Allocco stepped forward, planting his feet apart, crossing his arms. "Okay," he said. "Let's try it again. What's your name?"

Silence.

"Where are the rest of your men?"

Silence.

"How many explosive devices have you planted, and what are their locations?"

The man on the bunk closed his eyes, shrugging himself into a more comfortable position.

Allocco rocked back on his heels, exhaling in frustration. "The police are on their way. You're in deep, deep shit. You cooperate with us, maybe you can climb out of that shit. Now, let's start again. Where are the rest of the explosive devices?"

This question received the same response as its predecessor.

Allocco turned away.

"Mind if I have a try?" Poole asked.

Allocco glanced at him. "What are you planning? Matches under the fingernails? Cattle prod?"

"Just want to talk to him, that's all."

Allocco sighed again. Then he motioned Poole forward.

Warne watched as Poole smoothed his jacket, adjusted his tweed cap. But he didn't step forward. He stayed where he was, speaking across the cell to the man on the bed.

"Sorry about that little dustup back there," he began. "But you know how it is. I just couldn't let you go around breaking things, spoiling everybody's fun. What kind of an Eagle Scout would I be then?"

The man was silent, eyes still shut.

To Warne, the surreal atmosphere had suddenly increased dramatically. A few minutes before, these two had been attacking each other with murderous ferocity. Now one was lying motionless on a cot while the other was speaking in mild, almost understanding tones.

"Shy about your name, I take it?" Poole went on. "Then I'll call you Rogue Twelve."

The man's eyes flitted open, focusing on the ceiling.

"It's just a name. But you're clearly not Rogue One, or even Rogue Two. In fact, I'd guess you're low man on the totem pole. So how many of you are there? Twelve?"

The eyes slid away, then closed again.

"No, I don't think so. Your leader seems smart, I'll bet he'd use a small force. Five operatives, maybe half a dozen. Utopia's so big, people wouldn't be expecting that. A small, experienced group: you'd have your script in place and you'd walk it through. But it would have to be a very good script, carefully planned. You'd get all your placements in advance. But not too far in advance: couldn't take the chance of anybody stumbling accidentally over one of your little presents, could we?"

The eyes opened again, slid toward Poole.

Poole laughed. "How am I doing?"

The eyes slid away again, but remained open, staring at the wall.

"Of course, you wouldn't be expected to work the system alone. You'd have somebody on the inside. No—on second thought, if I were doing it, I'd have two. There'd be a grunt, somebody you'd bought and turned, to do the running and fetching. And then there'd be somebody highly placed, I think." Poole nodded to himself, one hand stroking the collar of his turtleneck as he spoke. "Yes. That would be your knight in shining armor. He'd know how everything ticks, how to circumvent intrusion systems, bypass the Park's natural defenses. But he—or she—wouldn't need to get their hands dirty. Pay no attention to the man behind the curtain, all that kind of thing."

The man stared back at the wall, his mouth set in an unmoving line.

Poole shook his head. "It's too bad, really. Because, at the end of the day, it's always Rogue One who walks away clean. And Rogue Twelve who gets the shaft. You feeling it yet?"

The room fell silent. Poole glanced over at Warne, winked. The silence dragged on.

"Well, well," Allocco said at last, a touch of sarcasm lacing his impatient tone. "Everybody else has weighed in. You got any questions, Lindbergh? Or you, Dr. Warne?"

At this, the man on the cot underwent a remarkable transformation. He had been lying, seemingly at ease, oblivious to the questions. Suddenly, he sat up on the cot. His eyes traveled around the group in the doorway, lighting on Warne.

"Warne!" he barked. "*You*! You're the one who fucked this up. Meddling *prick*!" And he leaped to his feet.

Immediately, Poole shot forward, pushing the hacker brutally back with his shoulder, slamming him against the wall of the cell, one elbow across his throat. The man uttered a strangling sound and Poole released his hold, letting him slide back down to the cot.

For a moment, the man sat there, hand at his throat, coughing. Poole took a step away, motioning Warne to stay behind him.

The hacker glanced over at Warne. The fit of anger passed as quickly as it had come, and now his lips parted in a disdainful smile. The teeth were shockingly yellow.

"I know all about you," the man said. "I watched you, tapping away, trying to figure out what happened to your little shit program." He laughed dryly. "Which, by the way, was *pathetically* coded. Whoever taught you to write in-line assembler did a piss-poor job."

As he listened, Warne was remotely aware that, though the man's features looked Mayan, his accent was distinctly American.

"You don't have a clue to what's going on. But there you were, tapping away. As if you could make a difference." He laughed again: cold, mirthless. "Well, guess what? You're fucked. Every last one of you is *fucked*."

Then he tented his fingers behind his head, closed his eyes, and would not speak again.

3:40 P.M.

THE CALL CAME as Sarah Boatwright was dismissing the line managers from a hastily called impromptu meeting. They'd filed in barely three minutes before: some impatient and preoccupied, others flustered and uncertain. Sarah had canceled the normal lunchtime State of the Park meeting, and rumors had been flying rapidly among the upper administrative echelons ever since. What had happened at Griffin Tower during the 1:20 show? What went wrong with the Waterdark ride? And what was this about some kind of security alert? She had brushed aside all questions with what she hoped looked like distracted lack of concern: the usual crises, nothing too far out of the ordinary. Then she'd asked for any new action items, holding her breath, expecting ominous harbingers of new mischief by John Doe. But all reports were benign and reassuringly commonplace. Unsanitary conditions in the ladies' room at Poor Richard's, the Camelot nightclub. Complaints about an overzealous ride operator on the Steeplechase coaster. And parking attendants had, once again, spotted a particularly bothersome lawyer, trolling for potential plaintiffs at the monorail unloading zone.

Sarah listened, then politely shooed the group away, pleading an unscheduled meeting. She watched as they gathered up their folders and clipboards and left her office. It had been pathetically easy to reassure them. They'd *wanted* to believe, because the alternative was almost unthinkable. For Utopia's supervisors, a smoothly running park was nearly as important as life itself. She wondered how she'd ever find a way to tell them the truth, if and when this nightmare ever ended.

Grace, her administrative assistant, stuck her head in the doorway. "Mr. Emory's on the line, Ms. Boatwright. And I have your ticket at my desk."

Emory, Sarah thought. She had just updated him half an hour

before, what could he want now, when the exchange hadn't yet . . .
She realized her assistant was still standing in the doorway.

"I'm sorry? What about tickets?"

"Your plane ticket. For San Francisco."

"Of course. Thank you, Grace." She smiled, waiting for
the door to close. She'd forgotten all about the entertainment
convention.

Her smile vanished as the door clicked shut. She picked up the
phone. "Mr. Emory?"

"I'm here, Sarah," came the CEO's voice. "There's something
you need to know. These new developments you informed me
of—well, the board is beside itself."

"The *board,* Mr. Emory?"

"After our last conversation, I had the board convene in emergency session."

She waited, listening. It was just like Emory. Unable to make a
crisis decision himself, he'd called in the board to back him up.
Now, instead of just Emory, there would be twelve of them, all
running around frantically, making long-distance judgments, is-
suing contradictory orders, inflaming the situation.

"They had to know, Sarah. You may be the one in the
trenches—and I'm sorry as hell it has to be you—but ultimately
the board is going to be held responsible for what happens. For
what *has* happened. Frankly, I'm surprised at Bob Allocco. Are
you still absolutely positive he isn't—"

"Yes. Mr. Emory, it was my call, and—"

"No need to explain, Sarah. What's done is done. I know you
were acting in the Park's best interests. But with this delay, those
injuries—and especially, the two deaths—they're demanding
action. They can't be seen as just sitting around, letting this
go down."

"But, Mr. Emory, I explained it to you. We're *not* just sitting
around. The exchange is set for four o'clock. We're so close to
resolving this situation. John Doe said—"

"I know. But this John Doe seems erratic, maybe unstable.
With the loss of surveillance, security and public safety are seriously compromised. We can't take any more chances."

Sarah opened her mouth to protest. But it was partly due to
her that Emory had taken this step. She remained silent.

"There's no unanimous position of the board, I'm afraid. But
this is the majority decision. We'll go ahead, use our backup

access codes to burn a second disc. But we can't wait more than another half hour. If Park integrity isn't fully restored by then, we're calling the feds."

"The *feds*?"

"The longer this goes on, the more dangerous it becomes. It's the board's feeling that, unless the situation is resolved immediately, Utopia will pass a point of no return. And there will be no way to contain bad press. If there's a calamity, better to let the cops share the rap. Am I clear?"

Sarah bit down on her lower lip. "All too clear, sir."

"Half an hour, Sarah. Be careful. And may God protect you all."

And the line went dead.

3:45 P.M.

JOHN DOE SAT beneath an awning at Chumley's, Gaslight's outdoor café, his slender hands turning the pages of a freshly printed 1891 edition of the London *Times*. He was in high good humor; so much so that he found himself unable to keep from greeting the guests that passed by along the cobbles. Most of these were moving between Soho Square, the upscale shopping district up the lane, and Mayfair Follies, the live show playing just a few doors down. "Hello!" he would say, smiling at them from behind his sunglasses. "Hello!" A few merely gave him blank looks and moved on more quickly. But the majority smiled and returned the greeting. It was remarkable, really, the transforming power of Utopia. It was almost like a drug.

Yes, it was a delightful spot, this outdoor terrace; just the place to relax with a soothing cup before an appointment. Chumley's tea proved disappointing, so he'd switched to coffee, which was better. He would have to ask Sarah Boatwright which restaurant served that delightful jasmine tea. Shortly, he'd have the chance.

His waiter, a tall fellow in tweeds and oversize four-in-hand, approached the table. "Another cuppa, then?"

"Gladly," John Doe said, sighing contentedly as he turned a page.

The waiter regarded him, an amused smile on his face. "You look chipper, mate."

"Oh, I'm just a man who loves his job."

John Doe watched the waiter thread his way back among the white tablecloths. The fellow's accent was quite good, though a true Cockney, born within earshot of Bow Bells, would probably object to some of the phrasings. Still, it was more than acceptable. The fact was, Gaslight suited John Doe more than any of the other Worlds. Camelot was all gaudy costumes and martial clamor, while Callisto had a burnished postmodern sheen that grated on him. Except, of course, for the distasteful Piccadilly, with its T-shirt shops and trinket emporiums, Gaslight seemed more civilized. And this little café was a real find. Unpretentious, cozy, and just a short walk from the Holo Mirrors. As he glanced around, he spotted first one, then two, well-concealed surveillance cameras. Both currently inactive, alas. John Doe's good humor increased.

The waiter was already returning with a fresh cup of coffee. "Right," the man said, placing it on the tablecloth with a flourish. "Get that down your gregory."

"Thank you," John Doe said, looking up from his paper. "And a right nice caff you have here," he said, slipping into a similar accent. "Not like some of the chippies down the way."

The man smiled. "Oh, ek, we do all right."

John Doe took the cup in both hands. "Little bit taters, though, with the rain and all."

"You fancy a table inside, then?"

"Nah, it's Uncle Tom Cobleigh and all in there. Wouldn't half mind a peek at your menu, though."

"Right you are. Fancy a Jim Skinner? Or just some afters, p'raps?" The man's smile widened, enjoying the challenge. "Unless you're totally boracic? No pictures of the queen about you?"

"No, I'm holding the folding. Just give us a butchers, that's a good lad."

"Good as done." And the man went off for a menu.

John Doe took another sip, greeted a few more passersby, replaced the cup in its saucer. Beyond the awning, the rain was starting again. Actually, it wasn't rain so much as a fine mist, barely enough to dampen the streets, give the surroundings a mellow sheen. John Doe knew that the rains in Gaslight were not timed, but rather set off by a complex set of conditions: crowd flow; ambient temperature of the air; the quality of light in the "real" sky above Utopia's dome, now obscured by the thick London fog. He watched as people rushed under curtains or doorways, waiting for it to pass. It never seemed to last more than ninety seconds. Already, in fact, the gentle patter was ceasing, and people were easing back into the lane, shaking the damp from their shoulders, chattering and laughing.

The truth was, this had all been disappointingly easy. Even this hiccup he'd just learned of was not an important failure.

Contingencies were in place. He sighed, feeling a trace of regret. This was his last job; he'd hoped that it would have proved more challenging, offered some real surprises. At least, that would have given him a chance to exercise his intellect. Something interesting to contemplate in his retirement. But no; that particular delight had been denied him. He watched the people moving by, chattering, oblivious. Like cattle. If he had not been in such a fine mood, he would have felt contempt for them all: contempt for human mores, human frailties, human suffering, human goodness. *Especially* human goodness.

Time to arrange the contingency. Putting the paper aside, he slipped a cell phone from his suit jacket and dialed.

"Ah," he said when a voice answered. "There you are."

The voice on the other end was subdued, furtive. And yet the nervousness, irritation, uncertainty it carried were unmistakable. "It's high time you called. This isn't working out as planned, and I for one don't like it."

"Not as planned? How, exactly?"

"I already told you." The voice was now barely more than a whisper. "That business in Griffin Tower, or in Waterdark. Nobody was supposed to get hurt. And that security specialist, backstage at Galactic Voyage—my God, did you have to *kill* him?"

"I'm afraid there was no choice."

"There's just been too many nasty surprises. And Tibbald never returned from the drop. I'm concerned he might have gone native on us."

John Doe took another sip of coffee, accepted the menu from the waiter, watched the man walk away. "I wouldn't worry about Tibbald. I'm sure he'll turn up."

"And what's this about the second handoff? It's entirely unacceptable, it was never in the script—"

"Perhaps it was. Perhaps it wasn't. That's not important right now." And here John Doe's voice lost a bit of its good humor. "What *is* important is that Cracker Jack has stopped transmitting."

"Why? What's going on?" The uncertain overtone in the voice grew more pronounced.

"I'm not sure. Perhaps somebody's getting frisky. Perhaps it's the work of our unexpected guest, Andrew Warne, who's been poking about where he's not welcome. Or perhaps there was some unforeseen circumstance. Whatever the case, Cracker Jack killed the surveillance feeds."

"I know."

"That's a signal his work upstairs is done, but that we can't count on him for the, ah, basement preparations. You'll have to hold up your end. *Personally*. Do you understand?"

"I got started once I heard about the video going down. I'll be finished in a few minutes."

"Good." Contingency arranged with—as expected—almost depressing ease. "We'll move up certain events to compensate for any loss of control. But this still leaves one open item. Your friend, Warne. Cracker Jack tracked him down earlier, and we went to have a talk with him. But it appears somebody else was wearing Warne's imagetag. And we tried that lab you mentioned, the robotics lab, but it was empty."

"I've been down here the last half hour. I don't know where he's got to."

"Then we need to *learn* where. This is the final act of our little performance. We have to convince him it's in his best interests not to meddle further."

There was a pause on the other end of the line. "You promise not to hurt anyone else?"

"Of course."

"Because I won't take blood money. There's no sense going forward if there's going to be more violence."

"No *sense*?" And here John Doe's voice became quite different: low, disdainful, menacing. Even the accent shifted subtly. "I warn you, don't sport with my intelligence. Expressions of altruism make my gorge rise. *Everything* we do, we do out of self-interest. You, my friend, are no exception. Assertions to the contrary would be mere self-delusion. Need I remind you whose idea this was to begin with? Who contacted *who*? Need I remind you, *again*, of the consequences of developing an eleventh-hour conscience? Remember who I'll be meeting, just a few minutes from now."

There was another pause, longer this time.

"In a few minutes," John Doe said, his voice mellowing, growing silken, "*we* will have everything we came for. Will *you*?"

At last, the silence on the other end was broken. "Warne has a daughter," came the strangled voice. "Her name's Georgia. She's down in Medical."

John Doe's eyebrows shot up. "Indeed? That's very interesting."

"Remember your promise."

"And remember yours. Screw your courage to the sticking place. Another forty-five minutes, and we'll all be gone." And with that, John Doe returned the phone to his pocket, picked up the cup of coffee, and continued his perusal of the newspaper.

ON THE OTHER end of the line, in a large but austere office far below Chumley's Café, the phone rattled slightly as it was replaced in its cradle. The hand that dropped it pressed against the handset for a moment, as if to stifle any further sound. Then it moved across the desk to a freshly burned disc, shimmering like pale crystal inside its protective housing. The hand paused there for a moment, fingers drumming anxiously. And then it reached for a nearby computer keyboard, dragged it closer, and began typing, hesitantly at first, then faster and faster.

3:45 P.M.

"LET ME GET this straight," Warne said. "*This* was your important stop?"

Poole stopped a passing hostess. "Sam Adams, all round."

"Make mine a mineral water, please," Warne sighed. The hostess nodded, then closed the visor of her helmet and glided away between the tables.

Warne turned back to Poole. "You know, Peccam isn't going to be pleased when he learns we gave him the slip just to grab a cool one."

Poole merely shrugged, smiled his distant smile.

They were in the Sea of Tranquility lounge, a large, circular space, dimly illuminated in black light. Guests chattered at nearby tables, sipping drinks and munching exotic-looking bar snacks. Warne could hear shouts and laughter floating in from Callisto's main concourse: from the rear came the clinking of coins and whirring of slot machines within the adjoining casino. Overhead, endless galaxies glittered against a midnight sky. The floor was made of some dark composite, through which gleamed a vast, apparently bottomless starfield. Despite his preoccupation, Warne found himself marveling at the illusion: it really appeared as if the tables around them were floating in an infinity of space. It was an unnerving sensation.

Terri hung her laptop on the side of her chair. "It's against policy for Utopia cast and crew to visit the casinos while working." It was meant as a joke, but her voice was strained.

"Who's visiting?" Poole said. "The casino's over there. And besides, who's working?"

"We *should* be working," Warne replied. "That's the problem."

"Oh, yeah?" Poole asked. "At what?"

"At that Trojan horse. Disassembling it, trying to learn which bots have been modified."

Poole shook his head. "You don't really want to go back to that office, do you? It's safer here—a public place, dimly lit. Besides . . ."

He finished the sentence with a mere wave of the hand, but it was enough. *These guys have run rings around you,* that wave said. *More computer time's not going to get you anywhere.*

It was something Warne had not cared to admit. But now he found his thoughts returning to the hacker, in the holding tank of the Security Complex. The way he'd lunged, sneered at him. His words, dripping with scorn and derision, echoed in Warne's head. *I know all about you, your little shit program. Pathetic. You don't have a clue to what's going on.* The code had been far cleverer than he cared to admit. It had been sheer chance they'd caught the guy at all.

You don't have a clue to what's going on.

He shifted restlessly in his seat.

The hostess returned with their drinks, placing them on the table with silver-gloved hands. Although the three of them must have been a sight—scuffed, bandaged, bruised—the woman merely smiled through her visor and walked away.

There was a sudden burst of laughter nearby, and Warne looked over. Two youths—teenagers, by the look of them—were guzzling tall, brightly colored frozen drinks at an adjoining table. One was wearing a long wizard's cape, obviously purchased in Camelot, over his T-shirt and frayed shorts. It was a fashion statement that would have looked hilariously incongruous anyplace but Utopia.

From the corner of his eye, he saw Poole tilt the beer into his glass, raise it to his lips, take a long pull. The red-spotted gauze bandage fluttered loosely at his wrist.

Terri broke the silence. "You still haven't told us why you're doing all this."

Poole put down his glass and wiped his lips with an oddly dainty motion.

"That's right," Warne added. "You could have been here all this time, relaxing. Instead of getting kicked at, shot at, God knows what else."

Poole smiled. "Think of the people who spend thousands of

bucks on those phony mystery weekends at hotels. This is much better. And the price is right."

"You act like it's just part of the entertainment."

"Isn't it?" Poole's smile widened. "Besides, it gives me a chance to keep my hand in, sharpen up the old skills." And he took another sip of his drink.

Warne looked at him with a sigh of resignation. He didn't think he'd ever met anybody quite so hard to read.

"You've got a point about that lab," he said. "So then if it's all the same to you, Terri and I will go visit my daughter." He started to rise.

"What's your hurry? In another fifteen minutes, John Doe will get his disc. And then he'll walk into the sunset, the houselights will come up, the music will swell. Happy ending, right?" Poole said this in an exceedingly unconvincing tone of voice.

"What?" Terri said. "What are you getting at?" She took a sip of the beer, made a face, pushed it away.

"I said this was an important stop, right? And I meant it. But much as I wanted a beer, it was the *stop* that was important."

Warne sat down again. He shook his head. "You're speaking in riddles."

"No, I'm not. Remember who I am here. I'm the observer, the outsider who doesn't really know what's going on." He took another sip. "That means, while you all have been racing around like headless chickens, I've watched. I've listened."

Warne glanced across the table at Terri. She shrugged in reply.

"What's your point?" he asked.

Poole picked up the bottle of Sam Adams, scratched idly at the label with a finger. "Haven't you noticed a pattern here?"

"No."

Poole continued to scratch. "They tell you to keep everyone in the dark about what's going on. And then they run you ragged, keep you reeling from one thing to another, never give anyone time to draw breath. To stop and ask a few basic questions." He set down the bottle. "Because this whole thing is like a jigsaw puzzle. You find the right piece, you see the whole picture. And they can't allow you to do that."

"Basic questions?" Warne asked. "What kind, exactly?"

"Here's one. If these guys are so good, why did they screw up on Waterdark? They intended to blow the whole ride, teach a lesson. What luck that retaining spar broke the way it did, keeping the ride from collapsing. But I disagree. I saw the blast signature from that charge, remember? Whoever set it was a goddamn *artist*. If they'd wanted to destroy that ride, they'd have done it."

So there was no miscalculation, after all, Warne thought to himself gloomily.

Terri shifted impatiently in her seat. "Okay. Call me dumb, but I'm not getting something here."

"These guys want to bang up some people, cause a lot of hand-wringing. But despite what John Doe says, they *don't* want a panic. Not now. That wouldn't fit into their plans. We have to assume that everything these guys do happens for a reason. The explosion in Waterdark? It was set to break *exactly* the way it did."

There was a brief silence while this was digested.

"If you ask me, that sounds nuts," Terri said. "But here's another question. You said everything these guys do happens for a reason. Remember how Allocco said that hacker in the Hub killed the video feeds? He shut down everything but the casinos and C Level. The casinos make sense, they have their own systems. But C Level is part of the central surveillance network. Why wasn't it shut down, too?"

"I don't know," Poole said. "What's down there?"

"Power plant. Laundry. Environmental Services, Treasury Operations, Food Services. Machine shops, attraction repair, data processing. Back-office stuff."

"That power plant you mention," Poole said. "It isn't nuclear, is it?"

Terri rolled her eyes.

Poole shrugged. "One hears rumors."

For a few moments, the table was silent.

"You called it a jigsaw," Warne said. "But we don't have any pieces. What kind of puzzle do you call that?"

"You're forgetting we have a critical piece," Poole replied. "Our friend in the cell. And he said something very interesting."

"What's that?"

"You remember how he reacted when he learned who you were? That, at least, wasn't a put-on. He wanted your throat. But it doesn't follow."

"Of course it does," Terri said. "Andrew here rained on his parade. Wrecked everything for him."

"Maybe. But do you remember *why* he was ripshit? Think

back to what he said. It was your *messing around* with the system that really riled him."

"So?" Warne asked.

"Why wasn't he mad about the trap they set in, what's it called, Galactic Voyage? That was their real problem. If it wasn't for that, they'd have gotten their disc and all been gone long ago. Right?"

Warne paused, thinking.

"*Inay*," Terri muttered beside him.

The shattered disc. He'd forgotten all about it. Warne reached into his pocket, pulled out the Ziploc bag Sarah had left in the medical bay.

"What's that?" Poole asked.

"Shards from the Crucible disc," Warne said. "Crushed in the scuffle." He laid it on the table. "So what are you saying, exactly?"

"I'm saying this whole thing sounds like a stall. A carefully orchestrated, carefully concealed stall."

"But why?" Terri asked, picking up the bag, turning it over curiously in her hands. "What are they waiting for?"

"Yes. That's the million-dollar question, isn't it?"

And in the silence that followed, he drained his glass and set it on the table with a sigh of satisfaction.

3:50 P.M.

ALTHOUGH THERE WERE no clocks on display in the public areas of Utopia, the time was precisely ten minutes to four.

In Gaslight, a large crowd had gathered outside the entrance to the Holo Mirrors. This was not the attraction's real name: on guidemaps, and on the ornate sign above the pre-show area, it was prominently labeled *Professor Cripplewood's Chamber of Fantastic Illusion.* It was a next-generation hall of mirrors, using Utopia's Crucible technology to render lifelike holograms from secretly taken photographs of those who stepped inside. The holograms were processed to look like mirror images, then displayed in real time throughout the chamber's dimly lit maze. Actual mirrors were used as well, creating a fiendishly baffling environment. Visitors, stumbling through the twisting corridors, were constantly confronted by images of themselves and other guests in the maze: yet they could never be sure if these were actual reflections, or holographic renderings of themselves, taken at earlier points in the chamber. Guests emerged disoriented, frightened, fascinated. Holo Mirrors—as it was universally known—was such an unusual experience that it had the highest same-day repeat percentage of any attraction in Gaslight.

Only the crowd currently outside was not full of the usual expectant eagerness. There were cries of frustration from guests who had waited in line nearly an hour, only to learn that the attraction was being temporarily shut down due to operational difficulties. Attendants in crinolines and foremen in frock coats worked the line, soothing tempers with return vouchers and casino chips. To one side of the brick-front entrance, Sarah Boatwright stood, arms folded, almost invisible in the mist. She was watching the milling crowd. One hand was pressed protectively against a disc in her jacket pocket.

* * *

FAR OVERHEAD, IN the pitiless Nevada sun, the cool moist fog of Gaslight was like a dream of a gentler world. The man known as Water Buffalo had finished his work and now sat in a gully, resting in the shadow cast by the smooth curve of the Utopia dome. A two-way radio lay beside one knee, a plastic water bottle by the other. From time to time he took his eyes from the dome and gazed over the rocky lip of the escarpment, down the long dusky road far below that snaked away from staff parking and vanished into the dry tableland of Yucca Flats.

FIFTEEN MILES AWAY, beyond the limits of vision, two vehicles were heading northwest along Highway 95. The rear vehicle was a late-model sedan, an amber flasher on its dashboard and a bulky takedown light fixed outside the driver's window. Long whip antennas bobbed on either side of the trunk. The car was painted white, but was now brown as a wren from the miles of dust thrown up by the vehicle in front of it.

The forward vehicle was an armored car, Ford model F8000, painted red with white accents around the muzzle ports and window cowlings. The ten-speed diesel rumbled unhappily, laboring under the weight of the quarter-inch ballistic steel that covered the body panels, laterals, and roof. A lone guard sat in the payload compartment, back against the wall, booted feet on the fragmentation blanket that covered the floor. A pump-action shotgun rested between his knees. Man and gun swayed together, jouncing in time to the heavy suspension.

In the forward compartment, the line-haul driver guided the vehicle up the grade. Beyond the dashboard, the browns, yellows, and greens of the high desert landscape looked slightly unearthly, their colors shifted by the bullet-resistant transparent armor that made up the windshield.

The driver adjusted his headset, spoke into it. "Utopia Central, this is AAS transport Nine Echo Bravo, over."

The headset crackled. "Utopia Central confirms."

"We've left 95, on approach. Expect arrival at 1610 hours."

"Nine Echo Bravo, 1610, understood."

The headset crackled once more, then fell silent. The armored car turned onto the unmarked highway exit that led to the access road; the grade steepened; and the driver ran the gears, accelerating the big truck toward the maintenance entrance of Utopia.

3:50 P.M.

KYLE COCHRAN STOOD outside the Sea of Tranquility lounge, resplendent in the violet and black cape of Mymanteus the Archmage. Although the light of the concourse was subdued, the bar had been darker still, and he waited while his eyes adjusted. Beside him, Tom Walsh, a little taller and much slimmer, stifled a belch. They'd just pounded down four Supernovas each. That would make a new school record. The fact that the drinks were nonalcoholic didn't really lessen the achievement: Supernovas were huge, multihued, crushed-ice concoctions, and Kyle's stomach had long since gone numb in indignation. As always, it was a little annoying that he wouldn't be able to take a legal drink for another year. But at a place like Utopia, it was probably just as well. They had a dorm buddy, Jack Fischer, who'd smuggled in a fifth of bourbon, gotten wasted, and then vomited all over his fellow riders on the Scream Machine, just a few weeks before.

Walsh belched again, loudly this time, turning the heads of several passersby.

"Nice one," Kyle said, nodding approvingly at his friend.

Coming to UCSB as a freshman, Kyle had heard horror stories of college roommates from hell: the party animal who cranked death metal on his stereo until dawn, the slob who changed his underwear once a week. Tom Walsh had proved a pleasant surprise. The two shared many interests: track and field, ska music, dirt bikes. Tom was a whiz in the hard sciences, while Kyle wrote decent papers and spoke fluent French, and they'd helped each other through what could have been a rough first year. As sophomores, their paths had diverged, but they still remained close friends. Tragedy struck at Christmas, however, when Tom's older brother was killed in a motorcycle accident. Throughout the winter, Tom remained moody and withdrawn, and Kyle had been half-surprised when his friend took him up on the idea of spending spring break in Las Vegas. But, very gradually, Tom was at last returning to his old self. At first it had seemed almost a conscious effort, as if he were just going through the motions of having a good time. But at Utopia especially, Tom had lapsed into easy banter, and his smiles were genuine. He'd even talked about applying here for a summer job.

Kyle yawned, stretched. "So, dude, what now?"

Tom patted his stomach. "I don't know. I was thinking, maybe, Station Omega?"

Kyle looked at him again, this time in disbelief. "You're shitting me. After downing four Supernovas? Get real."

Tom's only answer was a crooked grin.

Kyle considered this as he stood on the concourse, heedless of the streams of chattering guests surrounding them. Station Omega was Callisto's "free-fall," a relatively new breed of ride in which guests were allowed, quite literally, to drop from a great height. Commonly, riders were strapped into place, as if riding a vertical roller coaster. But Utopia's designers had taken the standard free-fall concept and made it their own. Guests would board an escalator at Callisto's Skyport and enter an elevator-like compartment that would—so the storyboard went—be transporting them to a waiting shuttle. But as soon as the elevator doors closed, something would go terribly wrong. There was a lurch, then a shudder. Ominous cracking noises would be heard. The lights would wink out, smoke would begin to fill the compartment. And then—without warning—the guests would hurtle straight downward a hundred feet before the lights came on, brakes were applied, and the elevator slowed to a quick but remarkably gentle stop.

It was a short ride, but effective; so effective that Station Omega had some of the most restrictive ridership requirements in Utopia.

And Kyle and Tom had already taken the drop six times that day.

Now Kyle glanced down the concourse, toward the crowds milling around the Skyport. Six drops in Station Omega was already a UCSB record. It looked pretty crowded down there. And the line for their last ride had been their longest of the day.

Still, seven times would cement their achievement. Especially after knocking back those four Supernovas.

Besides, Tom had been the one to suggest it.

Kyle looked over, gave the thumbs-up. And Tom's grin widened into a genuine smile.

"Come on," Kyle said, swinging his cape with a flourish. "Let's go for it."

"WAIT A MINUTE," Terri said. "Something's wrong here."

Warne lifted his head and looked across the table at her. Angus Poole, too, lowered his beer and looked over, drawn by something in her tone.

She'd opened the plastic bag and was holding one of the larger shards in her hand, turning it over and over. "This disc," she said. "It's blank."

"What?" Warne replied. "That's impossible. It's the Crucible technology; they were handing it over to John Doe."

"I'm telling you, it's *blank*. Look, under this black light you can tell." She handed him the shard. "See? If data had been burned to this, you'd see the pits and lands in the polycarbonate. But nothing. Nada."

Poole took the bag. "I don't see anything."

She looked at him sardonically. "Listen to a trained professional here."

"But that doesn't make sense," Warne said. "Why would we give him a blank disc?"

"Maybe we didn't," Terri replied.

Warne shut up abruptly, grappling with this fresh surprise, struggling to unravel John Doe's clever little knot. What was it Poole had said? *Stop and ask a few basic questions.*

And then, suddenly, he had an idea.

"Terri," he said. "That worm we found was inserted into your computer a month ago. Is there any way it could have been planted remotely, over the Net?"

"Nope. All Utopia terminals are individually firewalled. I can't even receive mail on that machine."

"It's ironclad?"

"No hacker could get through it."

"External *or* internal?"

Terri shook her head.

"Then that can mean only one thing: the worm had to be *physically copied* onto your machine. From inside your office." Warne paused. "Now, think carefully. Who could have had access to your terminal around that time?"

"Nobody."

"Not coworkers? Not your boss?"

"I would have known."

"You're sure?"

"Sure."

Warne sat back. The speculation that had been gathering dissolved abruptly into disappointment.

Then he had another thought. "What about you, then? Did you install anything? Any new programs, OS upgrades?"

"Nothing. They're very strict about production systems. No software gets installed without prior approval from IT. But there hasn't been anything, not since the Metanet itself. And that was close to a year ago."

Warne slumped further in his chair. Around him, the Sea of Tranquility was abuzz. The two rowdy youths at the next table had left, only to be replaced by a family of six. The children were drinking root beer floats and playing with foam-rubber swords.

"Wait a minute."

At the sound of Terri's voice, he sat up quickly.

"There *was* something. Just over a month ago."

Warne looked at her.

"But it's not the smoking gun you're looking for. In fact, it's just the opposite."

"Tell me."

"Remember how we said the entire Utopia system was recently white-hatted?"

"Yup. By KIS, the same outfit that did Carnegie-Mellon." Barksdale had mentioned this in the morning meeting.

"White-hatted?" Poole asked, draining his beer.

"Hackers for hire," Warne explained. "Legitimate snoops. Big firms employ them to try to break in, uncover security loopholes." He turned back to Terri. "Go on."

"Well, we got a good report card. They said our network was decently hardened. But they did distribute a system patch for some of the high-security terminals. To fix a bug in Unix that could potentially be leveraged by hackers, they said."

"A system patch? For how many terminals?"

"Not many. A dozen or two."

"And yours was one of them." It was a statement, not a question.

Terri nodded.

For a moment, Warne remained motionless. Then he stood up, the chair skidding back across the transparent floor.

"Where's the closest phone?" he asked.

"The public phones are in the Nexus. We'll have to go down the concourse and—"

"No," he interrupted. "We need to find a phone. Any phone. *Now*."

Terri stared at him in silence. Then she, too, stood up, motioning for them to follow.

Warne dropped some bills on the table and they half walked, half jogged toward the rear of the lounge, into a wide passage leading to Callisto's casino. Terri walked directly toward one wall, opened a well-disguised door. It was lined in the same dark material as the wall, invisible save for the gray rectangle of corridor that lay beyond it. He ducked through, followed by Poole.

Closing the door behind them, Terri led the way down a metal staircase and along a service corridor, turning into a large office labeled *Compliance*. A bank of secretaries sat in carrels along the far wall, typing. One or two looked up briefly, then turned back to their screens.

Terri pointed to a phone on an empty desk. Warne picked it up, pressed the button for an outside line, dialed.

"Directory assistance? I need a listing in Marlborough, New Hampshire. Keyhole Intrusion Systems."

A moment later, he was dialing again.

"KIS," a woman's voice said on the other end of the line.

"Give me Walter Ellison's office, please." Warne mentally crossed his fingers. It was almost four. As he remembered, Walt Ellison was a workaholic. There was a very good chance he'd be there, if he wasn't at a client's. *Pick up, damn you, pick up* . . .

"Ellison here," came the voice he remembered: loud, nasal, Bostonian.

"Walt, this is Andrew Warne. You tested our system at Carnegie-Mellon last year. Remember?"

There was a silence on the other end, and for a sickening

moment he feared Ellison had forgotten him. Then he heard a lazy laugh.

"Warne, sure. Robotics, right?"

"Yes."

"How's that ice cream vendor of yours, what's its name—"

"Hard Place."

"Hard Place, right. Sheesh. What a piece of work." Another laugh.

Warne leaned into the phone. "Walt, listen. I need a favor. It's about a KIS client."

"You mean Carnegie-Mellon."

"No."

Ellison's tone grew a little distant. "Hey, Dr. Warne, you know I can't discuss other clients."

"If I'm right, you won't have to. See, I don't want to know about work you've done. Just about work you *haven't* done."

There was a pause. "I don't follow."

"Remember who I was building Hard Place for?"

"Sure, the theme . . . I mean, yes, I remember the entity."

"Good. And you know I do work for that, ah, entity?"

"I gathered as much."

"Then you shouldn't mind answering one last question. Has KIS ever done a security audit for them?"

The line was silent.

"Look," Warne said urgently. "I *have* to know."

Still, silence.

"It could mean life or death, Walter."

There was a sigh. "Guess it's no secret," Ellison said. "We've never worked for them. Would be a peach of a job, though. Could you swing it, you think? Put a bug in the right ear?"

"Thanks a lot," Warne said, hanging up. Then he turned to face Terri and Poole.

"KIS never came to Utopia," he said.

Disbelief rushed into Terri's face. "That's impossible. I saw the team myself. They were here for the better part of a day."

"What you saw was John Doe's advance guard."

Terri didn't answer.

"And those system patches they handed out? Stealth software. When you ran the patch, you installed their Trojan horse *on your own system*."

"You mean—" She hesitated. "You mean the whole thing was a ruse?"

"A very clever, very brazen one. To infect certain Utopia systems, pave the way for what's happening today."

"But that can't be. KIS is a real company, you said so yourself. It can't be a ruse."

Terri was speaking quickly. *She's beginning to understand,* Warne thought to himself. *And she doesn't like where this is leading.*

"Yes, it *is* a real company. John Doe knew that. Utopia would never have fallen for a phony. But the people who showed up— who did the security audit, gave you those system patches— were impostors, not KIS employees. Instead of closing loopholes, they were creating them."

"*Sira ulo,*" Terri muttered. "No."

"KIS *was never here.*" Warne gestured toward the phone. "I just got it from the horse's mouth."

"But we would have *known,*" she said. "Fred arranged the whole thing himself. He would have smelled a rat, he would have known if something—"

She fell silent. Warne took her hands.

"Terri," he said. "Fred Barksdale *is* the rat."

"No," she repeated.

"He's the one. John Doe's man on the inside. He gave John Doe everything he needed to compromise your systems. Nobody else had the access, the authorization. Nobody else could have set it up."

With an awful, piercing kind of clarity, Warne saw the layers of deception peel away one by one. No doubt, early on, John Doe had had his men try halfheartedly to break into Utopia's computer network from the outside. That would have given Barksdale legitimate reason to contact Keyhole Intrusion Systems. Only it wasn't KIS who showed up to check Utopia's defenses, it was John Doe's team. Unwittingly, Utopia had not only allowed its systems to be hacked—it had even invited the hackers in. Those strange glitches Sarah had mentioned early on, the disaster on the Notting Hill ride, must have been by-products of the installation process—or, perhaps, cold-blooded field tests by John Doe. And yet even now, with proof staring directly at him, he did not want to face the consequences of such a complete, such a devastating betrayal. *No, not Barksdale, he knows too much about . . .*

As he finished the thought, he felt his heart begin to beat wildly within his chest.

Terri stared at him, a strange expression on her face. Then, slowly, her eyes fell away. She shook her head, not speaking.

"I know. It's a terrible, terrible thing. I don't understand it any more than you do." Warne tightened his grip on her hands. "But right now we don't have time to figure it out."

He turned to Poole. "You've got to find Barksdale. Get him to Security, stop him before he causes any more damage." He fished in his pocket. "Here's my passcard. I've got Sarah's tag, I won't need it."

Poole remained motionless. "Find Barksdale. And what if he hangs tough? You think they'll take my word over his?"

"You're the war hero, you figure something out. Tell them what I just told you."

With a grunt, Poole took the card, slipped it inside his jacket. When the hand came back out, it held an automatic pistol.

Warne glanced at it in surprise. Then he remembered how the hacker had fired at them, back in the Hub; how the man had dropped his weapon in the scramble that followed. Funny he'd forgotten about it all this time.

"What about you?" Poole asked, checking the weapon, returning it to his jacket. "I still want that lifetime pass."

"I'll be okay. I'll meet you in the Security Complex. Just get Barksdale."

"You take care." And Poole ducked out into the corridor.

Warne turned back to Terri, still silent and white-lipped. "Do you understand what this means? If that disc is blank, they must have planted it there. They have the good disc. *They already have the Crucible technology.* Why is John Doe asking Sarah to deliver another one, and deliver it herself? He wants her. Why, I don't know. But I do know she's in danger."

Even as he spoke the words, another, even more terrible image flashed across his mind: Barksdale, that morning, suggesting Terri take Georgia for a soda. *Barksdale knows about my daughter. But does John Doe?*

Terri was watching him intently. Suddenly, her eyes grew wide. It was as if her own thoughts had raced to the same question.

Warne spun away, clenching and unclenching his fists. He was in an agony of indecision. Sarah Boatwright was in grave danger. She was walking—unwittingly—into John Doe's hands. On the other hand, Georgia might be at risk herself. Perhaps it wasn't likely. But if they'd been searching for him . . . if they had already killed somebody, *believing* it to be him . . . and if John Doe learned . . . Georgia, *his only family* . . .

He could not reach them both. There was only time for one. One in certain danger; the other in possible danger. One loved, one once loved. He pressed his face into his hands. It was an awful, unthinkable dilemma.

He felt a hand fall on his shoulder. "I'll go," came the voice.

He turned back to Terri. "I'll go," she repeated in her low, uninflected voice. "I'll watch Georgia."

He let his hands drop to his sides. "You will?"

She nodded.

For a moment, the surge of relief was so strong that Warne felt physically weak. "You know where she is, right? Still in the Medical Facility, in a recovery bay." He thought quickly. "I want you to take her someplace where the two of you can hide. Get her to Security, if you can, but get her somewhere you'll be safe. Just to be sure. Will you do that?"

Terri nodded again.

"Thank you, Terri. Thank you. Thank you."

He embraced her, held her close against him for a moment, then pulled away. Terri's eyes did not leave his face as he headed for the door.

A moment later, he was once again in the corridor, running now, heading back toward the public spaces of Utopia.

CENTRAL WARDROBE WAS a sprawling warren of rooms on B Level. Though its halls were always teeming with cast members, Wardrobe seemed to grow particularly busy as four o'clock approached. Royal dukes and knights errant from Camelot, going off-shift, butted elbows with street vendors in straw skimmers and seersucker suits, bound for Boardwalk and the evening festivities. Courtiers in wimples and flowing dresses chatted with interstellar explorers wearing pressurized flight suits. Dressers, milliners, costume consultants, tailors, and speech trainers wandered through the hallways, adjusting and instructing. It was a bizarre, noisy, disconcerting mix of old and new, past and future.

The dormitory-size men's lavatory was sandwiched between Costume Storage and Cosmetic Prep. Inside, a lone male stood before a bank of sinks. He was washing his hands carefully, taking time to remove some caked material from beneath his fingernails. That accomplished, he pulled a paper towel from a nearby dispenser, glancing up at a mirror as he did so. A pair of taciturn, almond-shaped eyes stared back.

The door opened and a group of jugglers in brightly colored motley entered, laughing and chatting. Tossing away the towel, the man left the lavatory and threaded his way past dressing rooms and the Camelot prop repository—long ranks of swords, lances, mail suits, shields, pennants, and breastplates gleaming under fluorescent lights—to Men's Changing. Finding his locker, he spun the dial, lifted the latch, opened the gray metal door. He had already replaced his malacca cane—newly cleaned and polished to shiny perfection—on a rack of fifty identical specimens in Gaslight Prop. He'd deposited the Inverness cape and woolen suit into one of the numerous metal hatches of the HPLR, the high-pressure laundry removal system that lined the walls of

Central Wardrobe. Now he peered inside his locker, examining the shiny, almost iridescent suit of a Callistan shuttle pilot that hung on a hook, next to a set of dark blue coveralls.

There was a brief, muffled *chirrup*. The man glanced around, making sure he was unobserved. Then he plucked a radio from his pocket. He leaned casually against the adjoining lockers, shielding himself with the open door, snapped the radio on, and entered the descrambling code.

"Hardball," he said into the microphone.

"Hardball, this is Prime Factor," came the voice of John Doe. "Any curious onlookers?"

"Negatory."

"Your work in Gaslight?"

"We're all set."

"So to speak." A dry laugh sounded over the radio. "Listen closely, there's been a change of plans. Once you've completed the final assignment in Callisto, you'll need to make one more stop on the way down to C Level. Remember our evasive friend, Andrew Warne?"

"Affirmative."

"Turns out he brought his impedimenta to the Park along with him. His daughter's down in Medical. Recovering from the late unpleasantness at Waterdark, it appears. Her name is Georgia."

"Understood."

"You're to bring her to the regrouping waypoint. She may prove useful."

"Understood."

"There's still no word from Cracker Jack. I've got the backup transmitter, so that's not a concern. But I'm troubled by the way this Warne fellow keeps giving us the slip. Still, perhaps you'll find him with his daughter. That would make things easier. Either way, you can expect company."

The man called Hardball glanced down into the locker. A pilot's flight bag lay there, gleaming faintly silver in the reflected light. "Not a problem."

"I knew it wouldn't be. But time is of the essence. I've got an appointment to keep. And you've got a few of your own. Ready to light the candle?"

"Just dressing for it now."

"In that case: fire in the hole." There was a pause. "I've always wanted to say that."

John Doe's chuckle died away as the almond-eyed man dropped the radio back into his pocket. Then he took another look around, removed the pilot's suit from the hanger, and began shrugging into it.

4:00 P.M.

THE QUEUE HAD been surprisingly, mercifully short, and the last Supernova was still cold in his belly when Kyle Cochran saw the barrier rope draw away from the base of the escalator. It wasn't a rope, actually, but some kind of hologram: a slick, high-tech re-creation of those thick velvet cords you saw hanging across old theater lobbies. It brightened briefly, coruscating bands of purple flaring to yellow, then seemed to evaporate into thin air. A nearby shuttle attendant came forward, smiling and gesturing for the head of the line to step onto the escalator. As Kyle waited, he felt himself jostled from the rear by his friend, Tom Walsh.

"Easy, big fellah," he said with a laugh.

Even the escalator was cool: the handrails glowing a subdued blue neon, the moving steps made of some semitransparent substance. It was slow, but silky smooth, affording an ever-expanding view of the Skyport falling away beneath. Kyle turned around to look, drinking it all in. It was the seventh time he'd seen it that day, but it was a view that didn't get old: lines of guests snaking across the illuminated station floor; lasers and exotic lighting effects throwing the massive architecture into bold relief; the vast dome of stars arching over all. The only ride without a queue line was Escape from Waterdark, mysteriously closed for maintenance during the peak attendance period.

Seven drops on Station Omega. Goddamn.

At the top of the escalator, another attendant guided the guests into a hallway labeled *Transport Approach*. Tom walked along with the crowd, craning his head over the people ahead of him. There it was, doors wide open at the far end of the corridor, pale walls shimmering faintly: the shuttle transport. The so-called shuttle transport. A one-way ticket, straight down. The interior was illuminated a pale crimson, and it reminded him of a vast open mouth. He shuddered pleasantly.

A third attendant waited at the end of the passage. "Travel time to the shuttle will be approximately five minutes," she said as she guided people into the waiting transport. "Please have your boarding passes ready. The shuttle is due to leave spacedock in twenty minutes, so please move quickly once exiting the transport."

As he allowed himself to be herded into the chamber, Kyle grinned to himself. He loved being one of the insiders, listening to all this carefully practiced deception. It was like watching the skilled misdirection of a master magician. He glanced around at the other occupants. Several of them were also grinning knowingly.

For veteran riders of Station Omega, the drop itself was only half the fun. The other half was watching the reaction of fellow riders. Despite the notoriety of the ride—the magazine articles, the websites devoted to Station Omega trivia—there were always a few passengers who weren't in on it. They truly believed they were about to take a ride on a shuttle, and that this oversize elevator was merely transportation to the real attraction. Kyle's practiced eye roamed over the sixty-odd guests crowded around him, ferreting out the ignorant. That Japanese tour group, chatting animatedly to one side: maybe. That pair of adolescent lovebirds in the corner, more interested in groping each other than in their surroundings: another maybe. The middle-aged couple in matching shirts and hats, wondering out loud how long the shuttle ride would be: definitely. Kyle nodded smugly to himself. When all hell broke loose, those two would be the ones to watch.

Outside, in the access corridor, Kyle could see the third attendant, talking to a white-haired couple in a low, urgent voice. The couple wasn't all that old—maybe sixty, maybe a little more—but the attendant was obviously turning them away. Utopia took no chances. Kyle knew, from the websites he'd visited, that the shuttle attendants at Station Omega were more than just a glorified boarding crew—they were medically trained staff, on the lookout for anyone even remotely unfit for a free-fall drop. He watched the two move grudgingly away, fresh casino vouchers in hand. They could have been his own parents. A part of him was glad they wouldn't be going on the ride.

He glanced over at Tom, nudging him in the ribs and nodding

toward the tourists in the matching outfits. Tom glanced over, rolled his eyes. *Yup*, his expression seemed to say. *Victims*.

Kyle grinned. In addition to a mounting sense of expectation, he was aware, far back in his mind, of another feeling: a feeling very close to relief. Tom was acting like his old self again. Maybe it was just a one-day blip. But then again, maybe he was, at last, beginning to see some light at the end of the tunnel.

The transport chamber was almost full now, and people were shuffling back and forth, creating small oases of space, in the unconscious way they did in subway cars and elevators. In a few moments, it wouldn't matter: everyone would be screaming, clutching at whoever was closest, personal space forgotten in the terrifying plunge into darkness.

Once again, Kyle wondered, a little idly, how it was done; how they managed to keep everyone upright and level during the drop. In free-fall rides at other parks, people were strapped into cars like they were wearing straightjackets. But here—where the element of surprise was everything—seats and straps would have been a dead giveaway. He knew somebody, a graduate student at UCSB's engineering school, who had a theory; something about the use of compressed air. Kyle made a mental note to pay careful attention this time. But it was difficult: the fall was so abrupt, so brief and wrenching, that almost before you drew in breath to scream it was over. And then there was . . .

His thoughts were cut short as the transport doors whispered shut, sealing the crowded car from the corridor beyond. He heard a loud clang from outside, then a voice came over an invisible internal speaker. *Transport under way to shuttle dock. You may feel a small vibration as we leave the airlock.*

A small vibration, Kyle thought to himself. *Yeah, right.*

This was the moment he loved most: the last few seconds before the bottom dropped out of the world. He felt his nerve ends taut with anticipation. He caught Tom's eye, gave him a thumbs-up. Then he glanced at the faces around him—some smiling conspiratorially, some bored and blissfully unaware—before settling at last on the couple with the matching hats.

There was a humming noise outside the compartment, as if an engine had engaged. The hum rose in intensity as power increased. A sensation of gentle movement.

Then a sudden lurch.

"Shit!" came an involuntary mutter.

Abruptly, the sensation of movement stopped. There was another jolt, stronger this time, and the lights flickered briefly. Kyle watched as the couple in matching outfits exchanged glances of mild surprise. Naked fear would follow soon enough.

The whine of the engines increased; grew ragged; then cut out. In the sudden silence, tickings and creakings of metal sounded outside the transport. There was a crack, louder this time, and yet another jolt. And then, suddenly, the lights snapped out.

There was a moment of pitch-blackness. Then a bank of emergency lighting, thin and blood-red, came on near the floor. Kyle liked this touch especially: the light rose up, rather than down, throwing everybody's features into grotesque relief.

Attention, came the voice over the intercom. *We are experiencing difficulties with the main propulsion system. We will be under way shortly. Do not be alarmed.*

Please, do be alarmed, Kyle thought, sneaking another glance toward the matching couple. Their eyes were wide and staring now, their faces set.

Another, rending crack sounded from outside, followed by the brittle hissing of sparks. And then, right on cue, came the smoke.

Kyle tensed. This was it: this was the drop.

He waited, half-eager, half-apprehensive, for that indescribable moment when you suddenly realized there was no longer any floor beneath your feet, and you were hurtling downward into the void. He took one breath, then another.

And then something very strange happened. The red emergency lights winked out.

Kyle waited, listening to the rumblings and hissings outside the transport. He felt himself jostled gently as the bodies around him shuffled in utter darkness. He didn't remember the emergency lights ever going out before—not completely, anyway. Had he just failed to notice before in the excitement?

Around him, he could feel his fellow guests standing in place, some tense with anticipation of the drop, others mystified. He didn't remember this long a wait, at all. Maybe he'd just grown too used to the ride.

But there was something else. Every place he'd been in Utopia had been cool, almost chill. That went for the rides as well as the boulevards and concourses. It was something you took for granted, never even noticed. But it seemed hot inside this transport: hot, and getting hotter.

There were voices around him now, talking in low, urgent tones.

"What's up?" he heard somebody ask.

"When are we going?" came a plaintive voice.

"Are we on our way to the shuttle now?" asked a third.

Kyle tugged at his shirt, plucking it away from his chest. The cape around his shoulders seemed suffocatingly heavy. Christ, it was getting hot.

He felt himself jostled again, more forcefully this time, and as he flung a hand out to restore his balance, he felt the back of his arm slide along a man's face, sweaty and stubbled. He shrank away. *Probably some kind of goddamn breakdown*, he thought with a mixture of annoyance and concern. *The kind of money you spend to get into this place, you'd think this wouldn't happen.*

In the darkness, a small voice started to cry.

The murmur of voices began to rise, notes of tension unmistakable now. Kyle glanced around, eyes wide against the darkness; but the darkness remained, unvexed by any light. It was an unfamiliar and somehow awful thing, absolute darkness. Only once before had he been completely without light, on a spelunking trip with some fellow UCSB students. As a joke, the leader had all the cavers turn off their helmet lamps when they reached the bottom of the cavity. But that had been for just a moment. And they'd all had flashlights. And they'd been able to get *out*.

Why did we have to make it seven? he asked himself as the incorporeal forms around him grew more restless, the voices more agitated. *Why couldn't we have left it at six?* This would ruin everything.

Utter darkness was terrifying. You felt defenseless, helpless, disoriented. And how much worse to be here, in an oversize shoe box, sweating your balls off, hanging suspended over a drop that . . .

With an effort, Kyle mastered himself. *Maybe this is intentional. They probably monitor the fan sites on the Web, watching for guests getting too complacent, rides getting too familiar. Maybe they've changed the ride. To keep repeat riders guessing, keep things from getting stale. That would be their style.*

Even if it *was* some kind of breakdown, he reasoned, there was nothing to worry about. The whole place was crawling with engineers and mechanics. It had to be. A few more seconds and they'd go into free fall; he knew they would. And he'd have even more of a story to tell back at the dorm . . .

As if in response to his thoughts, the car gave another lurch. There was a tense, excited burst of chatter as sixty-odd people tried to keep their balance in the blackness. *Here we go*, Kyle thought. And the relief that flooded through him was almost overwhelming.

But they did not go. And now, as he waited in the sweltering, oppressive darkness, Kyle realized something must be terribly wrong. It was too hot, too stifling, for the close quarters, the crush of bodies, to account for by themselves. He could feel the smoke continue to tumble down upon them, but it wasn't like the fake smoke of the previous drops. That had been cool, moist, scentless, even refreshing. This was hot, almost scalding.

"I can't breathe!" somebody cried. There was a sudden, wild scuffling to his right.

Kyle tried to gulp air. His lungs felt parched. He wheeled around in confused desperation.

"Get us out of here!" cried another voice.

"We're trapped! Help, *help*!"

It was as if a dam had suddenly burst. In a single, galvanic action, dozens of panicked bodies turned toward the doors that had closed behind them just minutes before, crying, pleading, pounding frantically against the unyielding walls. Kyle felt himself buffeted, knocked back and forth by hysterical unseen forms. A heavy blow spun him around, sent him reeling toward the floor.

He fought desperately to keep his balance, grabbing at limbs, pulling himself upright. Even in this extremity, he could hear some inner voice quietly reminding him that to fall would mean being trampled relentlessly underfoot. The scorching air was full of screams, curses, ragged cries. He could hear a different voice coming over the speaker now—a male voice, quick and urgent—but it sounded distant, impossibly faint over the bedlam that surrounded him.

Something screaming ran into him with terrific force. Kyle felt hands tugging at his hair, nails raking across his face. He fell backward, knocking against slippery bodies and, despite a supreme effort, found himself sliding down, down into a region inhabited by boots and shoes and sandals. The floor was like a griddle and he turned over, trying to rise to his knees, but the press was too close around him and he was unable to struggle against the overwhelming pressure. He could hear the horrific impact of flesh on bone as people fought and clawed their way toward the closed doors. Something heavy hit him in the face—once, twice—and suddenly the panic, the confusion, even the blistering heat, seemed to fade away. Vaguely, he wondered what had happened to Tom. And then people were falling upon him, crushing him with their weight, and as consciousness began to flicker and his limbs relaxed involuntarily he realized he was sinking, sinking, like an old leaf, coming gently down to rest on earth.

4:00 P.M.

ANGUS POOLE SAT on a desk in the large outer office of Information Technology, arms crossed, whistling a jaunty if off-key arrangement of "Knock Me a Kiss." He was surrounded by at least three dozen other desks, most of them occupied. On each desk sat a keyboard and flat-screen monitor, set at the same precise angle. Despite its size, the room seemed quiet, and Poole's whistling easily overrode the quiet murmur of conversation, the tap of keys, the jingling of telephones.

At the far end of the room sat a brace of windowless green doors. Above them was a sign, its cautionary language legible even at Poole's distance: *Authorized Systems Personnel Only Beyond This Point. Use of Retinal and Hand-Geometry Scanners Required for Access.* On the far side of those doors lay the vast computers that were the brains of Utopia: a metropolis of silicon and copper that supervised the rides, robotics, pyrotechnic effects, holographic displays, live shows, surveillance, casino operations, electrical distribution, trash processing, fire-sensing devices, monorail, chilled- and hot-water facilities, and countless other systems necessary to keep the Park operational. It seemed incongruous that such a place of wonders would hide behind a facade as bland and colorless as this outer office.

As Poole waited, somebody stood up from a nearby desk and began to approach him. He glanced over: female, Caucasian, late twenties, slight build, five six, 110, green eyes camouflaged by tinted contacts. He continued whistling.

She came forward, a little tentatively, eyeing Warne's passcard clipped to his jacket. Clearly, she was unused to seeing external specialists within the sacred halls of Systems.

"Can I help you, sir?" she asked.

Poole shook his head and smiled. "No, thanks," he said. "Already been helped." And he resumed his whistling.

The woman stared at him for a moment. Then she nodded, turned away, and—with a single backward glance—returned to her desk.

Poole watched her go. Then he looked down at his watch. Four o'clock precisely. His whistle slowly segued to a hum.

As he hummed, he was thinking quickly. This was a distastefully inelegant operation, and it was taking longer than it should. Still, under the circumstances, it would have to do.

Warne's plan—not that, to Poole's way of thinking, it deserved to be called a plan—contained a number of annoying loopholes. To begin with, Warne's case against this Fred Barksdale seemed circumstantial, difficult to prove. But more to the point, Poole himself had no idea where to find the man, or even what he looked like. Luckily, Utopia had an internal telephone directory. And just as luckily, Poole's call—made from an empty office at the end of an adjoining corridor—had been answered on the first ring. Now, as he waited, Poole's eyes lighted on a small black attaché case, stuck beneath an unoccupied desk about a dozen yards away. Glancing around, Poole slid off the tabletop, walked casually over to the desk, and grabbed the briefcase. It would make an appropriate prop.

Something was moving in his peripheral vision, approaching with quick, deliberate steps. Turning, Poole saw a tall, thin man with blue eyes and a thick sheaf of blond hair, threading his way between the desks. He had come from the direction of the green doors. Although his well-tailored suit was immaculate, and his tie knotted beyond reproach, to Poole's eye he had the air of a successful man caught during an unexpectedly stressful day.

Poole extended his hand. "Mr. Barksdale, right?"

The blond man shook hands automatically. His grip was dry and very brief. "Yes." Poole recognized the same British accent he'd just heard over the phone. "You'll forgive me, but I'm rather busy. Now, what's this about—?"

Barksdale stopped abruptly as he noticed the passcard clipped to Poole's jacket. He frowned. "Just a minute. Over the phone—"

"Pardon me," Poole interrupted. "But would you mind if we talked out here?" As he spoke, he placed one arm smoothly beneath Barksdale's elbow and began guiding him toward the outer door—not enough pressure to push the man against his will, but enough to make resistance awkward. It was important to get Barksdale off his turf, into neutral territory.

Grasping the contraband briefcase in his other hand, Poole led Barksdale out of Information Technology and into the wide corridor of B Level. Barksdale allowed himself to be guided, clearly annoyed but otherwise silent. He was a Utopia bigwig: under normal circumstances, Poole figured, he would have raised a fuss at this unexplained interruption. But if Warne was right—if Barksdale was dirty—then the man couldn't risk a delay at this point in the game. He wasn't a professional at this kind of work: he'd be feeling worried, out of his depth, fearful of unexpected complications. He'd have no choice but to go along. And he *was* going along. Poole's instinctive skepticism began to ebb.

A few minutes before, when scouting the area, Poole had noticed a break room a hundred feet down the corridor. Now, he led Barksdale into the deserted lounge. Smiling, he indicated a bank of couches along one blue-painted wall.

Barksdale freed himself from Poole's grasp. "Now, look, I'm afraid I don't understand. Over the phone, you said you were one of Camelot's mechanical engineers."

Poole nodded.

"You said there was a problem with the governors on one of the rides. Systems tampering, you said. Suspicion of sabotage. You didn't want to speak to anybody but me."

Again, Poole nodded. That had been the bait: to lure Barksdale out with precisely the kind of red flag he wouldn't dare ignore.

Barksdale pointed to the passcard. "But you're an external specialist. Not Utopia staff at all. So what, precisely, is going on?"

Poole inclined his head. "You're right, of course. I'm not Utopia staff. I'm sorry about the phone call, but you're such a hard man to reach. I just wasn't making any headway through the usual channels."

Barksdale's blue eyes narrowed. Poole read a mix of emotions behind them: annoyance, uncertainty, anxiety.

"Who are you?" Barksdale asked.

Poole smiled deprecatingly. "I'm a sales consultant for an external vendor. Fact is, my boss said I *had* to see you, no matter what it took."

"You're a—what, you're a bloody *salesman*?"

Poole smiled again, nodded.

The mix of emotions left Barksdale's face, leaving only indignation in their wake. "How did you get in here?"

"That's not important, is it? The fact is, I'm here, and I'm here to help you." Poole patted the briefcase. "If you could just sit down for a minute, I'd like to give you a brief demonstration of our—"

"I will not," Barksdale said. "In fact, I'm going to call Security." And he turned away.

"If you could just *sit down* a moment." And with that, Poole's hand shot out, grasped Barksdale's shoulder, and pushed him onto the nearest sofa.

Barksdale's face darkened, but he remained where he was.

"Thank you. I promise I'll just take a minute." Poole went through an elaborate pretense of turning the briefcase, as if preparing to open it. "As head of Information Technology for this fine Park, you must be aware of the dangers of, ah, outside infiltration."

Barksdale remained silent, staring at him.

"The more automated, the more computerized, our infrastructures become, the more susceptible we are to attack." Poole went on in the singsong rhythm of a canned recitation. "It's a sad commentary on the times we live in. However, computer-based protection has become a business necessity. There are outside elements who would like nothing more than to penetrate your systems, Mr. Barksdale. And that's where we can help."

As quickly as it had come, the color drained from Barksdale's face.

"The firm I represent can diagnose your systems, check for weaknesses, suggest remedies. And today, today *only,* we're offering a special two-for-one sale. Can I sign you up?" Poole reached into his pocket for a pen.

"What firm did you say you worked for?" Barksdale's voice was as dry and thin as old parchment.

"Oh, I'm sorry, didn't I say? Keyhole Intrusion Systems."

A hunted look came into Barksdale's face. He looked sharply left, then right.

Any doubts Poole had now disappeared. He held the passcard up in front of Barksdale, close enough for the man to read Andrew Warne's name imprinted along its edge.

"Gotcha," he said lightly.

Barksdale leaped to his feet, spun away from the couch, and began to sprint out of the lounge.

"Mr. Barksdale!" Poole said in a commanding tone.

Something in Poole's voice made Barksdale stop in midflight. He turned around slowly. Poole had dipped two fingers into his corduroy jacket and withdrawn the butt of the hacker's pistol.

"It'll be much less messy if we do this my way, Mr. Barksdale," he said.

Then, with an encouraging smile, he relaxed his fingers and let the pistol slip back out of sight.

4:00 P.M.

TERRI BONIFACIO WALKED down the broad hallway, arms at her sides, eyes straight ahead. It was four o'clock, and—in the wake of the changeover from Red Shift to Blue Shift—the Utopia Underground had grown crowded with cast members. More than once she was acknowledged by a wave, a nod, a smile. Terri did not respond. She was lost in thought.

What had started as a normal day had turned into a kind of waking dream. Actually, waking nightmare was more like it.

And to think it had started with a *pleasant* surprise—Dr. Warne's arrival a week early. Day after day, as she'd monitored the Metanet, watched it subtly improve itself and the bots under its care—and as she'd relayed this information to Warne in countless phone conversations—she had grown increasingly interested in its creator. Here was a man who shared her fascination with machine intelligence, who'd actually made fundamental contributions to the discipline. Someone she could learn from. A witty, brilliant someone, with a wry sense of humor to boot. As gossip about his breakup with Sarah Boatwright surfaced, she'd even gone so far as to daydream about a future collaboration: Warne as the iconoclastic genius, herself as the technical wizard who could implement, *complement,* his visions, bring them into the mainstream. Hand in hand.

The surprises that followed, however, had been far less pleasant.

And the final revelation, Barksdale's treachery, left her stunned. Even now she could scarcely believe it. Could it all be some terrible mistake? Could Warne have made some profound error in judgment?

The double doors of the Central Medical Facility were closed, bright lights shining behind the frosted-glass windows. Terri slowed as she approached.

Even now . . . And what *about* now? Whatever the truth about

Barksdale, she'd seen that struggle in the Hub, the duffel full of ammunition. And now she was headed for Medical, volunteering for battle. *Sure, let me help. Let me save some bratty kid from an army of mercenaries. Nice going, Terri.*

She shook this thought away. The chances were a thousand to one against anyone coming after a fourteen-year-old girl. Even if they knew of her existence—which was unlikely—they had far better things to do. She was just making sure. For Andrew.

She took a deep breath, pushed the doors open.

Terri had only been in Medical a few times—once for a flu shot, once when she'd dropped a propulsion system on her foot—and each time it had been nearly empty. The facility was laid out in the shape of a square, its two wide central corridors forming a giant plus sign where they intersected. She imagined all too clearly the scene that was about to greet her: half a dozen nurse practitioners, standing around patientless, would immediately demand to know her business. But as she passed by the doors, she found something very different. A single nurse stood at the nurses' station—an open area ahead and to the left, at the intersection of the two long corridors—frantically balancing a phone on each shoulder while scribbling notes. Other nurses were running back and forth, pushing crash carts or gathering medical supplies.

Terri walked toward the nurses' station, looking around curiously. Now a group of doctors approached her, heads together, talking rapidly. As they passed, Terri strained to listen. It seemed there had just been some kind of freak accident on one of the rides in Callisto. Numerous casualties were reported, and the burn unit was on full alert.

Terri felt a chill course through her. *Not again . . .*

She caught sight of two security specialists. They were standing at the junction of the two main corridors, across from the nurses' station, talking in low tones.

Terri slowed her pace, forced herself to think. There were two ways she could do this. The first way was to be honest and upfront. She'd approach a nurse, or one of the guards, and say, *Hi, I'm Terri Bonifacio, from IT. You've got a casualty, Georgia Warne, recuperating here? Well, we're not sure she's safe here, and her father wants me to hide her someplace else, so . . .*

Terri dismissed this option without playing it out any further. She'd have to try the other way.

She walked forward and, as nonchalantly as she could, reached out and slipped a clipboard from the sorting tray on the near end of the nurses' station. She was still wearing her white lab coat; it could double as a medical uniform in a pinch. Tugging the lapels tightly around her neck, and holding the clipboard in prominent view, she walked along the station to the corridor junction. Ahead lay the operating theater and the ICU. To the right were the examination rooms and lab facilities. To the left lay the recovery rooms and support areas. And lining the walls of the transverse corridor were the patient bays, their privacy curtains drawn back, beds and chairs open to view. In a few of them, she could see orderlies changing linens, smoothing down sheets. It was as if they were expecting a flood of casualties. Perhaps they were.

She thought quickly, ignoring the beating of her heart. Georgia's injuries were minor, Warne had said, but the medication would keep the girl asleep a while longer. She was in one of the recovery bays. Terri glanced up and down as she approached the intersection. But all the bays were vacant, their curtains drawn back . . .

. . . except those few down the transverse corridor, to her left.

As she passed the security guards, she looked down at the clipboard, turning left into the intersecting corridor, keeping her movements as casual as possible. The guards glanced at her, but did not pause in their conversation.

She headed toward the closed bays. There were three together, jutting out from the right wall, light blue curtains shut tightly around each, shielding the beds from sight. As she came closer, she realized with a sinking feeling that all three were in clear view of both the guards and the nurses' station. *Goddamn it*, she thought, *I'll never get away with this*. She felt ridiculous, exposed.

Propelling herself forward by a conscious act of will, she approached the empty bed closest to the three closed bays. She turned her back to the drawn curtains, placed her clipboard on the bed, and pretended to check the placement of a blood-oxygen meter at its head. As she did so, she took a covert glance toward the intersection. Nobody was watching. She slipped behind the curtain.

Terri turned around, then drew in her breath sharply.

An old man lay in the bed, blankets tight around his chin, eyes unfocused and rheumy. Liver-spotted hands trembled as they clutched the sheet. A monitor beeped monotonously beside him. She worked her way around the foot of his bed, careful not to jostle the curtains or in any way betray her movement to those outside.

On the far side of the bed, she paused to draw another deep breath. Then, turning away from the elderly man and staying close to the wall, she pulled back the curtain separating him from the next bay.

Empty: the bed freshly made, the instrumentation screens dark. *This is a wild-goose chase,* Terri thought. *She could be anywhere.*

There was one more bay to try. After that, she'd head down to Security. Nobody, not even Andrew, could say she hadn't tried. *Besides,* she thought as she made her way around the empty bed and stealthily pulled the curtain from the far wall, *Georgia's probably safer here than anywhere. Probably.* Taking another deep breath, she slipped into the third bay.

Georgia was still peacefully asleep, chestnut hair spilled across the pillow. For a moment, Terri stood there, the world around her forgotten as she stared down at Warne's daughter. From this angle, she could see something of him, younger and foreshortened, in the face: the high forehead, the deep-set eyes, the rising swell of the mouth.

Then she forced herself to think once again. Andrew had asked her to take Georgia back to Security, if she could. Even if that proved impossible, there were plenty of other options: a place where she wouldn't be looked for, a place unlikely to attract unwanted attention. There were dozens of innocuous-looking offices, labs, utility spaces, all within a two-minute walk. At the far end of this hallway was an emergency exit that would take her out of Medical into a service corridor. Finding a hiding place would be the easy part.

But getting Georgia out unnoticed—that might prove impossible.

She stepped away from the bed, looking around the bay, hesitating. *This is nuts. What am I going to do, carry her out on my shoulder under the noses of the guards?* She should just sit here, wait for Georgia to wake up. What was going to happen, anyway?

She turned back, looking down at the sleeping form, at the

fresh, angry-looking bruise coming up on one cheekbone. Something about the girl reminded Terri of herself. It was not a physical similarity: she knew she wasn't as pretty, and she lacked Georgia's natural grace, so rarely found at the awkward age of fourteen. It was something in her manner; something in the way she presented herself to the world. At that age, Terri remembered, she'd been quiet, withdrawn. Newly moved to the States, she was the brainy Asian, shortest kid in her class. Adults might have seemed stupid to her, but they were preferable to her teasing, bullying peer group. Fourteen was a tough age.

She felt her will hardening as she stared at the girl. The chances might be a million to one that she was in any danger. But it didn't matter; she'd find a way to guarantee her safety. She'd do it for Georgia—and for her father.

Moving swiftly to the far side of the bed, Terri parted the curtains and looked out toward the end of the corridor, hoping for a gurney, a cart, anything on which she could wheel the sleeping girl. Seeing nothing, her heart sank.

Then her eyes lighted on a collapsed square of shiny metal: a folded wheelchair, leaning against the near wall.

Gingerly, she pulled back the curtain and eased out into the hallway, careful to keep the curtain of the recovery bay between herself and the view of the intersection. She could hear voices, the quick patter of footsteps; but thankfully, the hallway, with its empty bays and support areas, remained quiet. Grasping the wheelchair, she pulled it back into the bay as quietly as she could, pulling the curtain closed behind her. She yanked the handlebars downward, locking the chair into a sitting position.

Now she turned toward the bed, breathing hard. She had to do this quickly, without giving herself time to think about how crazy it might be.

She maneuvered the wheelchair toward the bed, then pulled the covers away from Georgia and—as gently as possible—raised her from the mattress.

"God, kiddo," she grunted. "You're as heavy as I am."

With an effort, Terri settled her into the wheelchair. Georgia sighed, muttered. Terri grabbed a pillow from the bed, propped the girl up as comfortably as she could, then covered her with a light hospital blanket.

She was almost there; she couldn't let her will fail now.

Moving around the bed, she parted the curtains just enough to glance toward the corridor junction and the nurses' station. The buzz of activity had lessened slightly, but the two security guards remained, still talking between themselves.

They weren't looking her way. It would be the work of thirty seconds to wheel Georgia out of the bay, down the far end of the corridor, and out the emergency exit. The guards would never know. If she kept close to the right wall, the closed curtains of Georgia's bay would shield her from view for part of the distance. Chances are, even if the guards looked toward her, she wouldn't arouse attention: just another nurse, wheeling a wheelchair.

Come on, Terri. Shake a tail feather.

Gripping the handles of the wheelchair tightly, she drew aside the far curtain and pushed Georgia firmly out into the corridor. The wheels wobbled, squeaking as they moved back and forth, and Terri bit down on her lip, reminding herself that, in a minute, she'd be out the door and gone.

And yet it was a longer walk than she'd thought. Pushing the wheelchair took effort, and the emergency exit seemed almost to recede into the distance, as if taunting her. Jaw set, she tried to quicken her pace.

It was then that she heard a new, louder voice behind her.

Something was happening back at the nurses' station. Was the first of the casualties arriving? Terri didn't dare look around to see. She felt naked, vulnerable. She was perhaps halfway to the exit—too far to return to the recovery bay. But she didn't dare go on without knowing what was happening behind her, without knowing if someone was watching her head for the emergency door. *Now you've gone and done it.* She felt her nerve begin to fail. Her eyes darted back and forth.

There: to the right she spotted a door, marked *Laundry Closet*. *No, no.*

But it was the only door nearby. They could hide inside until whatever it was had passed. Then she could ease back out into the hallway and guide the wheelchair through the exit.

Old fears, half-suppressed phobias, roared back. *No, please. Not a closet.*

The room would be small. It would be dark. It would be so much easier just to keep going, to gamble on not being noticed. *But a closet . . .*

More voices, louder now, behind her.

Struggling to master the panic that boiled up within her, Terri angled the wheelchair toward the laundry door. She could feel her hands shaking as she opened it and guided the wheelchair through.

Inside, the only light came from a single bank of fluorescent bulbs. Terri looked around, breathing fast. It was a large space—thank God—but it was dark, so dark. Green scrubs, white nurse's uniforms, and gowns of various sizes hung from rods or lay within countless wooden cubbyholes. The rear section of the room was dominated by a huge tube of metal and PVC plastic that ran horizontally from one opposing wall to the other. Rows of smaller tubes ran across its surface like veins. Two large hatches were riveted to the main tube, bolted in place and fitted with brass handles. This was the HPLR, the high-pressure laundry removal system that threaded its way throughout the underground areas of Utopia. All day—but primarily at the end of the two main shifts—costumes, uniforms, towels, napkins, tablecloths, and bed sheets were whisked by pneumatic pressure from hundreds of hatches to the central laundry service on C Level. Terri could hear the system working now, a faint hollow thrumming that echoed and whistled along the oversize tube.

She was breathing faster, hyperventilating. The dark walls seemed to crowd in on her. Forcing back the panic, Terri bent toward the wheelchair, adjusting the blanket and the pillow. Then she returned to the door, opened it slightly, and peered out.

A man was standing at the nurses' station. He was of medium height, muscular, and even from her distant vantage point his eyes looked somehow exotic. He was wearing dark-colored coveralls, and as he spoke to the duty nurse he looked around, slowly, as if disinterestedly taking in the surroundings. His gaze seemed to light on the laundry door, and Terri ducked back. Then she leaned forward again, trying to catch the words.

"I'm here to see a patient," the man was saying. He had an accent almost as exotic as his eyes.

"Name of—?" the nurse asked. Her head was down, staring at a computer terminal behind the desk.

"Georgia Warne."

Terri felt her grip on the handle stiffen.

"And who might you be?" the nurse asked, still looking at her terminal.

"I'm Mr. Warne. Her father."

"Of course." The nurse consulted a chart. "She's in—no, I

take that back, it appears she's been moved. You'll find her in recovery bay 34. It's down the corridor to the left, the last set of
closed curtains, Mr. Warne."

It's Doctor *Warne!* Terri wanted to cry out. *Doctor, not Mister!*
But the nurse had already trotted away, headed in the opposite
direction, and the man had rounded the station and was walking
along the corridor. As he came fully into view, she could see,
through the crack in the door, that he was holding a bulky duffel
bag. It shimmered silver in the fluorescent light.

Common sense screamed at her to shrink away. And yet Terri
found herself unable to move from the doorway and its vertical
crack of light, to creep back into the darkened, enfolding, stifling
laundry closet.

*Jesus, Mary, and Joseph, protect me from all harm. Jesus,
Mary, and Joseph, protect me from all harm.* Terri had not
prayed since convent school. But now she found herself saying,
under her breath, the once-familiar, once-comforting words:
*I believe in God, the Father Almighty, Maker of Heaven and
earth . . .*

Behind her, in the wheelchair, Georgia stirred. The man came
closer.

*O my God, I am heartily sorry for having offended Thee, and I
detest all my sins, because I dread the loss of Heaven and the
pains of hell, but most of all because they offend Thee . . .*

The man came closer.

4:00 P.M.

OUTSIDE PROFESSOR CRIPPLEWOOD's Chamber of Fantastic Illusion, gaslights reflected fitfully off the damp cobblestones. The waiting guests had dispersed, carrying ticket vouchers guaranteeing their entry starting promptly at 4:30. A thick purple rope, brocaded and tasseled, had been stretched across the ornate brick-front entrance. For the next half hour, the Holo Mirrors would be off-limits.

Twelve feet below the street, in the low-ceilinged spaces of Imaging Fabrication, Sarah Boatwright rubbed her arms against the chill. It was, incredibly, even colder here than in her office. She glanced around at the forest of outsize display systems and control housings, each branded with its own red identification label: *acousto-optic modulating array no. 10, superposition stream processor, fringe encoder A*. A small city of proprietary hardware, ensuring that the holographic hall of mirrors above worked its magic without hitch. Normally, five hundred people passed through the Hall every half hour. But right now, it was empty. And she was to be the sole visitor.

No—that wasn't quite right. John Doe would be there, too.

She turned to glance at Bob Allocco. The security chief's bulky form occupied a narrow space between two high-resolution modulators. Well behind him stood Rod Allenby, the Gaslight line manager, and Carmen Florez, attraction supervisor for the Holo Mirrors. Anxious looks were on both faces.

"Think he's already inside?" Sarah asked.

Allocco shrugged. "No way of knowing, with the cameras all out. He's a sneaky bastard. There's at least four service entrances to the Hall from down here, and Imaging Fabrication has access to both A Level and the Park." He glanced sidelong in her direction. "You specifically said no guards were to be posted. Inside the Hall or out."

"Look what happened last time. This time, we've got to do it his way. I give him the disc. No tricks. And then he leaves. And we start to pick up the pieces."

"Pick up the pieces. Nice image."

"Come on, Bob. It's John Doe's game now. And we've only got a few minutes left to play." In the back of her mind, Sarah could hear Chuck Emory's voice, mournful, resigned. *We can't wait more than another half hour. If park integrity isn't fully restored by then, we're calling the feds.*

"It may be John Doe's game, but that doesn't mean he's holding every last card." Allocco plucked something out of his pocket and handed it to her: a pair of glasses, the frames dark blue, the eyepieces thick as ski goggles.

"What's this?"

"Modified night-vision goggles. They sense heat, and they also filter out holographic images. The ride engineers use them for troubleshooting the Holo Mirrors. Once you're inside, put them on. The power switch is here." Allocco paused, looking at her. "We've got the technology, for God's sake. We might as well use it. You know how confusing that place is. With these, at least you have an edge."

"Very well." She looped the glasses around her neck, glanced at her watch. "It's time. I've got to go."

"One more minute, please." Allocco held out a radio. "Keep this on the open channel. I'll be monitoring it the entire time you're inside. You're familiar with the layout?"

Sarah took the radio. "More or less."

"Glasses or no, it'll be disorienting in there, so don't dawdle. Give him the disc and get out. One word from you will bring the cavalry."

"I don't *want* the cavalry. I want a hands-off operation. If we're going to save my Park, we have to get him the hell off the grounds as quickly as possible."

Allocco sighed. "Yes, ma'am. But this one goes on your rap sheet, not mine."

Sarah nodded, turned away.

"Watch your ass all the same."

She waved the radio in acknowledgment, then began threading her way through banks of renderers and holovideo display units, making for a staircase in the far wall.

Imaging Fabrication filled the entire space beneath the Holo

Mirrors. Each display unit here drove precisely one hologram in the Hall above. By Sarah's orders, the complex had been cleared of all but a skeleton staff, and, as she followed the twisting route to the staircase, she already found herself feeling more and more alone.

She reached the stairs, put her hand on the frigid railing. Then she paused. She placed her other hand against the breast of her jacket, assuring herself the disc was still there. Glanced at her watch again.

These were needless, delaying actions. Why had he asked for her, specifically? She realized, with a sense of dull surprise, that she really, *really* did not want to climb those stairs. She did not want to lose herself in the Hall's confusing maze of displays and reflections. But most of all, she did not want to see John Doe again; see those bicolored eyes staring back at her, that strangely intimate smile framing the closely trimmed beard. Not here. Not alone.

Then her grip tightened on the railing. *Look what happened last time*, she'd told Allocco. They'd been aggressive, reactive. It cost them a dead security specialist and a whole lot of injured guests. And it had been *her call*. Perhaps John Doe was telling the truth when he said he wanted her to deliver the disc to ensure no more snags. Probably he was. But it didn't matter. Because—after what went wrong at Galactic Voyage—this was her responsibility. Hers; no one else's.

Squaring her shoulders, setting her jaw, Sarah climbed resolutely up the staircase, grasped the door handle, and pulled it open.

Beyond was a large room, richly appointed in Edwardian excess. Textured paper lined the walls, vast swirls of crimson paisley rising toward the ceiling. Ornate gas jets in cut-glass bowls sprouted between gilt-framed oils, bathing the space in a rich, mellow light. The floor was decorated in a parquet mosaic of many-colored woods that formed a complex, spiral labyrinth. This was the pre-show area of the Holo Mirrors. Normally, it would be full of eager, chattering guests, waiting for the costumed attendants to let the next group enter single file into the Hall. Now it was still and empty. Long, gaunt shadows stretched across the floor. The corners of the room were consumed by darkness.

Sarah took a step out into the room, letting the door to Fabrication close quietly behind. Her step resonated against the wooden floor, and she halted, listening. She could hear the hiss of the gas lamps, the tick of the half dozen grandfather clocks lining the walls of the antechamber. To her left, faintly, she could make out the sounds of the Park beyond the closed double doors: laughter, snatches of song. To her right—where the entrance to the maze itself yawned wide—there was nothing but silence. Somewhere inside, John Doe waited.

She knew she should head for that entrance, walk in with businesslike stride, announce her presence. And yet something in the listening silence seemed to defeat her best intentions, paralyze her will. Throughout her adult life, Sarah had never allowed herself to fear anything or anyone. But now, standing alone in the watchful hallway, the metallic taste in her mouth was unmistakable.

She took a deep breath, then another. And then, quietly, she stepped toward the open doorway, radio gripped tightly in one hand. She had accepted it in passing, without thought: now, it seemed almost like a kind of lifeline.

No more stalling. She crossed the threshold, went through the doorway, and passed into the Hall.

It was subtly lit, but not dark. The gaslights of the antechamber gave way to hidden, indirect lighting that threw the passage ahead of her into soft focus. The walls were lined with large mirrored panels, framed in dark wood. As she stepped forward, Sarah watched her reflection follow on both sides.

The first section of the Hall, she knew, was comprised entirely of mirrors. But she also knew that, hidden within the moldings and behind one-way glass, cameras were scanning her image— sending it to the computers in Fabrication—which would in turn process it, perform a series of complex digital conversions, and send the result to the holographic renderers for display in other parts of the Hall. Sensors in the ceiling would take note of her approach, determine which direction to display the newly created holograms, even render their motion in real time as she came closer to them. The deeper you penetrated the Hall, the less clear it became what you were seeing: an image in a mirror or a hologram of yourself or another guest. It was a classic hall of mirrors, with a twenty-first-century twist. She wondered again why John Doe had chosen this, of all places, to make the transfer.

As she moved forward, Sarah could now make out an image of

herself, approaching: the corridor clearly took a sharp bend up ahead, so she must be looking at a mirror, blocking her path. She came closer, staring at the image that stared back. A woman, radio in one hand, mouth set. She raised her arm, the doppelgänger's arm rising in slavish imitation. She pressed her fingers against the hard cold glass.

The mirror image of herself was carefully detuned, fuzzy. Mirrors in the Hall were intentionally blurred, to more closely resemble holograms and thus heighten the illusion. Dropping her hand, Sarah turned away, heading down the new corridor. Once again, she felt images of herself following on both sides. In her hand, the radio made a faint squawk, then settled back into silence.

Abruptly, the corridor opened into a small, six-sided room. All around her, other Sarah Boatwrights returned her gaze. She thought back, trying to re-create in her mind the plan of the Hall. Three of the six walls were mirrors, she remembered; one was the corridor she had just passed through; the other two were holograms, concealing other corridors.

She looked more carefully at the surrounding images. All of them were holding a radio, arms at the sides of her tan-colored suit. She raised her arms, and three of the images followed her lead. That meant the other two were holograms. She could pass through those images, down one of two new hallways. But which one?

She considered stopping here, waiting, letting John Doe make the next move. Perhaps he was there, in the next corridor. Or perhaps this was all a ruse, and he and his cronies were already miles away, speeding down Highway 95. Whatever the case, it was easier to keep moving than to stay here, listening, waiting.

Sarah took a step toward the closest hologram of herself. It stared back at her. Abruptly, it raised one arm. She stopped instinctively at the movement. Now she understood: a camera had been hidden behind the mirror at the end of the earlier hall, recording her own act of lifting fingers to the glass.

Gingerly, she stepped through the hologram. It warped and distorted around her as she passed. On the far side, another mirror-lined hallway marched away into the distance. She paused, waiting for a sound, a sign of movement. There was none, and after a few seconds she moved forward once again.

She was deeper into the maze now, and it was increasingly possible that the walls to her left and right were no longer mere glass, reflecting her image. Some would be holograms, re-creations of herself passing by earlier mirrors. Beyond the first junction, her memory of the layout grew fuzzy. It was easier in some ways, being the only person inside the Hall: normally, the mirrors would be capturing images from groups of twenty different people, not just a single person. That made it even more difficult to tell what was a projected hologram, what was a mirror image, and what was a living body. Even so, her sense of disorientation was growing.

Then she remembered the glasses hanging around her neck. She switched on the battery, raised them to her eyes. The view of the corridor suddenly shifted: ahead of her, the holograms became dim, ghostlike. Now, she could tell illusion from reflection. A surge of renewed confidence passed through her.

The corridor took a sharp jog, then opened into a "Y." Sarah looked down the two hallways angling ahead of her, their mirrored surfaces winking. She hesitated, then on impulse chose the left-hand bend. As she started down it, her radio crackled into life.

"Sarah, do you read?" Allocco's amplified voice seemed unbearably loud in the hushed passage.

She quickly turned down the gain. "Yes."

"What's going on?"

"Nothing. No sign of him. Why the transmission? We should maintain—"

"Listen, Sarah. There's been some kind of accident over in Callisto."

"*Accident*? What kind of accident?"

"I don't know. With our video links down, we're slow getting a handle on exactly what happened. But something appears to have gone wrong on Station Omega. I've"—the voice disappeared in a brief wash of static—"reports of 904s."

Sarah felt herself go cold. In Utopia's emergency-traffic code, a 904 meant guest casualties.

"Sarah? Sarah, you there?"

"I'm here. You sure about this? It's not a false alarm?"

"I've had two independent reports. It looks serious. Crowd control might become an issue."

"Then get over there and stabilize the situation."

"I can't do that. You're—"

"I'm fine. Your responsibility is to the guests. Alert Medical, get a victim-recovery operation under way if necessary. Deploy Security and Infrastructure to the site. Get Guest Relations started on any peripheral containment."

"Very well. I'll hand the radio over to Florez, tell her to monitor this frequency." There was a pause. "Remember what I said, Sarah."

With a soft squawk, her radio went dead. Sarah turned up the gain once again, then stuffed it into a jacket pocket.

With Allocco gone, there'd be only the skeleton crew manning the Hall, all ignorant of her mission. Although Carmen Florez would have the radio, she, like the rest, had been kept in the dark.

Now, Sarah really was alone.

Despite what she'd told Allocco, she was *not* fine. She hesitated in the left-hand fork of the passage. Another accident, following so soon on the heels of what had happened at Escape from Waterdark. There was no way this was a coincidence.

Then what was happening? Was this all part of John Doe's plan? And if so, why? They'd agreed to his demands. They'd burned a second disc, she was here to deliver it. Was it possible he thought she hadn't shown up—that Station Omega was some kind of retaliation? But that was impossible—if Allocco was just learning of it now, this must have been set in motion *before* four o'clock.

For all she knew, it could have been set in motion hours before.

Either way, John Doe had clearly meant for it to happen *all along*.

She stood motionless in the glittering hallway. Anger, frustration, apprehension competed within her. What had gone wrong? How many casualties? Was Callisto now the scene of mass panic?

As anger got the better of her, she started down the left-hand fork, heedless of the rap of her heels against the floor. At least she had the goggles; that gave her an advantage. She'd find that bastard, find him and—

As quickly as she'd started moving, Sarah stopped again. Up ahead, at another bend in the maze, stood John Doe.

At least, she thought it was John Doe—in the glasses, the image was so faint it was hard to tell. She let the glasses fall away. Immediately, the hologram blossomed into life.

She drew in her breath. It was the first time she'd seen him—

actually seen him—since he'd dropped by her office, perched on her desk, drunk her tea, caressed her cheek. She felt the muscles of her jaw harden. He looked even more relaxed now than he had then: slender hands at his sides, expensive suit draped impeccably over his frame, the small self-amused smile displaying perfect teeth.

"Sarah," came the voice. "How good of you to come." The voice was still distant—the real John Doe was someplace deeper in the maze.

She waited, motionless, staring at the image.

"I love the way you've decorated this place. It appeals to the narcissist in me."

Still she waited.

"Have you brought the disc, Sarah?"

Slowly, gingerly, she walked up to the image. He was standing, his strange bicolored eyes glancing first left, then right. Perhaps one of the cameras had caught him pausing at a junction, wondering which way to go.

"I said, do you have the disc?" The lips on the Doe-image did not move.

"Yes," she replied. Suddenly, she did not want to see that face anymore. She placed the goggles over her eyes, and the holograms around her grew faint and spectral once again.

"Good. Then we can proceed."

"What did you do, Mr. Doe?"

"Excuse me?"

"The Callisto attraction, Station Omega. What did you do?" She could hear her voice shaking with emotion.

"Why?" came the voice, laced with the faintest hint of mockery. "Is something wrong?"

"I've done everything you asked!" she shouted. "I trusted you. Don't *fuck* with me!"

"My, my. And to think I believed you well bred."

Sarah gasped, felt her fists balling involuntarily.

"We're almost done here, Sarah. Let's finish our business, then you can attend to that unpleasantness yourself, and—just a minute, just a minute, I'm seeing a new image of you now. What's that fashion accessory you're wearing? Ah, I understand. Those glasses don't do anything for you, Sarah. They're much too heavy for your delicate features. We'll have to do something about that."

There was a brief silence. Then—from somewhere deep in the shrouded darkness—there came a clicking noise.

For a moment, nothing changed. Then Sarah noticed a green glow along the edges of her goggles. In the corridor ahead, the holograms that a moment before had been almost too dim to see now began to glow: green wraiths that grew brighter and brighter. Sarah blinked, turning away from the painful glare. As she moved her head, bright heat trails streaked green across her vision.

With an exasperated cry she tugged the goggles from her eyes and lifted the radio. "Carmen?" she spoke into it.

There were a few seconds of silence. "Yes, Ms. Boatwright," the radio crackled.

"Carmen, is something happening down there?"

"A few seconds ago, the gain on the holographic generators suddenly quadrupled. They're overheating, all of them."

"Can you stop it?"

"Yes, but it'll take time. Everything's under computer control. We've got to figure out where the command's coming from. Until we've pinpointed it, I don't even dare pull the plug on the generators."

"Keep on it." Sarah lowered the radio. *He was prepared for the goggles, too. He's prepared for everything. Everything we can think of, he's thought of already.*

"See what I mean, Sarah?" came the smooth, distant voice of John Doe. There was another distant clicking noise. "How can you speak of trust when you display none yourself? Just deliver the disc to me, and I'll be out of your life forever."

Sarah did not answer. There was nothing more to say. All at once, she felt defeated.

"What post are you at now, Sarah?"

She did not respond.

"Sarah?"

"Yes?"

"What post are you at?"

"I don't understand."

"Look at the frame of the mirror nearest to you. The left edge of the upper crosspiece. You'll see a number branded on the underside."

Woodenly, Sarah looked over. It took her a minute to spot, but then she saw a small series of numbers, burned into the wood.

"Seven nine two three," she murmured.

"I'm sorry?"

"Seven nine two three, I said."

"Very good. Now listen, Sarah. I'm going to guide you to where I'm waiting. We'll keep in voice contact at all times. Understood?"

"Yes."

"Good. You should be . . . you should be in a left-hand corridor, following a Y-intersection. Follow the corridor to the end. Let me know when you're there."

Sarah moved forward unwillingly, watching her reflections move alongside. Suddenly, the image of John Doe reared up to her right. She froze: another hologram, different this time. He was holding what looked like a set of plans, glancing up, then down, up, down, in a continuous-loop ballet.

"I'm at the end of the corridor," she said.

"Look up at the mirror on your left. Is the number you see 7847?"

A pause. "Yes."

"Now take another left and proceed down the corridor. A hall will lead off from the right, concealed by a hologram. Watch for it."

Sarah turned down the hallway, her step slow and resigned. John Doe was not lost, not uncertain of his way. If anything, he knew the Hall even better than its designers. He knew about the troubleshooting goggles. He had the plans for everything, right down to the numbers of the individual mirrors lining the hallways.

All her better instincts shouted at her not to go on. But there was no other choice: she had to give John Doe the disc. No matter what.

Suddenly, she stopped again. Her own image—sometimes a reflection, sometimes a hologram captured earlier—was all around her. But up ahead and to the left, there was a different image: the image of a man. And it was not John Doe.

She stepped closer, staring hard, as the framed image came into focus.

It was Andrew Warne.

She whirled around. *Andrew? Here?*

There was no time to think, only to react. She was supposed to be unaccompanied. If Warne was here, there had to be a reason—

a *pressing* reason. He must be somewhere between herself and the entrance. Since John Doe was deeper in the maze, it would take a little more time for the image servers below to relay Warne's image to him.

Quickly, she retraced her steps to the last intersection, then veered right, heading back in the direction she'd come. From somewhere ahead came the patter of approaching footsteps.

"Sarah?" She heard Warne's voice: a fierce, impatient whisper. "Sarah?"

The voice grew fainter for a moment, then came again, closer this time: "Sarah? Where are you?"

"*Here!*" she whispered back.

A figure loomed into view at the fork of the Y-intersection. And this time it was not a hologram, not a reflection in a mirror. It was Andrew Warne, bandage hanging loose on his forehead, anxiety clear in his gaze. And then he caught sight of her. He frowned a moment, as if trying to tell reality from artifice. She stepped toward him. Immediately, his features cleared.

"Sarah," he said, rushing toward her, clasping her hands. "Thank God."

For a moment, the touch of another, sympathetic human being overwhelmed everything else. She closed her eyes.

Then, with a start, she pushed herself away.

"What are you doing here?" she whispered fiercely. "How'd you get in?"

"I had to stop you," he whispered back. "You're not safe here."

"You can't be here. I have to give John Doe the disc, alone. I—"

Warne grabbed her arms. "It's a trap."

Hearing him echo her own worst fears, Sarah went numb. "How do you know?"

She felt his grip tighten. "This isn't going to be easy for you. Sarah, we've discovered the mole. John Doe's inside man."

She waited, not daring to breathe.

"It's Barksdale."

Sarah's first impulse was to slap Warne's face. She yanked herself away.

"*Liar!*"

Warne stepped forward again. "Sarah, please. You must listen, listen quickly. There never was any outside security check. KIS never visited Utopia. Barksdale made it all up. Those technicians who came to check Utopia's firewalls last month were John

Doe's men. That's how they infiltrated your system, set their traps."

She shook her head violently. It couldn't be true. It was *impossible*. There had to be some other explanation.

"No," she said. "I don't believe you."

"I'm not asking you to believe me. I'm just asking you to leave this place now, right now, learn the truth for yourself. That disc you found, crushed beneath the guard's foot? It was *blank*. That means John Doe took the real disc, substituted a blank of his own. It was all a setup. Why do you think John Doe wants a second one? Why do you think he asked for you *specifically*? You have to—"

"Sarah?" came John Doe's voice.

Immediately, Warne fell silent. He glanced sharply at Sarah; she put a finger to her lips.

"Sarah, I told you to remain in voice contact. Why have you stopped?" The voice was more distant than before. Among the reflections along the hallway, a new one flickered into view: John Doe, plans now at his side, ear cocked, as if listening. Mutely, she watched the holo image repeat its brief visual loop, over and over.

"Sarah, you know what I think? I think we're no longer alone."

Sarah waited.

"In fact, now I *know* we're no longer alone. I see a third hologram, Sarah: it isn't you, and it isn't me. Who is that man?"

The Hall was silent.

"I think I can guess. It's the troublesome Dr. Warne. The *meddlesome* Dr. Warne. Am I right?"

Sarah glanced at Warne. He was staring back at her.

"This was not part of our arrangement, Sarah. First the goggles, now this. I'm seriously displeased."

The hologram of John Doe wavered, then changed, as the renderer updated the display with a newer image: John Doe once again, a snub-nosed pistol hanging loosely in one hand.

From deep inside the maze came the sound of running feet.

"He's coming for us!" Warne whispered urgently.

Beckoning for him to follow, Sarah raced headlong down the corridor, past the reflections and the holograms, away from the sound of John Doe's voice. Dimly, she could see images of herself darting by as she passed. The sound of their heels against the floor, the intake of breath, filled the narrow hallway. She turned one corner, then another.

And then she halted again.

"Stop," she heard herself order Warne.

Something within her was changing. Maybe it was the shock of Warne's unbelievable tale; maybe it was the sight of John Doe's gun. But the storm of emotions was clearing, leaving only a strong, steely anger behind.

She pulled the radio from her pocket. "Carmen?" she spoke into it, breathing hard. "Carmen, are you there?"

"Yes, Ms. Boatwright," came the answer. "Can you please tell me what's going on?"

"Later. Can you do something for me? I need you to cut the lights inside the Hall."

"Cut the lights?"

"All of them. *Right now*. Can you do that?"

"Yes . . . Yes, I can."

"Then do it."

She slid the radio back into her pocket. Then, leaning toward the nearest mirror, she took note of the number burned into its frame. Taking the fresh disc from her pocket, she placed it against the mirror's base. Then, motioning Warne to follow, she led the way back, more slowly now, to the six-sided room. From here, she knew she could find her way out. Even in the dark.

She took a deep breath. Then she turned and spoke in the loudest, most commanding tone she could muster.

"Mr. Doe! Stop! If you want that disc, stop right where you are."

She stopped to listen, but the only answer was silence.

"You once told me that I betrayed your trust. Well, this time you've betrayed mine."

"Indeed," came the voice. It was closer now. "I'm intrigued."

"You've sabotaged another ride, hurt more people. For no reason. I've followed your orders, I've brought the disc. So why the gun?"

Silence.

"I can answer that!" Warne said sharply. "You were planning to take the disc and Sarah as well. As a hostage. Or maybe you'd just kill her, escape in the pandemonium. Right? So much for your element of surprise."

"Surprise, Dr. Warne?" came the silky voice. "I'm not out of surprises quite yet."

"Then surprise me by doing the unexpected. Just let her go. Show us you can adapt."

Abruptly, the lights snapped out, plunging the corridor into darkness. Sarah grasped Warne's elbow.

"Mr. Doe!" she called as she began backing away. "Listen to me! The disc is here. It's at post 6942. Hear me? Post 6942. You'll find it at the base of the frame. But I'm leaving now. You've broken the rules, and I'm not going to play anymore. It may take a little while in the dark, but I'm sure you'll find it. And I'll keep the Hall clear for another twenty minutes. So do as you promised. Take the disc and get the hell out of my Park. Or I'll hunt you down and kill you myself."

At this, a laugh came out of the black: slow, cynical, amused. "Now, that's my kind of game, Sarah. Count me in."

If there was more, Sarah didn't hear it. Because they had turned down the hallway leading out to the anteroom of Professor Cripplewood's Chamber of Fantastic Illusion, and all she could hear was their feet, rapping against the darkness, running for the stairwell that would take them away from this haunted place.

4:03 P.M.

TERRI STOOD IN the shadow of the door frame, paralyzed by fear and indecision, as the man in the jumpsuit approached. Already, he was passing the first of the closed recovery bays. Another moment, and he'd reach Georgia's bay, realize the empty bed was still warm, and . . .

"Excuse me! Mister!"

It was one of the security guards. Terri cracked the door open a little wider, craning for a view. She felt her heart hammering against her ribs. The guards had stopped talking and were looking toward the man in the jumpsuit. He stopped, hand on the curtain of the third bay, and turned slowly back to face them.

"I'm sorry, sir, your name was—?" one of the guards asked as the two began to move down the corridor toward him.

Terri watched, relief surging within her. Perhaps the guards had been specifically told to watch for anybody coming to see Georgia. They'd snag this bastard. Everything would be all right now.

Behind her, she heard Georgia stir again. Terri looked around, and her heart gave a huge lurch. The girl was awake and sitting up, blinking at her inquiringly.

Quickly, Terri forced herself away from the door and ran to the wheelchair.

"Listen, Georgia," she whispered, kneeling beside her. "I'm here to take you to your dad. Okay? We have to wait here a minute—just a minute. Then we can go."

Georgia stared back, confused eyes luminous in the dim light.

Terri gave her hand a reassuring squeeze. Then she returned to the door.

The guards had surrounded the stranger now. "Very well, Mr. Warne," one of them was saying as he eyed the man's coveralls curiously. "But before you can take your daughter, we'll need to see some ID."

"ID?" the man asked. As he spoke, he casually drew aside the curtains of the third bay, peered inside.

"If you please."

The man peered inside the bay—Georgia's bay—for what seemed a long time. Then he withdrew, letting the curtains fall back together. "May I ask why?" he said. He spoke slowly, as if considering something.

"I'm sorry, sir," the first guard said. "Orders. Check the ID of all guests or external specialists entering or leaving Medical."

Shit, shit, shit. So they weren't looking out for Georgia, after all. They were just at a heightened state of alert. *Of course. Otherwise they'd have been keeping a closer eye on Georgia's bay, seen you enter it, come out with a wheelchair. Dolt. Now you're stuck here, stupid with claustrophobia, in this closet, with—*

Her thoughts faded as the stranger swiveled around, glancing quickly up and down the corridor. Once again, it seemed as if his gaze fell directly upon her. She shrank back.

"Very well, gentlemen," he said, swinging the duffel up around his shoulder and easing his way between them. "If you insist."

And he began to walk, with the same easy, confident step, toward the laundry room door.

Terri half walked, half stumbled backward into the room. She pivoted, glancing around in fresh desperation. Other than the banks of folded clothes, hanging uniforms, piles of towels, and a few small tables, the room was empty. There was only one chance for concealment: the dim, cramped recesses behind the HPLR tube.

The thought of hiding in such a confined place made her faint with terror. But there was no other choice.

She turned back to the girl. "Listen to me, Georgia," she said as calmly as she could. "Listen very carefully. There's a bad man out there, a very dangerous man. We have to hide here until he goes away."

Georgia stared at her mutely, as if in shock. From the hall came the approaching clatter of feet, voices raised in protest.

"Can we do that, Georgia?"

Still the girl stared.

"Can you help me? *Please*?"

"All right," Georgia murmured slowly.

Terri maneuvered the wheelchair toward the back of the room, angling it under the huge white tube and pushing it into the darkest corner she could find. Then she crouched down beside it, clasping Georgia to her side.

"Be very quiet now," she whispered. "Don't make a sound until they're gone. No matter what happens."

The HPLR tube now lay directly in front of her: three feet wide and three feet high, it ran completely across the room, heavy brass rings surrounding it at the points where it disappeared into the walls. She could hear the hum of pressurized air whistling dryly through it.

Then the door opened, flooding the room with light from the corridor. Terri crouched even further below the tube, hugging Georgia. Her heart beat faster and faster. She could see shadows striping the walls as first one man, then another and another, stepped into the room.

"What's this?" one of the guards was saying.

"It's a big nuisance, is what it is," the man replied in his strange accent. "Having to show ID to visit my own daughter. My wallet's at the bottom of my duffel. I need a place to put it down, sort through my equipment."

There was a clump as something heavy landed on one of the tables. Leaning cautiously to one side, Terri strained for a look.

"We're sorry, Mr. Warne," came the voice of the first guard, "but as I told you, our orders—"

"I doubt if your orders included harassing one of your visiting scientists. Bad enough that my daughter ended up here in the first place, due entirely to Park negligence, no doubt. I plan to take this up with your superiors."

Angling her head, Terri could now see: the security guards had again surrounded the almond-eyed man, who had placed his duffel on a table and was tugging open the zipper.

"That's certainly your right, Mr. Warne," the first guard said again. "But I must insist that we continue this conversation back at—"

With a smooth, fluid movement, the man reached in and slid something out of the bag. For a moment, Terri did not recognize it: long and slender, a sharply angled cone at one end. Then the man swung the thing at the guards. Flame spurted from its end.

The first guard jerked sharply back, gouts of blood arcing from holes in his uniform. Terri stifled a gasp, covered Georgia's eyes.

Pivoting in front of the door and closing it with the heel of his boot, the man swung the machine gun toward the second guard. There was a stuttering, stitching noise. Dust and bits of plaster fell from the wall, raining down upon Terri and Georgia. The guard fell back silently, fingers scrabbling at his own throat, billy club and radio spinning away across the floor.

The wheelchair squeaked as Georgia stiffened, clutching one of Terri's hands in her own. Terri held her still more tightly, staring, transfixed by horror.

The man took a step to the side. Then he angled his weapon downward and sprayed fire over the inert guards. Their bodies twitched in time to the spurting flame. There was no noise; she could not understand why there was no noise. Had the shock, the panic, deafened as well as paralyzed her? The only sound was a stiff mechanical clicking—the clatter of an infernal sewing machine—and the ringing of metal on concrete as empty cartridges rained down.

And then it was over. Silence returned to the room as a pall of gunpowder curled toward the ceiling. Terri watched, unable even to breathe, as the man lowered the smoking weapon and gazed down at the carnage. With swift, professional motions, he replaced the gun in the duffel, then cracked the door open—as she herself had done scarce moments before—and peered out into the hallway.

Beside Terri, the wheelchair creaked again. Georgia gave a sob of terror.

Terri lowered her hand, covering the girl's mouth as the man turned back, his gaze following the contours of the room. In the poor light, his eyes glowed pale as a cat's.

There was a sigh of escaping air, the clinking of metal, as one of the guards jerked, then expired, among the scatter of spent cartridges. Terri saw the twin gleams as the man's eyes swiveled toward the body.

The hoarse chatter of static suddenly sounded in the room. The man closed the door, reached into his duffel, pulled out a radio. "Hardball," he said.

"This is Prime Factor," came a garbled voice. "Position?"

"Medical."

"Condition?"

"The girl's gone."

"Where?"

"Unknown."

There was a pause.

"We can't afford any more time," came the voice over the radio. "There's a problem with Snow White, I need you back at the rally point. Right away. Understood?"

"Roger." The radio snapped off.

The man stepped away from the door, rolling the bodies back beneath the table with the toe of his boot. Then, reaching up to one of the overhanging shelves, he toppled a stack of towels onto the floor, covering the spreading pools of blood in a careless heap of linen. As Terri watched, still pressing Georgia to her, the man peeled out of the jumpsuit, exposing the silver and platinum outfit of a Callisto shuttle pilot. It matched the duffel perfectly. The jumpsuit went carelessly on top of the towels.

With a final look around, the man picked up the duffel and slung it, zipper still half-open, around his shoulder. Then he grabbed the door handle, pulled the door open, and stepped into the hallway.

There was a gentle click as the door closed, and the bright light faded away once again. For a moment, all was silent. Then, with a low trundling noise, a series of garments came down the HPLR tube, rolling and tumbling on their way to Central Cleaning. In their wake came the hiss of compressed air. At last, this sound, too, faded away. Terri felt her limbs begin to shake: faintly at first, then violently. In her arms, Georgia made no sound, did not cry. She simply held on to Terri's hand; held on so very tight that it seemed she would never, ever consent to let it go.

4:03 P.M.

AS THE MAIN entrance to the Security Complex came into view, Poole stopped abruptly. It took Fred Barksdale, walking in front, a moment to realize this. Then he, too, came to a halt.

"Now, listen." Poole walked up behind Barksdale and spoke quietly into his ear. "We're going to do this nice and easy. Don't say anything unless I tell you. And don't try anything. If I have to, I'll shoot you first and sort out the red tape later."

If Barksdale heard, he gave no sign. He began moving forward again. Wordlessly, Poole swung into step behind him.

So far, everything had gone smoothly. The brief display of force, the sight of the gun, had been enough. Poole had seen the effect before, especially with people who were into something over their heads. Young rebel soldiers—unfamiliar with automatic weapons, paralyzed with fear at the thought of combat— sometimes seemed almost relieved by capture. Barksdale had reacted the same way, submitting without struggle. At least, that's the impression he'd given. But the hardest part lay ahead: convincing Allocco and his merry men that Frederick Barksdale, systems overlord for all of Utopia, was in league with the enemy. If Barksdale wanted, he could make this very messy. It would be his word against that of a meddling guest. Poole frowned at the blond head before him: the head that looked resolutely, woodenly forward. He wondered what was going on inside of it.

LESS THAN AN hour before, Security had been a scene of frenetic activity. At least a dozen specialists had been bustling around the complex: entering incident reports, answering phones, peering in curiously at the unusual sight of a detainee in the holding cell. But now—as Poole opened the doors and led Barksdale across the bright, cheerfully colored anteroom—he was surprised by what he saw. The place was almost empty. Only three guards could be seen, and they were all behind the main desk, speaking at once: two into telephones, one into a radio.

Tucking one hand between the buttons of his corduroy jacket and placing the other on Barksdale's elbow, Poole propelled the Englishman firmly toward the desk. The quicker he did this, the better. He recognized one of the guards from his earlier visit: Lindbergh, a kid with black hair, pale gray eyes, and the legacy of a bad case of acne. The guard obviously recognized him, too; Poole could see it in his eyes, the way he put down the phone as they approached. The man opened his mouth to speak.

"Where's Allocco?" Poole interjected.

"He's in Callisto," Lindbergh said, looking from Poole to Barksdale and back again. "At the accident site."

"Accident?"

The guard nodded. "One of the attractions at the Skyport. Station Omega."

"What about it?"

"Don't know the details. Something malfunctioned."

"Sweet sister Sadie." Poole thought of his cousin, Sonya Klemm; her husband, Martin; their three foulmouthed boys. He'd sent them back to the Skyport, urged them to try the other rides. The chances were small, vanishingly small . . . but he had to ask nevertheless. "Any casualties?"

"Lots, I understand. It's pandemonium up there."

Poole turned to Barksdale. "Hear that, you bastard?" he muttered, yanking brutally at the man's elbow. "You know about this?"

But Barksdale had gone deathly pale. He made no reply, not even a gesture. It was as if he had gone someplace far, far away.

Poole turned back to Lindbergh, who was still shifting his gaze between the two of them. "I need to speak to Allocco."

The guard continued to stare, but gave no other response.

"I *said*, let me talk to Allocco."

This time, Lindbergh turned toward the guard on the radio. "Hey! Who're you talking to?"

"Tannenbaum."

"Tell him to put Mr. Allocco on a moment."

The second guard spoke into the radio, then handed it to Lindbergh. "Make it fast," Lindbergh said, passing it over the desk. "They're kind of busy up there."

Poole took the radio.

"Christ, what is it now?" he heard Allocco boom. There was a riot of background noise: cries, sobs, incoherent shouts. "Suit up! Suit up!" someone was calling.

"Mr. Allocco, it's Poole. Angus Poole. You remember?"

"Yeah. I can't talk, Poole."

"What happened? What went wrong?"

A fresh storm of noise drowned Allocco's first words. ". . . don't know, not yet. It's like a slaughterhouse up here."

"A *what*? You mean, people are, are *dead*? How many?"

"We're still counting. Medical's just coming on-scene now."

"Look, there's a chance I may have had relatives on that ride. A woman wearing a wizard's cap, a man in a green T-shirt, three boys—"

"I don't have *time* for this," Allocco interrupted, gravelly voice tight with exasperation. Poole heard a huge sigh. "Look, I haven't seen anything like that, okay? I'll let you know if I do. Is that why you called?"

"No. Not exactly." Poole hesitated, thinking. "I don't know how to tell you this, but I have Fred Barksdale here, and—"

"I know all about that."

Poole stopped again at this fresh surprise. "You do?"

"Yeah. Andrew Warne tracked me down by radio a few minutes ago, on my way over here. Told me all about it."

"And?"

"And it sounds crazy to me, but I don't have time to sort it out now. Keep Barksdale confined until I get back, we'll work it out then. Heaven help you if you're wrong."

"You'll give those instructions to your men here? It would be better, coming from you."

"Pass the radio over. Hurry up, man. *Hurry*."

Poole handed the radio back to Lindbergh. "This is Eric Lindbergh," the man said.

Poole could hear Allocco's tinny bark sounding in Lindbergh's ear. As the guard listened, his gray eyes widened. He stared at Barksdale again.

"Yes," Lindbergh said. "I understand. Very well, sir."

He lowered the radio, then slowly handed it back to the second guard. All the time, he kept his eyes on Barksdale.

"You heard the man?" Poole said.

Lindbergh nodded.

"Then you know what you have to do. Put him in the holding cell, just to be sure."

The guard nodded again. He looked almost as dazed as Barksdale.

Turning, Poole pulled Barksdale away from the desk, then propelled the man brusquely before him. Gesturing for one of the other guards to follow, Lindbergh picked up a baton and walked around the desk, opening a door in the front office and coming out to meet them.

Out of the public areas of the Security Complex, the bright color scheme and comfortable sofas gave way to gray brick walls and linoleum-tiled floors. "You'll get a chance to see a buddy of yours," Poole said, giving Barksdale another push as they made their way down the corridor that led away from the anteroom. "It'll be like Old Home Day, a regular reunion."

The corridor gave onto a rectangular room, surrounded on all sides by doors. One of the doors to the left was different from the rest: heavy steel, with a small meshed-glass window set into it. The second guard approached the door, peered through the window, then unlocked the door and opened it gingerly. Lindbergh took up a position on the other side of the door, palm resting on the handle of his baton. Poole glanced inside. The young hacker was still lying on the cot. At the sound of the lock turning, he had leaned forward on his elbow, looked disinterestedly up at the door.

As they walked, Barksdale had remained detached, seemingly in shock. The moment the cell door opened, however, a change came over him. He glanced inside, saw the occupant, and started visibly. The prisoner sat up on the cot, a crooked smile coming over his bruised and swollen face.

"Get in there," Poole said, pushing Barksdale through the door. He stepped away as the second guard slammed the door shut, twisted the lock, and removed the key.

The systems chief wheeled back toward the small window. "I don't want to be locked up!" he called from inside. *"Please!"*

"Don't worry," Poole said. "I'm going to be right here, watching. I'll be watching like a hawk."

He stepped back from the door, crossing his arms and keeping his eye on the wired glass. The two guards stepped away also. In his peripheral vision, Poole caught them exchanging glances.

It would be interesting to watch Barksdale's reaction to the rogue hacker. Their interaction might provide more clues. As it was, the entire business had been much easier than he'd expected, especially Allocco's having already heard the story from Warne. Things might have been very tricky otherwise. That was clever of Warne; it showed foresight. Perhaps he'd been underestimating the man, after all.

Now Barksdale was anxiously pacing the far wall of the cell, darting occasional glances toward the hacker. Poole watched through the glass with amusement. He'd be enjoying this if it weren't for the nagging seed of doubt in the back of his mind. The chances of his cousin or her family being anywhere near Station Omega were close to nil. And there was nothing he could do about it either way. Still, he wouldn't rest entirely easy until he'd heard that . . .

"Hey!"

It was the third guard. He was halfway down the corridor from the front desk, motioning with one hand.

"Are you Poole?"

"That's right." Poole turned from the window, Barksdale temporarily forgotten.

"There's someone on the radio for you, here at the desk."

Poole walked back to the anteroom, then took the radio that was handed over the desk. "Poole here," he said.

He listened for a moment to the anguished, incoherent voice that came crying over the transmitter.

"Who is this?" he said. "*What?* Calm down, calm *down*. Terri, where are you exactly? Are you hurt? No, stay put—I'll be right there."

Poole spun around, letting the radio drop to the desk. He dashed to the door, yelled down the corridor. "Lindbergh! *Lindbergh!*"

The mop of black hair appeared. "Yes?"

"Listen, I've got to go. I'll be back as soon as I can. Guard those two, you hear? *Guard* them."

Lindbergh scratched his face perplexedly. "I'll do that," he replied. "Mr. Allocco said—"

But Poole was already gone.

4:08 P.M.

THE WORST THING, strangely enough, was the music: the sterile, ethereal New Age music that seeped from hundreds of hidden speakers, suffusing Callisto with its promise of a tranquil future. Normally, it was barely audible beneath the clamor of numberless guests. But there were no longer any guests in the Skyport. The queue lines had all been dispersed, the would-be riders asked to return to Callisto's other attractions. A silver curtain—part of a system for isolating sections of the Park in civil emergencies—now hung at the end of the concourse, shielding the Skyport from outside view. Though it looked ethereal, light as gossamer, it was completely opaque, heavily reinforced with layers of soundproofing. Two security specialists, dressed in Callisto's twenty-second-century uniforms, stood guard before it.

Bob Allocco walked across the Skyport, hearing the rap of his shoes against the reflective blue pavers, the icy cadences of the ambient music. It was cruelly, diabolically out of place here, and he wished he could get it out of his head. He wished, too, that he could get the other thing out of his head—his first glimpse of what had once been Station Omega—but he knew already that was one sight that had been seared into his memory forever.

At night, when the Park was closed and there were no lines of guests, the walk across the Skyport always seemed long. Today it seemed even longer. Allocco glanced over, saw a security foreman trotting toward him.

"Status?" Allocco was already asking as the man came up.

"We've completed another sweep, sir," the foreman said, panting slightly. "No guests anywhere. The Skyport's totally secure."

After what he'd seen in Griffin Tower, Allocco no longer believed any place in Utopia was totally secure. But he grunted his approval. Under the circumstances, the evac had gone remarkably smoothly. There had been no panic, no outraged refusals to leave the Skyport. All the guests—on line, entering or leaving the rides—had seemed to buy the story of a federally mandated emergency drill. The barrier curtain had come down unobtrusively, the posting guard set up. Such a procedure had only been simulated in the past, and the best evac time in the drills had been four minutes. Today, the real thing had taken perhaps four and a half. On another occasion, Allocco might have been pleased.

But none of this efficiency would be of any help to the riders on Station Omega.

"I want three roving patrols, six men each," he told the foreman. "Is the forward command post established?"

"By the entrance to Moon Shot."

"Good. Have the teams keep in radio contact with the post, ten-minute call-ins. Keep running them through the Skyport until mop-up's complete." He glanced around. "Did anybody see anything unusual before this happened? Anything out of the ordinary?"

The security foreman shook his head. "One of the loading attendants saw a cast member she didn't recognize. That's about it."

Allocco pounced on this. "She didn't recognize? What made her remember?"

"She just said it was funny, seeing a cast member in a shuttle pilot's suit leaving the off-loading area."

"What's this attendant's name?"

"Piper, sir. She's still back there, with . . . with the others."

Allocco thought a minute. "I want plainclothes teams dispatched through the rest of Callisto. All the other Worlds, as well. Small groups, low profile, two teams to a World. Atlantis, too."

"The other Worlds, sir?" The foreman looked surprised. "Looking for what?"

"Anything. I'll take their reports in thirty minutes, then we'll re-evaluate."

As he veered off in the direction of Moon Shot, Allocco glanced at his watch: 4:09. My God, was it possible he had been here only seven minutes? He felt as if he'd aged at least a year.

When he'd first arrived on the scene, racing up the maintenance stairway, the exit area of Station Omega—out of sight from the main Skyport, thank God—had been a pandemonium of frantic activity: desperate rescue workers, off-load specialists either crying or shocked into senselessness. But it had been different then, of course: people still thought there was a chance to save lives. Now, over the course of just seven minutes, the atmosphere had changed completely. A kind of grim, spectral pall lay over the Skyport.

Except, of course, for that damned music.

A small group had gathered at the hastily constructed forward command post. As he approached, Allocco saw representatives from Guest Relations, Operations, Human Resources. All hovering out here, away from the accident scene, like wallflowers at a frat party. They all wore the same expression of white-faced disbelief. When Sarah got here, she'd . . .

He realized he'd forgotten all about Sarah and the Holo Mirrors, and felt a momentary stab of concern for her. Then it vanished as several phones on one of the portable desks began ringing at once and Malcolm Griff, head of Guest Relations, plucked at his sleeve.

"Yes?" Allocco said, turning to him.

"I've got that report on the containment activities," the man said over the ringing of the phones.

"Let's have it."

"The emergency-drill story seems to be working. I haven't gotten word of any sizable hot spots."

"Good." While he listened, Allocco's eyes were constantly on the move. He watched security specialists answering the phones, watched another specialist unroll a large spool of fiber-optic wire, watched the foreman dispatch the first roving patrol.

"With the help of Operations, we're encouraging outflow from Callisto to the other Worlds. We've slowed inbound traffic at the portals. Just to speed up witness dispersal, retard any rumor clustering."

"Yeah, yeah." Witness dispersal, rumor clustering. Guest Relations used more fancy in-speak than a sociology convention. And yet Allocco sensed the man was keeping something back. He brought his roving eyes back, homing in on Griff.

"What else?"

The man hesitated. "We planted some of our people in the exit lines as the guests left the Skyport. To listen, you know: gauge the mood, what people were saying."

"Go on."

"One of our specialists overheard two guests talking. Apparently, some tourist was wandering near the backstage areas, looking for a bathroom. She caught a glimpse inside the Station Omega exit corridor before the off-loading site was cloistered."

"A *glimpse*?"

"Um, yes. From what our specialist overheard, it sounded pretty accurate."

Jesus Christ. Just what we need. "You get a description of this witness?"

Griff shook his head.

"Any other similar reports?"

"No, just the one."

Allocco's eyes were on the move again. He spotted Tom Rose, Infrastructure chief, emerging from the Skyport backstage. "We'll have to hope it doesn't spread. People are always hearing things like that—with any luck this will be chalked up as another shaggy-dog story. But have your people keep mingling with the guests, keep their ears open. I want to know if this story pops up again somewhere else."

Griff nodded, then turned and walked quickly toward the bank of telephones.

Tom Rose was coming toward him. He was walking slowly, his face pallid. The collar of his shirt was dark with sweat.

"Tom," Allocco said, nodding in solemn greeting.

The Infrastructure chief simply looked back in reply.

"Any idea yet how this could have happened?"

Rose chewed his lip, seeming to think about this. "I've got ride inspectors and engineers looking at it right now," he said. Then he stopped. Allocco stood, waiting for him to continue.

"They're not sure exactly what it was yet. But it has nothing to do with the heat effects, like we thought it might. It seems to be related to the safety design."

"The *safety* design?"

Rose nodded. It looked as if the man was about to burst into tears.

"You know the hydraulic retarding system on Station Omega, how it kicks in after a hundred feet of free fall? It's massively over-engineered; it has to be, because of the way the drop is propelled by the injector mechanism." Rose was talking faster now, as if he wanted to get the painful explanation over with.

"I've seen the specs. Go on."

"Well, normal operation seems to have been reversed. The retarding system didn't kick in at the bottom of the ride, like it was designed to. It came on at the *beginning,* at the top, just as the injector was trying to launch the ride compartment."

"And?"

"Well, there was all that pressure pushing the compartment down, and all that pressure trying to retard it at the same time . . . It generated tremendous heat."

"How much heat?" As soon as it was out, Allocco was sorry he'd asked the question.

Rose looked sorry, too. "My engineers estimated about 500 Celsius. And it vented . . . it vented—" He stopped abruptly.

"Into the ride compartment," Allocco finished for him.

There was a brief, terrible silence.

"But how could that happen?" Allocco asked.

Tom Rose's lips trembled. "We engineered that ride to be failsafe. Everything was done to triple the original specs."

"So?"

"Can't you understand? Our main concern was safety. We designed the ride to be as safe as possible. Not as *tamperproof* as possible."

Suddenly, Allocco understood what it was Rose didn't want to say directly. The ride's own safety design had been used against it. It was a diabolical irony.

"How could such a thing be done?" he asked.

"If someone knew exactly what to do, it would be relatively easy. Reverse half a dozen switches, change the wiring in one of the control panels. The work of a minute, maybe two. But the safety governor would have to be in override mode. That's a systems job, and much more complicated. You need high privileges, all sorts of things. That would have to be done remotely."

Allocco took a step backward, his jaw working. In his mind he saw John Doe, thumbing through pilfered engineering diagrams, determining just which ride could be most conveniently sabotaged against itself. And he saw something else: the unauthorized person in a shuttle pilot's outfit, the one the loading attendant had witnessed walking away from Station Omega just before the calamitous drop. And he remembered what Poole had told him about the hacker; about how he'd just sat there in the Hub, typing, as they approached. As if he'd had to finish something important before . . . Dimly, he realized Tom Rose was asking him a question.

"Sorry?" he said, turning.

Now, Rose *was* crying. "Who?" he asked in a whisper. The tears were coursing down his cheeks unchecked. "Who would do such a thing? And why?"

Allocco could not bear the pleading look on that face. He turned away again.

John Doe had said to keep things quiet. But it was John Doe who had done this. So fuck John Doe.

"My friend," Allocco said quietly, "we've got some very bad people in the Park today."

When he turned back, Rose had gone.

Allocco sighed, blinked, wiped his arm across his forehead. Until Sarah showed up, he was in charge of line operations. For at least the fifth time, he went through the emergency preparedness drill in his head. He'd just touched base with Security, Infrastructure, Guest Relations. That still left Medical and Emergency Response.

But that would mean going back to the scene. Allocco had already been there once. And he really, really did not want to go back.

He sighed again, took a balm stick from his pocket, ran it over his lips. Then he looked around, slowly, as if trying to take comfort in the deceptively calm Skyport around him. And then he left the command post, worked his way along the perimeter to Station Omega's exit corridor, and stepped back into hell.

THE EXIT CORRIDOR smelled like a pig roast. A large, long tent of clear plastic had been hastily erected around the base of the drop shaft, concealing the spot where—once the fail-safe mechanisms had finally been overridden and the power cut—the ride known as Station Omega had come drifting down to earth and at last opened its doors. Allocco was grateful for the tent. The music was fainter here, and he was grateful for that, too. Involuntarily, he thought back to the first moment he'd seen those open elevator doors, the contents of the transport exposed pitilessly to view: the river of tumbled limbs, grotesque against the singed lines of shirts and pants and shoes . . .

As the image lanced its way across his mind, he stopped. Then he forced himself forward once again, in the direction of the tent. It would be better now. There would be some semblance of order.

To one side of the tent's entrance, he could see a wheeled rack, hastily appropriated from Costuming. Dozens of heavy plastic garment bags, black and oversize, hung from its upper bar. Already, the rack was half-empty.

Large banks of life-support equipment stood to one side. Beside them were several wheelchairs, empty, unnecessary. A video specialist passed him, walking quickly away from the site, face set in a greenish cast, evidence camera and video recorder swinging from his shoulders. Small knots of people were scattered around the off-loading area: ride attendants, mechanical engineers, security guards. There was sobbing, of course, but less than before. Most of the Station Omega crew were sitting together, heads bowed. Allocco recognized Dickinson, the tower operator, and Stevens, the ride foreman. A knot of security guards surrounded them. He made a mental note to track down the attendant named Piper, listen to her story before he left. As he passed, Allocco could hear someone talking. It was the young woman who'd been working off-load. She was still recounting the same story he'd heard already, over and over, broken-voiced, as if unable to stop herself. He glanced over. A nurse was kneeling by the woman, wiping her hands and face with a cloth.

"It was quiet, so quiet, as it came down," she was saying. The metallic cloth of her sleeve had been rolled up, a blood pressure cuff placed around her arm. "There was nothing, *nothing,* after all that screaming, and I couldn't understand it, I just knew that something terrible had happened. And then the doors opened, and . . . and they were stacked up so high against it they just tumbled out, past me, *past* me, and there was no sound but they just kept coming and . . . Oh, *God* . . ." and she lapsed into silent, racking sobs. The nurse stroked her bent head, whispered to her. One member of the group stood up and began walking, stiff-legged, toward a far corner of the off-load area. Retching sounds reached Allocco's ears.

Jaw set, he walked past the security detail, put out a hand to pull the tarp away, and stepped into the medical tent.

Here, in this plastic longhouse, the smell of burned flesh was much stronger. Stretchers and gurneys had been set up in two rows, allowing for the processing of corpses to be handled as efficiently as possible. When Allocco had first arrived on the scene, this effort had been slow to get started: Medical, under the assumption a massive influx of casualties was on its way down from the ride, was being prepped for triage. But now the doctors, medical attendants, orderlies, and nurses who'd been ready to save lives were up here, helping to arrange the dead with as much dignity as possible.

Dr. Finch, head of Medical, was at the near end of the left-hand row, bending over one of the oversize plastic bags. Like the others, he wore latex gloves and a double set of surgical masks. Allocco walked toward him, careful to keep his eyes away from the vast, oddly mounded tarp that covered the floor at the far end of the tent, where the ride doors lay open.

"How do we stand, Doctor?" he asked as he approached.

Dr. Finch zipped the bag closed, made a notation on a chart, and turned toward him. "We've got medevacs flying in from Columbia Sunrise and Lake Mead."

"Due when?"

Above the mask, the doctor's eyes were already haggard, red-rimmed. "They're about twenty-two minutes out."

Even if they were here now, it wouldn't make any difference, Allocco thought. *What we need is a fleet of coroners.*

"We've contacted the sheriff's office and the Clark County ME," the doctor said, as if following his thoughts. "They're due in the next half hour, forty minutes, tops."

Allocco nodded. He wondered what John Doe would think when he saw half the uniformed officials in Nevada descending upon the place. He realized he didn't much care.

"What's the procedure here?" he asked, waving his hand along the rows of stretchers. Although Utopia's emergency procedures manuals were exhaustive, there were no guidelines for anything quite like this.

"We're just stabilizing the site, organizing the bodies for the MEs to identify."

"Got a count yet?" The automatic counter showed that sixty-one people had entered Station Omega before the doors were shut, but there was always a hope the count was wrong, that there were actually fewer people on the ride than they thought.

"No. Not in the state *that's* in." The doctor made the merest motion of his head toward the huge, lumpy tarp that covered the rearward floor of the tent. "So far, we've processed twenty-seven."

Twenty-seven, Allocco thought. Throughout the 1990s, there had been a total of twenty-one deaths at all amusement parks across all fifty states. Last year, there had been only five. Here, in one incomprehensible tragedy, the number was more than ten times as large. It would go down in history, forever haunt the Park. People would always be wondering, when the doors of some thrill ride whispered shut around them, if the same thing might happen again: the sudden stop, the darkness, the panic, the indescribable merciless heat . . .

He shook himself back. "Thank you, Doctor. Don't let me keep you. Until we get an official presence here, I'll be monitoring the situation from the command post outside. If you need anything at all, just let me know."

The doctor glanced at him a moment, then nodded and returned to his chart. Allocco turned away, letting his gaze fall across the tent. At the far end, a man wearing an A-level hazmat suit was lifting a zippered bag from one of the stretchers. The bag was clearly light, maybe forty or fifty pounds. As Allocco watched, the man backed away, pivoted, then carefully laid the bag at the end of a long row of similar bags. Then he turned toward the massive tarp covering the mouth of the ride, held out a heavily gloved hand, lifted an edge to reach beneath. Allocco caught a fleeting glimpse of something—glistening, bright as boiled lobster—before he turned away and ducked back out of the tent.

4:10 P.M.

IT SEEMED HE had been pacing—down eight steps, turn, eight steps back—for an hour. Probably it hadn't been more than five minutes. As he'd paced, Fred Barksdale had tried very hard not to think. Thinking would be too painful. And yet despite his best efforts, shame and rage, fear and bafflement and mortification, had begun to settle over his shoulders like a cloak.

The other occupant of the holding cell had lain down again, closed his eyes. Although they'd met for planning sessions half a dozen times, Barksdale did not know the man's name. He was simply Cracker Jack. But then, he didn't know any of their names—they were just aliases, like Water Buffalo, Candyman, or that really frightening chap, Hardball. Barksdale had always felt reassured by this anonymity, as if his ignorance were a kind of protection. Now, he didn't feel so sure.

When that strange unknown fellow in the corduroy jacket had appeared out of nowhere—tricking him with that fraudulent KIS story, showing him the gun—Barksdale had simply shut down. The agitation that had been growing inside him over the past week had abruptly dissolved into, strangely enough, a kind of relief. It was over. For better or worse, at least it was over.

But by the time they'd entered the Security Complex, this numbness had given way to a terrible inner conflict. He hated himself for having started all this; for letting things spiral out of control, for letting John Doe alternately charm and threaten him to such an undignified conclusion. And the talk of casualties in Callisto, vague as it was, felt like a dagger piercing his heart. And yet he'd tried hard to suppress his surprise when they had opened the cell door and revealed Cracker Jack on the cot within: any signs of recognition would only work against him. Despite his pain and self-loathing, Barksdale knew, deep inside, that he was still hoping to beat the rap.

Cracker Jack opened his eyes, took in the pacing. "So, how 'bout them Lakers?" he asked.

This drollery received no reply. Barksdale simply quickened his pace, back and forth, back and forth.

" 'I am a man whom Fortune hath cruelly scratched,' " he said to himself, too quietly for Cracker Jack to hear.

He hadn't been entirely truthful with Sarah, back in Medical. A line of Shakespeare's *had*, in fact, come to mind. *All may be well*. But it had been spoken at such an inappropriate time, and by such an inappropriate person—Claudius, murderer of Hamlet's father—that he could not bring himself to utter it.

O, my offense is rank—it smells to heaven . . .

He pushed these thoughts away. There would be no consolation in Shakespeare today.

How had it all gone wrong? It had seemed so simple. All the pieces had slipped so easily into place, almost as if somebody else were assembling the puzzle for him.

But then again, someone *had*—if he'd only seen it. And that someone was John Doe.

It all started with a great anger. Despite being an ideal candidate, he'd been passed over for head of Operations. Even more galling, the powers-that-be had hired someone from Carnegie-Mellon in his place. Sarah Boatwright's impeccable credentials—positions as executive administrator at Busch Gardens and VP of Administration at a Silicon Valley microchip manufacturer—hadn't mattered to the outraged Barksdale. The point was that they had hired *out of the Park*. Chuck Emory, arrogant swine of a CEO, had never really liked him. Barksdale had almost quit in disgust.

But then, something had occurred to him. Something better than quitting.

At first, it was just an idea he liked to toy with; an intellectual challenge he found interesting to solve. It was only after he realized just how clever, how perfectly simple, the solution was—and how he, as head of Systems, was the only one in a position to implement it—that he began to think more seriously.

The answer lay in the high degree to which every process within Utopia was automated. Automation was all-pervasive: from the movement sensors that tracked crowd dispersal throughout the Park; to the computers that monitored and readjusted light, temperature, humidity, water pressure, and countless other environmental variables; to the system that ran the collection and processing of money.

This last—the Financial Processing System—was a beautiful system indeed. As he spearheaded its development, supervised the implementation, he'd used as his model the networks of Roman roads that once strode across Europe and Asia. He remembered being fascinated by these roads as a child in grammar school. Straight, paved, uniform—the Domitian Way, Aurelian Way, Appian Way, countless others—and all leading back to the *milliarium aureum*, the Golden Milestone, at the Forum in Rome.

Utopia, with its imagetags and Park credit cards for guests, had tried to dispense with paper money as much as possible. But there were still countless places throughout the Park—the food vendors and souvenir sellers, holographic photo galleries, T-shirt emporiums, cash-only Embarkation booths—that accepted it. And, unlike other theme parks, Utopia had something else: four vast casinos, whose slots, video poker machines, blackjack tables, and roulette wheels had proved insatiable magnets for cash.

Barksdale's Financial Processing System drew money from countless far-flung sites across the Park, channeled it without human intervention to a variety of collection and processing substations, and ultimately deposited it in the central vault on C Level: Utopia's own financial *Forum Romanum*. And from there, once a week like clockwork, it was taken off-site by an escorted armored car. It all happened automatically, autonomously, under Systems control. In fact, nothing could interrupt this weekly cycle of collection and delivery but the head of Operations. Only a call from Sarah Boatwright could cancel an armored car pickup. And she would only make such a call if there was a perceived threat to the integrity or stability of the Park.

But what—Barksdale had wondered to himself—if an armored car came *anyway*?

The regular truck from Utopia's chosen carrier, American Armored Security, might be canceled by Sarah Boatwright. But it was Barksdale's responsibility to cancel the *internal* processing, the actual financial disbursal. If it was done cleverly, the systems personnel on C Level would never know that the *real* armored car had been canceled. Because Barksdale would not act on, or *pass on*, Sarah's order. Knowledge would stop with him. And when a replacement armored car rolled in, it would be filled within minutes, as usual, and sent on its way, as usual—with what, over the last two months, was averaging a staggering hundred million dollars a week . . .

Barksdale paused in his pacing. *A hundred million dollars.* If he was completely honest with himself, he had to admit that it wasn't just a noble anger that motivated him. It was the money as well.

The facade he had always presented to staff and superior alike—Frederick Barksdale, born to the first water of English nobility, rider to hounds—was a sham. He'd grown up in a miserable semidetached house in Clapham, reading moldering books, fantasizing that he was one of the privileged lads attending Eton, or Harrow, or Sandhurst. The idea of working for a living seemed distasteful, beneath him. His real calling, surely, was to tread the boards as a Shakespearean actor, like Gielgud or Olivier. Of course, his parents had no money for such a childish indulgence, despite his obvious flair for acting. So he got a scholarship to Canterbury Technical College, where he soon found he had another aptitude—an aptitude for computer design. After graduation, he secured a systems management position in the States, and his star rose quickly. He soon learned he had yet another aptitude: to don the affectations of an upper-class Englishman. With his gift for voices, his inbred love for the finest things in life, it was easy. The persona developed subtly. Nobody ever questioned him. In time, Barksdale stopped questioning himself. And he began to indulge himself in the way he'd always known he deserved.

This turned out to be very expensive. Debt multiplied with frightening rapidity. And yet the things he most wanted—the kind of luxury, the civilized life he merited—still remained out of his grasp.

A hundred million dollars.

Of course, it could never be done. Not really. Barksdale couldn't be seen messing with his own systems. And besides, it wasn't a job for one man. It would require a skilled team, men who knew where to procure such things as uniforms, the truck, everything else. Things that Barksdale himself wouldn't have the first clue about.

Although Barksdale was enterprising, rather desperate for

money, and full of righteous indignation, he was not particularly brave. The discreet, cryptic advertisements he placed in the *Times* of London, *Punch,* and a few other journals known to be read by ex-MI5 members were more a private joke with himself than anything else. *Unusual investment opportunity. Successful candidate will have performed with distinction in one of the Special Branches. Sangfroid, high organizational and leadership skills necessary. Small initial investment, large return possible. The fainthearted and morally scrupulous need not apply.* Barksdale's advertisement had satisfied his sense of outrage: *look what I could do if I wanted to,* it said.

But then, the ad was answered. And one thing led to another. And now he was here, inside this cell.

Inside this cell . . .

There seemed to be some kind of activity going on beyond the door. Barksdale paused in his pacing to listen. Apparently, still more guards were being called away to deal with whatever had happened in Callisto. The guard that had been visible through the small meshed-glass window was no longer there. At the thought of Callisto, of the security specialist named Chris Green, Barksdale felt a fresh stab of pain. *Nobody was supposed to get hurt. That was the promise.*

Cracker Jack, too, was intrigued enough by the noise to get up from his bunk. He walked toward the window, took a look around. Then he rapped on the door. "Hey!" he yelled.

Nobody answered.

"Hey!" he yelled, more loudly this time.

The youthful, acne-scarred face of Lindbergh, the guard, appeared in the window.

"Where's the bathroom?" Cracker Jack asked.

"Later."

"Fuck later, man. I gotta go *now*. What are you going to do, make me shit my pants?"

On the far side of the window, Lindbergh looked first left, then right. A key jangled in the lock, the door opened slowly.

"Keep your hands in front of you," Lindbergh said. He was holding his billy club at the ready. "And don't try anything. I don't want to use this on you, but if I have to, I will."

Barksdale watched the door shut again, heard the rasp of the lock. He turned away with a sigh. Unlike Cracker Jack, he was unaware that Lindbergh was now the lone remaining guard in Security.

Barksdale resumed his pacing. Now he could see that the ease with which things had come together—the way the plan had almost assembled itself—was illusory. It was like that terrible kind of dream where one seemingly innocent event leads naturally into another, and then into another, and you go along without thinking until suddenly you're locked into a nightmare from which waking is the only freedom. A nightmare that had been carefully, deceptively engineered by John Doe.

Abruptly, Barksdale stopped again. Turning toward the wall, he touched his head to it gently, once, twice. If only he could wake up *now*.

And yet it *should* have worked. Every little problem that cropped up, every potential snare, had been quickly solved. The man who had answered the advertisement, who called himself John Doe—mysterious and elusive though he was—proved supremely shrewd and clever. He was clearly of good breeding, highly cultured, student of Bach and Raphael and Shakespeare, a man that Barksdale could understand. John Doe seemed to genuinely sympathize with him. As planning went on, the man assumed greater and greater control, telling Barksdale precisely what systems needed further explanation or what schematic he wanted copies of. He'd taken care of recruiting, luring Tom Tibbald on board for the lighter inside duties. And it was John Doe who had seen the *real* potential, beyond anything Barksdale had ever dreamed of. At first, it had been just about the money. But soon it grew into much, much more. John Doe showed him how the very ruse that would convince Sarah Boatwright to invoke emergency procedures—to, among other things, call AAS and cancel the armored car run—could be used to procure the Crucible, a technology worth even more than the cash itself. It would all be quick, almost effortless. Best of all, it could be accomplished without violence.

In fact, by that point, Barksdale's only reservation didn't involve the plan at all. It involved Sarah Boatwright, the woman he had so resented for landing the job as head of Operations. He'd never planned on liking her. He wasn't even sure how, exactly, it had happened. She wasn't his type, at all—so sure of herself, so American. He hadn't tried to charm her, particularly; he had merely been himself. Oddly enough, that was what did it. It was funny, the way their relationship seemed to have developed in lockstep with his own plans for the Park. If either one had come markedly first—his feelings for her, or his scheme to enrich himself—the other would probably never have come about. As it was, he grew increasingly conflicted. But every time he decided to call it off, John Doe would reason with him, cajole him, remind him just how huge his cut of the take was, show him the fallacy of his fears. And Barksdale would realize the man was right. Perhaps, when it was all over, he'd find a way to contact Sarah, to explain. Perhaps—he liked to believe—he could even convince her to join him. Madeira was a beautiful spot, a green nugget of paradise in an azure sea, and . . .

But here the train of thought grew very painful. Barksdale shook his head, resumed his pacing.

He'd almost told her, back there by Georgia Warne's bedside. He'd come within a heart's beat of asking her to forgive him, come with him. But now, here in this stark cell, he realized he'd been deluding himself. Sarah would never be able to forgive his betrayal: of her, and perhaps to her mind even worse, of her Park. He could only hope that she'd be able to find happiness elsewhere—perhaps, despite her denials, with Andrew Warne.

He thought back to what she'd said about John Doe; about the way he seemed to see into her soul, say precisely what she wanted to hear. The same thing had happened to him. John Doe had appeared as the well-bred Britisher Barksdale had always secretly ached to be. His credentials had been impeccable. He'd treated Barksdale as an equal, in social class as well as intelligence. How surprised Barksdale was to finally learn that this chameleon-like performance was as fraudulent as the credentials were genuine.

Other surprises were to follow. The boy who got hurt on Notting Hill Chase—that wasn't supposed to happen. John Doe had been contrite, assuring him no other such glitch would occur. But the biggest surprise of all had come today, when Andrew Warne showed up a week early.

Warne's arrival was a given, of course. The very nature of the plan assured he'd show up, sooner or later, to debug the Metanet. It had been Barksdale's idea: to use John Doe's team, posing as KIS operatives, to insert rogue software into the Utopia Net. And John Doe had come up with the clever scheme of having Cracker Jack pose as an outside hacker, feeling around Utopia's firewall, trying half-heartedly to break in. His attacks had been unsuccessful—of course—but they'd had the desired result of a sudden demand among Utopia's board for instant action. That had allowed Barksdale to involve KIS—or, rather, the phony KIS—at somebody else's behest. It kept him above suspicion. And the board's habitual secrecy allowed him to make all the necessary contacts himself. Utopia had a ten-week billing cycle, and eventually somebody would question why KIS never sent a bill for their services. But by that time the operation, and Barksdale's own role in it, would already be well known. And Barksdale himself would be far, far away.

Warne was supposed to arrive a week from today. But instead, he'd shown up this morning, the very worst time for a surprise. And that was when the first feelings of real foreboding had begun to crawl up Barksdale's spine. But by now, of course, John Doe was alternating his affable reassurances with rather terrifying threats. He made little attempt to disguise, any longer, his true contempt for Barksdale. Even the man's own allusions to Shakespeare had taken on a cynical, taunting edge. So there was nothing for it but to continue the operation, despite his feelings of . . .

There was a noise in the hallway. It was Cracker Jack, on his way back from the bathroom. *Spent quite some time in there*, Barksdale thought disinterestedly. The key rattled in the lock, the door opened. Barksdale turned to see Lindbergh framed in the doorway, one hand on his billy club, the other grasping the door handle. Beside him stood Cracker Jack. This time the hacker's hands were not in front of him, but behind his back.

As Barksdale watched, Cracker Jack quickly swept his arms forward, raising them above Lindbergh's head. A thin piece of metal wire was stretched tightly between his hands. It glistened briefly in the light, as if it had been freshly washed. Staring, time suspended, Barksdale had the sudden clear realization that he did not want to speculate on where the wire had been hidden.

And then Cracker Jack's hands jerked downward and the wire disappeared into the flesh of Lindbergh's neck.

The guard instinctively raised his hands, rasping and choking. His baton fell to the floor, rolling across the tiles and coming to rest half inside the cell. Barksdale watched in frozen horror. The guard lurched one way, then the next, but Cracker Jack stayed close behind him, one palm crossed over the other as he sank the garrote deeper into Lindbergh's neck.

Then he eased back on the pressure slightly. The guard's fingers dropped and he gasped for breath, coughing and retching.

Keeping his hands against Lindbergh's neck, Cracker Jack leaned in toward the man's ear. "Where's my duffel?" he asked.

"Locker . . ." Lindbergh wheezed. "Locker."

"Where?"

Lindbergh rolled his eyes toward the end of the corridor.

"Locked?"

The purplish face nodded almost imperceptibly.

"Keys?"

". . . Pocket . . ."

"Take them out."

The guard lowered one hand toward his pocket. He was unable to look down, and it took him a moment. Barksdale watched, thunderstruck, as the fingers twitched and jerked their way along the line of the belt. Fresh hope, all the sweeter for being unexpected, surged within him. He was going to get away, after all. He was going to make it.

Lindbergh had found his key chain, holding it out between his thumb and index finger. The keys rattled noisily in his trembling hand.

"Which one?"

With an effort, Lindbergh raised the chain to his eyes, sorted through them, held up a small, bronze-colored key.

Cracker Jack took a good look at it. "You wouldn't be bullshitting me now, would you?"

The guard gave his head a single shake.

"Good." And with a grunt of effort, Cracker Jack tightened the garrote once again.

Lindbergh began struggling wildly, his hands tearing at his neck, his feet skidding across the floor. Cracker Jack fought to keep himself level, arching the guard's body backward under the pressure of the wire. The air was filled with a terrible wet rattle.

Barksdale stared, rooted in surprise and horror. "No," he murmured.

Cracker Jack tightened relentlessly, his face contorting with the effort. Lindbergh had jerked himself around now to face the open door of the cell. He looked in, mouth open and full of blood, eyes wide and pleading.

"This isn't right," Barksdale said, more loudly now.

Lindbergh's eyes rolled up into his head, ghastly white within crimson sockets.

"No!" Barksdale shouted. And barely knowing what he was doing, he leaped forward, grasped the baton, and, rising, sent it on a long, looping swipe across the side of Cracker Jack's head.

There was an ugly noise of wood against bone, and the baton shivered out of Barksdale's hands, clattering to the floor. For a terrible moment, Cracker Jack's grip held tight. Then he slumped to the ground. Lindbergh immediately collapsed on top of him, arms sprawled out, fingers twitching spasmodically.

Barksdale knelt beside the guard, rolled him gingerly to one side. The garrote had sunk so deeply into the guard's neck that it had remained fixed in place even after he fell. It was slippery with blood, hard to get a grip on. Barksdale peeled it away, loosened the man's collar, stroked his forehead.

"Come on, old fellow," he muttered, shaking him gently. "Come on. You'll make it."

There was a sudden blow to the small of his back, and pain exploded in his spine like a mortar round. Barksdale fell to one side, crying out. Cracker Jack was getting to his feet, a little unsteadily. The man looked around. Barksdale followed his glance, but by the time he realized the hacker's intentions, Cracker Jack had already spotted the billy club. He dove for it, pushing Barksdale's reaching hand out of the way. Then he rose a second time, much more quickly now. He glanced down at the guard, spotted the keys, moved to scoop them up.

Barksdale took a scrambling step backward, across the floor. At the movement, Cracker Jack turned toward him again. He lifted a hand to the side of his head, winced. Barksdale saw the man's knuckles whiten as they gripped the baton.

"Mother*fucker*," he muttered, stepping quickly toward the retreating Barksdale.

4:12 P.M.

AS THE ARMORED car and its escort sedan ground up the long approach route to Utopia, the exit traffic slowly increased. Huge semis, tall-sided refrigerated vans, and produce trucks shot past them, lighter now, their loads ferried away into the endless warrens of the Park's underbelly. The trucks were soon joined by a procession of cars, SUVs, and pickups: Red-Shift Utopia cast and crew, leaving for the day. The faces looked happy, unfettered, heading back for the north Vegas suburbs or the nearby party community of Creosote.

Now, as the last curve was turned and the massive rear wall of Utopia came into view, the line-haul driver glanced at his watch: 4:12. Right on the money.

He reached into a reinforced compartment and pulled out a radio. One eye on the road, the other on the radio's keypad, he punched in a descrambling code, then lifted the transmitter to his lips.

"Prime Factor, this is Candyman, do you read?"

He let his finger slip from the transmit button, listening. After a moment, a voice replied, reedy and artificial through the wash of static: "I read, Candyman. Do you have a visual?"

"Coming in sight now."

"Excellent." The reply was still faint, but it would soon get stronger. "Proceed with contact. We'll meet you at the rally point."

"Out." The man put the radio to one side. For a moment, he consulted a small list of typewritten commands that had been taped beneath the dashboard. Then he pressed his other hand to a button on his radio headset. "Utopia Central, this is AAS transport Nine Echo Bravo, over."

A very different voice came crackling over the headset. "Utopia Central."

"We're on final, requesting an entrance authorization."

"Nine Echo Bravo, stand by."

The headset went silent and the driver slowed, working his way down the gears. The shift change was over now, and the procession of cars was ebbing. Ahead, past the guard station, the road widened into an endless ocean of blacktop. The vehicles of Utopia cast and crew stood to one side, in long, shining, unbroken rows. To the other was a motley assortment of trucks and other service vehicles. Far to one side sat a windowless van, brown against the pitiless sun. *Exotic Bird Trainers of Las Vegas* had been painted on its side in palm-leaf letters. As if in advertisement, a large buzzard sat on its roof, wings outspread and drainpipe neck erect. Once or twice it tapped its beak, inquiringly, against the van's roof.

Beyond the staff parking and the maintenance ports rose the endless bulk of Utopia. Officially known as the Service and Administrative Zone, it was a sight not shown in any tourist brochures or videos, and only occasionally seen in covert pictures taken for fan magazines and websites. Yet it was aweinspiring in its own way. The Park's rear facade curved gently from one canyon wall to the other like the face of a vast dam, unbroken save for a scattering of tiny windows. Above it arched the graceful lines of the dome, glittering in the late afternoon sun. Its monstrous shadow was just beginning to fall over the leftmost edge of the lot.

"Utopia Central confirms," came the voice over the headset. "You may proceed. Approach corridor being cleared now."

"Nine Echo Bravo confirms," the driver said. "Thanks. Out."

At the checkpoint, the lone guard waved the armored car through. The driver responded with a chuff of air brakes, then trundled across the tarmac toward an oversize bay set into the base of Utopia's main structure, between twin loading docks. The letter *B* was stenciled above it in ten-foot-high black paint. Though the bay was large enough to fit the truck easily, it looked like little more than a mouse hole in the wall that rose above it.

The escort sedan peeled away from the truck and drove to one side of the bay, where it waited, engine idling, amber blinker on its roof turning idly. The line-haul driver looked in his rearview mirror, caught the eye of the messenger guard in the rear compartment. The guard returned the glance, grasped his shotgun. Nodded.

This entrance had to be done right the first time: any mistakes or deviations from the norm would be immediately noticed. But it had only been eighteen months since he'd stopped driving armored cars for the company, and it had become second nature again very quickly. Besides, the maneuver had been practiced dozens of times, between lines of cones in the arroyos and dry washes of Esmeralda County, and there was no hesitation. The driver approached the bay, then pulled the wheel over hard and brought the big Ford into a slow turn. Then, sliding the transmission into reverse, he smoothly guided its rear toward the bay. As the end of the truck slipped into the belly of Utopia, the growl of the engine, the insistent bleat of the backing tone, grew harsh and echoing.

Slowly, the blue sky disappeared and the roof of C Level came forward to take its place. Now the armored car was fully inside, backing carefully down the wide, gently curving passageway. As the driver passed by the guard station, the man inside nodded.

"Check the oil and tires, willya?" the driver shouted through the gunport.

The guard smiled, gave him a thumbs-up, and gestured him on.

4:15 P.M.

THEY HALF WALKED, half ran through B Level, Sarah striding forward, Warne struggling to keep up. Sarah looked straight ahead, mouth set, eyes rarely blinking. A radio, appropriated from Carmen Florez in Imaging Fabrication, swung in her right hand. Approaching cast and crew, catching sight of the expression on her face, gave the Park chief a wide berth.

"Tell it to me again," she said brusquely, over her shoulder.

"There's no more to tell," Warne panted. "I don't have all the answers. I just knew that, with that disc you found being blank—"

"How do you know?"

"Terri told me."

"Well, Terri must be mistaken." The confused, uncertain look he'd seen on Sarah's face in the pale glow of the Holo Mirrors was now gone.

"If she's right, that means John Doe already *has* one disc. Why would Barksdale give you a blank disc—especially since he's involved? That's when it occurred to me that maybe it wasn't just another disc John Doe was after. It was *you*."

"Me?" Sarah's voice was tight, laced with skepticism.

"He clearly needed you, for some reason. You're the Park chief, after all. No doubt he intended to kidnap you—or worse. A confusing place like that, a maze, was the perfect spot. Why would he let you see him, face-to-face, up close, in your office? He doesn't seem like the kind of guy to leave such a loose end behind." This conversation wasn't going the way he'd planned. Warne realized, with an uncomfortable hollow feeling, that he had been acting impulsively; that, really, he couldn't prove any of this at all. But nothing else made sense.

"And why *now*, of all times?" Sarah asked skeptically as they turned down a new corridor.

"Maybe this is a critical point in their plans. Something must be happening we don't know about. They must need diversions. Why else would they damage that ride—what's it called, Station Omega—after you've agreed to deliver the second disc?"

"Yes, why would they?" The way she put it, it didn't sound like a question. "After we locked up one of their crew, thanks to you? That's where I should be right now, by the way: Station Omega. Instead, I'm on this wild-goose chase."

Warne felt agitated. Until this fusillade of questions, Sarah had said little since they left Gaslight. "Why do you call it that?" he asked.

"Because that's what it is. Your little theory has one problem: Fred's guilt. Without that, everything falls apart. And I don't buy it. Not for a minute."

"But I explained about KIS, about how there was no—"

"Yes, yes. I heard. I could see you were jealous of him, Andrew, but this is *completely* unacceptable." She quickened her pace. "I'm going to stop by Security just long enough to hear Fred's explanation. And then I'm going to order him released, of course. And get back to what I'm supposed to be doing: running this Park. In about five minutes, Chuck Emory will be phoning the feds. And when they get here, all your little theories are going to become academic." She gave Warne a brief, baleful glare.

Warne's agitation deepened. He'd been feeling relieved, even—if he dared admit it—a little pleased with himself. He'd figured it out, unraveled the knot. He'd saved Sarah from an unknown fate at the hands of John Doe. The only concern he'd felt had been over Georgia's and Terri's whereabouts. This withering blast of anger and disbelief was the last thing he'd expected.

Ahead, the double doors of the Security Complex had come into view. *She's in denial*, he told himself. *She can't accept what Barksdale's done.* But there was that other voice in his head, quieter, but colder and more insistent: *What if you got it wrong? What if there's some other explanation you've been missing? Did you let your feelings cloud your judgment?*

Sarah pushed through the doors, stepped inside. Then she stopped, frowning.

The anteroom was empty. The brightly colored plastic chairs were unoccupied; the long front desk, polished and gleaming, was vacant. A strange, watchful stillness seemed to hang over the room. In the distance, a telephone was ringing.

"What—?" Sarah began. She stepped forward, looking around.

Warne followed. Where was Poole? Why hadn't Terri returned here with Georgia? Was it possible they were all waiting in one of the rear offices?

He opened the door beside the front desk and looked down the corridor beyond. No sign of anyone, no sound or movement. Mystification began to turn to alarm.

He started down the corridor. Still nothing. The tick of a clock, the low rumble of air-conditioning. The phone began ringing again. At the far end of the corridor, one of the doors was open. Inside, Warne could see a bank of large steel lockers. One had swung open, key dangling from its lock.

Then Warne stopped moving. It had been instinctual, that sudden halt.

On the wall of the corridor, something glistened. He approached it cautiously. It was a spray of blood, still wet, bright red against the gray brick.

Heart thumping in the back of his throat, Warne crept forward, peered into the open area ahead. There was more blood here, spattered across chairs and a duty desk, climbing the walls in narrow traceries.

Had John Doe come for the prisoners? What terrible thing had happened?

Still, no sound. And then, the pattering of feet from behind.

Warne had forgotten about Sarah. He turned, saw her approach quickly.

"Sarah!" he said, trying to keep her back. *"No!"*

Ducking around him, she ran into the open area. She stopped when she saw the blood.

"Oh, Jesus," she muttered.

Warne looked around once more, struggling to master himself. His eye landed on the door of the holding cell. It was ajar. Blood was pooled before it.

Slowly, almost mechanically, he approached, put his head to the security window, gazed in.

Two bodies lay motionless, facedown, on the floor. Through the window he could see heads, shoulders, little else. They both wore the black blazers of security guards.

They've escaped, he thought. *Both of them, Barksdale and the hacker. They killed the guards and escaped.*

But Poole? Was his body stashed elsewhere? And where—he

felt a sudden, terrible chill—where were Terri Bonifacio and Georgia?

Suddenly, he felt himself pushed to one side. Sarah peered through the window. As she did so, Warne could hear her gasp. Then she threw open the door and went inside. Immediately, she cried out in what sounded like physical pain. Without another thought, Warne ducked around the door to follow.

Sarah was down on her knees beside one of the guards. Only now, Warne realized the man wasn't a guard. He was wearing a light-colored suit, but the top half of the jacket was so darkened by blood it looked black. Sarah leaned forward to cradle the figure and a blond head lolled back.

It was Barksdale.

For a moment, Warne stood still, rooted in horror.

Sarah turned toward him violently. "Help me, for God's sake!" she screamed. "Get some water, get a cloth. *Call Medical!*"

Stung into action, Warne wheeled away, running down the corridor toward the front desk.

In the anteroom, he saw movement. It was Poole, arm around Terri. He was leading her gently through the double doors with one hand, guiding a wheelchair with the other.

Warne's gaze fell on the wheelchair. There was Georgia, eyes closed, a hospital blanket around her shoulders.

For a moment, relief overwhelmed all other emotion. Then Warne looked at Terri. She was pale beneath her bronze skin. Her eyes caught his, darted away. And then, with an effort, returned. Her right hand was slick with blood.

"Are you hurt?" he asked instantly.

"She's okay," Poole said. "There was blood on the radio she used to contact me."

"What happened?"

"We were hiding," Terri said. "In the closet." There was a tremor in her voice, and she struggled to maintain her composure.

"We'll get to that later," Poole interjected. "I think it's more important you tell me what's going on *here*." And, significantly, he let his gaze fall toward the ground.

Following it, Warne saw that his own shoes were covered in blood; that a bloody trail led back through the door and down the corridor. He motioned Poole to one side.

"Barksdale's back there," he murmured in the man's ear. "I think he's dead. He and one of the guards. And the hacker's gone."

With a single, blistering expletive, Poole moved past him, racing back toward the cell.

Warne went to Terri, put an arm around her shoulder.

"Are you okay?" he asked. He stroked her cheek, lifted her eyes toward his. Tried to keep her from looking down at the trail of footsteps.

She nodded. "I'm okay."

"And Georgia—?" Something in Terri's eyes would not let him continue.

"She woke up. Briefly. She's asleep again."

The double doors opened and a very young man stood framed between them. Warne recognized him as Peccam, Allocco's video tech.

"Where have you been?" Peccam demanded. "I've been looking all over for you. All hell broke loose in Callisto, and this place emptied out, so I . . ." He stopped at the sight of the bloody footsteps.

"Poole's back there," Warne said, pointing over his shoulder. "He'll fill you in. Maybe you can be of some help. Meanwhile, I've got to make a call."

As Peccam moved away, Warne guided Terri into the area behind the front desk. There were two smaller rooms here, an office and a bathroom. He gently wheeled Georgia into the office. She was restless, stirring in her sleep. She cried out once and he stroked her hair soothingly, kissed the warm forehead. She muttered something, seemed to grow calmer.

"I love you, princess," he murmured. Then he stepped outside and returned to Terri.

Terri raised her eyes to him. "She didn't cry," she said. Her voice was a monotone, still full of shock. "After that man with the gun left. It was dark there, so dark, where we hid. She dozed again. I think it's the—I think it's the medication."

"Thank you," Warne said in almost a whisper, taking her hand. "I'll never forget what you've done for me today."

Terri looked at him.

"Can you do one more thing?" Warne stared at her closely, trying to read the emotions on her face, wondering how best to say this. He decided to tell her everything. "Two men have been hurt here, very badly. One's a security guard. The other is Fred

Barksdale. Could you please call Medical, have them send a doctor down right away?"

At the sound of Barksdale's name, Terri flinched, seemed to grow even paler. But without another word she turned away, toward the central desk. She located a phone, picked it up. It trembled slightly in her hand.

Ducking into the bathroom, Warne grabbed half a dozen towels and dampened them in the sink. Then he ran back down the corridor.

With both Sarah and Poole kneeling beside Barksdale, the holding cell was cramped. Mutely, Warne handed a couple of the towels to Sarah, then retired to the doorway, stood beside Peccam. The guard had been rolled over onto his back—probably by Poole, checking his condition. The man's face was grotesquely swollen, the tip of a blackened tongue peeping almost coyly between parted lips. Sarah, still cradling Barksdale in her arms, began gently swabbing his face. The Englishman was so badly battered his fine features were almost unrecognizable.

"Terri's calling Medical," Warne said.

Poole took the rest of the towels from him, exchanged them for Sarah's bloody ones. "He's still alive," he told Warne. "Barely."

Carefully, with infinite gentleness, Sarah dabbed at the face. Barksdale stirred and moaned slightly.

"Freddy," she said, drawing closer. "It's me, Sarah. I'm here."

Barksdale stirred again.

"Just relax."

Barksdale's mouth twitched. "Sarah." The voice was slurred, barely comprehensible.

"Don't try to talk. Everything's going to be fine."

"No. Must talk. Sarah—so sorry . . ."

The towels were now exhausted, and Warne retreated to get more. At the front desk, Terri was speaking into the phone in low, urgent tones. Warne rooted through a few cabinets, looking for a first-aid kit. Unsuccessful, he went to the bathroom for the fresh towels. Then he headed back down the corridor. To his surprise, he was met halfway by Poole and Ralph Peccam.

"I thought you should know," Poole said. "He's confessed."

"What did he say?"

"Not much, yet. He's in an awful lot of pain."

"Let's go." Warne started back down the corridor, but Poole put a restraining hand on his arm.

"What is it?"

"Look. I'm not a doctor, but it doesn't take one to see that guy isn't going to make it."

Warne looked at him. "What are you saying?"

"I'm saying, let's give her a couple of minutes' peace with him." Warne hesitated a moment.

"Whatever he says, she'll tell us when she's ready. If it's any of our business."

"You're right." Warne turned, began walking slowly back toward the anteroom. Peccam stood, blinking stupidly, stunned motionless.

Terri was replacing the phone as Warne returned. In the over-size leather chair, she looked small, vulnerable. Her eyes were red, but dry. Although he wasn't sure what had happened in Medical, the blood on her hand made guessing all too easy. Warne felt a stab of guilt. Somehow, he would try to make it up to her.

He knelt beside the chair, using the towels to clean the spattered blood from her hand. He felt a pressure on his shoulder as she leaned her head against him. He raised his other arm, pressed her close. Her shoulders began to shake in silent, rhythmic sobs.

"It's all right," he told her. "Everything's over now."

He knelt there, holding the woman in his arms. Minutes passed, he wasn't sure how many. He felt her slowing sobs, smelled the clean scent of balsam in her hair. It was over. For better or worse, it was over. It *had* to be.

That's when he heard the voice—Sarah's voice—shouting his name. "Andrew! *Andrew!*"

As gently as he could, Warne detached himself from Terri. Then, giving her cheek a final caress, he turned away and raced for the cell.

Poole was there before him, crouched once again beside Barksdale, listening.

"The armored car," Sarah was saying as she stroked Barksdale's hair. "That was the real target. That, and the Crucible technology. Everything else, the glitches with the bots, were just ruses to keep us off balance."

As Sarah spoke, she rocked back and forth slightly.

"To keep you from seeing what was really going on," Poole

said to Sarah, nodding. There was a sympathetic expression on his face. "What's this about an armored car?"

"It makes one run a week, on Mondays." Sarah did not look at either Poole or Warne. Her eyes were on Barksdale, her voice a monotone. Blood had soaked the sleeves of her jacket, making them cling to her forearms. "The whole process is automated. Only myself or Chuck Emory in New York can cancel it. Which we're supposed to do if there's an emergency, or a threat to public safety. I canceled the milk run this morning, but the word was never passed on by Freddy. The people in Vault Control downstairs still expect a truck. And he says one's coming. *Where's that goddamned doctor?*"

"On his way," said Warne.

"What time is the truck due?" Poole asked.

"Right now."

"Now?" Poole echoed in surprise. He glanced at Warne. "That would explain why they didn't kill the video cameras on C Level: couldn't let the boys in the subbasement get too suspicious. And it would explain what just happened at that ride in the Skyport. One final diversion. No fooling around this time, either."

Sarah turned abruptly. "Freddy didn't know about that," she said, drilling him with a glare. "He was tricked. There weren't supposed to be any casualties. He just told me so." She turned back to the unresponsive Barksdale.

There was a brief silence.

"That's not why I called you back here." A quaver came into Sarah's voice, but she quickly mastered it. "They've rigged the dome with explosives."

The small room filled with sound as both men spoke at once.

"*What*?" Warne cried.

"How do you know?" said Poole, rising to his feet.

"That bastard left Freddy for dead. But he heard him, talking over a radio. They're all meeting up at the phony armored car."

There was a moment of stasis, of horrified incredulity. And then Poole ducked out of the cell, motioning Warne to follow.

Peccam, who was standing out in the hallway, came over at Poole's impatient signal.

"Remember that high-powered transmitter we found in the duffel?" Poole said to Peccam. "The one you couldn't figure out?"

Peccam nodded.

"It could send a signal over a relatively long distance, you said." Poole turned to Warne. "But to do that, it needed a clean line of sight. It couldn't go through walls."

"Right, right, I remember."

Poole leaned away with a look of surprise. "Well, don't you *see*?"

Warne had to work to keep his focus. "No."

"Once they're clear of the building, they're going to use the transmitter to implode the dome. Bring the whole thing down on top of the guests, then escape undetected in the aftermath." A strange kind of smile came across his face. "They must have intended to do it from the very beginning. Security, any arriving law enforcement, will have their hands full coping with the carnage. Now, that's what I call a *real* diversion."

Briefly, Warne's sense of reality wavered. *Blow up the dome?* He struggled with this fresh surprise.

"You almost act as if you admire it," he said.

Poole shrugged. Then he turned away, ducking back into the cell. Warne followed. He still felt numb. *Blow up the dome . . .* For a moment, his only panicked thought was to grab Georgia and Terri and run for safety. But just as quickly he realized that, even if he knew where to run, there simply wasn't time.

"What else did he say?" Warne heard Poole ask Sarah.

"That's it. He's resting now." And Sarah rocked Barksdale's ruined head softly in her arms.

"What's the turnaround time for loading the armored car?"

"I don't know. Treasury Operations was, is, Freddy's area. Ten minutes, something like that."

Poole looked at Warne. "Ten minutes. We're in deep kimchi, brother."

He raced out into the anteroom, Warne and Peccam at his heels. Poole looked around a moment, then grabbed an internal directory and began leafing through it. "Vault Control," he murmured under his breath. "Vault Control." Finding the number, he reached for a wall phone, dialed. A moment later, he hung up with a curse. "It won't let me connect," he said. "Of course."

"But Terri was able to call Medical just now."

"Is that so surprising? John Doe's obviously cut phone communication to the vault."

"But we know about the armored car now. We can stop it."

"The operative word in that sentence was 'armored,' pal.

They've got guns, remember? Lots of nice, big guns. I've got a pistol with a few rounds left."

"What about Allocco?" Warne could hear the desperation in his own voice.

"Can't get him down here in time."

"Security guards?"

"It would take us more time than we have just to convince them. Besides, Utopia's guards are *un*armed. What do you suggest? Spitballs? A human chain?"

"We've got to do *some*thing," Warne rounded on him. The sense of unreality was gone, leaving only a grim determination behind. "We *can't* let that vehicle get out of the Park. Whatever it is, we'll have to do it ourselves."

"You're filling me with confidence."

"Peccam here said that transmitter needs a clear line of sight," Warne continued. "Right? That means they have to be *outside* the Park. So if we can stop the armored car *before it leaves the building*, they won't be able to use the transmitter. That's the key. They're not going to bring down the dome until they're clear, until they can get away safely."

Poole considered this. "Makes sense. But I'm not throwing my body down in front of an armored car in hopes it'll stop. Why don't you get that mechanical doggy of yours to nip it to death?"

"Maybe I will." Warne thought quickly. "What do you know about explosives?"

"Uh-oh. I know where this is leading."

"Answer the question. What do you know about explosives?"

"What do you think? A hell of a lot more than your grandmother does."

"Leave my family out of this. Why don't you go up there, see if you can defuse them?"

"I can give you about forty reasons why. Because that's the number of charges it would take to bring down that big old dome. I don't know the architecture, the delivery system, the—"

"It beats staying here."

"I don't know about that. At least it's safe down here."

"Safe?" Warne cried. "What makes you so sure that collapse wouldn't pancake the Underground? Besides, you're the one who signed on for bodyguard duty, remember? Only now it's not just me. It's about seventy thousand people. Including a few I think you know."

Poole glanced at him sharply. "Okay. You've got a point." He paused. "If they're using standard shape charges, I might be able to pull enough detonators to destabilize the pattern, keep the dome from collapsing. But it's a balancing act. You'll need to find a way to slow down that armored car."

Warne nodded.

"They're not going to set off the charges until the car is clear of the building. You have to keep it from leaving. Everything depends on how much time you can buy me. Understand?"

Warne nodded again.

"Good. Because if you screw up your end of the job and I get blown sky-high, my ghost is going to haunt your ass for all eternity."

"Fair enough."

"In that case, we're wasting time talking."

Poole trotted through the anteroom. At the far door, he paused to look back. "You watch yourself, friend."

"You, too," Warne replied.

Then the doors closed behind Poole and he was gone.

Warne turned to Peccam. "Wait here for me a minute, please," he said.

More quickly now, he walked around the front desk. The leather chair was vacant, and he felt a brief surge of fear. But then he saw Terri, through the open doorway of the office beyond. She was standing beside Georgia.

As he entered the office, she turned, noticed instantly that something was wrong. "What is it?" she asked.

He hesitated, just for a moment. "I was wrong when I said it was over. There's something I have to do."

Terri swallowed painfully, gripped the handle of the wheelchair. At the sound of their voices, Georgia sighed, shifted.

He placed his hand on Terri's shoulder. "Listen," he said. "I need to lean on you one more time. You've got to be strong, just once more, for me."

Terri returned his gaze but said nothing.

"Stand guard here, while I'm gone. There's no time for you to get out of the Park, but I think you'll be safe here." He hesitated. "Terri, I love my daughter more than anything, more than life. It's so hard for me to leave her now, you can't know how hard. But remember what I told you earlier—how afraid I was something would happen to Georgia, only to see that something did?

Well, I'm not afraid now. And I *can* leave, because I know I can trust you to look after her. There's no one I'd trust more. So will you do this for me—look after Georgia, look after *each other,* no matter what? Will you do that?"

Terri nodded again, brown eyes not leaving his face.

"You understand me, right? No matter what?"

She brought her face toward his. He hugged her, closed his eyes, whispered a prayer.

Then he ran back to the anteroom, where Peccam was waiting.

"I need you to take me somewhere," Warne told him. "Can you show me the fastest way?"

"Where?" Peccam asked as they, too, ducked out into the corridor. The door swung closed behind them, and the Security Complex fell into deep silence.

4:15 P.M.

FOUR-FIFTEEN P.M., mountain standard time.

IN NEW YORK, Charles Emory III, chairman and CEO of the Utopia Holding Company, had picked up the phone and was dialing the Las Vegas field office of the FBI. His actions were slow and automatic, and his normally tanned face looked gray and very old.

IN THE HIGH desert south of Nellis Air Force Base, atop the sandstone escarpment that surrounded Utopia, the man known as Water Buffalo lay in shadow. He had seen their armored car come up the rear approach, right on schedule. Taking his eyes off the horizon for a moment, he glanced over his shoulder, up at the mountain of glass and steel that rose in a perfect logarithmic curve behind him. The charge placements were not visible at this distance, but in his mind he reconstructed the blast pattern, searching the design once again for hidden faults or structural weaknesses. The dome had been exceptionally well built, the load perfectly distributed across its members. Normally, he would have preferred a three-tiered design, fired bottom-to-top at quarter-second intervals. That had always served him well in taking down steel-reinforced bridges, whether he'd been working for Chechen rebels or the Congolese. But given the size of this particular job, and the limited amount of C-4 he'd been able to carry in, he'd striven for maximum efficiency. A single ring of twenty charges spaced evenly along the base would break the dome's back; a second set of elliptical charges, placed in a smaller ring about halfway up, would explode simultaneously, collapsing the crown, imploding it in upon itself.

He took a swig from his canteen, simulating the geometry of the explosion at high speed in his mind, dropping the dome, rebuilding it in reverse, up, down, up, down. The design was perfect. He grunted, pleased. Demolition was an art form, beautiful in its own way. It was like reverse architecture. And, like sniping, it was a solitary art, suited to solitary people.

He looked away from the dome, locating his radio. John Doe would be calling any moment. He replaced the canteen in his canvas duffel, following it with the copy of Proust. Then, hunkering back into the shadow, he returned his eyes to the horizon, watching, waiting.

FAR BELOW, IN the cavernous spaces of the Callisto Skyport, Bob Allocco stood behind the makeshift series of desks comprising the forward command post. In one hand, he held a telephone; in the other, a two-way radio. He was talking into both. As the recovery and investigative operation matured, the teams of medical, security, and engineering personnel had swelled to ever-larger numbers. And yet, despite the dozens of workers clustered around the entrance and exit areas of Station Omega, the vast Skyport seemed empty and echo-haunted. Allocco finished talking and replaced the phone, but almost as quickly as he had done so, another began to ring.

Amid the frenzy, he had completely forgotten about Sarah Boatwright.

NOT FAR AWAY, in the cool celestial twilight of the concourse, lingered John Doe. He was leaning against a luminescent pillar, one of many that lined the entrance to *Atmosfear*. The lines here had grown much longer since the Skyport had been so abruptly closed down. Folding one arm over the other, he leaned in toward the queue line to catch the chatter of the guests.

"I heard it was a bomb," somebody was saying. "A neutron bomb, placed by terrorists."

"I heard it was a gas attack," said somebody else. "Like that place in India. Killed three hundred people. They're still lying in there."

"That's crazy talk. This is Utopia, nobody dies here. If something had really happened, you think the rides would still be open, we'd still be here?"

"I don't know. Hey, see those people heading for the exit portal? They look worried, they're practically running. Maybe they know something. Maybe we'd better leave, too. It's after four already, and it's a long drive back to the hotel."

"No way. I've been waiting to watch this holomovie all day. It's just some bullshit rumor. Probably FantasyWorld employees, get paid to come over here and spread that kind of talk."

John Doe smiled broadly as he listened. Bombs and explosions had their place: there was nothing quite like the loud report, the sudden sight of scorched clothes and viscera, to stir immediate panic. But rumor could be so much more insidious. It was wonderful to see it at work. It was like placing a single drop of blood on the smooth, placid surface of a pond. The ripples spread out, slowly but unstoppably. Exactly as intended.

He glanced over as a security detail trotted down the concourse, heading in the direction of the strange-looking starry curtain that had been lowered over the entrance to the Skyport. They were in plain clothes, of course, but to a practiced eye they stood out like eunuchs in a Turkish harem. What tourists frowned like that, or walked practically in lockstep? He'd seen a number of publicity flaks, too: cruising the crowd, observing, taking notes. As rumors began to spread and guests grew more restless, they'd have more on their hands than they knew how to handle. That's what made it all so perfect. You could contain an explosion. But contain a rumor? Like trying to shackle a moonbeam.

Ever since his first inquiring little tap—back when he'd encountered the guard on first entering the Underground—Security had responded with precisely the knee-jerk reaction he'd hoped to see. In every incident that followed—the explosion inside Waterdark, the loss of security cameras, the unpleasantness at Station Omega—his confidence in their zombified dedication to going by the book had grown. He glanced at his watch. In a few minutes, Allocco's minions would have a far, far larger job on their hands: and thus, unwittingly, ensure that his own departure was worry-free.

He pushed himself away from the pillar and eased out into the throngs of passing guests. There it was again: that sense of something almost like disappointment. In the end, everything had worked out precisely as expected. He'd done his research exhaustively, interacted impeccably, shown a different face to at least half a dozen people. He smiled to himself. If they only knew the truth, knew the real John Doe. Now, *there* would be a shock, indeed.

His walk slowed. Actually, *precisely as expected* was not completely true. He glanced toward the Big Dipper, where the absence of Hard Place continued to disappoint guests. Dr. Warne had caused more than his fair share of trouble. Much more, in fact. No doubt he was responsible, directly or indirectly, for Cracker Jack's temporary incarceration. But the way he'd arrived out of nowhere and spirited Sarah Boatwright away from the Holo Mirrors had been even more annoying.

John Doe had been particularly proud of Sarah Boatwright. Over the course of numerous conversations, Fred Barksdale had, quite unwittingly, provided a very detailed character analysis of the Park chief. John Doe knew the type: headstrong, overachieving, territorial, a little defensive. He felt certain that—if he pushed just the right buttons—he could provoke her into premature action. And he'd been right. Her placing security guards in the Galactic Voyage ride had allowed John Doe to react, show righteous anger, plant the fake disc and take the real one. More important, it meant he did not have to *invent* reasons for the necessary delay—such as, say, claiming the disc was garbled. They would think he *had* no disc; they would never think to refuse a second handoff. Best of all, it meant Sarah would blame *herself* for what happened—and thus certainly agree to meet him for the second handoff.

John Doe had counted on her death—at his own hand, fittingly, in the dark passages of the Holo Mirrors—to add the final dollop of confusion, a crisis of leadership, that would further ease his own exit from the Park. But Andrew Warne, fly in the ointment, had spoiled this beautiful piece of manipulation.

Of course, in the larger scheme of things, it made no difference. Now that Cracker Jack was back in operation, the team's casualty count was once again down to zero. True, Fred Barksdale had expired a bit earlier than expected, but that simply saved trouble down the road. Quite literally; John Doe was never one to share his hard-gotten gains. And they already had *two* discs, two priceless glass masters which—thanks to Imaging Technology's copy-protective overburning—could not be duplicated. That meant *two* sales of the Crucible, twice as much profit. And speaking of profit, the armored car was approaching the vault at that very moment.

John Doe stared down the concourse, sighing once again. He realized he was reluctant to leave the place. After all the preparation, the planning and execution, the successful end of an op always seemed anticlimactic. The difference here, of course, was that—for the first and only time—he was acting as his own client. And putting together this retirement package would be his last piece of work.

Although, if he found retirement too confining, he might just come back long enough to pay Andrew Warne a visit. Reward him for his uninvited contribution to the day's events. Time would tell.

He lingered another moment, drinking in the crowds, the costumed cast members, the otherworldly air of the place. Then he turned away and entered a nearby rest room.

Approaching the bank of sinks, he washed his hands carefully, waiting for the sole occupant to leave. Then he walked to a maintenance door in the rear wall. He punched in the day's access code and the lock clicked open. Reaching into a pocket, he withdrew a passcard and a fresh imagetag—courtesy of Tom Tibbald, now deceased—and fixed them to his jacket. Then he opened the door and walked through, closing it tightly behind him.

The concrete-lined maintenance corridor beyond was cool and smelled faintly of refrigerant. Pausing in the empty space, John Doe glanced first left, then right. Then he pulled his radio from a jacket pocket, tapped in a frequency.

"Water Buffalo, this is Prime Factor," he said into the mike. "Come in."

He waited a moment, listening.

"Water Buffalo, over."

"How's the view?"

"Outstanding. Rolled in right on time."

"So I heard. Anything since? Arrivals of a more official variety, perhaps?"

"Negatory. Just routine deliveries."

"Very well. Your job's done there. Meet us at the waypoint, double time."

"Roger, out." Any arrivals after this point—and there were sure to be arrivals, sooner rather than later—would make no difference. Ten minutes, and they would be driving away from Utopia at seventy miles an hour, in the safest means of transportation possible.

John Doe replaced the radio. As he did so, he noticed that the trousers of his linen suit had become creased. It must have happened in the Holo Mirrors. An annoying development. Then again, it didn't really matter: he'd be burning the suit in the hotel incinerator that evening, anyway.

He turned and, with jaunty step, made his way down the maintenance passage toward the stairwell to A Level.

4:16 P.M.

WILLIAM VERNE YAWNED, then leaned back in his chair, stretching languorously. He had barely moved for the past hour, and he could feel the joints in his shoulders shift and pop. He realized—at some distant, barely conscious level—that his movements were being captured on a security monitor. But it didn't matter. An occasional stretch wasn't excluded from his job description. Besides, the whole business had become so damn routine he doubted anybody was watching. And if anybody was, they'd be looking at the truck, not him.

Leaning forward again, he swept his eyes across the control board. As always, everything was green. Vault status okay, delivery chamber okay, access corridor okay, Financial Processing System okay. Okay, okay, okay. Sometimes he almost found himself wishing something would go wrong. At least it would be a change.

Five months had gone by since Verne had been lured away from his job as a software developer in Palo Alto. The position had sounded too good to pass up. Not only would he be working at Utopia, and not only would he be working in their New Technology department, but the job had some hush-hush high-security aspect that intrigued him. He'd had to sign all sorts of waivers and nondisclosure forms, submit to an extensive background check. What a surprise, then, to find himself doing the same kind of work here at the Park as he'd done in Palo Alto. Systems development and maintenance was the same, it seemed, whether you worked for a theme park or a small start-up company. More money here, cooler toys, but much less creative responsibility.

And the "high security" portion of the job? It consisted of watching a control board, sniffing diesel fumes, and staring at the ass end of an armored car for about seven minutes, once a week.

There was a low tone, then a buzz as somebody outside Vault Control activated the retinal scanner. The heavy door clicked open and Tom Pritchard, representing the Auditing and Controls department, stepped inside.

Verne looked over at him without interest. "How're we doing?"

"Locked up tighter than your sister's chastity belt," Pritchard said as he closed and locked the door. He'd just returned from the obligatory visual inspection. During the few minutes that the actual exchange took place, the section of C Level surrounding the vault and the access corridor was closed off from the rest of the Utopia Underground.

"Good. Let's get this over with." From the corridor beyond, Verne could hear the insistent chirp of the armored car's warning tone as it backed the three hundred feet down the corridor toward them. He hit a switch, engaging the powerful exhaust fans that would send the engine fumes back into the desert where they belonged.

"Where's our baby-sitter?" Pritchard asked as he stepped toward the observation window. Although only two crew members were required for the transfer—a Treasury Operations specialist and a liaison from Controls—normally at least one security specialist sat in during the exchange.

"Guess we're on our own today," Verne replied. "They're probably all back at that damn machine again." The week before, one of the security grunts had won eight grand on a high-stakes video poker machine in the Boardwalk casino. The money had been confiscated, and the guard disciplined for gambling while on duty, but it had caused a huge stir among the junior security specialists.

"Maybe they're all at that accident scene in Callisto. Whatever it was."

"*If* it was, you mean. That's the third accident story I've heard today. Wonder who makes them all up." Of course, even if it was true, they probably wouldn't hear about it for days, stuck down here in the damn bilge. Verne had once read a story by Joseph Conrad in which these two Englishmen were stranded, working in some really remote outpost in darkest Africa. Eventually, they couldn't take it anymore, went crazy, and killed each other.

That's how he remembered it, anyway. It had always seemed pretty far-fetched to him. But maybe it wasn't, at that.

"I don't know, it sounded like the real thing to me. I heard somebody died."

"Hey, who knows? Maybe a hundred died."

"Stop messing around. I even heard talk of terrorists."

"You're *always* hearing talk about terrorists," Verne said, looking at him derisively. "You're in the wrong end of this business, pal, you know that? You should be working with the ride designers and creative engineers. Anyway," he went on in a more placating tone of voice, "if there was anything really wrong, His Lordship would have canceled the run."

"His Lordship" was how much of the Systems staff referred to Fred Barksdale, who was known as a hardworking and talented boss but also as a stickler for protocol. Barksdale had designed much of the financial control system and always took personal control of the weekly exchange between Utopia's automated vault and the armored car. During orientation, Verne had been told of the precise chain of command. If anything went really wrong, Barksdale would notify them that the weekly pickup had been canceled. But nothing had ever gone really wrong, and Barksdale had never called to cancel. He'd called for plenty of other reasons—to criticize a slow or sloppy exchange, for example—but never to cancel.

The radio speaker set into the control board crackled. "Utopia Central, this is Nine Echo Bravo." It was the voice of the armored car driver. "I have a visual on the chamber."

Verne leaned toward a gooseneck microphone. "Utopia Central confirms. We're green for the exchange."

He glanced at his watch: 4:18. Right on time. At least Barksdale wouldn't be calling to complain today.

Verne stood up and joined Pritchard at the observation window. Down the gentle curve of the access corridor, the rear of the armored car could be seen approaching at a slow, steady pace. *American Armored Security* was emblazoned in large gold letters on its flanks. Verne stared without interest. Already, Vault Control was beginning to stink of diesel fumes, fans or no fans. And the smell would remain for at least twenty minutes after the truck had gone. He wondered if diesel fumes were carcinogenic. Maybe he could put in for hazard pay.

The truck drew level with the control room, then stopped with a sharp protest of brakes. It sat there a moment, as it always did, the invisible occupants going through their checklists. Then the driver worked the door release and the heavy passenger-side door swung open. A man stepped down lightly, shotgun in one hand and clipboard in another. He turned toward their window and waved.

Verne pressed a button, and a small door facing the access corridor popped open. He pushed the door open and descended the ten steps into the high-ceilinged corridor. The grinding noise of the diesel was much worse here, and he wished fervently that they'd turn it off. But no; that was against regulations.

The armed guard was approaching him now. Verne looked at him, frowning slightly.

"How's it going?" the guard asked. He was in his late thirties, smiling, with a short coppery mustache and a deep tan. He had an easy, assured Texas drawl that matched his demeanor.

"It's going," Verne said.

The man smiled, nodded. He was chewing gum.

"You're not the regular driver," Verne said.

The man kept smiling. "Nope. I'm Earl Crowe, route supervisor for AAS. I conduct runs myself sometimes, make sure everything's operating efficiently, the customers are happy. And, damn, you're our biggest customer."

He passed the clipboard over. Verne took it, still looking at the man.

"Johnny's here, actually," the man named Crowe went on. "Outside. Some of the boys were out helling around late last night, and he got himself pretty drunk. So I had him drive the escort car instead of the truck today. Nothing like eating forty miles of dust to sober a body up, right?"

At this, Verne finally chuckled. He plucked a pen from his pocket, glanced down at the form without reading it, scribbled his name.

"Are you happy with the service?" Crowe asked as Verne returned the clipboard. "Any problems or concerns I should take up with senior management?"

Verne, so used to being on the receiving end of orders, was surprised and pleased by this. "Well, no," he replied. "Nothing I can think of."

"I'm real pleased to hear that. You be sure to tell us, though, if there's any little thing we can do to serve you better."

"I'll do that, thanks," Verne said, managing to sound a little more managerial. "If you're ready, I'll open the delivery chamber now."

He stepped back into Vault Control, hastily closing the door against the noise and fumes. As the door clicked shut, a red light on the panel blinked back to green. He turned to Pritchard, who'd been watching the exchange through the observation window. They nodded to each other: the visual "handshake" with the truck was complete.

"Engaging the delivery chamber," Pritchard said, typing a series of commands on a keyboard. Moving to another keyboard on the far side of the control panel, Verne typed in a separate access code.

There was a brief hum of machinery, and beyond the control room wall the door of the vault began rotating on its silent bearings. Both Pritchard and Verne moved to a smaller window in the side wall to observe. For Verne, this was the one part of the job that never grew stale.

From the moment that money was received by Utopia's Financial Processing System—whether it was at a casino counter in Gaslight, a hot dog vendor in Boardwalk, or a seller of wimples in Camelot—it remained untouched by human hands. Whisked away to collection stations, scanned and sorted, counted, taped and bagged, and ultimately delivered to the vault, it was always under machine control, human handlers kept far out of temptation's path. Now the heavy curved door moved aside, sealing off the corridor that led deeper into Utopia and exposing the delivery chamber and the vault beyond to the armed guards. There was a boom as the door came to rest on the far side of the corridor.

Verne looked through the small window. Normally, the vault was sealed off from human eyes by the huge semicircular door. But once their twin set of commands had been entered, the door revolved ninety degrees, turning the access corridor into a closed tube. Now daylight lay at one end, and vast sums of cash at the other. And in between sat the armored car.

The two men watched as Crowe stepped through the delivery chamber into the vault, two empty canvas bags in his left hand. He reappeared maybe twenty seconds later, the bags now bulging, slung over his shoulder. The stacks of money had been sorted by machines into brown-wrapped bundles exactly eighty bills high: the ideal size, Verne had learned during orientation, for handling and transporting by the automated system.

Now Crowe was coming back for another load. He was moving quickly, clearly experienced at this work. *Pretty tan for a manager*, Verne thought absently. *Must get in plenty of golf time. Or maybe he punches cows, with an accent like that.* Though Verne could not see him behind the transparent armor, he knew that the driver of the truck would be watching Crowe carefully, maintaining visual and radio contact at all times.

Crowe returned with another load, disappeared inside the truck, came out again, shotgun still tucked under his right arm. Verne glanced indifferently at the shotgun. It was a nice little setup, very neat, very clean. The Utopia crew never handled the money, never handled the guns. They could hire outside specialists for that, seal themselves hermetically away during the entire transaction. No doubt the insurance adjusters loved it.

Yet again, Crowe reappeared. Even at his energetic rate, it would take several minutes to move a hundred million dollars. Curiosity waning, Verne moved away from the window, sat down heavily in his chair behind the control panel, and stretched luxuriously once again.

EARL CROWE STEPPED up into the armored car, ducked into the rear compartment, and let the heavy canvas slide off his shoulders. The driver, who was waiting in the rear, overturned the bags, letting dozens of identically wrapped packages spill across the steel and rubber floor. It was not exactly standard procedure—the driver should have remained at the wheel, supervising the loading, keeping a vigilant eye out for potential robbers or hijackers—but inside this sealed, tenantless corridor they were hidden from view.

Crowe swung the now-empty bags back onto his shoulder, then turned to watch the driver as he hastily stacked the brown packages into the car's side-mounted compartments. "So, you like driving armor again?" he asked.

The driver nodded without pausing in his work. "Damn straight. And for the first time, I get to keep what I'm driving."

Crowe gave a low chuckle. Then he turned away, trotted down the steps, and headed back toward the vault.

4:16 P.M.

THE PHALANX OF security specialists at the VIP Hospitality Center had dwindled significantly since Warne's last visit. As he approached, he could see only two: one watching the entrance, the other inside, in the shadow of an alabaster column, hands behind his back. The thoughtful, melancholy strains of the string quartet sounded from still deeper within.

The guard at the entrance glanced at the management tag on Warne's lapel, nodded, and ushered them through.

"What are we going to do, exactly?" Peccam said as they trotted across the marble floor.

"I don't know," Warne said. "Ask me again in five minutes."

But in fact he did know. At least, he hoped he did.

Poole's words came back to him over the sounds of the quartet, the low whisper of the fountains, the chatter of a few restless guests sitting on leather divans: *That high-powered transmitter we found in the duffel? It needs a clear line of sight, it can't go through walls. Once they're clear of the building, they're going to implode the roof. Bring the whole thing down, escape in the aftermath.*

Perhaps Poole could get to the charges in time, disable enough to keep the dome from collapsing. But they couldn't count on that. And that meant there was only one other thing to do. Stop the armored car from leaving the Utopia Underground.

Once again, Poole's voice sounded in his head. *They've got guns, remember? Lots of nice, big guns. Utopia's guards are unarmed.*

It was true. Utopia had no weapons to use against the armored car. But maybe—just maybe—they had something else.

Warne pushed his way through the double doors and down the carpeted corridor, trying to reconstruct the layout of the place in his mind. He'd been rushed, then as now, and the memory of his previous visit was a blur. *This is the door. I think.* Not bothering to knock, he grasped the knob, turned it, pushed the door open.

In the room beyond, the short, slightly built man named Smythe turned at the sound of their entrance. The thick spectacles hung down on his nose, and the thin strands of hair—so carefully combed and brilliantined on the monorail that morning—were askew. He had been pacing, apparently for quite a while.

There was a rustling sound, then a blur of movement from behind the table that held the coffee machine. Wingnut emerged, panning his head assembly around. Fastening twin cameras on his master, the robot lurched forward, emitting a loud, belchlike bark. Warne patted the head array, relieved to see him. And the man was still here, too: thank God.

"Mr. Smythe," he said, "I'm Andrew Warne. Do you remember me?"

The short man frowned behind his spectacles. "Ah, yes. You were on the monorail with me this morning. And then again, here, I believe. Ms. Boatwright called you after I . . . after I . . ." He stopped.

"That's right," Warne said hastily. "And this is Ralph Peccam. He works as a video technician for Security, reporting to Bob Allocco. You met him here, too."

Ten minutes, the cold little voice whispered in his head. *You've got ten minutes, maybe less.* This small talk, this cordial round of introductions, was agony. But it was vital: if there was the least chance of this working, Warne knew he needed Smythe's trust.

"Mr. Smythe," he went on, "I hope you'll forgive me. We're in a bit of a hurry here. I wonder if you could help us out with something."

The man took off his spectacles and began polishing them with the end of his tie. Without glasses to shield them from the outside world, his pale blue eyes looked exposed, startled.

"Of course," he said. "If I can."

"Mr. Smythe, can you tell me . . . well, can you tell me what kind of fireworks are stored here at the Park?"

Smythe went on polishing. "Oh, the usual sort. You know. Class B."

"Class B?"

"Of course. Orange Book classification 1.3." When this was

greeted by silence, Smythe added, "That's one of the U.N. classi-
fications for dangerous goods. One point three. Fiery projectiles.
Display grade, not consumer grade, naturally." He seemed
shocked at such gross ignorance.

"Are there many?"

"Many? Oh, you mean fireworks? Oh, my, yes. You'd be surprised at the number they go through, with the coordinated
shows every evening. Especially the gerbs, comets, and—"

"I see. What kind explode?"

The wiping slowed, then stopped.

"Explode?" Smythe asked. He had an annoying habit of re-
peating the last word of a question. "Well, let's see. All fireworks
explode, that's their nature." He began explaining in the slow,
patient tone one might use with a small child. "There are two
kinds of black powders, of course: the unglazed meal powder
you use for lift, and the one for burst—"

"No, no," Warne interrupted. "I mean, what kind blows up?"

"Blows up? Well, that depends on what you mean by blowing
up. We have crossettes and tourbillions, which you know are
moving displays. They blow up, down, sideways. Or the kind of
colored fountains that—"

"*No!*" With an effort, Warne controlled himself. "What kind
does damage?"

Smythe looked shocked. He replaced his glasses. "I would
have to say that, ah, most of them do. Or would, if improperly
used." He hesitated, looking more closely at Warne. "But the
outdoor aerial displays, the multi-break star shells and maroons,
would probably . . ." His voice tapered off.

"And where are they kept?" Warne asked, almost prancing
now with impatience.

"In the storage magazines on C Level."

"You've got access?"

"Naturally. I supervised their installation."

Warne glanced back at Peccam, who had been listening to this
exchange with increasing disbelief. Then he turned once again
to Smythe.

"Look," he said. "We really need your help. It's related to
the—what you found back in the Specialists' Lounge. Could you
please show us these storage magazines?"

Smythe hesitated again, longer this time.

"Please, Mr. Smythe. It's vitally important. I'll explain on the way. We have to hurry."

At last, Smythe nodded.

"Come on, then," Warne said, taking Smythe by the arm and almost propelling him toward the door. "As quickly as possible, please."

Then he stopped, looked back. "And Wingnut," he said briskly. "Heel."

With a klaxon call of delight, Wingnut shot forward, following the group out of the room.

And as Warne hurried down the hall, he massaged Wingnut's echolocator thoughtfully, turning it round and round on his wrist.

4:20 P.M.

ANGUS POOLE TOOK the narrow metal stairs two at a time, pulling himself up by both handrails. It had been too many years since he'd done forced marches in full kit, and he was more out of breath than he cared to admit. To his left, the concrete wall of the stairwell curved away out of sight overhead, fluorescent lights bolted to its face at a rising angle. To the right, beyond one-way observation glass, the green lawns and parti-color tents of Camelot fell away below, a lush tapestry of battlements and pennants and gaudy medieval spectacle. Poole paid no attention.

It had taken longer than it should have to find the access stairwell: he'd had to sweet-talk a cast member from Camelot, bluff his way past a security specialist with the aid of Warne's passcard. As he climbed, he didn't want to think about how many minutes had already been wasted.

He also didn't want to think about how crazy all of this sounded. The idea that the massive dome was rigged to implode—to scatter countless shards of glass and chunks of steel down over the interior of the Park—seemed too extreme for even a piece of work like John Doe. Poole wondered if the woman, Sarah Boatwright, had understood what Barksdale's broken mouth was saying. Or if Barksdale could even be believed. Maybe he was raving, delusional. Or maybe it was some ploy of his to escape, get them to leave him alone in Medical. But in his gut, Poole didn't believe this. Barksdale had been desperate to talk, gargling on his own blood in an effort to warn the Park chief about what was going to happen. Just moving those shattered jaws must have been agony. The man had to be telling the truth.

The corridor angled around a gentle bend, the spectacle of Camelot vanished, and up ahead the stairs ended in a metal door. A thin line of sunlight traced a rectangular outline against the dark frame. An infrastructure worker in a beige jumpsuit was coming down the staircase toward him, oversize duffel in one hand. He glanced over briefly as Poole ran past. Poole returned the glance but kept climbing as quickly as he could: the last thing he wanted now was to stop and play twenty questions with some drone. Thankfully, there was no shouted warning, no demand to stop, and Poole kept climbing toward the door, his thoughts bent on the task ahead.

If the dome really *was* rigged, what exactly could he do about it in the few minutes left? *You're running in the wrong direction, jerkoff*, every self-preserving instinct shouted within him. These guys were obviously pros—whatever awaited him up there, it sure as hell wasn't going to be a fertilizer bomb wired to a windup clock. This was a job for a disposal team with first-class resources and time to spare . . .

And then he thought of his cousin and her family—an obnoxious family to be sure, but family all the same—and the countless thousands of other guests that packed Utopia, blissfully ignorant, smiling and chattering as they walked beneath the shadow of that vast dome . . . and Poole found himself redoubling his speed as he climbed toward the door.

Perhaps it wasn't that hopeless. This wasn't a war zone; they probably had only one or two grunts to lug up the explosives and equipment; there wouldn't be multiple redundancies. And if there was a transmitter, that meant there also had to be a receiver somewhere. Finding it would be faster, surer, than dismantling a few of the detonators in hopes of saving the dome. The receiver would be on the rear side somewhere, facing the maintenance road that led away from the Park—he was sure of that. That tech with the head cold, Peccam, had said the transmitter needed a clear line of sight.

Four more steps—two—and he was at the door. For a sickening moment he feared it would be impassable, that it would have some kind of hand-geometry reader like the door he'd convinced the cast member to open, but with relief he saw it had only a simple steel knob. A savage kick was enough to burst the lock and open the door.

Blinding light and baking heat rushed forward to embrace him. For a moment, Poole hesitated, face turned away and eyes tight shut, stunned after the cool darkness of the staircase. He took one step forward, and then another, as the painful white glare receded and the scene came into focus around him.

The access stairs ended in a small metal shed, set down like a child's toy atop a vast, flat escarpment. Sparse high-desert vegetation, juniper and straggly sage, clung to the fissures and gullies that ran away through the sandstone before him. The reddish surfaces looked wounded and gouged, as if scarred by some terrific battle. This was the mesa top surrounding the circular bowl that held Utopia. And ahead, arching over that bowl, rose the dome, the roof of the Park, steel ribs and hexagonal glass panels shimmering like dragonfly wings in the sunlight.

Seeing it, Poole stopped dead once again. It was so massive—the smooth curve of its surfaces so precise, so achingly regular above the pocked uneven sandstone—that it seemed to possess the distant otherworldliness of a dream-tower. Poole forced himself to look away, glancing toward the sky to orient himself. Then, with a deliberate effort, he trotted forward.

As he approached the dome, he made out a network of catwalks and ladders, cunningly set into the supporting ribs and crosspieces. There was no sign of tampering, no suspicious-looking emplacements. He almost grunted with relief: perhaps Barksdale had been wrong, after all . . .

And then he saw the det cord.

It had been strung beneath the lowest walkway, following the metal as it curved around the base of the dome. Poole came up to the catwalk, knelt beneath it, reaching to turn the plastic-coated cord gingerly between his fingers. It was professional grade, thin and light but very reliable. He resisted the urge to cut it, certain it was rigged in such a way that any tampering would set off a premature explosion.

He rose again and, with a sinking feeling, ran along the base of the dome, following the cord. After fifty feet or so, he reached the first charge: a small mound of plastique, expertly shaped around the base of a truss. At another time, he would have appreciated the subtle beauty of the placement. The field agent in him approved of the economy of material. The demolitions expert—for Poole no longer had any doubt that such a person was responsible—had clearly opted for a surgical attack, emphasizing precision over sheer volume of explosive.

He continued along the base of the dome, toward the rear of the Park. He came across another charge, then another, all expertly placed to do the maximum amount of structural damage with the minimum amount of explosive. One man had done this;

two at most. It was a highly disciplined job. All too disciplined: there would be no shoddy workmanship here, no weaknesses to exploit. The sinking feeling grew stronger.

As he ran, Poole had kept his eyes on the line of det cord as it snaked beneath the catwalk. Up ahead now, low along the curve of the dome, he could see a larger control box, lines of det cord attached to it. *Must be the receiver*, he thought with a fresh surge of hope.

Suddenly, an object came into view in the bottom of a shallow gully before him, and he swerved to avoid it. Then he stopped, turning back quickly to kneel beside it.

"Sweet sister Sadie," he muttered.

It was the body of a man: late thirties, tall, wearing the uniform of a maintenance worker. His rubber-soled shoes were drawn up beneath him, and some kind of electronic device dangled from his utility belt. A large bloodstain was splashed across the white fabric of his work suit. Poole reached out a finger to touch the fabric: it was stiff, the fatal wound hours old.

On the underside of the catwalk, not five feet from where the dead man lay, another shaped charge had been carefully molded into position. Poole leaned in for a closer look.

Movement registered in his peripheral vision. Old, half-forgotten reflexes took over, and Poole immediately flattened himself in the rocks beside the corpse. He glanced up cautiously, using the body as cover.

At first, he saw nothing: the gnarled, wizened surface of the mesa top seemed utterly still. And then the movement came again. It was a man, out in the sunlight beyond the vast shadow cast by the dome. He was hugging its base, moving slowly, only the left side of his body visible from Poole's angle. He wore the beige jumpsuit of an infrastructure worker, and Poole cursed under his breath as he recognized the man he'd passed on the stairway. He'd been so wrapped up in the problem at hand, it hadn't even occurred to him to question who would be coming down those access stairs. He'd assumed all of John Doe's men would have regrouped by now, ready to leave in the armored car. But he should have known better: John Doe was thorough; he'd have kept a spotter watching the escape route until the last possible minute. *Never assume*, they'd taught him. *Always question. Take nothing for granted.*

Motionless behind the corpse, he watched the man slow for a

moment, glance around, then come forward once again. Poole recognized the halting, deliberate movements: the man was stalking someone. And it was all too clear who it was.

As the man approached the line of shadow, he stepped briefly away from the dome to avoid some unseen obstacle. His right side came into view, and as it did, sunlight glinted off the barrel of a heavy rifle.

Poole cursed again fervently under his breath. A weapon like that changed the rules of the game entirely. He couldn't afford to go one-on-one against a sniper. He'd have no choice but to take a defensive posture, try to avoid being picked off at a distance. Besides, there wasn't any time for fun and games.

There was only one thing to do—surprise the man, get him in close enough so that the rifle wouldn't give him any advantage.

He glanced up again: the man in the jumpsuit was about to cross out of the sunlight and into the shadow of the dome. Quickly, while he still had the advantage of concealment, Poole ducked further behind the corpse, molding himself to its stiffening curves. The man knew there'd be a body here: no doubt he'd been responsible for its presence in the first place. He wouldn't be expecting to find a second body behind it.

Reaching into his jacket, Poole carefully drew out the hacker's pistol. Keeping his movements to a minimum, he did a press-check to make sure a cartridge was in the chamber. Then, bringing his arm back across his chest, he waited, lying below the lip of the gully, listening. He couldn't rely on his eyes anymore: the man was in shadow now, too, and if Poole raised his head, the man would notice the movement. So he waited in the gully, waited to hear the telltale sound of approaching footsteps. Sharp stones dug into his back, and the smell of the dead man's cheap aftershave filled his nose. *Nice choice, Poole,* he thought. *You could have been having another beer in the Sea of Tranquility right now. Instead, you're snuggled up next to a stiff, about to get your ass either shot off or blown up . . .*

There was the sound of footsteps. They slowed, stopped, then began again, measured, coming closer. Poole waited, breathing slowly. Five seconds. And then the shadow of an approaching figure loomed over the gully.

As the figure's head came into view, Poole raised the pistol, bringing his left arm up to steady his gun hand. "Hold it," he said.

The man stopped abruptly, then slowly allowed his upraised boot to settle back to the ground. Poole lay there, in the hard-scrabble gully, his gun pointed toward the man's head. For a long moment, the two simply looked at each other.

"Nice day if it don't rain," Poole said at last.

If the man heard, he made no response. He was powerfully built, with short hair that fell across his temples and down the back of his head in tight, corrugated waves. The rifle was in his right hand, held away from his body, flash hider on the barrel pointed earthward.

Now, very deliberately, Poole rolled forward and rose to his feet, keeping the pistol aimed at all times. He could feel the pebbles falling away from his back. He took a couple of rearward steps, planting his feet carefully, making sure he did nothing to upset his balance. Then he nodded toward the M24.

"Only one kind of person I know favors that particular rifle. Were you in the Corps?"

The man looked back without replying.

"Ninety-Sixth Marine Expeditionary Unit myself," Poole went on. "At least until they tired of my company, I was. Story of my life."

Still, the man remained silent, staring back at him impassively.

Poole sighed. "Well, if you can't carry on a civil conversation, why don't you just drop the weapon instead?"

The man remained motionless, and after a second or two Poole jerked his gun downward, toward the man's legs. No more time for pleasantries: he'd take out a kneecap, incapacitate his opponent, then get the information he needed.

Immediately, the man's right hand relaxed, letting the rifle slip, butt-first, to the ground. Poole smiled. The man had read his eyes: very clever.

"That's a start," he said. "Now, put your hands over your head, spread your fingers, and tell me the fastest way to deactivate all this busywork of yours."

With insolent slowness, the man began to raise his arms. Poole was about to complain when he saw the right arm jerk backward with the speed of a striking snake, disappearing behind the man's back.

Poole raised his gun and immediately fired. There was no crack of explosion, just a low, dry click, and by the time Poole realized the round was a dud and racked the slide to clear the chamber, the man's hand was in view again, filled with a .45, and then the big gun was obscured by a gout of flame and Poole felt something like the burning hoof of a horse pass through his gut and his own gun went off but he was already falling backward, the black curve of the dome and the blue of the sky wheeling dizzy above him, and then the cruel unyielding rock of the escarpment rose to meet his shoulders and all the breath fled from his lungs and everything went abruptly dark.

4:20 P.M.

THE HEAVY STEEL door was labeled *High Security Area: Authorized Personnel Only*. Warne stood beside it, stealing a nervous glance up and down the hallway, while the man named Smythe typed a code into the adjoining keypad, unclipped a passcard from his jacket and swiped it through a scanner, then placed his palm in a geometry reader. There was an audible click and the door sprang open. Dry air whistled out. Warne noticed that the edges of the door were coated in stripes of rubber.

"Seems deserted down here," Warne said. The remark sounded inane even as he made it, but he felt a need to say something, *anything*. He'd evaded most of Smythe's questions on the way down, saying merely that the Park was in grave danger; that Smythe was the only one now who could help them. Better to fill the silence with idle chatter than face more questions. On the far side of the door, Peccam waited. The look of disbelief had been slow to leave his face.

"The area's off-limits while the armored car is in the building," Smythe said. "Only specialists or crew members with level 2 security or higher have access." He stepped inside, Warne and Peccam at his heels.

The room seemed large, remarkably so: its length and relative emptiness reminded Warne of a gymnasium. The floor was covered with squares of black rubber matting. The walls were bare, save for a variety of posters and warning signs: *No Synthetic Clothing. Minimize Bare Skin. Complies with APA 87-1*. In the center of the room, spaced perhaps twenty meters apart, stood a long line of metal containers. They were identical, each about seven feet high by fifteen feet long, bolted to a concrete platform that ran the length of the room. Heavy padlocks were fastened to their front faces. Beside each sat a small green plastic trash can, *Live Waste* stenciled in black letters.

"Are those the storage magazines?" Warne asked, pointing to the containers.

Smythe nodded. "As you can see, they meet the separation distance mandated by the Bureau of Alcohol, Tobacco and Firearms. In fact, everything here meets or exceeds all regulatory standards. Except for one thing." He walked over to a small door on the far side of the room and jiggled its handle. "See?" he said, frowning, as he returned. "Locked."

"So?"

"It's locked electrically. A security measure while the armored car is being loaded. And a flagrant violation of OSHA's multiple exit requirements. I've complained about it on several occasions, but I'm always told it's only for ten minutes, once a week. Once the vault's closed and the car is on its way, the electric lock is cut off. But it's a violation, nonetheless." Smythe looked over at Warne suddenly, as if a new thought had hit him. "Maybe you can put in a word about this to the right people, hey?"

So the car's still here, Warne thought. He turned toward Smythe with renewed urgency. "Show me the magazines, please. The ones with . . ."

"High-level shells," Smythe completed the sentence for him.

Warne nodded. Smythe pursed his lips disapprovingly, but led the two men across the rubber floor toward the line of storage magazines. Wingnut followed in their wake, moving more cautiously than usual, cameras panning around the walls and ceiling as his processors constructed a topological map of the vast space.

Smythe stopped at the fourth container, digging into his pocket for his keys. There was a wet-mat on the ground before the container; a waterproof GFI light switch on its face; and a large orange placard on its side panel that read *Explosive 1.3g*.

Opening the padlock, Smythe switched on the light, then wrenched open the heavy metal door and stepped inside. Warne ducked in after him. A hygrometer sat on the floor, and strips of wicking paper hung from the ceiling. Tall wooden platforms ran along both walls of the magazine. On their shelves sat dozens of cardboard boxes, stamped with identical labels: *Fireworks UN 0771. Handle Carefully—Keep Fire Away*. Long series of numbers had been scrawled onto the side of each box in black Magic Marker. At the far end of the magazine, Warne could see countless tubes of what looked like thick black cardboard. The top of each tube had been painted a unique color, according to height.

Smythe turned to a nearby shelf, ran his finger down the series of handwritten numbers on one of the boxes. Then he pulled a box down from the shelf, placed it on the floor, and opened it carefully. Inside, sealed in individual plastic bags, were several spherical-shaped parcels wrapped in brown paper. "These are the outdoor fireworks," Smythe said. "For the above-the-dome displays we shoot at Park closing." He removed one of the parcels and gingerly freed it from the plastic wrapping. He held it up to the light, turning it around in his hands, as if inspecting for tears or imperfections. Then he held it out to Warne.

It was surprisingly heavy. As he hefted it, Warne noticed that a fuse of twisted paper was fastened to its side by white string. Several small labels had been glued to the casing. *Warning,* one read: *Extremely Dangerous. For Professional Use Only.*

"It's a golden willow," said Smythe. "Not especially bright, but very high—rises a thousand feet before it releases its composition—and quite spectacular. It's got a heavy lift charge, needs at least a ten-inch mortar for all that black powder."

Hastily, Warne handed it back. Smythe placed it on the floor beside the box, then walked deeper into the magazine. "And here we've got double chrysanthemums, very large shells, usually used with cakes and illuminators during a finale." He moved to the opposite bank of shelves, pointed to a stack of boxes. "And these are silver dragons, full of aluminum or magnesium flash powder. Magnesium in particular is remarkably bright; the composition burns at an incredible temperature. A perfect accompaniment to maroons."

"Maroons," Warne repeated. "You mentioned those before."

Smythe blinked at him, wiped his glasses. Then, motioning them to follow, he stepped out of the storage magazine and walked down the line. Stopping outside another magazine, he unlocked the padlock and let them in. Wingnut remained outside, muttering electronically, rolling restlessly back and forth.

The walls of this container were lined in panels of wood. There were no platforms or shelving. Instead, rows of heavy metal ammunition boxes sat on the floor, two deep.

"Maroons," Smythe said, opening the nearest box. "Salutes, as you Americans usually call them. Made entirely of gunpowder. No stars, no illuminators, just a huge bang. Very brutal and powerful. A favorite of Spanish pyrotechnists, you know."

"Gunpowder," Warne said, looking down at the cylindrical packages lying inside the box. "Pure gunpowder."

"Or flash powder, yes."

At that moment, a low beeping noise sounded through the room.

"That's the vault tone," Smythe said. "It means the vault's sealed again, and our escape route's unlocked. We'll hear the all-clear in a couple of minutes, I imagine. Once the armored car has left the Underground."

Warne spun around. *"Left?"* Then he pointed at the open ammunition box. "We're going to have to borrow some of these."

Smythe blinked through his glasses. "I beg your pardon?"

"And some of the shells in that other magazine, just in case. The golden willows, the mortars."

"Borrow," Smythe repeated, still blinking.

"Hurry, man! *Hurry!"*

Smythe carefully scooped a few salutes out of the box, then left the magazine, trotting back in the direction from which they had come.

Warne turned toward Peccam. "How long do we have until the armored car's gone?"

Peccam returned the gaze. "I don't know, really. Not long. If the vault's been sealed, that means the car's already on its way out."

"Shit!" For a moment, Warne felt despair wash over him. "Look. You know what I'm planning to do. Right?"

Peccam's eyes narrowed. "I think so."

"And you agree we've got no other choice?"

Peccam nodded slowly.

"I've got to go with Smythe, see that he gets what I need. There may still be time, we have to pray there's still time. Meanwhile, there's something I need you to do."

He unfastened the echolocator from his wrist. "This is a homing device for Wingnut," he said, handing it to Peccam. "If I order him to, he'll head for it, wherever it is."

The security tech took it, a little gingerly, almost as if Warne had handed him one of the explosives from the ammunition case. Wingnut waited outside, watching the transfer with great interest.

"You know what to do with it?"

Peccam nodded.

"Then go ahead. Run. Don't put yourself in any more danger than you need to. I'll get Smythe to show me where to set up. If there's still time, if we're not too late, I'll see you there."

Peccam nodded once again. His face was pale, his expression grim but determined. He turned and, without another word, ran from the magazine, heading for the emergency exit.

Warne stepped out of the magazine. "Come on, boy," he said gently to Wingnut.

He glanced at his watch. It was twenty-four minutes past four.

4:24 P.M.

THE LAST CANVAS bag of brown wrapped bills had been stowed in the belly of the armored car; the checklist was complete and the transfer amount verified; and smiling, mustached Earl Crowe had given the go-ahead to the monitors in the control room. Verne waved back. Crowe clambered up through the passenger-side door of the truck; the door slid closed with a heavy thud; and—after a series of commands had been entered on the vault control board—the vast semicircular door of gleaming steel rolled back into place, opening the corridor while sealing off the delivery chamber and its now-empty vault from human access. The low chime of the vault tone was lost in the growling of the diesel.

With a final wave, the driver put the truck in gear and slowly eased back down the access corridor. Fifty yards ahead, out of sight around the gentle curve of the passageway, lay a single intersection. Another fifty yards ahead was the guard checkpoint. And beyond that, the tarmac of the crew parking lot; the maintenance road that led down off the plateau to U.S. Highway 95; and an infinity of possibilities.

But the truck did not continue down the corridor. After a few more yards, it stopped. Then it crept forward again, very slowly, until it cut off the view of two nearby security cameras. Then it stopped once again.

Almost immediately, an electrical access panel opened in the nearby wall. It banged softly against the body of the truck. The door of the armored car cracked open with a chuff of air.

John Doe emerged first from the access panel. He looked both ways, smoothed his shirt, then climbed up the stairs and into the truck. And then, another figure emerged from the electrical access. It was Hardball, once again wearing the leather jacket he'd worn when he met Tom Tibbald in the van that morning. He, too, glanced first one way, then another, almond-shaped eyes veiled and expressionless. He mounted the steps, disappearing into the armored car. Last to appear was the young hacker, Cracker Jack. His face was puffy with bruises, and the knuckles of one hand were gashed and bleeding, as if cut on a sharp object or—perhaps—teeth. He hoisted out a duffel, then closed the panel behind him. He followed the duffel up the three steps, and the passenger door closed once again.

Inside, John Doe maneuvered his way past Earl Crowe into the back of the truck. Crowe watched as John Doe opened one of the side panels, ran first his eyes, then his hands, over the stacks of evenly wrapped bills, four deep, that filled the shelves within.

"As George Bernard Shaw said, lack of money is the root of all evil." John Doe closed the panel. "This should keep us all good little boys for a long, long time."

"Got the discs?" Crowe asked.

John Doe nodded, patting the pocket of his linen jacket absently. He looked at his watch. "Water Buffalo didn't show up at the rally point. Has he radioed?"

The driver, Candyman, shook his head. A squawk came over his headset, and he raised one hand to the transmit button.

"AAS Nine Echo Bravo, over."

"Nine Echo Bravo, this is Utopia Central. We show you stopped in the approach corridor. The vault tone's sounded, and we're waiting to give the all-clear. Report nature of your delay, over."

"Utopia Central, nothing major. The motor's seizing a bit. I think the air intake is clogged. Trying to clear it now."

"Nine Echo Bravo, understood. If the problem continues, request you continue examination on the outside, repeat, on the outside."

"Utopia Central, I say again, nothing major. We should be rolling any second."

Candyman switched off the radio headset, glanced back into the payload compartment.

"I've been on the scanner, monitoring the internal security chatter," he said. "Word of Station Omega's filtering down through C Level. The natives are getting restless."

"Not to worry," John Doe said. "We'll give Water Buffalo a few minutes more. Then we leave."

"Shall I get out, open the hood?" Crowe asked.

John Doe shook his head. "Don't bother. The cameras are neutralized. Right?"

The driver looked out the transparent armor of the window. He peered into the oversize rearview mirror, then into the convex mirror on the cowling above the front wheel well.

"That's affirmative," he said. And then he looked away again, glancing back toward the scanner monitoring Utopia's security traffic.

As a result, he did not see a man—little more than a youth, really: freckled, scared, with rheumy eyes and a nose almost as red as his hair—creep nervously out of an emergency exit behind the truck, affix something resembling a watchband to the underside of the rear bumper, then creep back out of sight once again.

4:24 P.M.

WARNE MOVED DOWN the corridor as quickly as he dared. Beneath one arm, he held half a dozen empty mortars: resin-bonded black tubes, with stenciled numbers on their ends designating charge capacity. Beneath his other arm were a variety of aerial shells, encased in their clear plastic wrapping. He hugged them protectively against himself: Smythe had warned him, in unpleasant detail, about what could happen to Goex powder or flash composition if it was rudely dropped onto a concrete floor.

Behind him came Smythe himself, arms full of bulky, brown-wrapped maroons and a variety of other things Warne didn't recognize. And behind Smythe came Wingnut, moving forward with short, swift jerks. Four heavy salutes had been taped to his locomotion array, long fuses of tightly wrapped tan-colored paper trailing away behind.

The corridor was deserted. In an absent, detached kind of way, Warne noticed that the doors they were passing—props for seasonal performances, holography and video storage, water filtration substation—were all infrequently visited areas not inconvenienced by being sealed off during the weekly armored car runs. Since the vault tone had sounded, Smythe's high-security passcard had allowed them access to the restricted area. But it wouldn't be until the all-clear was given that the bulk of Utopia's cast and crew would be allowed back into these corridors.

"You're sure this is the way?" Warne called over his shoulder.

Smythe, who was out of breath and struggling to retain a tight hold on his burden, did not reply. Warne glanced back. The pyrotechnist's face held a variety of emotions: dismay, disapproval, concern. He wondered what the guy would have done if he'd explained his plan in detail. Would he have agreed it was the only possible way? Or would he have refused point-blank?

As they ran, an odor was gradually introduced into the cool, normally unscented air of the Underground: the stench of diesel fumes. *Are we too late*? he wondered with a sudden spasm of anxiety. Too long a time had passed, the all-clear should have sounded. John Doe and his boys would have been eager to leave. If they already had the money, why would they still be here?

And then he heard something over the echoing clatter of their footsteps: the sound of an idling diesel. It was a low, throaty growl, intensely out of place in these concrete corridors. He remembered what Amanda Freeman had told him during his entrance processing: *The only nonelectric vehicle allowed is the armored car that makes a weekly pickup.*

Warne slowed. Up ahead, the hallway dead-ended in another, wider corridor that ran away in opposite directions. To the left, Warne saw, or thought he saw, the faintest hint of daylight illuminating the concrete walls.

He turned back toward Smythe, pointing, asking a wordless question. Smythe nodded in reply. That was it: the access corridor.

Warne continued toward the T-intersection at a much slower pace. The idling of the diesel was clearly coming from the right side of the access corridor. That meant the armored car would have to pass directly across Warne's line of sight in order to exit the Underground.

A strange rush of feelings passed through him. One was relief: against all hope, they'd arrived in time. Another was naked fear. And still another: what was *he*—rebel theoretician of symposium and laboratory—doing here? Right now he should be trying to resuscitate a sinking career: writing for a scientific journal, doing lab research. Why was he here, of all places?

He'd asked himself the question before. And again, the same answer came back. He *shouldn't* be here. But there was nobody else. He was the only one who had any chance of stopping these people from imploding the dome. And to do that, he had to keep them from leaving the Underground.

A hundred feet from the intersection, he stopped. Kneeling, fingers trembling slightly, he set the tubes on the ground. Wingnut waited nearby, his normal seesaw motion subdued. He seemed to be still trying to adjust his movements to the added weight of the four large cakes of black powder, wrapped in cartridge paper and strapped to his back. If he could have looked unhappy, he would have.

Warne placed the shells beside the mortars. "What comes next?" he asked Smythe as calmly as he could.

The little man was placing his own burden carefully on the ground. "Well, in a manually fired show, you'd sandbag the mortars. Check each shell in the display for loose powder. If there are broken suspenders, you'd need to repair them so the lead is secured to the end of the shell."

Warne listened, gritting his teeth. The stink of the diesel exhaust, the growl of the invisible truck, seemed to intensify. And yet he sensed there was no way to rush this: Smythe had to explain.

"And how do you angle the shell?" he asked.

Smythe looked at him, smoothing his tiny mustache with the fingers of one hand. "Pardon me?"

"I said, how do you *angle* the shell? Say you want to shoot it horizontally, not vertically."

"But that's just not done." Smythe looked surprised, almost affronted, as if the idea had never occurred to him before. "These shells have propelling charges that lift them hundreds of feet in the air. That's the equivalent of several sticks of dynamite. No fire marshal would allow it. Why, the separation distance, the fallout area, would be exponentially greater than a normal—"

"*Mr. Smythe,*" Warne interrupted. "We're not dealing with anything normal right now. Tell me how it's done."

Smythe's fingers froze, but the look of surprise remained. "Well, I suppose the procedure would be about the same. Lower the shell into the mortar, make sure it slides freely. Make sure the shell rests squarely on the bottom. Then you would—" Smythe stopped, and a sour expression came over his face. "Then you would place the mortar on its side. Not directly horizontal, of course. That would . . ." He shook his head, clucking to himself at the thought.

"I see." Warne pointed to one of the largest shells. "Show me, with that one there. The—"

"Golden willow."

"Golden willow, right."

Smythe carefully tore the plastic wrapping from the shell, checked the heavy lifting charge fixed to its base, untied the twist holding the quickmatch fuse, unlooped it. And then, holding the shell by the end of its fuse, he lowered it gingerly into one of the large black mortars, raised it again, lowered it. Satisfied with the fit, he draped the end of the quickmatch over the side. Then he took one of the smallest mortar tubes, lay it perpendicularly on the ground, and—much more slowly—lowered the charged mortar so it was resting at an angle atop the little tube.

Warne nodded. "I see. Now, how do you light it?"

"Light it?"

Warne nodded. The roar of the diesel was louder now, the driver revving his engine.

"Why would you want to know?"

"Because I'm going to fire it, Mr. Smythe."

The pyrotechnist's look of surprise deepened abruptly. "Fire it? But why?"

There was time only for a brief explanation or a threat. Warne chose the former.

"Because some very dangerous men are about to come down that passageway. In an armored car. If we let them escape, they'll blow up the dome over Utopia. Destroy the Park. We're not going to let them escape."

Behind them, a maintenance hatchway opened and Peccam appeared. He glanced down the hall in both directions, then came forward to join them. There was dust on his knees and a hunted look in his eyes.

Smythe didn't bother to look over. "You're going to fire a golden willow—in *here*?"

"If I have to, Mr. Smythe. That, and the, the whatever you call it, the double chrysanthemum, if necessary. But first I've got Wingnut here, loaded to the gills with black powder, as you can see. I'm going to send him into the truck."

Smythe's eyes had grown wide. "So you mean . . ." he began. "You mean that this might be *dangerous*?"

Warne shut up. The look of shock and disbelief on the pyrotechnist's face was ludicrous, indescribable. Perhaps the man had been fooling himself into thinking this was all some kind of emergency drill. Or maybe he thought it was some undercover test by Utopia management. Whatever the case—with his heart hammering double time in his chest, the stink of diesel fumes swirling around the exhaust vents, the grinding of the truck around the corner—Warne suddenly began to laugh. He laughed until the sound echoed off the walls of the Underground, drowning even the noise of the idling diesel. And then, as the laughter died away, a single, choking sob took its place.

"Yes, Mr. Smythe," he said, dabbing at his eyes. "I guess it might be dangerous, at that."

Peccam came up behind the pyrotechnist. "Just show him how to light these before you run away," he said.

Smythe looked back at Peccam, then at Warne. He nodded quickly several times, wordlessly, then removed his glasses and began wiping them unsteadily with his shirttail.

"You okay?" Warne asked Peccam. "The echolocator's in place?"

Peccam nodded.

"Okay." Warne moved toward Wingnut, flipped a battery of switches on the robot's processing panel. Then he stepped back. "See those buttons on Wingnut's upper housing? When I give the signal, press the second switch from the left. Normally, he's programmed to follow his avatar. That's me. But I've just modified things so that pressing that switch will override the programming, go right to the firmware. He'll home in on the echolocator, wherever it is. Those heavy charges on his back are what will take out the armored car; we'll just use the fireworks to keep anybody inside from escaping. Got it? So when the car—" He stopped as he noticed the expression on Peccam's face. "What is it?"

Peccam gestured down the corridor, toward the intersection. "It won't take that armored car more than a second or two to pass by our field of view. How are you planning to do all this in such a short space of time?"

Warne stared back, aghast. In the frantic burst of planning, he'd never even stopped to consider this.

"We've got to find some way to stop the thing, then," he said. "Make it stop for a moment when it reaches the intersection."

But, with a rising despair, he realized there *was* no way to make it stop. Poole's words came back to him: *I'm not throwing my body down in front of an armored car in hopes it'll stop.* He'd been right. There wasn't any—

And then, suddenly, he remembered something.

"Stay here," he told Smythe. Then he turned to Peccam and beckoned urgently. "Come with me."

Warne ran back down the corridor, Peccam at his heels. He came to a stop before the door he'd noticed earlier: *Holography and Video Storage.* He grasped the knob. It was locked; Peccam swiped his passcard through the nearby reader and the door clicked open. Warne darted inside, flicking on the light and frantically scanning the crowded storage room. *They've had the upper hand all day*, he thought. *We've never had a chance. Once, just once, cut us a break.*

There it was: the low black cylindrical housing he'd hoped to find. It was sitting in a far corner, beside two others just like it—a portable holographic display unit, like the one Terri had demonstrated to him in her office that morning.

He ran up to it, then rolled it forward on its large wheels. Peccam watched him curiously, eyes narrowed. They widened suddenly as understanding dawned.

"Do we have time?" he asked.

Warne stopped to listen. The diesel was fainter here, but he could hear that it was still idling. "We've got to try," he said.

"But if that truck starts to move before—"

Warne made a silencing motion with his hand. "One thing at a time. Let's go."

And, pushing the low cylinder ahead of him as quickly as he could, he led the way out of the room and back down the corridor.

4:25 P.M.

TERRI PACED THE small front office of the Security Complex. She realized that, unconsciously, she was clenching and un-clenching her fists. She forced herself to stop. Where was Andrew? What was going on? Was he all right? It was agonizing, this waiting, this uncertainty. She glanced out of the office, over the front desk, toward the door leading out into the corridors of C Level. The doctor had left it wide open when he'd come rushing in a few minutes earlier. She felt her fists balling again. Then she glanced back at Georgia, stirring restlessly in the wheelchair.

No matter what, she reminded herself. *No matter what.*

A minute before, maybe two minutes, the crying had started. It was faint, muffled by the intervening walls. Although Terri could not picture the Park chief shedding tears for anyone, she knew the voice could only be Sarah's. Her agitation increased, and she quickened her step.

There was a rustling behind her, and she looked over. Georgia was standing up, supporting herself with the wheelchair. The girl blinked once, twice, stupidly. *Still groggy*, Terri thought. Whether from the sedative or the shock of the day's events, she didn't know.

Georgia took a shuffling step forward, then another. She was headed toward the door of the office. Toward the sound.

Terri put a gentle hand on her arm. "Where are you going, Georgia?"

"I'm looking for my dad. I thought I heard his voice."

"Your dad's not here right now."

Georgia looked at her for the first time. The eyes were growing clearer, the fogginess beginning to lift. "Where is he?"

Terri licked her lips. "I'm not sure, exactly. He—he's gone to take care of something."

Still looking at her, Georgia blinked.

"He left a message for you. He said he'll be back soon. He said that we're supposed to take care of each other until then."

Suddenly, Sarah's voice cut through the dead air: "Freddy, you can't leave. Do you hear me? *Stay*, Freddy. *Please*."

Georgia's head perked up. "Who is that?"

Terri was silent as the crying recommenced.

"It sounds like Sarah." Georgia turned back. "Is that Sarah? What's the matter?"

Still, Terri hesitated. *What should I say?* She had no idea how Warne would have responded, what he'd want her to do.

If it was me, I'd want to know the truth.

With a slight pressure on the girl's forearm, she turned Georgia toward her. "Do you remember that meeting this morning, with the other grown-ups?"

Georgia nodded.

Terri reached out for Georgia's other arm. "You remember the man, the one with the accent?"

Georgia nodded again.

"Well, he's been hurt, badly. Sarah is upset. She's trying to take care of him."

"Shouldn't we help them?"

"I think Sarah needs to be left alone right now. But it's nice of you to offer like that. I know she'd appreciate it."

From the rear of the Security Complex, the crying increased. It was a harrowing sound: inconsolable, utterly alone. Georgia listened a moment. Then she turned back, raised her eyes to Terri's, alive with a look Terri did not fully understand. Slowly, her eyes dropped toward the ground.

Through everything, even the ordeal in the medical laundry, Georgia had maintained an outward stoicism. But now, the beautiful face suddenly crumpled. Her lips trembled, then parted. Tears welled in her eyes.

Impulsively, Terri drew the girl close—much as Warne had done for her, in this same spot, not long before. And then, abruptly, Georgia dissolved into tears. It was as if a dam, long under pressure, had finally given way. For a minute, perhaps two, she simply let Georgia sob, stroking her hair lightly.

"Grown-ups aren't supposed to cry," the girl said at last.

"Grown-ups cry, too," Terri replied, still stroking her hair. "Haven't you seen—I don't know—your dad cry?"

Georgia answered with more sobs. "Once."

The room fell silent, save for Georgia's slowing sobs, the distant crying.

"Do you have any sisters?" Georgia asked with a sniff.

The question was so unexpected that, for a moment, Terri stopped stroking Georgia's hair. "Nope," she said after a moment. "I'm an only child. Not too common in a country as Catholic as the Philippines, either."

"I always wanted to have a sister," Georgia murmured.

Terri's only response was to resume stroking her hair.

"What was it my dad told us to do?" Georgia asked a few moments later.

"To stay here. Watch each other, stand guard. Protect Sarah."

Georgia pulled away. "Stand guard?" The fear had come into her damp eyes so quickly that it could never have been far. "Do you think he's going to come back—that man with the gun?"

Terri drew her close once again. "No, honey. I don't think so. But we need to stand guard, just the same."

Georgia stirred in the embrace. "Don't you think we should close the door?"

Terri glanced over. In her own lingering shock, she had forgotten the doctor had left the main entrance to Security open.

She nodded. "You know, that's not a bad idea."

Gently, she detached herself from Georgia, made her way out into the waiting area.

"Maybe . . . maybe you should lock it, too."

Terri walked across the sparkling tile floor of the anteroom, stuck her head warily out the door, glanced up and down the corridor. It was deserted. Somewhere far away, an alarm was ringing. She closed the door, locked it carefully, made sure it was secure.

The sounds of crying had ceased, and as she made her way back to the front office, a shroud of deep silence lay over the Security Complex.

4:25 P.M.

OCEAN. PROFOUNDLY BLUE, deep inviolate azure, troubled only by infrequent flecks of white. It was serenely still, the distant sound of surf rising and falling in an ageless monody: that perfect beach every dreamer knows lies at the antipodes of the earth, ours for the possessing if we could only find it.

Then Poole's eyes fluttered into focus and the illusion fled far away.

For a moment, he was sorry to see it go. There was no tranquil ocean; only the blue-black dome of Utopia, curving away above him, vertices along its bulk shining in the afternoon sun. The call of surf was his own blood, rushing through the portals of his ears. There was no alabaster beach; only the hard ridges of unforgiving sandstone pressing into his back and the hollow of his neck. Instead, there was a fierce, throbbing pain at his temples, and another—deeper, more pervasive—in his gut.

And then he remembered everything. Abruptly, he tried to sit up.

Pain lanced through his abdomen like a spear of fire. With a groan, he fell backward again.

He'd been played for a sucker. A side arm tucked into the small of the back was the oldest trick in the book. He'd used it himself on more than one occasion. He was getting too old for this game.

But there was no time to lie around, moping.

Rising again, Poole crawled backward through the gully, propelling himself with his feet and the palms of his hands. The pain in his belly grew unbearable, and with a sound between a gasp and a sob he threw himself at last between two massive bolts at the base of the dome, beneath the lowest catwalk. A shaped charge had been placed here; nobody would dare shoot him if he could keep himself close enough to it.

Grasping the catwalk overhead, he pulled himself slowly upward. Black spots danced across his vision, and unconsciousness threatened, but it was critical that he know.

Leaning against the side of the dome, he glanced around. He saw the dead workman, lying in the gully a few feet away. Beyond the gully, the man in the infrastructure uniform—the one with all the weapons—lay sprawled on his back. Over the projecting brow of the rock, Poole could only see the legs, the outflung right arm. But none of the limbs were moving. He must have hit the demolitions expert as he fell backward from the impact of the shot.

He tried to think through the fog of pain. There might be others. The first thing he had to do was arm himself. But to do that, he'd have to move.

Get a visual, he remembered an instructor once saying at an advance camp's training tent. *Learn the extent of the wound*. A slide had flashed on the screen: a black-and-white of an old battlefield, soldiers lying in trenches, little hats and funny boots and layers of clothes in disarray. *Look at those dead Confederates*, the instructor had said. *Why do you think their shirts are all torn up like that? It's not battlefield looters, it's the grunts themselves, looking for entrance or exit holes. They knew that if they'd been gut-shot, they'd die. Get a visual. Learn the extent of the wound. And take it from there.*

All this went through Poole's mind in a tenth of a second.

Taking short, choppy breaths, Poole glanced down. His corduroy jacket seemed untouched save for the gray dust of the mesa top. Then he saw the neat little hole a few inches above the left pocket. Gritting his teeth, he took hold of the jacket and very carefully peeled it away from his body.

The first thing he saw was blood: lots of blood. It had soaked the lower part of his shirt, and for a moment the sight made him light-headed. He bit down on his lower lip, forcing himself to concentrate. He unbuttoned his shirt, plucked it gently away from his flesh. As he did so, a fresh torrent of blood welled out.

He could see the wound now, a ragged little hole in the lower left quadrant. It seemed to have missed any vital organs, but it was bleeding freely. The exit wound, he knew, would be much bigger. And it hurt like a sonofabitch: Poole had been trained in gunshots, told what to expect. But he'd never expected such relentless, overwhelming pain.

His hand fell away from the wound as he slid back to the ground. Once again, he thought back to the field instructor. *If you're in a hot-war situation*, he'd said, *there's no lying down and waiting for a medic. You've got to work through the pain. Pain is your friend. It means you're not so far gone that you're useless. So put your pain into a box. Lock the box, throw away the key. Then you put that box inside a bigger box. Lock that one, too. Throw away the key. Then put that box into a still bigger box. Lock it up, but this time don't throw away the key. Put it in your pocket. And then put that box aside. You'll unlock it later, when there's time.*

Poole remained still a moment, panting. Then he raised his right hand, checked his watch: 4:27.

Grasping the catwalk again, he pulled himself first to his knees and then, with a supreme effort, to his feet. The world tilted around him dangerously, and he closed his eyes, grasping the catwalk tightly, waiting for things to steady. After a few seconds, he opened his eyes again.

Here in the shadow of the dome, the hollows and ridges of the mesa top seemed shallow labyrinths of brown and gray. He looked for his pistol, but all he could spot in the monochromatic landscape was the M24 sniper rifle, lying where he'd told the man to drop it. Twisting his neck to the right, he could see, maybe fifty feet farther along the curve of the dome, the small square shape of the control box he'd seen earlier, just before discovering the corpse in the gully.

He took a step forward, then another, closing his eyes once again to steady himself as the world reeled. Slowly, like an old man, he knelt to retrieve the rifle. The pain bent him double, and he bit down hard on the involuntary cry of pain. Blackness threatened to wash over him again and he waited, in the shadow of the gully, for it to pass. Then he rose unsteadily to his feet and, rifle at the ready, approached the man in the infrastructure uniform.

He lay spreadeagled, right arm flung wide, left arm across his chest. There was no sign of any wound. For a moment, Poole wondered if this was all some weird figment of his imagination: if in fact he was the one still lying in the gully, dying, reality long since fled far, far away.

And then he noticed the red-rimmed hole where the man's right eye had been; noticed the small dark stain ponding beneath the head, flowing into the dry fissures of stone.

Poole turned away, his breath coming short and shallow, trying hard to lock the pain away. He knew he was still bleeding
freely, but there was no time to worry about it. The rifle was
heavy, useless in his hand. What he really needed was to deactivate that control box.

He moved slowly back to the base of the dome. Grasping the
rail of the lowest catwalk, he pulled himself forward, one agonizing step after the other, following the line of det cord as it
snaked its way toward the box. Directly ahead of him now, about
thirty yards from the base of the dome, he could see the top of
the rear wall of Utopia. Behind it, a long, flat, concrete roof
swept from one edge of the canyon to the other. Ventilation
tubes, smokestacks, display launching platforms, elevator housings, and aerial masts pocked its surface, creating a man-made
forest of spars and booms. Beyond the rear edge, and perhaps
two hundred feet below, lay the cast parking lot. And, farther
still, the access road that curved its way down the desolate high-
desert plains toward Highway 95.

Poole gave all this merely a cursory glance. His eyes were on
the control box, now just a few feet ahead. He tried not to think
about the time; about the fact that, at any moment, the armored
car would emerge from the Underground, John Doe or one of his
cohorts would activate the transmitter, and people would be
picking up little pieces of Angus Poole for a long, long time. If
he could just get to the control box, neutralize it, they might have
a chance.

The unit was fastened securely to the lower rail of the catwalk,
delicate fingers of det cord streaming away in several directions.
Poole tried to kneel beside it, but a fresh whiplash of pain sent
both him and the rifle sprawling in the dust. He pulled himself
up, willing the agony away just long enough to reach up, pluck
out the receiver, and deactivate the infernal device.

His fingers pawed uselessly over a slick, smooth surface.
Forcing his eyes into focus, he looked more closely at the box.

It was not a receiver, at all. It was merely a relay box, a split-
ting junction for the leg wires.

Poole blinked, numbed by surprise and disbelief.

A few feet away, an access ladder had been bolted above the
catwalk. A line of thinner wire led away from the relay and
curled upward along one of the ladder's rails. Poole's eye followed the wire, traveling slowly up the dome . . . And there, leer-

ing down at him, sat the receiver he'd been searching for. The demolitions expert had strapped it to the underside of a second catwalk, circling the dome some fifty feet above the first, ensuring a clear line of sight for John Doe's transmitter.

Poole's knees gave way and he fell back onto the rocky ground. "Christ," he moaned. "Oh, no. No, no, no."

Fifty feet up the ladder, but it might as well have been five thousand. There was no way he could climb. He closed his eyes. It was too late: too late to reach the receiver, too late to defuse the triggering mechanism, too late to attain safe distance. Too late, in fact, for anything.

4:28 P.M.

IN THE DRIVER'S seat of the armored car, Candyman had one hand pressed against his headset. There was a puzzled expression on his face. After a few moments, he dropped his hand and shook his head slowly.

"What is it?" asked Earl Crowe, sitting behind him.

"I don't know. I could have sworn I heard somebody laugh."

Crowe exchanged glances with Hardball and Cracker Jack, then shrugged dismissively.

Sitting alone at the rear of the payload compartment, John Doe had removed one of the countless stacks of currency and was making origami cranes from the contents. The infrared transmitter lay ready at his side. He glanced at his watch.

"Still no word from Water Buffalo?"

Candyman shook his head.

"We'll give him sixty seconds more."

A silence settled over the interior of the armored car. John Doe finished folding the crane, put it carefully to one side, pulled a second note free, and folded another. A minute ticked by. Then he glanced forward.

"All right, let's move," he said. "Water Buffalo can walk back to Vegas."

Candyman adjusted his headset, spoke into it. "Utopia Central, this is Nine Echo Bravo. Problem resolved. Repeat, problem resolved. Rolling now."

"Utopia Central confirms," came the responding crackle. "About time. Report when you're in the 95 driveline. Over and out."

Reaching overhead, Candyman turned on the high- and low-band police scanners. Then he glanced toward a panel to his right, pressed a yellow switch marked *load manager*. The truck went into high idle, bringing additional electrical power to bear. He disengaged the parking brake and gave another look back.

"We're rolling, gentlemen," he said.

THE SOUND OF the diesel changed just as Warne and Peccam were running back toward Smythe. It grew lower, throatier. Air brakes chuffed and hissed; there was a protesting squeal. A clutch released, gears knocked their way through a transmission. Warne and Peccam exchanged quick glances.

For a moment, the only sounds were the roar of the engine and Peccam's noisy breathing.

"Are we really going to do this?" the video tech asked.

"I don't know. I guess so." Warne turned to Smythe. "So how do we fire?"

Smythe's mouth was working, but the words were inaudible. Warne leaned closer.

"No supply tender," Smythe was saying to himself, shaking his head. "No fire suppression equipment. No loading personnel. No spotters, no monitors." He seemed to be counting something on his fingers; perhaps it was all the local, state, and federal regulations that were about to be broken.

The entire corridor seemed alive with the rumble of the approaching vehicle. Any minute and the armored car would come into view.

"*Smythe!* Show me *how!*"

Smythe looked at him, startled. "You remove the protective cap from the quickmatch."

Warne tore the perforated ends away from the fuses trailing below the mortars.

"You light the fuse with a portfire. At full-arm extension. There's a very short delay, perhaps a half second, so be sure to get well away. Turn away from the glare. It's likely to blind you—"

"You light the fuse with a *what*?"

"A portfire." Smythe waved his hand at a bundle of small, red, flarelike objects. Warne grabbed one, turned it over in his hands.

"It's not lit," he said stupidly.

Smythe blinked at him.

"*It's not lit!*" Warne cried over the growing roar.

"Of course not. You wouldn't light the portfire until you're ready to launch a shell, would you?"

"Then give me the matches. I'll light it myself."

Smythe looked at him blankly.

A sudden, terrible fear came over Warne. "The matches, Mr. Smythe."

Smythe blinked again. He spread his hands as if to say, *Why should I be carrying matches?*

Warne went cold. *Oh, God. After all this . . .*

He slumped back against the concrete. His vision seemed to dim. And then he felt something being placed in his hand.

It was a plastic cigarette lighter.

He looked over to see Peccam, withdrawing back into position beside Wingnut. The video tech shrugged, laughed nervously. "I like the occasional cigar," he said.

Warne crouched over the end of the portfire, holding it just above the lighter's small flame. The portfire came to instant life, sparking and flickering with an angry hiss. He tossed the lighter to Peccam, turned back to the line of mortars just as the nose of the armored car came into view.

Against the backdrop of the tunnel it seemed impossibly huge, elephantine, invulnerable. Bands of heavy, red-painted steel surrounded the wheel wells and gunports, the transparent armor of the windows. Tall steel rods, topped with white, rose from the reinforced bumper. Amber lights on its roof, the roar of its engine, drenched the corridor in light and sound. Warne stared, portfire dangling from his hand. The driver's compartment appeared, reflecting green in the fluorescent lights. Warne held his breath, waiting. Now the entire intersection was filled by the truck's bulk. For a moment, he was afraid something had gone wrong; that the truck would keep going. But then, with a shrill protest of brakes, it ground to a halt and sat, idling, the entire frame shaking.

"Shall I light?" Peccam yelled from behind Wingnut.

Warne glanced over. Wingnut held the real charge: four huge cakes of black powder. He'd had to guess at the fuse length; for all he knew, it might well go off too early. But there was no time to worry about that now. He nodded, watched as Peccam lit the fuse, then pushed the button on Wingnut's processing panel. The head of the robot panned around, searching for the echolocator's signal. Then it froze, aimed directly at the armored car.

Warne watched it. Despite everything, he felt a pang of regret and guilt that he had to sacrifice the robot like this. "Good-bye, Wingnut," he murmured. "I'm sorry."

For a moment, Wingnut remained still, head assembly pointed at the armored car. Warne had the strange thought that perhaps it knew what was about to happen; that at some deep, atavistic level it would refuse to obey a command tantamount to suicide. And then, with the deep purr of its powerful motors, it shot forward, heading for the distant bumper.

And, just as quickly, it came to a stop again, the fuse still spiking and sputtering behind it.

Warne stared at the robot in horror, trying to determine what had gone wrong. Was it possible that he was right? That Wingnut would refuse to follow his programming? And then—as he lifted his gaze to the end of the corridor—he understood.

Beneath the rear end of the shuddering truck, something that looked like a huge plastic watch lay on the concrete floor, broken into pieces. The shaking of the vehicle had jarred the echolocator loose. It had shattered in the fall. And now Wingnut was stranded in the corridor, ten pounds of heavy explosive on his back, with no instructions on how to carry out his directive.

"WHAT IS IT?" John Doe asked from the rear compartment. Leaning back against a metal locker, he threw his arms behind his head. As he did so, his suit jacket draped open to reveal an elegant silk lining, the holster snugged beneath one arm.

"There's somebody up ahead in the corridor," the driver replied. "He came into view as I rounded the bend."

"Well, give him a minute, he'll get out of the way."

"He's not moving."

"Give him a bit of the horn."

Candyman complied. "Still there. He just doesn't want to move."

John Doe let his arms drop to his sides and leaned forward. "Is he deaf?"

"The guy's looking right at us."

"Is he a guard?"

"No. Just some civilian in a suit."

John Doe frowned at this. "Is it possible, even *conceivable*, that—" He rose and, holding an overhead rail for support, peered forward, out through the windshield.

"I've seen that man before," he murmured. And then, suddenly, his features contorted with anger and surprise.

"It's Warne!" he cried. "Step on it! Run him down, now, *now*!"

* * *

AS THE ENGINE revved and the driver threw the truck into gear again, Warne dropped his eyes from Wingnut to the canisters propped on the ground before him. He leaned his portfire toward the fuse of the golden willow. With Wingnut frozen, lacking instructions, he knew what he had to do: fire a shell at the truck himself. And yet, a strange lassitude filled his limbs. For a moment, time hung suspended.

A parade of images flashed through his head, an accelerated magic-lantern show: Norman Pepper on the monorail, gesturing expansively, smile impossibly broad as he rubbed his hands together. Sarah, wide-eyed, in the hall of mirrors. Terri Bonifacio, sobbing against his shoulder in the Security Complex. Georgia standing in Metamorphoses, staring at the magically aged image of herself. And then, later, in the recovery bay in Medical . . .

In a single stroke, Warne moved forward and touched the portfire to the fuse.

There was a brief white light as the fuse caught, and then the flame traveled up the line of the quickmatch with surprising rapidity, sparking and spitting. At the last moment, Warne remembered to avert his eyes. There was a strange noise, like compressed air being released underwater. And then, with a ferocious hiss, the shell shot from the tube. Warne looked back to watch it coruscating down the corridor at unbelievable speed, a comet of light with an intense smoking tail that caromed from wall to wall until it hurled itself into the ceiling above the armored car.

For a millisecond, there was nothing. And then the world turned white.

With a terrifying, shattering report, the remainder of the lift charge exploded. A hundred tongues of golden composition jetted down the corridor, hissing and snaking along the walls and ceiling, curling around the armored car in a fiery caress. There was an incredible fusillade of sound, like countless grenades exploding in rapid sequence. The white light became obscured by a strange smoky corona of gold, awe-inspiring and terrifying at the same time. Warne ducked as fiery tendrils shot over his head, growing brighter and brighter before at last fading into nothing.

As the echoes died away, Warne could hear another sound: the distant clamor of warning sirens. Now the ragged curtain of smoke began to drift away, and Warne struggled to see past it.

The front end of the armored car had been knocked to one

side by the blast. As he watched, Warne could see the tires rolling, the driver working desperately to get the truck back on course.

His aim had been far too high, and the shell had exploded over the truck.

Warne glanced over his shoulder. Smythe, the pyrotechnist, was lying on the floor behind him, curled up in a ball, arms wrapped protectively over his head. Peccam crouched nearby, frozen disbelief on his face.

Warne turned back. The spent mortar lay beside him, smoking. Wingnut still stood a few yards down the corridor, the fuse growing alarmingly short. He saw its big head pivot back toward him, as if in inquiry. At the end of the corridor, the truck was still trying to align itself, the diesel roaring as the driver rocked the big vehicle back and forth. Another moment and it would disappear down the corridor.

He dropped his eyes to the remaining mortars. The support tube had been knocked away by the ferocity of the launch, and the cylinders lay at angles across the floor. He would not be able to prepare another in time for a second shot. Even if he could, aiming with any accuracy had proved almost impossible. He glanced ahead at Wingnut. If only there was some way to reach him, to alter his programming. But there was no time. And so the robot sat there, the charge they needed to disable the armored car about to explode on his back, with no directives to follow . . .

Ahead, at the intersection, the snout of a rifle poked through one of the gunports of the armored car.

Warne ducked down. A sudden thought had occurred to him. Maybe there *was* a directive Wingnut could follow. It was no command he had ever been given before; in fact, it went against everything he had been taught. And yet maybe . . .

"Wingnut!" he barked, pointing at the armored car. "Chase!"

Wingnut remained motionless.

"Chase!" Warne cried again. *"Chase!"*

Still the robot hesitated, as if trying to process this unfamiliar command. Then it began to move forward, slowly at first, but quickly gaining speed. Warne sat up, speechless. The fuse glowed and sparked between the robot's knobby rear wheels. As Warne watched, Wingnut seemed to gain purpose as well as speed, moving faster and faster as it approached the huge truck.

Warne shut his eyes, turned away.

There was a blinding light that scorched his eyeballs even through the closed lids, followed by a violent thunderclap that seemed to shake Utopia to its very footings. Warne felt a wave of overpressure boil past him. He gasped, tried to raise himself up. For a moment, his muscles refused to obey. And then, with an effort, he staggered back onto his hands and knees.

He could see that the armored car had been thrown onto its side, the radiator grille guard irreversibly wedged into one wall of the corridor. The uppermost wheels were turning lazily, run-flat inserts going round like drunken tops, the composite of the side panels blackened and steaming. He could see that the heavy armor that covered the truck's underside had been torn and petaled, peeled away in one section like aluminum foil. The sprinklers at the end of the corridor had gone off, and curtains of water rained down through the rolling palls of gunpowder.

Warne crouched, staring, his breath coming in sharp gasps. For a long moment, there was only the labored sound of his breath, the distant patter of the sprinklers on metal and concrete, the drone of the fire alarms.

And then the door of the armored car shifted.

Warne stared, wondering if he'd been mistaken; if the sheets of water, the roiling streamers of smoke, were playing tricks with his eyes. But then the door moved again, as if pushed up from below.

Someone was trying to get out.

Warne's breath came even faster. He looked at the mortars lying before him, their contents scattered and askew, quickmatch fuses trailing away like tails. He tried to force his brain into action. He made out the double chrysanthemum, the heavy, cake-like lifting charges. What had Smythe said about them? *The equivalent of several sticks of dynamite.*

The door of the armored car flew upward, banging against the rear wall of the corridor. Warne saw a man's head emerge, then the upper part of a torso, clad in a tight leather jacket. The man was forcing himself up, struggling against the crazy tilt of the vehicle. In his hands was a stout, ugly-looking submachine gun.

Warne fell back, looking around desperately. The portfire lay to one side, still sparking and sputtering, flaring crimson against the concrete floor.

There was no time to think, no other options to consider. He grabbed it, then reached wildly for the nearest mortar, dropped in a lifting charge, then another, frantically tugging their quick-match fuses into position. The man raised the gun, steadying himself against the frame of the door. A gout of flame erupted from the muzzle; something whined past Warne's head.

Gasping, he dropped the huge chrysanthemum shell into the mortar, then angled it away and held the portfire to the end of the fuses, his fingers stupid, refusing to work. Another stuttering flash from the gun, another whine of bullets, concrete chips flying across his face and stinging Warne's eyes, but the fuses were lit now, and—holding the mortar as far in front of him as possible—he aimed it directly toward the shooter.

There was another angry hiss, and then smoke boiled back from the mortar tube and a brutal recoil knocked him to the floor. Another comet of light, brighter than the first, arrowed down the hallway, swerving first up, then down, a searing shaft of brilliance that sped directly toward the open door of the armored car. Warne fell to the floor, covering his ears, shielding his head with his arms.

For a millisecond, silence. And then there came a terrific double report; a concussive blast of incendiary color; a sudden flowering of fire—one within another—that stretched out into brilliant pinpoints of light, incandescent red and yellow and turquoise, a hundred tiny suns too bright and terrible to look upon. Warne felt almost violated by light. He tried to rise, but the brutal shock wave forced him back to the floor, where he lay a moment, stunned. Next he felt—or thought he felt—confetti landing around him, falling gently to earth. He lay still, trembling, eyes tight shut, afraid to move.

For a moment, he could hear nothing but a harsh buzzing in his ears. As that faded, other sounds came slowly back: the rolling thunder of the salute as it echoed and reechoed deeper through the halls of C Level; the distant sound of a hundred car alarms blaring out in the employee parking lot. "I can't see!" Peccam was crying behind him. "I can't see!"

More sprinklers came on now, water running through Warne's hair, down his neck, into the hollow between his shoulder blades. And then, at last, Warne pulled himself up the side of the wall, opened his eyes, and looked ahead.

The truck lay as it had before, wheels slowly spinning, water trickling down its flanks in spidery streams. The stench of gunpowder and phosphorus hung heavy in the air. Shreds of money lay everywhere, covering the sides of the truck, the floors and the walls, darkening as water soaked it. The man with the submachine gun had vanished. The truck's open door was now awash in blood and matter, and a curtain of blood ran up the wall behind it, fan-shaped and huge. Warne watched as the sprinklers traced clear lines of water through the crimson.

He sank back against the wall, too numb to feel anything: no relief, no fear, only an uncomfortable sensation in his hands. He looked down and noticed with a kind of detached surprise that his hands were raw, the skin burned away by the heat of the shell. He let them fall to his sides, then looked back down the corridor, his motions slow and dreamlike. There was Peccam, sitting against the wall of the corridor, hands clasped over his eyes. Smythe was nowhere to be seen.

Warne exhaled slowly, letting his head come to rest against the cool wall of the corridor. The portfire lay in his lap, soaked through, spent. The pain in his palms was becoming more intense, but he felt very tired. The bleating of the alarms, the trickle of water down his face, seemed very far away. Maybe, if he closed his eyes, he could sleep.

He let his gaze fall once again on the armored car. And abruptly, as if galvanized by an electric current, he sat up, portfire rolling from his lap and across the floor.

John Doe was clambering out over the hood of the armored car. His face was blackened, his hair burned. Steam rose from the shoulders of his linen suit. Blood was running freely from his nose and ears. He seemed not to notice Warne, or the scatterings of currency, or anything else. His gaze remained locked on the tunnel exit.

Warne stumbled to his feet, staring at John Doe's hands. One held a pistol; the other, the black oblong of the long-distance transmitter.

Warne looked around wildly. His hands were too burned to light another fuse. Even if he could, there was too much water; nothing would light. He had nothing, could do nothing.

He looked back toward the truck in desperation. But John Doe had already slid off the front grille and vanished out of sight down the tunnel.

4:32 P.M.

JOHN DOE WALKED down the corridor, away from the smoke and water and confusion and the indescribable horror that lay within the armored car. His gait was unsteady, but his grip on the transmitter remained firm. Fire, smoke, and emergency alarms were going off but he did not hear them: both eardrums had burst in the third shell's explosion. Blood and gore covered the front of his suit, but most of it was not his and he paid no attention.

A guard was running down the corridor toward him, his face a mask of shock and concern. He was mouthing something— *What the hell just happened? Are you all right?*—and John Doe raised the gun and shot him. His eyes were bleeding and powder-burned, but he was still able to make out the semicircle of sunlight that lay at the end of the access corridor. *Not much farther now.*

Another guard came down the hall and John Doe raised his arm, fired again, and moved on. He passed the security checkpoint—deserted—just a few more steps—and then he was out on the tarmac, the vast rear wall of Utopia rising above and behind him. The shadow of the dome lay across the lot, but even so, the light was almost too much for his damaged eyes. He staggered forward, feeling the blood trickling from his ears. Some crew members, who'd raced from the loading docks at the sound of the explosions, stopped and stared at him. He walked on, not bothering to glance at them. One or two vehicles were moving across the tarmac, vague indistinct shapes, but he was interested in only one: the escort car that would take him away from this place, from the deadly confusion he was about to rain down upon the Park. What was that line of Vishnu's quoted in the Bhagavad Gita? *I am become death, the destroyer of worlds.* At least, that's how he believed it went: his mind was not as clear as it should have been.

There was no hard cash, of course, but he had the discs; that was more than compensation enough. Ahead now he could make out the vast, curved line that marked the edge of the dome's shadow. He gripped the transmitter more tightly. When he reached that point, he'd turn around. He'd have all the angle he needed from there.

Not much farther now.

BALLING HIS SEARED palms, Andrew Warne clambered painfully over the hood of the armored car and began staggering down the hallway. He did not know what he planned to do: he knew merely that he had to stop John Doe any way he could.

The portable holographic projector he and Peccam had placed to stop the truck lay on its side in the passage, knocked over by the explosions. It was still projecting a hologram of himself: feet apart, arms crossed, sprawled drunkenly against the ceiling. He passed beneath it quickly. Ahead, there was a guard lying motionless in the passageway, shot; and then another. To the rear he heard a confusion of shouts, the sound of running feet. He moved on, past the checkpoint, past the roaring fans of the air purification system, and out into Cast Parking.

He stopped for a moment, looking around, trying to spot John Doe. And then to his horror he saw him directly ahead, perhaps a hundred yards away, his narrow form bisected by the shadow line of Utopia's dome as it fell across the tarmac. *How had he moved so fast?*

He saw the blood-drenched arm swing up slowly, deliberately. "No!" Warne cried, taking off at a dead run. But even as he ran, he saw the transmitter aim toward the sky, saw the empty, glassy smile on John Doe's face, and he knew he was too late.

And then, quite abruptly, John Doe's head disintegrated in a cloud of blood and brain matter.

The body fell backward, transmitter clattering across the asphalt. Only then did the crack of the shot reach Warne. It echoed across the lot, rolling and rumbling above the blare of car alarms, tossed back and forth like a ball between the opposing canyon walls.

He ran up to the transmitter, stamped it into fragments with his heel. Then he turned back, his gaze traveling up the broad concrete posterior of Utopia. Far above at the roofline, silhouetted against the shadow of the dome, a figure in a tweed cap and corduroy jacket leaned against a long-barreled rifle. He waved once, weakly, down at Warne. And then he sat down very abruptly, the rifle falling away out of sight.

Warne, too, sat down, the tarmac in shadow now but still hot from the day's exposure to the sun. A few yards away lay John Doe's body, ruined, motionless.

Warne glanced around, arms across his knees, blinking stupidly. Not far away, a late-model sedan with a flashing amber light was peeling rapidly away, heading for the interstate. Warne ignored it. His gaze was fixed on a more distant point: the scribbled red line of the horizon, where a row of squat shadows was approaching above a thin ribbon of cloud. If he listened closely, he thought he could hear a throbbing murmur, like the beating of giant wings against the air. The cavalry had arrived.

EPILOGUE

WARM SUNLIGHT SPLASHED over the canyon walls, dappling the sandstone with a profusion of reds, yellows, and ochers. Warne sat alone in a window seat, enjoying the reflected warmth on his face. This time, he'd remembered the dark glasses. The gentle rocking of the car was comforting, almost familiar somehow, like cradle memories of early childhood. The canned speech coming over the speakers was the same mellow, sophisticated voice, only now a pitch had been added for the Callisto Skyport, reopened with new rides just two weeks before.

Somebody was speaking over his shoulder, and he roused himself from the enshrouding fog of memories and looked around. It was a man in his mid-forties, with thinning hair and a florid complexion.

"I'm sorry?" Warne asked.

"I said, is this your first trip here?"

Warne shook his head, recalling the last time he'd viewed these red walls: from within a medevac chopper tearing back toward Vegas, his hands packed in ice, a uniformed man shouting questions at him. For a moment, the rocking of the car grew less comforting.

"It's mine. My first trip, I mean. And I still can't believe I'm actually here." The man's words seemed to tumble out in a breathless rush. "And it's all because of that article I wrote."

The feeling passed, and Warne forced the memories aside. "Really?"

"For the *Epicurean Quarterly Review*. On medieval cuisine. I'm a food historian, you know?"

"Food historian."

But the man needed no encouragement. "Yes. And so last week I get this call from Lee Dunwich, head of Food Services Utopia—can you believe it, Lee Dunwich himself, gave up that three-star Paris restaurant and everything to come to the Park? Anyway, he wanted me to come and review some of the Camelot menus, you know, they're opening those two new restaurants, and apparently guest sampling showed people weren't happy with some of the dishes, you know, medieval food tends to be a little . . . Oh, my God, there it is!"

The monorail had swung around a narrow curve in the canyon, and up ahead lay the vast copper-colored facade of Utopia, winking and shimmering in the sunshine like some monumental mirage. The flow of words halted abruptly, and the man stared at the spectacle before him.

Watching that look, Warne smiled despite himself. "Have yourself a good time," he said.

INSIDE THE NEXUS, all the clocks read 0:50. The long, echoing galleries seemed to be waiting, as if holding their breath against the sudden influx of guests. Warne stood on the off-loading ramp, gazing around at the vast conflation of brushed metal and blond wood, the empty restaurants and boutiques, the graceful blue band of the dome arching far overhead. He took a slow breath, then another. The food historian—Warne had already forgotten his name—was hurrying down the ramp toward the line of white-blazered hosts, all standing as if for a military review. The line began to break up as the external specialists and assorted VIPs approached, and Warne watched a young woman step toward the historian. He thought he recognized her as Amanda Freeman, the woman who had processed his own entry nine months before.

Then—as he turned to follow—he saw, to his surprise, that Sarah Boatwright was coming briskly up the ramp toward him.

At first he was struck, as usual, by the simple, strong lines of her face. But as she drew nearer, he noticed something else. The way the corners of her mouth drooped ever so slightly, the faint dark lines beneath her eyes, seemed to speak of a deep and private sorrow.

In the weeks that followed his return to Pittsburgh, he had spoken to countless law enforcement officials, ATF agents, Utopia guest relations flaks. More recently, he'd had dozens of phone conversations with park designers and system techs. But this would be the first time he'd spoken to Sarah Boatwright. The last time he'd seen her, she had been on the floor of the holding cell, cradling the dying Fred Barksdale.

He debated embracing her, offered his hand instead. "Sarah. What a nice surprise."

She shook his hand, her grip brief but firm. "I saw your name on today's list of visiting specialists. I thought I'd greet you myself."

"Don't you have to be somewhere?" he asked. "That morning meeting, what's it called—?"

"The Pre-Game Show? They can handle one without me."

They started down the ramp, following the line of specialists and their white-jacketed charges fanning out through the Nexus. Warne caught a glimpse of another clock. It read 0:48.

"Actually, it's kind of nice to get away for once," Sarah said. "Things are frantic, what with the plans for the second anniversary celebration. And there's all this new red tape. If it isn't one functionary, it's another. Nevada Health and Safety Code, environmental assessors, industrial hygienists. Sometimes it feels like we're playing bureaucrat of the week."

"That bad?"

"Worse. But it hasn't hurt business. Park attendance is up 15 percent over the last quarter. We're now third in overall draw."

There was something comforting in this chatter, Warne knew: this quotidian talk of numbers and ratios. Something was different about Sarah, something beyond the bittersweet eyes, but he was unable to quite identify it.

They walked between a brace of fountains, past the holographic Attractions board and the entrance portal to Camelot. Cast and crew members trotted by, emerging from hidden doors or disappearing through access panels, intent on last-minute duties. Farther ahead, near the entrance portal for Callisto, a musician in a mercury-colored jumpsuit was carrying an instrument that looked something like a futuristic cello. "Come on," Sarah said, breaking a silence that was just threatening to become awkward. "I've got something I think you'll want to see."

They walked past a cluster of emporiums and the Mind's Eye gallery, and then Sarah directed them toward the far wall of the Nexus and a massive, hexagonal portal. The word *Atlantis* stood over it in letters that seemed to ebb and flow, like water. *Of course*, Warne thought as he glanced at it.

At the sight of their approach, a group of portal attendants stood aside, smiling and nodding at Sarah. The two passed through a wide, low-ceilinged passageway, then emerged into what looked to Warne like an equatorial beach. A vast archaeo-logical project was under way here; he stared in surprise at the grids and balks, the bar scales and baseplate compasses, the carefully stratified soil profiles: all the trappings of a large, professional excavation. At this early hour, it was deserted.

"What *is* all this?" Warne asked.

Sarah looked at him curiously. "You didn't see the concept renderings?"

"Just brief descriptions. I was busy going over the technical specs."

"It's modeled after the current digsite at Akrotiri. It's an actual working archaeological dig, right down to the photogrammetric recording. The idea is, guests first have to pass through this modern-day excavation of Atlantis. That's the 'decompression.' Then a portal will take them back in time, to the city's golden age. We've tried to make this particular immersion as realistic as possible. Fabrication's complete; we just delayed the opening a month to make a couple of . . . *refinements*." She shot him a glance.

"The delay wasn't my fault," Warne replied.

"I didn't say it was. We're completing phase-three testing, you know, and all the reports we're getting are incredibly enthusias-tic." She beckoned. "Let me show you the World itself. If you haven't even seen the color boards yet, you're in for a treat."

At the far end of the digsite, they entered one of several large, cylindrical compartments. As the doors closed around him, Warne found himself briefly in darkness. Then side panels opened on both sides of the cylinder, and he realized they were surrounded by water. Reflected light danced, greenish blue, off the ceiling and floor. There was a hum, then a subtle shudder, and bubbles teased up the sides of the cylinder in tiny storms as they began to descend.

Warne turned to Sarah. "We're not really moving, are we?"

"Quiet. You're spoiling the illusion."

Far below, on what looked like the ocean floor, Warne could make out indistinct shapes just coming into view. He pressed his face to the Plexiglas window. It was the spires and minarets of a fantastic city, lights winking like tiny jewels, distorted and mis-shapen in the deep currents. The light grew dimmer and the im-age vanished. Warne stepped away.

Then, with a gentle lurch, the cylinder came to a stop. With a whisper of air, the door on its far end slid open.

"Come on," said Sarah, beckoning him on with a small smile. And Warne stepped out into paradise.

At least, it occurred to him that—had he ever stopped to imagine what paradise would be like—this would be his vision.

They were standing on a wide quay of pearlescent white. Surrounding them, lapping gently before their feet, was the edge of a tranquil sea: a sea of such an intense, rich blue Warne wanted to dip a paintbrush into it. Wide, gracious walkways of the same pearlescent material fanned out in myriad directions, arching gently over the water, curving toward larger clusters of buildings, towers, and silvery ramparts, extending back into what seemed a limitless distance. Exotic palms and knots of brightly colored flowers lined the verges. A cluster of wooden boats bobbed at anchor nearby, prows tall and graceful, carved into the semblance of swans. Here and there, small silver fish leaped from the water, sunlight glinting off their scales. And over all curved the dome and the clear empty sky beyond.

Wordlessly, Sarah led him to a nearby marble bench, set beneath a spreading palm.

Warne sat, entranced by the vision that lay around them. There was a fresh breeze blowing, cool and bracing, that somehow carried on it the scent of infinite promise. It seemed to him almost as if this timeless city had risen out of the sea as his private gift.

"What do you think?" he heard Sarah ask.

Warne shook his head. "It's magnificent. It's perfect."

Sarah smiled, clearly pleased by the compliment. "That's good, seeing as you'll be spending most of the week here. No expense was spared. Some of the water effects our engineers have created must be seen to be believed. One water ride, Last Moments of Pompeii, is expected to be the biggest single draw in Utopia. Maybe you've heard about it. They've leveraged the portable hologram technology to put an image of Eric Nightingale into every single passenger car, and—"

There was a sudden commotion in the water before their feet. A storm of bubbles erupted on the surface, and then a long, narrow head emerged, foam streaming down its scaly sides. Lidless yellow eyes stared, unblinking, back at them.

Warne grinned. "There you are," he said.

The sea creature looked attentively at him, raising itself still farther out of the water, foot upon foot, tall and sleek as a giant snake. It glistened with an iridescent platinum sheen, mirroring the sparkling surface below. Gemlike drops fell from the webbing of mechanical fins that ran down its sides. For a moment longer it remained still, balancing on the foam. Then in a flash it turned away, pinwheeling and cavorting across the surface.

Warne shook his head. He'd only been able to test the creature in the double Olympic pool at Carnegie-Mellon, over the protests of the swimming coach. Seeing it here, in this vast expanse of water, was a revelation. Building an aquatic robot impressive enough for Atlantis—with the intelligence of a dolphin, the fluidity of an eel—had been his greatest challenge yet. At least he'd had the assistance of a very helpful colleague. Still, there had been more false starts, more late-night coding marathons, than he'd care to admit. But the end result—Lady Macbeth, as this prototype had been named—had been his most successful demonstration of machine learning yet. And seeing it in this environment made all the work worthwhile.

Abruptly, the robot stopped its capering and disappeared beneath the surface. For a moment, all was quiet. Then at a distance it shot far out above the water, jaws opened to expose rows of jewel-like teeth. With a roar, it spewed a long tongue of purple flame. Then it dove back into the water once again, leaping several times up into the warm sunlight before at last returning to their bench, balancing on the foam, looking at them as if awaiting approval. Thin streams of smoke rose from its nostrils.

"What would Atlantis be without sea serpents?" Warne murmured. He turned to Sarah. "Has she been behaving herself?"

"She's been in beta-test ever since you sent her. From what I hear, the hourly performances have all gone off without a hitch. There's been one bad habit, though."

"Bad habit? What's that?"

Sarah nodded at the serpent. "Keep watching. You'll see soon enough."

Warne frowned. "Hmm. Anyway, the first two production models are waiting at the airport. They arrived yesterday, on a cargo plane. After I see them installed, I'll take Lady Macbeth here down to the lab, check for leaks or anomalous behaviors."

He fell silent. When he stopped to think, it seemed impossibly strange to be here again, in Utopia, beside Sarah. Last time, he'd been summoned to remove the Metanet, to lobotomize his misbehaving robots. But other events had intervened. And now, ironically, things had come full circle. He'd made tangible progress in his work on machine learning. His theories, once considered radical, were moving into the mainstream. And today, he was back to install newer, better, more intelligent robots.

He cleared his throat, waved his hand over the glittering cityscape. "Well, it's truly amazing, Sarah. You should be proud."

Sarah nodded. "We've created a state-of-the-art circulation system that purifies and distributes 200,000 gallons of water a minute—the city of Venice has asked for a monograph. When Atlantis opens next month, every other water park in the world will immediately become obsolete."

She paused, looking around, brown hair stirring in the gentle breeze. "We're going to be fine," she said in a very quiet voice.

Warne turned to look at her. The smile remained on her face; the sad, strong eyes were clear. And now he realized what it was that seemed different. Since the first day he'd met her, Sarah had always exuded an instinctive, almost aggressive self-assurance. He could still feel it now, like heat radiating from a brazier; but it seemed to have been tempered, veiled, as if by bitter experience.

On the trip from Pittsburgh, he'd wondered just what he would say when this moment came. Somehow, here in this watery splendor, only the simplest words found their way to his lips.

"But how are you, Sarah?" he asked.

She continued looking out toward the spires of Atlantis. "I'm okay. Not at first. But I'm okay now."

"When I didn't hear from you early on, when you didn't return my calls, I was afraid that—" He stopped for a moment. "Well, I was afraid that you couldn't forgive me. For Barksdale."

"I couldn't, Drew. At first, I couldn't. But I do now."

At last she turned to look at him. "I mean, you helped save all this. This Park is my life now, I should be grateful. But it's hard, you know. Sometimes, it's very hard . . ."

She turned away. Warne watched her, then turned back to the water, to the leapings and divings of Lady Macbeth.

"You know," he said, speaking slowly, "it wasn't me who saved Utopia, in the end. It was Wingnut." He stopped, replaying in his head the final scene in the corridor of C Level.

Sarah threw him a questioning glance.

"Peccam must have explained the situation to your people. The explosives on Wingnut's back, the echolocator we'd placed on the armored car for him to home in on."

Sarah nodded.

"But the echolocator stopped transmitting. And Wingnut stopped dead when he lost its signal. The whole plan was jeopardized. Almost without thinking, I ordered Wingnut to 'chase.' And that's just what he did. He chased the armored car. And he stopped it."

Sarah nodded again.

"But, Sarah, Wingnut *was never taught* a 'chase' command. It was just the opposite: I hardwired him to obey the command 'no chase.' Yet somehow he was able to parse the directive on his own, determine the action that had to be taken. I couldn't understand it. Was it my tone? My gesture? Or had the ad hoc ability been there all along, lacking only some unknown precipitant? So I got curious. When I learned that Hard Place wasn't going to be reactivated, I asked Terri to send his logical unit to me in Pittsburgh. See, I assumed that the reason he abruptly turned dangerous was that he'd been infected with John Doe's rogue code, which I prematurely triggered. Luckily, I'd managed to turn him off before he could hurt me or anybody else at the ice cream counter. Or so I thought."

"Go on," Sarah said.

"When I examined his internal logs, I found I was right about the rogue code. It did exist, it had been triggered prematurely. But I was wrong about something else. Sarah, *I never switched him off*. The kill switch hadn't been activated. And yet that made no sense. Hard Place couldn't just shut himself off. He didn't have the capability."

"But he could overload his neural net," Sarah replied. "Force a shutdown. He realized what he was doing was wrong, out of line with his original programming. And he took corrective action. In other words, he *learned*."

Warne stared at her. "You knew?"

"I read the confidential white paper you sent us on the subject—and your trade article, 'Machine Learning Under Perceived Stress.' " She nodded at Lady Macbeth. "That's why we wouldn't have considered asking anyone else to build her."

"Yeah? And all along I thought it was that cover story on me in *Robotics Journal*."

Sarah smiled briefly.

Warne stretched out his feet, put his hands in his pockets. Out in the still water, a school of fish passed by. Lady Macbeth gave a great belch of fire and took off after the fish, which scattered in all directions.

"What was that?" Warne said, shocked. "That's not part of her programming."

"It's the one glitch the techs have logged," Sarah replied. "The bad habit I told you about. She likes to chase fish."

THE BLOND AND chrome space of the Embarkation Building was filling up with guests, milling around impatiently beyond the ticket windows, waiting for the magic hour of nine to arrive. Warne moved among them, Sarah at his side, scanning the crowd, looking for Georgia. Abruptly, he spotted her, standing beside a metal column near the exit doors. She was swinging one leg back and forth, looking around, headphones bobbing in time to some unheard rhythm.

Standing beside her was Terri Bonifacio. The bright sunlight, streaming in from the skylights overhead, gave a gilt finish to the rich dark shine of her hair.

Out of the corner of his eye, Warne saw Sarah pause. She, too, had seen them.

Sarah walked up to Georgia with her swift, purposeful stride. "Hi, Georgia," she said, placing a hand on the girl's shoulder. "How are you?"

"Not good," came the response.

"Why not?"

"Because I'm out *here*. My dad wouldn't let me go inside."

Sarah glanced inquiringly at Warne.

"I thought we ought to take it slow the first day back," he said. "You know, test the waters, go only as far as Embarkation. Turns out I needn't have worried. So we'll come back tomorrow, do it right."

Sarah turned back to Georgia. "If you get some free time, look me up. If I'm not in a meeting, I'll show you Atlantis."

Georgia glanced at her with interest. "Dad's been telling me about it. Sounds cool."

Sarah allowed her hand to linger on Georgia's shoulder as she turned to Terri.

"It's nice to see you," she said. "How's the new job?"

"Carnegie-Mellon's throwing me more work than I can han-dle," Terri replied, with a smile that seemed to lend a glow to the rest of her face. "I love it. Andrew's got me up to my—up to my chin in research." Warne felt her give his hand a small, private squeeze. "If only there were casinos and a midway nearby, I'd be in seventh heaven."

"Well, you can't have everything."

"I know. So I'll settle for three free passes to the Park tomorrow."

"You've got them."

Warne watched this interplay intently. But there was no sense of awkwardness between the women.

Now Sarah turned back toward him, smiling. "I ought to put the dogs on you, helping Carnegie-Mellon steal Terri away from us like that."

"You could always steal her back."

"I'll remember that," she said, looking at them closely. "Give us time."

ON THE TARMAC outside the Embarkation Building, the lot at-tendants were already in motion, choreographing the parking of a hundred cars a minute. Armadas of yellow trams snaked their way between the rows, leaving their loading docks empty, re-turning full of smiling, sunglassed faces. Sarah walked them toward the rental car, chatting with Georgia. It was that rarest of Nevada days, pleasantly warm but not hot.

Warne pulled Terri to him as they walked. "You added that chase routine to Lady Macbeth when I wasn't looking, didn't you? Naughty girl. You're getting a spanking when we return to the motel."

"Promises, promises. Besides, Wingnut wouldn't have wanted it any other way."

Warne turned to look at Sarah. "You know," he said in a louder voice, "I never did hear from Poole."

"I did."

"You did?"

"Got a postcard a few months ago. No name, no return ad-dress, just a Juárez postmark. He wanted to know if that lifetime pass was still good."

Warne laughed, shook his head.

"You'd better sit in back," Georgia called out to Terri as they approached the car. "I'm not finished."

"Finished what?" Warne asked.

"Making Terri ride the Scream Machine with us tomorrow."

"No way," Terri said instantly.

"You've got to. It won't be any fun if you don't."

"I told you, I can't stand roller coasters."

"Come *on*."

Terri hesitated, glanced sidelong at the girl. "You'll give me back that Brubeck CD you 'borrowed' three months ago?"

"Okay."

"*And* the Art Tatum?"

Georgia made a face. "Okay."

"I'll think about it."

Sarah laughed, held the door for Georgia. She watched the girl strap herself in, then ducked inside and hugged the girl tightly.

"Bye, Georgia," she said.

"You mean it?" Georgia asked. "About Atlantis, I mean?"

"Of course. Stop by Guest Services. Your dad has my extension."

Now Sarah came around the car, leaned against Warne's open window. She wore no makeup, and the bright sunlight turned her eyes a pale jade.

"Good luck with the install," she said.

He bent toward her, kissed her cheek. "See you round the Park."

She smiled, straightened. Nodded.

And as he pulled away from the lot—headed for the interstate and Las Vegas—Warne could still see her in the rearview mirror, motionless as a gilded shadow, framed against the low Art Deco lines of Embarkation, arm raised in farewell.

And don't miss Lincoln Child's explosive thriller

DEATH MATCH

Available in paperback wherever books are sold

Please turn the page for an exciting preview . . .

IT WAS THE first time Maureen Bowman had ever heard the baby cry.

She hadn't noticed right away. In fact, it had taken five, perhaps ten minutes to register. She'd almost finished with the breakfast dishes when she stopped to listen, suds dripping from her yellow-gloved hands. No mistake: crying, and from the direction of the Thorpe house.

Maureen rinsed the last dish, wrapped the damp towel around it, and turned it over thoughtfully in her hands. Normally, the cry of a baby would go unnoticed in her neighborhood. It was one of those suburban sounds, like the tinkle of the ice cream truck or the bark of a dog, that passed just beneath the radar of conscious perception.

So why had she noticed? She dropped the plate into the drying rack.

Because the Thorpe baby never cried. In the balmy summer days, with the windows thrown wide, she'd often heard her cooing, gurgling, laughing. Sometimes, she'd heard the infant vocalizing to the sounds of classical music, her voice mingling in the breeze with the scent of piñon pines.

Maureen wiped her hands on the towel, folded it carefully, then glanced up from the counter. But it was September now; the first day it really felt like autumn. In the distance, the purple flanks of the San Francisco peaks were wreathed in snow. She could see them, through a window shut tight against the chill.

She shrugged, turned, and walked away from the sink. All babies cried, sooner or later; you'd worry if they didn't. Besides, it was none of her business; she had plenty of things to take care of without messing in her neighbors' lives. It was Wednesday, always the busiest day of the week. Choir rehearsal for herself, ballet for Courtney, karate for Jason. *And* it was Jason's birthday; he'd demanded beef fondue and chocolate cake. That meant another trip to the new supermarket on Route 66. With a sigh, Maureen pulled a list from beneath a refrigerator magnet, grabbed a pencil from the phone stand, and began scrawling items.

Then she stopped. With the windows all closed, the Thorpe baby must really be cranking if she could hear . . .

Maureen forced the thought from her mind. The infant girl had barked her shin or something. Maybe she was becoming colicky; it wasn't too late for that. In any case, the Thorpes were adults; they could deal with it. The Thorpes could deal with anything.

This last thought had a bitter undertone, and Maureen was quick to remind herself this was unfair. The Thorpes had different interests, ran in different circles; that was all.

Lewis and Lindsay Thorpe had moved to Flagstaff about a year before. In a neighborhood full of empty nesters and retirees, they stood out as a young, attractive couple, and Maureen had been quick to invite them to dinner. They'd been charming guests, friendly and witty and very polite. The conversation had been easy, unforced. But the invitation had never been returned. Lindsay Thorpe was in her third trimester at the time; Maureen liked to believe that was the reason. And now, with a new baby, back full time at work . . . it was all perfectly understandable.

She walked slowly across the kitchen, past the breakfast table, to the sliding glass door. From here, she had a better view of the Thorpes'. They'd been home the night before, she knew; she'd seen Lewis's car driving past around dinnertime. But now, as she peered out, all seemed quiet.

Except for the baby. God, the little thing had leather lungs . . .

Maureen stepped closer to the glass, craning her neck. That's when she saw the Thorpes' cars. Both of them, twin Audi A8s, the black one Lewis's and the silver one Lindsay's, parked in the breezeway.

Both home, on a Wednesday? This was seriously weird. Maureen pressed her nose up against the glass.

Then she stepped back. *Now listen, you're being exactly the kind of nosy neighbor you promised you'd never be.* There could be any number of explanations. The little girl was sick, the parents were home to tend to her. Maybe grandparents were arriving. Or they were getting ready to go on vacation. Or . . .

The child's cries had begun to take on a hoarse, ragged quality. And now, without thinking, Maureen put her hand on the glass door and slid it open.

Wait, I can't just go over there. It'll be nothing, I'll embarrass them, make myself look like a fool.

She looked over at the counter. The night before, she'd baked an enormous quantity of Toll House cookies for Jason's birthday. She'd bring some of those over; that was a reasonable, neighborly thing to do.

Quickly, she grabbed a paper plate—thought better of it—replaced it with a piece of her good china, arranged a dozen cookies on it, and covered them with plastic wrap. She scooped up the plate, made for the door.

Then she hesitated. Lindsay, she remembered, was a gourmet chef. A few Saturdays before, when they'd met at their mailboxes, the woman had apologized for being unable to chat because she had a burnt-almond ganache boiling on the stove. What would they think of a homely plate of Toll House cookies?

You're thinking about this way, way too much. Just go on over there.

What was it, exactly, she found so intimidating about the Thorpes? The fact they didn't seem to need her friendship? They were well educated, but Maureen had her own cum laude degree in English. They had lots of money, but so did half the neighborhood. Maybe it was how perfect they seemed together, how ideally suited for each other. It was almost uncanny. That one time they'd come over, Maureen had noticed how they unconsciously held hands; how they frequently completed each other's sentences; how they'd shared countless glances that, though brief, seemed pregnant with meaning. "Disgustingly happy" was how Maureen's husband termed them, but Maureen didn't think it disgusting at all. In fact, she'd found herself feeling envious.

Steadying her grip on the plate of cookies, she walked to the door, pulled back the screen, and stepped outside.

It was a beautiful, crisp morning, the smell of cedar strong in the thin air. Birds were piping in the branches overhead, and from down the hill, in the direction of town, she could hear the mournful call of the South-west Chief as it pulled into the train station.

Out here, the crying was much louder.

Maureen strode purposefully across the lawn of colored lava and stepped over the border of railroad ties. This was the first time she'd actually set foot on the Thorpes' property. It felt strange, somehow. The backyard was enclosed, but between the boards of the fence she could make out the Japanese garden Lewis had told them about. He was fascinated by Japanese culture, and had translated several of the great haiku poets; he'd mentioned some names Maureen had never heard of. What she could see of the garden looked tranquil. Serene. At dinner that night, Lewis had told a story about the Zen master who'd asked an apprentice to tidy his garden. The apprentice had spent all day at it, removing every last fallen leaf, sweeping and polishing the stone paths until they gleamed, raking the sand into regular lines. At last, the Zen master had emerged to scrutinize the work. "Perfect?" the apprentice asked as he displayed the meticulous garden. But the master shook his head. Then he gathered up a handful of pebbles and scattered them across the spotless sand. "*Now* it is perfect," he replied. Maureen remembered how Lewis's eyes had sparkled with amusement as he told the story.

She hurried forward, the crying strong in her ears.

Ahead was the Thorpes' kitchen door. Maureen stepped up to it, carefully arranged a bright smile on her face, and pulled open the screen. She began to knock, but with the pressure of her first rap the door swung inward.

She took a step.

"Hello?" she said. "Lindsay? Lewis?"

Here, in the house, the wailing was almost physically painful. She hadn't known an infant could cry so loud. Wherever the parents were, they certainly couldn't hear her over the baby. How could they be ignoring it? Was it possible they were showering? Or engaged in some kinky sex act? Abruptly, she felt self-conscious, and glanced around. The kitchen was beautiful: professional-grade appliances, glossy black counters. But it was empty.

The kitchen led directly into a breakfast nook, gilded by morning light. And there was the child: up ahead, in the archway between the breakfast nook and some other space that, from what she could see, looked like a living room. The infant was strapped tightly into her high chair, facing the living room. The little face was mottled from crying, and the cheeks were stained with mucus and tears.

Maureen rushed forward. "Oh, you poor thing." Balancing the cookies awkwardly, she fished for a tissue, cleaned the child's face. "There, there."

But the crying did not ease. The baby was pounding her little fists, staring fixedly ahead, inconsolable.

It took quite some time to wipe the red face clean, and by the time she was done Maureen's ears were ringing with the noise. It wasn't until she was pushing the tissue back into the pocket of her jeans that she thought to follow the child's line of sight into the living room.

And when she did, the cry of the child, the crash of china as she dropped the cookies, were instantly drowned by the sound of her screams.